"The world is woven of secrets."

For a moment I could not remember which way was east, and panic froze me. Then I remembered, and sprang over to the eastern side, to slice Raphael's sigil into the space between the lines. The archangel who is the great healer first, who holds the trumpet of the Apocalypse, Raphael's name was one I knew as well as my own. Then the warrior general Michael for the south—

Something pale and green flashed. I leapt away from it, careful to remain in the circle. Dropping the athame into the goblet, I grabbed one of the longest logs, whirled and slashed at the dripping, glowing thing—arm. The blow connected with a satisfying, terrifying thud and crunch.

Oh, Lady, it's real, it's real, it's real—

๑·ᵭ·๑

Praise for Katharine Eliska Kimbriel's *Night Calls* Books:

๑·ᵭ·๑

Advance praise for *Spiral Path:*

"Magic and treason form a deadly maze for Alfreda, one of my favorite heroes, returning to public life in one of my favorite fantasy series. It's alternate early America; Alfreda is savvy to the life and magic of the forest, the rivers, and winter, but powers know she is alive and able, to be recruited or destroyed."
—Tamora Pierce, #1 *New York Times* Bestselling Author

"Having already faced darkness early on, Allie's struggles at first come from culture shock, fear of failing in school, and even press gangs. ...readers will appreciate the chance to breathe before a climactic sequence where Allie is sent to ferret out a traitor to the young America. ...enjoy the total immersion in Kimbriel's alternate early America."
—*Publishers Weekly*

D1289976

"**Much of the adventure here** is the adventure of boarding school with a magical twist, but there are other things going on in the background, and Allie can no more avoid trouble than she can avoid breathing. She's just far too intelligent, inquisitive, and brave, not to mention impetuous. This is a lot of fun. Recommended."
—*Lis Carey's Library*

"**A gem: *Spiral Path* lays an** enchanting spell as young Allie Sorensson continues her fearless exploration of her magical powers at an exclusive school for practitioners of the arcane arts. Crafted with precision and heart, this tale shimmers with imagination, adventure, and characters who burst alive from the page. More, please!"
—Sara Stamey, author of *Islands*

۞

Praise for *Kindred Rites*:

"**With a clear, distinctive voice,** Katharine Kimbriel invents and re-invents magic on America's frontier, a place hardly explored by writers and long overdue for a visit. (Or should I say a visitation?) Love the book."
—Jane Yolen, award-winning author of *Briar Rose*

"**It is good to see this back**—the Alfreda stories are one of the reasons YA is so dynamic today. ...*Little House on the Prairie* meets Harry Potter, with a dash of Stephen King."
—Sherwood Smith, author of *Crown Duel*

"**...and I am very happy to report** that Kimbriel made me almost miss my bus stop at work because I had to read just one more page."
—*The Book Pushers*

"**Allie is a compelling character...** Her world feels real, her studies feel real... This is one of the best historical dark fantasies I've ever read. I deeply enjoyed Allie's second tale, and plan to re-read it many, many times over the years to come."
—Barb Caffrey, *Shiny Book Review*

"A skillfully woven tapestry of American history, multicultural folklore, and dark fantasy for readers of young adult and above. *(Kindred Rites)* is one you will revisit from time to time when you need an old friend."
—Rebecca McFarland Kyle, Amazon Top 500 Reviewer

"She has a real gift for taking a story into interesting situations, and in directions you don't expect. I keep dipping back into the book!"
—Ru Emerson, author of the *Night-Threads* books

"Katharine Eliska Kimbriel's Allie books do Harry Potter one, or two, maybe even three better. ...These are the kind of good books that help a reader get through a bad night."
—Alexis Glynn Latner, author of *Hurricane Moon*

"Take *Little House on the Prairie*, mix in a large dose of magic, shake well for adults and settle in for a very fun ride. I want the next installment of Alfreda Sorensson's adventures right now."
—Laurell K. Hamilton, *NY Times* best selling author

࿐

Praise for *Night Calls:*

"If you can imagine *Little House on the Prairie* with werewolves, vampires, and magic, you've got an idea what this dark fantasy novel is like. ...The strong characters, the matter-of-fact tone, and the strong sense of place make this something special."
—*Locus Magazine*

"I am so glad that Katharine Eliska Kimbriel's *Night Calls* is getting out into the world again. If anything, I believe this story's time has come—it's the dark fantasy with an underlying glint of the numinous that I think so many readers are looking for and not finding."
—Sherwood Smith, author of *Crown Duel*

"To protect those she loves, a pragmatic young witch finds faith and magical lessons in the natural world—compelling, fantastic tale, beautifully, wondrously written!"
—Patricia Rice, best selling author of the *Magic* series

"Kimbriel's *Night Calls* is a fresh, immersive take on magic and the supernatural in a young America."
> —Maya Kaathryn Bohnhoff, *NY Times* best selling author

"*Night Calls* combines genuinely chilling occult elements with a believable, gritty context that both convinces and compels. Allie is a real person, living in a sort of alternate-history setting, and her character, companions, and problems pull the reader into her story."
> —Ardath Mayhar, author of
> *The World Ends in Hickory Hollow*

"*Night Calls* is the kind of book I needed most when I was a tween. ...Along with Terry Pratchett's *Wee Free Men, A Hat Full of Sky, Wintersmith,* and *I Shall Wear Midnight,* this is a story rich in regional historical detail, voice, and charm. I feel gypped that I didn't get this book when I was that age. But I can have it now."
> —Jennifer Stevenson, author of *Fools Paradise*

From a cherished letter....

"It has been a very great pleasure for me to have been, this past week, introduced to your two books dealing with the Craft... The likeness of your people to those of Manly Wade Wellman is strong—though he dealt mainly with male characters and I found your women really more interesting and thoroughly believable.
"I have on order both volumes to send to a Wiccan friend who I am sure will find them absorbing reading. Do you intend to continue this series? I trust that is so. And I want to thank you very much for introducing me to your world."
> —Andre Norton, author of the
> best selling *Witch World* series

SPIRAL PATH

SPIRAL PATH

KATHARINE ELISKA KIMBRIEL

ILLUSTRATION
MITCHELL DAVIDSON BENTLEY

BOOK VIEW CAFE

Spiral Path
Copyright © 2014 by Katharine Eliska Kimbriel

ISBN 978-1-61138-436-9
All rights reserved.

Book View Cafe Publishing Cooperative
  PO Box 1624 , Cedar Crest, NM 87008-1624
Dragonrain Studio
  PO Box 202045, Austin, TX 78720-2045

Cover art "Surprise Visit" ©2014
by Mitchell Davidson Bentley
Used under contract, all other rights reserved
Cover design by Atomic Fly Studios
www.atomicflystudios.com

Interior design by Hypatia Press
For information address: alanbard@alanbard.com
Dragon Illustration page 135
by Leslie Newcomer
©1987 Hypatia Press
www.fantasyCatArt.com

DEDICATION

To Andre Norton, Barbara Burnett Smith, & Lori Wolf

They waited a long time for it. I know they've
been reading over my shoulder as I work.
Hope you like it, folks...

A Work of Fiction

All medicinal and culinary references in this novel are for entertainment purposes only, and are not intended for actual use. Herbs, if used improperly, can be harmful or fatal. Do not attempt self-treatment with herbs without first consulting with a physician or qualified medical herbalist. Neither the author nor the publisher can be held responsible for any adverse reactions to the plants mentioned within.

This story is a work of fiction. All characters are fictitious, and any resemblance to actual persons, living or dead, is purely coincidental.

Acknowledgements

Never let it be said I am not determined. I had to become a wizard to get this book written.

Allie never would have returned to the world without the help of so many people. Their assistance varies in how they helped, but at some point, they were all crucial to the cause. Some people are obvious, like my parents and my sisters Beth and Karen. Others are not so obvious, but whether they were proofing a manuscript, babysitting a cat, or nagging me about my health--all necessary.

Alan, Alexis, Amy, Andre, Ardath, Barb, Beth, Bev & Michael, Bobbi & Tom, Carla, Carrie, Cathy, Charlene, Deborah, Deborah, Doranna, Ginger, Ginny, Glen, Gordon, Jane, Jen, Judy, Julie, Julie & John, Karen, Kasey, Katie, Keith, Kirby, Kit, Laura, Laura Anne, Laurell, Lynne, Marla, Maya, Michael, Michelle, Mindy, Mitch, Nancy & Liten, Pat, Patrice, Patricia, Richard, Roy, Ru, Sheilagh, Sherwood, Silona, Sofia, Susan & Matt, Vonda, Wanada, Whit
...along with every fan who found me through Live Journal, Facebook, Twitter, Goodreads, Book View Cafe...you have all helped in so many small and large ways. You know who you are. Pat yourselves on the back. The reason Allie Lives is because you believed.

You'd think I was Peter Pan asking if you believe in fairies.

Good thing you believe in Alfreda.

Also many thanks to the best production team ever: Jennifer Stevenson, Sherwood Smith, Vonda N. McIntyre, and the wonderful members of Book View Cafe who kibitzed on cover and back copy. Thank you all.

SPIRAL PATH

ONE

IT IS SAID AMONG FOLK OF DIFFERENT GIFTS—those who cannot straddle the worlds—that when a wizard is born, the very church bells announce the blessed event.

Practitioners know better than that.

Gifts are not so easily recognized, and how they reveal themselves is tricky. Shifting wind might announce the birth of an Air child. We see a sudden thunderstorm for Water children, a ghost for a Medium...a plant blooming out of season for an Earth babe. Even attracting a Good Friend, a friendly spirit that aids the practice of magic, can show magical potential. It's more like that, and if the child's future power is great, the sign can be felt from many miles away.

Occasionally—such as during the birth of my sister Elizabeth—the wall between worlds rips open and the mysteries drop into your arms.

Sometimes literally.

From the first labor pain to her last ancient breath, my sister Elizabeth was a surprise. She always looked so normal, so agreeable, so docile...and then her gift seized her by the throat, and you fell back before the terror of it all. Momma wasn't due until the month of Flowers, but when my kinswoman Marta and I arrived from the south, worn thin with winter travel, the fact that it was a month early mattered not at all. Marta laid her practiced hands upon my mother and announced: *It's true labor.*

Suddenly the household was in a tizzy. Marta was my teacher in the Wise Arts, and healthy babies were her life. She set Papa on the road to fetch Aunt Dagmar from Sun-Return, the boys to tending the animals and trap lines, and me to scrubbing clothes and grinding herbs. Momma hadn't spoken about where we'd been; she'd just hugged me and said, "Alfreda, child, thank God you are safe."

Papa had given lots of thought to his own home, and had anchored our log cabin with a huge chimney open on two sides. We had a great central fire that allowed cooking in the kitchen and warmth and company for the main living area. This island of light in the midst of organized labor saved us wood and made the flow of people much easier to manage.

Three months ago, about when I was kidnapped from Marta's home, Papa and the boys built another room of our house. This small room was next to the main room, and larger than the still-room off the kitchen. There would be a chimney when this became our parlor, Papa told us, but not yet. For now, Marta and I would carry hot water and bricks to Momma in this snug little room while she had her baby on the birthing mattress Papa made.

Aunt Dagmar arrived and took over the kitchen, and I took up the spinning wheel, so we were ready for Momma's confinement. Momma's oldest sister didn't always approve of me—I was much too outspoken for her, plus she was a tad jealous of Momma having the only wizardly child in the current generation—but while Momma was lying in, we called a truce. I complimented Aunt Dagmar on her cooking (which was very good) and she exclaimed over my thin, fine wool thread and tight weaving. Momma was pleased to have peace in her house, and Marta merely smiled and held her tongue.

This was Momma's seventh baby to go almost the full time, and the more you had, the less time you spent in labor. Usually. Elizabeth's birth was different. Fortunately we'd made it back in time—I shudder to think of Aunt Dagmar delivering Elizabeth by herself. Of course we weren't supposed to know that Momma and Papa had decided on "Elizabeth" as the name for a girl. But the universe had already whispered it to me, long ago. I had seen Elizabeth standing by my side as I looked into a dark mirror one night. She had Momma's dainty form and dark hair, and a shy smile all her own. My reflected self could have passed for Marta in her youth. Tall and golden like my father, I represented the Norwegian side of this Sorensson family, while Elizabeth looked very Irish.

As time crawled on, pressure built throughout our big log home. Elizabeth took her time arriving. It wasn't until the second day of slow, intermittent labor that things fell into a rhythm. The boys went up to the loft room or tended stock, which kept them busy. As Momma paced, Marta carded wool, and I worked at the huge spinning wheel before the fireplace in the living room. In the kitchen Aunt Dagmar cooked and talked non-stop, but Papa sat and kept her company—and away from Momma, Marta and me.

Momma knew why we'd come from the south. A family of sorcerers had taken me down to the Indiana Territory for "who knew what reason." But Momma feared the dark on the other side, and had quit training in the Mysteries after she learned herb lore. We didn't tell her anything about how we bested the sorcerers of Hudson-on-the-Bend. I do not know if she suspected there had been a battle, or thought Marta, Cousin Cory, and Shaw Kristinsson simply took me back from those who had kidnapped me. I was alive, healthy (if thin) and not throwing up, so I wasn't pregnant. I was back with kin—nothing else mattered.

We were very practical people, back then.

What of Shaw Kristinsson, you might ask, from my own village of Sun-Return, fifteen year old son of a blacksmith and an innkeeper? I suspected he was a shape shifter, like his parents before him. Now I knew he was an apprentice practitioner, and believed he was my friend. He'd come with Marta, Cousin Cory, and old Joseph to rescue me. Shaw had stopped talking to me for a while in there, his shyness overcoming him. I wasn't even a woman grown, and yet he was always looking at me and blushing.

But five days into our trip home, our tales of Hudson-on-the-Bend spent, Shaw had finally begun to talk to me again.

He'd started by handing me a letter he'd written to me.

He had words...he just had trouble getting them out to my face.

"You did just fine, Allie," was where he began.

Those words had meant the world to me.

Momma's voice filtered into my thoughts. "I tell you, Marta, this doesn't get—" A contraction folded Momma over in the midst of her pacing around the kitchen and living room.

"Breathe, Garda," Marta said, moving to the table. "Slow and deep; try to keep your shoulders down." Marta just stood there, tall and straight as an ash tree, hands on Momma's shoulders. Momma's face eased, and I wondered if Marta had used a small magic, or just the power of her presence. "Let's check how far along things are." Bending her fair head over Momma's dark one, she walked my mother back to the new parlor room and the birthing bed.

In moments Marta peered around the doorway. "Allie, come bring the linens, quickly."

I rushed to get the towels, which were warm and wrapped around a pot of coals. By the time I was across the main room and into the parlor, Marta was holding Momma's hands through another contraction. Elizabeth was coming soon? I glanced at Marta and then went down to the foot of the bed.

Papa had made a long mattress, so the baby would come out on solid padding. I felt a bit shy about helping my mother with a new baby, but I'd helped others before—Lord and Lady, I'd delivered twins! So I checked—

Pressure hit me in the face, like rising steam or opening the door to an oven. It was magic, not real heat, so I just ignored it. "Marta, I can see her!" Oops—I wasn't supposed to know the sex yet. As the top of her head peeked out, I set my fingers lightly on her hair to make sure she didn't come out too fa—

Heat seared my fingertips, roaring up my arm as if I had run up to a solstice fire on a cold winter's night. I could see nothing but flames, the mass heaving like a cauldron of molten sugar. Shiny black and golden flames. The vision was much like a bright bed of coals. The baby was coming out fast, so fast—

Allie, catch her! The mental words rang out like a command.

Blinded by the blazing light, I fumbled to seize hold of little Elizabeth, cursing my gift and praying I wouldn't somehow fail and hurt my mother or sister.

Earth heaved beneath my feet, trying to throw me to the ground. I could no longer separate magic from Now. The stench was awful, then choking, the rain of ash burning. I held on to the baby and leaned into the plump mattress, trying to flatten us into the softness of herbs and husks, trying to keep us from sliding off the face of a mountain—

And then the top of the mountain blew off.

Clouds—no, steam—rose into the heavens, miles into the sky, carrying rock and ash and liquid stone halfway to the rim of the world. Winds churned above, carrying evidence of the deed far and wide.

Whimpering called me back. Stunned, I realized that *Elizabeth* saw with my eyes. She cast her Vision out into the beyond, trying to channel something she had no possible chance of understanding. *A seer. Powers that be, my baby sister is a seer.*

It's all right, I whispered to her mind, hugging her into the clump of toweling and cradling her bloody body close. *We're safe, it's all right, it hasn't happened yet, and we will warn people that it's coming.* Over and over I tried, with silent words and warm hands, to reassure her that there was nothing to fear.

Finally I could see again. Time had not stood still.

Marta bent over Momma and gently slapped her cheek.

"Marta?"

"Clean up your sister, Allie. I need to wake your Momma. Is the placenta—ah, good. Take care of her, dear. Do you have your embroidery thread with you?" Marta was watching carefully, her hand on Momma's shrunken, wrinkled belly, but there was apparently nothing to fear—no bright blood, no change in her breathing, no sudden swelling. My cousin's other hand checked Momma's pulse, and since Marta did not look concerned, I bent to tie off the cord and, when the last of the blood had drained into the baby, tied the knot.

Elizabeth was much calmer, now, as if nothing strange had happened. She made cooing noises as I wiped her clean and bundled her into a soft diaper and a warm flannel gown with a draw at the feet. My little sister looked just like one of the baby dolls with china hands and head. She'd have the Sorensson trademark, the soft, pale curls of childhood. I knew that Elizabeth would start growing dark hair around five or six—although I wasn't going to volunteer that. Once we had her in her christening gown, her pale gold hair dry and fluffy, she'd be a beautiful baby.

Had Marta felt what had happened, or had she only noticed my distress? I decided not to say anything until we were alone. My mother wanted a daughter who could be a normal little girl—at least for a time—and I didn't want to spoil the first few years for her.

Marta revived my mother, and helped her freshen up with a clean sleeping gown. My cousin even stripped off the birthing sheets and put fresh linens on the bed. No need to get them both upstairs— we'd move them and burn the straw mattress later. I brought the baby over and placed her in Momma's waiting arms. "You have another daughter, Momma," I told her.

"Elizabeth," was Momma's response, her eyes full of her joy. "We decided on Elizabeth if it was a girl."

I hurried to the kitchen to announce the news. This brought both Papa and Aunt Dagmar to the new parlor to see the baby. Papa, as always, turned to Momma first, kissing her cheek, his sky blue gaze only for her. Glowing, Momma showed off the latest addition to the family.

I helped Marta bundle away the sheets and my apron to the kitchen, where we plunged them into a basin of ice cold water. I thought about shouting up to the boys, but decided to let Papa tell them. A new sister was interesting, but probably not as interesting as a new brother.

After we'd made sure there were no iron stains from blood separating on the sheets, I turned to Marta. "You felt that?" I asked as we dumped the wrung linen into a second basin.

"Oh, yes," Marta said. "Perhaps not as strongly as you did, since you were touching her, but I felt it!"

"Why? It means she's a seer at the least, doesn't it?" I went on.

"It suggests that her primary gift will be seeing," Marta answered, stirring the sheets with a pole. "I hadn't told you about that little trick of nature, because you haven't helped deliver a baby practitioner. I apologize. Until now, you were the only one of Garda and Eldon's children to have talent—the only Schell in this generation with magic, and the first born to great power in three generations."

"Our blood has thinned—that's what some say," I muttered, squeezing out Momma's nightgown.

"I don't think so." It was quite definite. "More like concentrating itself, Allie. Why only the daughters this time, I have no idea. But I predict that your brothers also carry the potential."

We stirred for a while, checking the bloodstains and rubbing cloth together to get rid of as much as we could. Bleaching was difficult in winter, since a day of sunshine was a rare event. We would use soap after we got the stains out.

"What did it mean?" I finally said aloud.

At first my cousin was silent. I worked at keeping my mouth shut. "I would guess one of two things," Marta finally said. "What we saw was either an earthquake, or a volcano exploding. But it didn't feel like it was...now. It felt like an echo."

"Was it an echo from the past or future?" I stopped stirring, overwhelmed by alarm. I twisted so I could see her face. "Could it happen here?"

"Could a volcano erupt here?" Marta gave me one of her crooked smiles. "There have been volcanoes on this continent in the past, and there will be such explosions in the future. We are more likely to have an earthquake, right here." She actually shivered, and I didn't think it was from the cold water. "A seer on the Silk Road once passed along the vision of an earthquake. The ground cracked open, and heaved like the swell of the ocean."

"I wonder if we would have known about this so soon, if Elizabeth hadn't arrived," I murmured into the washbasin. For a moment, the water surged and glimmered, flowing like lava. I stirred the brightness, and the glittering image was gone. It appeared that the glimmer had also taken out the last stains.

Perhaps I should check my great-grandmother's *Denizens of the Night* before I troubled Marta with this little glimmer vision.

"It depends on how far away it is in time and space," Marta said, her voice calling me back. "If we get more information about it soon, then soon it will come. If we don't get anything for a season or two, it may be years away. We watch, and we wait." She started twisting the sheet, and I moved to help her.

Aunt Dagmar returned in time to hang a clothesline for us, and we draped the bed linen and nightgown near the kitchen fire. My aunt warmed some milk for cocoa, and we three had a celebratory cup.

As I sat on a huge pillow before the fire in the main room, I looked around and made sure Aunt Dagmar had retired to the still-room, and then turned to Marta.

"Does that sort of thing always happen when a new practitioner is born?"

Marta gave me a weary glance from her chair, and she didn't stop her slow rocking. "Not necessarily a vision, but something, yes. The people delivering the baby know, and maybe a few miles beyond."

"Do you think Cory heard Elizabeth?" I asked, referring to Momma's cousin Corrado, a practitioner who lived ten days away, in the orchard country.

A faint smile, a slight shake of the head— "I would say not," was the reply. "It usually doesn't travel far—a protection thing, I think. Family will protect a new practitioner, but there are others who might want to kill it." At my lifted eyebrows, she added: "Competition, Allie. Or there are darker users of the Arts. They might want a child of power for other reasons, as you well know."

No one had ever mentioned this to me before. "What else can happen at a birth?"

"Usually a child reveals a hint of whichever element is their strongest. A thunderstorm might erupt when Water is dominant or high winds for Air masters."

It was a vision, not an explosion. Visions were...Air? "So Elizabeth is of Air? That means...she can do more things with Air?"

"Most seers are of Air." Marta sipped again. "It means that she will be able to master all powers associated with Air. Even if she's not good at all of them, she'll be able to use them in a pinch." Marta glanced at me. "Air and Fire are usually men's powers, so she will be unusual in that."

"Do you have an element?" I squirmed around to face her as I spoke, because talking about a practitioner's element was very personal business. I'd never dared ask her that before. There was always something else to discuss, things that seemed more important. But my Grandmother's book hadn't mentioned much about this...yet.

Of course, I suspected the book actually hid pages from me, until I was ready for the knowledge.

I hadn't asked about the book's changing page count, either.

Marta dimpled. The crease was startling against her tanned skin and white temples. "Six animals gave birth when I was born. Earth is surely my element, if anything is."

I thought about it, and decided it seemed appropriate. "Marta, you delivered me, didn't you?"

"I have been present for every one of your momma's confinements."

"You never told me any such thing happened when I was born. In fact, people seemed surprised when I started seeing things and hearing werewolves and all." I poured myself a tiny bit of cocoa from the copper pan sitting by the fire. "What's my element?"

My cousin paused to drain her mug. "I don't know."

I blinked at her. "Nothing strange happened when I was born?"

This time, Marta's smile was only slightly twisted, that smile that meant more than one thing. Her gaze was riveted to the firepit before us. "I didn't say that. I just don't know which element, if any, is your strongest talent."

"What happened when I was born?"

Marta stared into the glowing coals of the fading fire. "You rushed out of your mother's womb, and in the moment between your birth and your first cry...the world took a sudden breath."

I sat there a while, and then said: "I don't understand."

"Neither do I, Alfreda. It was as if all creation gasped at the sight of you. I have no idea what it means." She finally looked my way. "Your momma labored long with you, and you were born with the dawn. That night, the northern lights were dancing among the stars, and we don't see them often, down here. I'd never seen them in summertime. Sheer curtains of vivid pink, sky blue, the deep blue of a butterfly wing, veils of pale green and white...someday, we'll find out if you can see the memories of another practitioner. I'll show you, then. It was worth seeing."

Marta leaned over and grabbed a folded towel. She seized the handle of the pan and poured herself the last of the cocoa. "How is your spinning coming?"

I blinked at the turn in the conversation. "Even with all the excitement, I finished nine more full skeins today." Marta smiled her pleasure. "I think I can finish in maybe three days."

"Good," Marta said. "Let's get some sleep while we can. Morning will come early, with a new little one in the house." She rose slowly and took the cocoa pan back into the kitchen.

I banked the fire for the night, and made sure that the finished wool skeins were far from the fireplace, and that the great wool wheel was lashed tight so it would not spin on its own. The dead would rise at the sound, I promise you, a sound like the rush of a mighty wind. Then I headed for the back stair to join Marta in my old room.

There was no time to waste with the spinning. Momma squawked about how much time my study of the Mysteries took from my chores when I still lived home in Sun-Return. But truth was I had gotten a great deal of work done. All the wool should have been spun by now, and the flax wheel humming. But wool remained to be spun, the flax untouched.

I was trying to make up for it now. We'd been in Sun-Return three days, and I had already spun nearly forty skeins of wool, all high-quality twist. I'd had to re-learn my mother's wheel, and being left-handed had not hurt me. Once I'd learned control of the speed of the wheel with my right hand, my left hand did everything else.

Truth to tell, I still hated plain sewing. But quilts and fancy work I could do. Fortunately for me, there was a greater demand for complicated weaving and embroidery. And a big demand for wool thread as thin as a British mill could spin.

What Momma needed was a daughter with my talent for dyes and fancy work, and no hint of the Gift that clung to our family tree. Momma hated the fact that I had power—so much power I was tingling with it by my eleventh birthday. I knew she hoped this child would be free of power.

Not likely. But there would be breathing room for Momma, who needed some years spent with a daughter who wouldn't be charging off into the woods every other minute. I didn't think Elizabeth would be the same kind of practitioner as I was shaping up to be.

Whether that was a good or bad thing remained to be seen.

❧ 🐦 ❧

"Wake up! Please wake up!"

The voice was insistent, the hands tugging at my arm strong and smooth as glass. It was the oddest dream I'd had in weeks, so vivid I could smell lavender. I shook my head to clear it of sleep, and found myself looking up at a dainty young girl with flaxen-colored hair and huge dark blue eyes. She wore soft, indistinct clothing and a scarf tied over her loose hair, as if she'd roused from sleep herself.

"It's Sister! It's her time, and she's having trouble! Please come! You must help Sister!"

Well, you know how it is, in a dream. You don't question anything, you don't wonder why things are happening—you just follow along until something tosses you out of the dream. Somehow I found my clothes, and then my stork scissors and several packets of herbs. The girl didn't want me to pause for anything, but I wasn't running out the door without scissors and embroidery thread, at the least. I put on the old shirt I'd been wearing when I'd been kidnapped by the Hudsons. Why did I choose that old thing?

I could not remember ever having such a detailed dream. I could still smell lavender.

I realized as I followed her that I had no idea where I was, nor where I was going. Somewhere off in the forest I heard the unique bird call, like a flute trilling, that told me my Good Friend, the spirit that had chosen me as its companion, was somewhere beneath the shadowy trees.

"How far are we going?" I said aloud. Was there something uncertain in that song...something like an alarm?

"Not far," the girl assured me as she reached for my arm once more. Half pulling, half coaxing, she led me through the darkness as if she had cat eyes. I could smell wood smoke and old snow, the cold fecund promise of spring just around the bend, but I could see almost nothing. A blanket of stars showed a clear night, but the moon either had already set, or was dark.

Ahead a pinprick of light promised our destination. The cabin rose out of the forest as if it had popped up like a mushroom, the trees crowding it against a stone outcrop. It looked as if the family had built their home against an opening in the rock. Not a bad idea—a cave would be an even temperature all year round, and fireproof.

"This way." The girl threw open the door and rushed in; I followed without question. When a baby is due, you don't ask questions, you just go. I suddenly realized I hadn't even asked my guide's name.

"I found her! Sister, I found her!" The girl hurried past looming, shrouded shapes of furniture and into the back room, and I pushed to catch up.

Crossing the second doorsill, I stopped short. One beeswax candle lit the cave beyond, throwing stark shadows into the crevices above us. The maiden who had fetched me from my dream sleep had her arms tossed around the neck of the prettiest little gray mare I'd ever seen, round as a tun, ready to pop with her foal. Turning back, tears in her eyes, the girl said: "Please! I know you can help her! Only you can help her!"

Well, truth be told, my father would have served the mare better, and I almost said so. But this was a dream, so perhaps I had power here. The child was so upset that I slowly reached over to touch the pale mare's damp shoulder. Dark eyes glinting like deep pools of water turned to me, and I suddenly had the strangest feeling. Something odd about this mare...could she be a practitioner who had shifting ability? The magic woven through her was foreign to my small experience.

Well.

I'd delivered foals before, and I'd delivered human babies. They were more alike than different, those little ones. I could do this thing.

"It will be fine," I murmured. "Let's just let her move around."

And she did move—that start-and-stop gait of a female grass eater restless without knowing why. The mare would pause, looking for a comfortable position, then move again, nibbling at soft new grass the girl had found somewhere. The waif still had not introduced herself, and in my dreamlike haze, I did not ask her name. I waited for the mare to progress, for labor had begun, and her coat was slick with sweat.

It felt like hours, so long that I asked the girl to build up the fire in the main room of the house. This caused me to remove my coat, for we had warm air at our backs. Finally the mare knelt in the deep straw, her sides heaving, and I knew I should check to see if the hooves had presented yet. Baby foals come out folded down against their forelegs, hoof first. *Please Lord and Lady, no breech.* I had no idea how to turn a foal. Would burning mugwort work as it did for human babies?

I moved the mare's tail to see how far along we were, and then the strangest part of the dream occurred. For a brief moment I could have sworn that I saw a human baby's hand peeking from the mare's womb! I blinked, and then I saw pearly gray hooves, which disappeared when the mare stopped straining. All this made me hesitate to take hold of the hooves to help her in her labor. Was this magic, or the dream?

It didn't matter what I was seeing—there was a baby to deliver. When the hooves and fetlocks stayed solidly outside the mare, I wiped down the feet with some straw and then took hold above the fetlocks to gently pull at the next contraction. Another push, the nose of the foal was visible—

Suddenly my vision changed; I saw repeating images from many points in the room.

The only thing I could use as an anchor in my thoughts was that this was how a spider might look at things with her eight eyes. The scene before me fractured and multiplied. Colors danced, opening and closing like a lady's fan. It was as if the stained glass in the Kristinsson family's front door spun before me. I'd heard that cathedrals in Europe had such jeweled windows, more than the front door of the boarding house. The mare gave a couple of strong pushes, and abruptly I fell backward to land in the straw with a newborn colt in my lap.

Only a moment...then the colt dissolved into a flaxen-haired baby boy, his face scrunched up in protest at this rude arrival into the world. My dream self took this calmly, reaching in my pocket for my embroidery thread and scissors to tie off the belly button cord.

There was movement next to me, and the mare surged back onto her feet. I looked up at her, and realized she had a long, glossy polished horn sticking out of her forehead. For a moment I just stared, for she'd gone from a pale gray coat to one of glimmering white. The horn was barely as thick as fine paper, with a twist and sheen like a shell. I could see the glow of candlelight through it.

Suddenly Marta was there, guardian of my life, even into my dreams, it seemed. Had I called her, or had she come because of something she sensed in the upper plains of existence?

"This goes too far, Suletu," Marta said to the girl, her expression stern. From my position on the floor, Marta looked formidable indeed. I held my head still to calm the floating images, and let my eyes look first to one, and then the other speaker.

"Would you rather that we asked you?" the young girl replied, swooping down to take the baby from my lap. "We thought that someone removed from Circle politics would be best, and you cannot deny that we chose well."

"You needed a powerful practitioner," Marta said flatly. "You would have gone halfway around the world for Alfreda, if that was where she was born, because you thought that you could control her. You have put her in a position of peril from any unscrupulous magic-user powerful enough to notice this night. Did you think I would not find out? You might as well have hung a sign on her saying 'Challenges Accepted.'"

You underestimate her. I blinked, for the thought came from the direction of the mare—the unicorn. Who was a...shape shifter? I crossed my legs to sit comfortably.

Marta just threatened a girl and a unicorn. This is not a dream.

"Who are you, and why did you choose to have your baby while shifted?" I said, looking up from the mound of straw that I'd tumbled into while helping the...baby...arrive.

She misses little, the mare went on. *It took all the attention I could spare to help Suletu keep Alfreda's mind in the dream place. We meant and mean her no harm. She has done us a great favor, and my house will remember, whatever comes of this deed.*

"Witnessed." Marta and the girl—Suletu?—said the word together, as if they had planned it in advance. I had the vague feeling that this word was important, but decided to keep my mouth shut. My head was starting to clear, and I could feel blood on my hands. I hadn't ever "felt" in a dream, so it turned out that this was magic after all.

"Congratulations on your son, Namid," Marta said as she offered me a hand up from the ground. "I would wish him a long and peaceful life, but your choice has already denied him that fate. I hope you do not regret this night's work."

We had no choice. Others have placed their pieces upon the board of life. If we had not moved a pawn, we would not be in the game.

"Perhaps." Next Marta picked up my coat and slipped it over my shoulders. "Alfreda is not your pawn to move. Do not attempt to coerce her again." Marta had her palm against the small of my back, and with a strong arm swept me out of the warm cave. Yes, the cave was real; the house had been illusion.

It was my second magical baby delivery that night.

I hoped that there wouldn't be a third.

❧ 𝒟 ❧

I had no idea which way we were walking through the dark, and tried to place myself by the stars. Apparently it was still the same night—I did not feel as if I had missed several meals, or a bath. "Why did they want me to deliver that...youngling? Why not you?"

The sound that came out of Marta was the closest I could remember to hearing her snort. "The horned ones have their own traditions, legends and superstitions, just as we do. The birth of a horned one, a unicorn or a Ki Lin, is a rare and blessed event. Few people know they are shape shifters. But unicorns believe that the stronger and more important a newborn will be, the more powerful the person who serves as midwife must be. Namid sought you for the task because she believes you will be a powerful practitioner."

"But she doesn't know that," I pointed out. "I may be very average, after all is said and done." I was shivering now, grateful for my coat but hesitant to pull on the sleeves. I did not want to have to explain blood on my coat to my mother or Aunt Dagmar.

"Who knows what Namid knows?" Marta responded. "Unicorns are long-lived, intelligent and secretive. They also have their own power, and we know little about that strength. I suspect many of them are Seers. Perhaps she is right—or at least she knows that on one path, you may become a powerful practitioner."

"But if I'm not...." I started slowly.

"Then she has opened you up to attacks by other powers who crave the title of strongest mage." Marta's words were flat. I did not sense any room for discussion.

"What do we do?" I asked, my voice soft and tight. I had been tricked by a magical creature. Could anyone just walk into my mind and cause me to do things against my will?

"We can get you immediate training in ritual magic," Marta replied, and she sounded tired. "Plenty of time for me to finish your work with herbs and basic elemental magic when you return. You're going to need to jump ahead to setting permanent wards and other protections." Marta stopped walking, her arm still around me. I could see the dark bulk of my parents' house against the starry night. Smoke lingered on the faint breeze, that blend of oak and apple wood my parents liked best.

There was something in her voice that made me say: "We're leaving tomorrow for Cat Track Hollow, aren't we?"

"I want us on the road before noon. We need to get back and pack your trunk and get you to Esme as swiftly as possible."

Cousin Esme? My mother's mysterious cousin Esme, the wizard of Manhattan?

The blood on my hands was finally dry. I shivered and pulled my coat closed. "It's a long way to New York," I murmured.

"Sometimes," Marta said in turn. "Don't worry about it, dear. We'll explain it to you later. Right now, you'll just have to trust me."

❧⫶❧

I rinsed the blood from my old skirt and let it dry by the banked fire. My parents were unhappy that we were leaving so soon, but Marta must have told them something about the night visitors, for they did not coax us to stay. We packed Marta's few things and were on the road by mid-morning. Ironing could wait until we reached Marta's home. It seemed wasteful to take any of Momma's clothes, since I had my things at Marta's house, but Momma insisted I take one of her older dresses *and* a sponge bath.

I wish we could have stayed longer. I scarcely got to talk with Momma and Papa, or let the boys show me what they're been making and learning. I could have sat for hours holding Elizabeth. A baby is the only miracle most people ever get to share in, and it had been a long time since we'd had a newborn in the house.

I hoped that she would remember me—would we know each other's minds?—but I would be a stranger to her when we met again.

My heart was heavy.

֍·𝕯·֍

It was a full day's ride to Cat Track Hollow in good weather. It was dark when we finally went east past the small town and followed the trail edging Wild Rose Run, the creek tracing Marta's south border. Snow was still heaped, though it had been a few days since the last storm. The ice was packed enough to walk upon, but the stream had broken through and gurgled a greeting. I was very tired, and glad to reach my cousin's home at last.

Marta and I rubbed down the horses and left them together in the big stall in the lean-to so they wouldn't be lonesome. Sweet William, Marta's walker, was over at a neighbor's place with the rest of her stock. That neighbor always took over when Marta left her home, and she had headed off to my rescue over a moon ago. My cousin had not known how long she would be gone in her efforts to retrieve me from Hudson-on-the-Bend, or if she would return at all. Practitioners are the most levelheaded of the magical world. You always know there's a chance you'll lose, when you challenge another.

We try not to leave loose ends.

By the time I had hauled in the last of our things, Marta had built a fire in the main fireplace and was setting an iron in the fire to heat. "Unpack my bag, Allie," she said. "We should set a small fire to warm up the bedroom."

I blinked. Another fire? I would be happy to roll up in a blanket in the big room, but I could see that wouldn't please Marta. Dragging the clothes bag behind me, I headed to the largest bedroom.

It didn't take long to start a fire in the pit in Marta's bedroom. Like my Papa, Uncle Jon had built some unusual things into his house, including two bedroom fireplaces, one for the master and one shared by the smaller bedrooms. I laid out all our clothing and shook out wrinkles, which didn't take long. All I had brought back from my family home was the one change of older clothes Momma insisted I wear, and the breeches, skirt, shirt and sweater I'd been wearing the day Erik Hudson snatched me and took me to his family's compound hundreds of miles away.

I also went into the guestroom closet Uncle Jon had built and pulled out every stitch of clothing I had brought from Sun-Return months before. I folded carefully, since I knew Marta would check to be sure I had not wrinkled things. She'd already started loading my trunk, which I found interesting.

Did Marta sometimes have prophetic dreams?

If she did, what had those dreams told her, while I was in Hudson-on-the-Bend?

As if conjured, Marta was suddenly there. "Are you finished packing your trunk?" she asked as she stepped into the guest room.

I paused. This question told me how worried Marta was about what had happened last night. She usually told me to do something, and then trusted that I was doing it.

"Yes, ma'am," I replied, holding up the tucker I was folding. I had several, all linen, as they extended how long you could wear a dress by many days. They also filled in any gaps that were not modest for someone my age. We'd designed the necklines for the bosom I would eventually have, not the one I had at the moment.

"Everything that we've finished," I added. "Not the ones laid out that we haven't cut."

"I added the uncut material and a few other things while you were gone. Now, let me check your height," she said, and I stood so she could take my measure. By her sudden smile, I knew that we had guessed right. Every scrap of clothing, new or old, had been cut or trimmed longer in case I was still growing. Marta had even left the chemises fuller than usual. "Good. You'll need to make up some new things when you get there. People pay more attention to fashion back east, although New York is not as style conscious as Philadelphia or London. Still, Esme may send you to Pennsylvania, so you need material to make clothing. Your parents will send more as you need it—or money."

The idea that my parents would give me silver coin for *anything* was humbling.

"You may need your Momma's old skirt for cleaning day, so press it now, and we'll pack things tightly. Tomorrow, we go to New York." With a nod, she went back to heat us the stew and corn bread we'd brought from Sun-Return.

I was so addled I barely had the sense to go make sure the horses were cool enough to be given more water and food. If we were hitting the road at dawn, we weren't even stopping to pick up Marta's favorite horse! When I passed through the stillroom to the main room, I asked if I could help her with dinner.

"Yes, stir it, and when it's hot through, and the cornbread is shining, serve it up. I'll just go check your trunk."

Definitely leaving at dawn. Believe my words—life with a practitioner can be nervy.

Dinner was hot and tasted wonderful, and we drank the last of the cider from Hudson-on-the-Bend. My cousin would not let me fuss further with the trunk or any food sacks, and insisted I get some sleep. The rooms had warmed enough that we banked the fires and both slept in Marta's room, instead of preparing the guest bed.

Tomorrow, the journey would begin.

I fell asleep to the whisper of wind about the eaves of the cabin. My first dream was only a flash, a shining unicorn looming above me, much taller than the ones I saw earlier that night. Then I was back on the dark, meandering trail from the southern Indiana Territory, reaching a place for our group to spend the night.

It was still late winter. I shook from the bone-chilling temperature as I helped break off dry branches from oak trees. Marta used precious magic to start a roaring fire, and Cory brought in a huge armful of wood. Shaw set up a small cauldron for cooking dinner, while the Hudsons tended the horses and rolled out our blankets.

In a blink it was later, our bellies full; most of us drowsed by the fire before seeking our beds. I walked away from the light to see the stars above us, the Milky Way spilled across the sparkling sky.

"The Magyars call it the Skyway of Warriors," came Shaw's voice behind me. "The stars are sparks from the hooves of the horses as Csaba's army returns to save their people."

"In some legends, Coyote tosses the stars into the heavens, creating the Milky Way," I said automatically as I turned around to face him. The fire was only a few strides away, and we were dark shapes outlined by intense flame.

We were the same height now—or was Shaw taller? In the darkness I couldn't tell. He was older, but girls grew up faster. We stood so close together I could smell the wood smoke clinging to his hair and deerskin jacket, and a hint of the rosemary I knew his family put in their soap.

It was a dream. I couldn't really smell those things. But I remembered smelling them.

Paper rustled and crinkled as Shaw pulled a pale scroll from his jacket. "Here," he said quietly, handing it to me.

"What is it?" I asked, taking the rolled paper from his gloved hand.

"It's a letter," he replied, his voice still hushed.

Shaw actually looked at me, something he barely did that night on the trail. Sometimes his eyes were like mist, and sometimes they shone like sunlight on water. In my dream they glinted like silver reflecting candlelight.

"What did you write that you could not say?" I said, matching his gaze with my own.

His breath caught—then he relaxed and exhaled.

"Things," was the hoarse answer. "My grandfather called the Milky Way the Pathway of the Birds. He said his grandfather told him that was how birds found their way south for the winter."

My mind scampered after the turn in the conversation. "I wonder if they really do use the Milky Way as a sign post?"

"Someday we'll know."

I smiled at him, although I could not see his expression. "Of course we will."

Marta's voice came out of the darkness. "Allie, time to get some sleep."

"You always want to know why and how," Shaw said, and touched my hand holding the letter. "Here's how."

It was my turn to hold my breath.

Then the fire hit a pocket of sap and popped, embers dancing into the sky, and Shaw moved back into the circle of light.

I could not read the letter until the next day. It began, *"You did just fine, Allie,"* and told me how Shaw and the others found where I was taken and followed, riding the wind to reach me.

I would keep that letter always.

He understood that *knowing mattered*.

Next I dreamt of walking through the forest with only Marta. We had my trunk dragging behind us on a small sledge and moved well down the snowy forest path. I was surprised we had no horses or a bag for Marta, but accepted the dream as it presented itself.

We'd walked for quite a while when we reached a small clearing, and Marta smiled and raised an arm in greeting. The air shimmered before us, the way heat rises from a freshly plowed field on a summer's day. We walked through sparkling air that tingled against my bare hands and face. Beyond the clearing was a snowy path with high green walls, and as I fell deeper into sleep, I heard the call of my Good Friend the White Wanderer, as if he followed in my wake.

.

TWO

THIS TIME I DID NOT FEEL THE HEAT. I did not fall out of my bed in terror. But the vision was not a good one.

I had snippets of dreams, like etchings in a book. There was one flash of a large, reddish cat, with gold and dark markings in his fur. He looked at me as if he understood what I said, but he was gone before I could blink. Another moment captured was of ladies and gentlemen in fine clothing, glimmering by candlelight as they moved in the patterns of a country-dance. A third vision was of a group of men quarreling inside some sort of tavern, fists flying everywhere, strong spirits only fueling the fight.

Next, I saw a village of Indians, a great gathering of men. I saw not only warriors, but also their families, and there were white traders present as well. Finally, I saw a group of young warriors moving past the long-house dwellings to the council fire. They wore loincloths, their faces painted black. Eagle feathers decorated their hair, and buffalo tails dragged on the ground behind them. It was very ceremonial, and I think it amused some of the traders.

But at night, after the traders had gone, the tall, handsome leader of that group began to speak. I did not know his language, but I knew he was a riveting speaker, because when he paused, you could have dropped the proverbial pin and actually heard it land.

The warrior gestured above their heads, and then I saw a sight I had yet to see in life, a splash of light across the night sky: what my grandmother's book called a comet. The old men he addressed nodded at the sight, and held their own counsel. Younger men murmured among themselves, but they kept listening.

My last dream was only a feeling. I was weary; weary to the point I could barely walk. I knew that I could not keep going…that no one person could solve this problem so dear to my heart. But I had no idea why I grieved.

If there were other dreams, they did not mark me.

჻ 𝕯 ჻

When I finally opened my eyes I found myself in the dark. Marta had already risen. She was often up before sunrise, but that wasn't hard at the end of winter. I could smell fresh bread, that lovely scent of baked flour, sweet and toasty, but I did not remember her putting dough out to rise.

It was when I stretched that the strangeness began.

My left hand touched heavy hanging fabric. I yanked my arms back and under the covers. What in Heaven? After a moment, I slowly reached out into the darkness. Again, my fingers touched draped material…wool, at a guess, and a nice, fine weave. I pinched and rubbed the cloth…no slubs in the fabric.

Sitting up in the bed, I strained for some light to see by, but no—either it was still dark, or this mystery place had no windows.

Lord and Lady, will I ever stop waking up in strange places?

Surely this happened to other practitioners.

At that moment, I heard footsteps on wood. Freezing like a hare, I waited for the sounds to fade away.

The footsteps came closer. A door swung open…its hinges creaked slightly. I heard a thud and some clinking of metal against metal, and then the scraping of metal against stone.

All right…I admit I am worse than a cat at curiosity. Carefully I ran a finger across the drapes until I found an opening and moved one fold to the left. Cold slid slowly and steadily into my dark cocoon. I reached back for some blanket to use as a stole, and looked out at what I could see.

So—not Marta's guest room. It wasn't the Kristinssons' boarding house, either, the only place I had ever seen hanging draperies around a bed. I could see a cold, pale light from an area to the left

and a form, maybe a tall dresser, by the wall opposite the foot of
the bed. A hand—a woman's, I thought—brushed the top of a candlestick sitting on the high dresser, and the wick suddenly lit, as if
a poltergeist were in residence. There was the sound of creaking
metal, the scrape of metal across wood, and then the "whoomp" of
a large fire igniting.

Well, whatever had happened, I wasn't supposed to freeze. I
waited until the person carefully placed a metal fire screen before
the chimney opening. Female, fairly tall although not a tree like
me.... As she shook wrinkles out of her long skirts and turned away
from the growing blaze, I asked: "What is the day, and the time?"

The girl let out a squeak and shrank back. I pushed the fold to
one side so she could see me. Only then did she relax.

"Gracious, miss, you startled me! I thought you would sleep for
hours yet, after so long a trip."

"The time?" I repeated.

The girl walked out of sight, and I heard fabric sweeping across
the floor. Weak morning light gave definition to the furniture in
the small room. As she returned to the bed's foot, this new daylight
showed me a bird-boned, pale girl not much older than myself. Her
hair was what you noticed about her—dark, thick and coiled in a
braid about her head.

"It's after eight o'clock, but on Saturday the students are allowed
to sleep in," she finally said. "There is a brunch, but...." She paused,
as if thinking over her answer. "If you'd like cocoa, and something
while still a-bed, I'm sure it would be all right."

"Has Mrs. Donaltsson had breakfast yet?" I heard myself saying.
Might as well act like I knew what was going on.

"I don't know, miss, but she was with Professor Livingston, and
Mary took them both scones and tea, so they have had the chance
to break their fast. I could see if any scones were left, or you can
go...to the buffet." The young servant (or so I thought she must
be) had on a full white apron to protect her clothing, but her high-
necked dress was a medium gray, so she wasn't in danger of ashes
marring the wool.

"I think I need to find Mrs. Donaltsson," I replied. So Marta *was*
here. And this young woman seemed to have reservations about the
morning meal.

I was pretty sure we were already at mysterious Cousin Esme's
house.

"Then I'll—Do you have any more questions? I will either answer them, or find someone who can."

Well, there was probably a chest with my clothes in it somewhere in this room, so that answered my first question. How we got here was another question entirely. My other needs were simple. This was New York, not Sun-Return, so.... "How do people dress for brunch?"

"A simple afternoon carriage gown is recommended for winter classes," she replied.

That wasn't a lot of help, but I had too much pride to ask what she meant.

"Anything else, miss?" She still held her place, neither picking up her metal can, nor arranging the open top of the fireplace screen.

"What is your name?"

The girl smiled and said, "Elizabeth, miss."

I smiled, too. "My baby sister was just named Elizabeth, so I should be able to remember that." *I have a sister! And she's a seer!*

I didn't say it aloud, but I realized that this might be a place where I could someday say those words. But I could not say them yet. I couldn't chance it getting back to Momma.

I pulled the curtain back a foot or two. "My name is Alfreda Sorensson."

"Yes, miss," Elizabeth said, bobbing into what I recognized from country-dances as a curtsy. "Thank you, miss!"

I hoped she didn't do that all the time.

Shivering, I pulled the blanket closer. "Thank you for the fire!"

Beaming, Elizabeth picked up her metal can.

"Oh, Elizabeth. Where is...how do I get to the privy?"

Elizabeth's blue eyes widened. "We don't need to use a privy here, miss! We have water closets! Dr. Livingston went to England for them! And then he did something special with them so they never back up or overflow or smell or—"

I could tell Elizabeth thought this was the best idea she'd ever heard. Having visited a few privies that I had to gather up my long skirt to even enter, I had a lot of sympathy with her feelings.

"Wonderful! How do I get there?"

♪·🎵·♪

It *was* a rather astonishing contraption with ceramic pipes everywhere, including into the floor and ceiling, and a polished wooden seat.

Elizabeth had demonstrated by pulling on a chain with a smooth glass bauble attached, draining and refilling the "necessary." Then she left after scenting the air by running her fingers through some dried flower petals in a bowl.

Well, I didn't intend to gape like a rustic, so I used the impressive throne and found it worked just as she promised. As I turned to leave, I paused and touched the water pipe descending from the ceiling. This was wondrous...something that existed, if imperfectly, improved by magic. Lots of magic, if they had multiple necessary rooms, and candles that lit by themselves.

Where did that much power come from?

Would they tell me?

I'd noticed a basin and pitcher in my room, so I shut the door to the necessary and made my way back down the hall, wondering how they handled bathing here.

I passed Elizabeth on my way into the sleeping chamber, and nodded to her, smiling my thanks. She had recovered her metal pail of hot coals and left the cinder guard on the fire screen folded to the stone fireplace. I didn't have time to judge anything else, even with the candle once again lit, because someone was busy in the bedroom. I shut the door and found Marta at the wardrobe pulling out my golden wool dress.

"Isn't that...Sunday best?" I asked as she laid the dress on the bed. We had altered it slightly after our trip to Cloudcatcher, raising the waist and moving the ribbon to tie in the front.

"Yes," Marta said, "But for your first appearance in the house it is better to be overdressed than underdressed. And you'll find the hallways in these huge places are very cold. You'll appreciate the warmth, believe me." She turned and surveyed me by the pale morning light. "I think you should meet Esme first—then you'll feel more like having breakfast."

"Do I get any explanations?"

Marta gave me that look that said, *You have to ask?* "Did you understand the water closet?"

I sighed. "Elizabeth showed me the water closet. It's very fancy magic." I went to the wardrobe to find my shift.

"A small magic, carefully applied," Marta replied, settling in the rocking chair near the window. "That's often the best kind of magic, subtle and undetected. You'll learn about that kind of magic here."

"Like candles that light themselves?"

"Exactly. Some things they don't change—for instance, they don't block every draft, because they couldn't explain it to visitors—but things like sewage and kitchen chores are improved by delicate spell casting."

The Hudsons used magic to kill the smell of the pig sty and guard the fires. I had not thought of my former captors in days, but all this magic had me anxious to know the source.

I quickly peeled out of my nightgown and pulled my shift and the dress over my head. Then I put on my silver necklace, which was under the high neck, and looked over my silver bracelets and the delicate gold necklace that bore the few trophies of my fledgling apprenticeship. Amber, tiger-eye and a tiny diamond caged in gold threads showed that I was not a new initiate, but on my way to knowledge and power.

I turned to Marta and held up the necklace. She nodded, and I slipped it on.

Marta stood and reached for my brush. "You have little ritual training, so you will mostly be with younger children for that class. But you will undoubtedly be in the advanced class for herb work, or midwifery and small injuries and illnesses. This is not a rigid school—it is common for students to have vast differences in skills, and study with others not their ages. Your necklace reassures your classmates that you are a practitioner, even though your teaching was different from Esme's lessons."

I was silent while she smoothed the tangles out of my hair and then started braiding it high on the back of my head, pulling hair from the front to join the sides and back strands. Since my hands were free, I decided on the bracelets as well.

Who knew if I'd need to protect myself with silver here?

Well, nothing ventured, nothing gained. "Are you going to tell me how we got here?"

"No, not yet," Marta answered. "If I tell you how we arrived here, you'll be so curious about it you'll be experimenting with that spell instead of learning proper ritual magic. That secret will keep until Esme is ready to share it with you." Holding the end of my long braid, Marta asked: "Where is your string of rawhide?"

"Tied to the brush, unless it fell off," I replied. My head was still full of questions. So...there was a spell to get here. Was there just one spell, or multiple spells? Did we ride the back of the wind, the way the others did when they came to rescue me from Hudson-on-the-Bend? Or was my dream reality, and had we walked from the Michigan territory to New York with only a comfortable stroll in the woods? Did—

It was hard to admit to myself that Marta had a good reason not to tell me about the spell.

I stood up straight, and Marta's gaze slid over me. Nodding, she handed me my dancing shoes and waited while I slipped them on and tied them to my ankles.

"Very good. Now—Esme has agreed to teach you ritual magic. She hasn't had a descendant of your great-grandmother Emma Schell to teach at that level, so this pleases her. But I know she isn't totally prepared for the reality of Alfreda Sorensson. So you need to be courteous of her. Call her Professor Livingston when others can hear, and let *her* tell people you're related, if she desires to. You must trust her for this—if she doesn't tell you something, there's a reason. Esme does not make decisions like that capriciously."

"I will." At least I hoped I would.

Marta gave me another of her "looks." I didn't see those looks often, but today was not like most days. "And please, Alfreda, try not to attract attention with your wanderings. I know this city will feel like walking in a dozen petticoats after living in the Michigan territory. But you can't ride astride here and leave Esme to deal with the gossip. You can't even eat an apple without cutting it up first. People expect a young girl to behave with decorum—in fact, they expect someone your age to have a governess watching over her. Think at the fussiest level you can; you can't go too high with town busybodies." She paused, and then added, "What you do when no one looks is different."

"Yes, ma'am," I said, nodding once decisively. I had learned how to keep the village of Sun-Return from talking about me, so I was determined to master this, too.

Marta turned to the wardrobe and then touched my shoulder. "Now, before I forget—" She pushed my heavy coat and bathrobe aside. "The pale blue dress is a walking gown, for class, for weekend days when you're only dining with fellow students, for walking in the maze and labyrinths." I blinked and stared at the simply styled, square-necked dress in a pale indigo. Where had *this* come from?

And then followed the most incomprehensible speech I had ever heard from Marta, about several other dresses in the wardrobe I did not remember making, much less possessing. They changed clothes during the day? Just for *dinner*?

I was in trouble.

"Remember, Alfreda, you aren't the most careful mender and patcher, but you can use your embroidery and sewing to trade services or earn actual coin," Marta finished, letting go of still another garment I'd never seen before. "This ancient green dress will serve you for cleaning and brewing herbs, if you line it with a chemise— a shift."

While I stared at the rainbow of surprises, Marta turned to the dresser and pulled out a drawer. "I have a gift for you. It didn't arrive until after Christmas, so I was waiting for your birthday. Now you need it so it's a very early birthday present." On top of my unmentionables was something else I didn't recognize. It was loosely woven, like knitting or crocheting, in shades of ivory, tanned leather and golden deer hide. My cousin unfolded it as she removed it from the drawer and let it hang to its full length.

It was a shawl—a woolen, knitted shawl, its ends smooth and nicely finished. Marta held it up. "Turn around and let's see how it works."

I let her slip the shawl over my shoulders, and pulled the front closer before I turned around. Oh, the softness of the wool! I didn't know what it was made of, but I wanted some of it for gloves!

Marta steered me toward a looking glass on carved eagle feet. I looked at the tall, slender woman in gold and ivory, and knew it had to be me, though I couldn't imagine I'd changed so much since the last time I'd looked into a mirror, before Christmas. There was a pattern in the shawl that gave it texture, woven in a Celtic or Greek key design. I watched the ripple of light over ridge and dale, giving the garment depth.

"It's...beautiful," I said, pulling the shawl closer. And it was *warm*—I knew I would be grateful for it in this house.

"I traded a quilt for it, to a practitioner in the south continent," Marta said with satisfaction. "And I spelled it, so if anyone tries to take it, they'll have a surprise coming to them. Spelled your jewelry as well."

"Oh, Marta—thank you!" I turned and impulsively hugged her. "Thank you for everything," I whispered in her ear.

"Thank *you*, dearheart. You've given me light and laughter when I thought only duty was left to me." She smiled as she straightened, and it wasn't one of those wry smiles—it was a big smile. "I know you will make us all proud, and I look forward to your return. Write us—Esme allows students to use a ritual circle to send letters. Tell me about life in the big city! You may write Cory and Shaw about your lessons, too. And—" She touched my cheek again. "We will come to visit. I will encourage your parents to bring the baby. She won't be a stranger, child. We have resources."

Somehow I managed not to burst into tears. Marta had a gift for touching my deepest fears and then easing them. Some people acted like they'd forgotten what it was like to be young. With Marta, you knew that somewhere deep inside she remembered.

Before she hustled me away, I *had* to know—"The dresses? Where did they...come from?" I gestured toward the wardrobe, because these were *not* the pieces of clothing I had cut out after my stay in Cloudcatcher. Had they been under the material in the bottom of the trunk? Had she put them in after I went to sleep?

Marta just looked at me with her famous impassive stare. "Where do you think?"

"Momma?" It was unlikely, but still....

"She was working on something for you, but it's not finished yet. Try again." Marta must have seen something in my expression, because she abruptly satisfied my curiosity. "I was frantic when you disappeared and we couldn't find you. I had to do *something* with my time."

"You left me the hems?"

Marta raised an eyebrow. "You got more sleep last night than I did. I left three for you. Two are cotton and linen, and easy—rolling the silk one will be good practice."

Silk?

How were we going to *pay* for all these things?

Well, there wasn't much more to say except to thank her, and I'd already done that. I just had to grow into someone she spoke of with pride.

"Are you coming with me when I meet Cousin Esme?" I really didn't want her slipping off while I kept my cousin busy.

"Of course. She will be nothing like you expect, and as full of surprises as a Beltane fire. I want you to feel like you have reinforcement!" Smoothing a few stray tendrils of hair away from my face,

Marta gave the fireplace a last look and then opened the door and
gestured for me to follow her.

The lit candle died as we passed it.

I will always follow her.

She has that effect on people.

❧·🕮·❧

The walls of this floor were made of wood painted white or white-
washed, and that pale color kept the hallway from being gloomy. All
candles were positioned on hinged brackets above our heads, glass
chimneys protecting them from drafts and us from flame. I looked
sharp as we walked, but I did not see dust on the bronze arm or
grime on the glass. Clearly my cousin was a formidable housekeeper—or she had an army of helpers keeping up the place.

I hoped none of them were slaves.

The third candle chimney caused me to look twice.

Did I see something look *back* at me?

I stopped and stared at the candle a long time. A steady, yellow
flame, nothing out of the ordinary....

"Allie, come along!"

I hurried to catch up to Marta.

We reached a staircase that was wider than the hallway. "This
is the family wing of this mansion, which also houses students and
servants. If you keep walking down that hall, you will reach the central part of the house. That central staircase takes you to the guest
rooms, the professors' private workrooms, and the room warded for
major spell casting. You won't need that for a while yet. For now,
this staircase takes you to your world." Taking hold of the smooth,
square banister, Marta moved quickly downstairs.

Only Marta would guess that this place felt like a strange forest to me. I had no landmarks, knew none of the noises.... I looked
around as I walked downstairs and realized that I was looking *for*
someone. I had the strangest feeling that I was being watched.

Our destination was close by. Pausing before a door, Marta murmured: "This is the north room. During winter Esme uses it for
private conferences with students and their families, and as a gathering place in the evening. You do not have to curtsy, but you may
if you'd like, it's proper and formal for a young girl." With that, she
knocked three times and then opened the door.

We walked over polished oak floorboards into a room with high
walls painted robin's egg blue. There was a mural painted on the

ceiling and the designs carved around the fireplace were beautiful, but I wasn't going to gawk like someone going to see the lions.

A cheery fire was burning, the occasional flame of blue or green hinting at mineral salts sprinkled over the seasoned firewood. My gaze skipped past a sewing chest, cloth, and hoop frames to the windows. They were huge, and clear, and I cannot begin to tell you how wonderful those windows were to me! I wanted to walk over and look through that glass. It was a physical aching, remaining next to Marta and keeping my feet nailed to the floor. Finally I turned my head, facing toward the fireplace and the slender woman seated near the screen.

Cousin Esme was closer to Marta's age than to my mother's age, but she looked no older than mother's eternally beautiful older sister Aunt Sunhild. Dark brown hair twisted gracefully from the knot up on her head, ringlets cascading to brush her neck and shoulders. She had huge dark eyes rimmed with dark lashes, and eyebrows that canted like bird wings.

Those eyes looked right through me and out between my shoulder blades. There was nothing threatening in that look, precisely, but I felt like I was being assessed like a cupboard—one layer at a time, top to bottom.

Marta had mentioned once that Cousin Esme did not tell people she was half Irish. There was some prejudice against those poorer cot holders who had come to the new world for a different life. I did not know how she hid this—she looked very Irish to me.

But then what those of different gifts—those without magic—saw when they looked at Cousin Esme might be very different. Even other magic-users might see only what she chose to reveal.

The woman stood, the serenity of confidence wrapping her like a cloak. It was as if she was in the heart of her power, and feared nothing within its walls. She was shorter than my mother, but her presence made her *feel* taller.

"Esme, I want to introduce Garda's daughter Alfreda to you. Alfreda, I make you known to Professor Esme Aisling Perry Livingston, your cousin through your mother's family."

Good thing I'd practiced a curtsy.

I wasn't sure if I should rise or not—she wasn't a queen, not in the sense most people used the word—so I bent my knee and my head, trying not to bounce, and said, "Ma'am," as I tried to lower myself enough to become, if only for a moment, the same height as my mother's cousin.

Cousin Esme extended a hand to me. "Stand, child. I am sure that is hard on your knees." I did as she requested, and tried to stand straight, hoping the shawl would not take a flying leap off my arms.

Shaking hands with Cousin Esme was not like anything I had previously experienced. Touching her hand reminded me of the time I struck at a demon with an iron poker. A crackle of energy sparked from our hands. I didn't know if Marta knew; I didn't see the movement of energy, I only felt it.

Cousin Esme's eyes widened, then narrowed, and I felt a tiny stab like a needle trying my defenses. For a moment the shield enclosing my mind and soul slipped. The resulting shift in energy made both women flinch back from me. I hastily threw up a wall against probing from anything watching our meeting, and hoped neither Cousin Esme nor Marta would try that again.

Marta was smiling gently. She and Cousin Esme traded knowing glances, and then Cousin Esme said: "I can see that Alfreda will help keep the school lively! Sit, if you please." Gesturing at the opposite chair and the small couch, she sat down and poured tea.

And next? Well, I can tell you that I worked hard for my tea and scones. One minute she was asking about the proper dosage of teas made for ladies who were increasing, and the next she wanted to know would I make a decoction, or perhaps a cold compress when using the herb boneset?

Oh, dear. I surely hoped this was a trick question. "Boneset has a lot of uses," I started. "But we use the herb, not the rootstock, so I learned to make an infusion or a tincture of it. Cold, it is a mild laxative, and warm it's a diaphoretic and emetic, and is useful for breaking up a cold, or for fever, and even for flu. Hot, you need to be careful, because it's both cathartic and emetic." When no one spoke, I added: "It tastes nasty, very bitter, so I would add honey to it to kill some of the taste."

"Good," Cousin Esme replied. "And how about wild carrot seed?"

"Important to lots of folks," I started. "Infusion or decoction for the seeds, but the rootstock can also be made into a soup or juice. Carrot seed starts up your moon time, so you don't want to use it when you want to be increasing. It is very effective for most women in preventing a pregnancy, but you *must* take your dose of seed every day. You miss a day, and it won't prevent you from ending up in the family way."

Cousin Esme smiled, and those expressions made her look very much like Marta. For a moment, these two merged in my mind, and I found myself wondering whose smile it was that had marked them. Had they shared a teacher at one time? Or was it something women who were practitioners gradually acquired? Then I thought back to see if Cory ever looked that way, which meant I missed half her next question.

"Ma'am?" I said quickly; she'd caught me woolgathering.

Cousin Esme's smile slightly opened her mouth; her expression was amused. "Yes, we did," she answered. "Now, your cousin tells me that you have delivered several babies, including twins. Let's speak of that."

I wasn't sure if she was answering my thought about being caught flat-footed, or...the thought before it, about a former teacher they'd shared. So I just plowed on.

I told her about delivering twins on Twelfth Night, with Marta too far away to advise me, and the Wild Hunt between the Moore's cabin and Marta's home. I gave Marta a quick glance, to see if she was starting to frown—meaning I could leave that part out of my story—but Marta just sat there, nodding her agreement at various points.

"You can mention your Good Friend," Marta said when I reached a place to pause. "And the poltergeist."

I did not need to tell Cousin Esme that a Good Friend was a spirit who willingly chose to help a practitioner work magic; she undoubtedly had her own Good Friend. More than one Good Friend could appear for someone overwhelmingly Talented.

And so I explained about losing Marta's horse in the snow, and my Good Friend, in his guise as a white stag, rescuing me from ghouls and then carrying me through the horde of dark faery. The story about the poltergeist that fled when my troubles with the Hudsons began was woven in there somewhere.

"Wild Magic follows you," Cousin Esme said abruptly, glancing at my cousin Marta.

"More than once," Marta agreed. "Tell her about controlling the tornado in the snow storm."

Well, I was surprised I was jumping ahead of the story, but I did, explaining how I'd caught a wisp of wind as I moved through a snowstorm, holding onto it in case I needed a weapon. Yes, it sounds strange now, but then I didn't think about it. I had never willingly harmed anything, especially a man—but that night Death itself used me as its weapon to reach an ancient and corrupt evil that had once called itself human.

As I found a rock to cling to in the river of narrative, Cousin Esme suddenly asked: "What is the first rule of wizardry?"

I just stared at her.

Marta said: "Actually we taught her the second rule first—in her case, we thought it best. Do you remember, Alfreda, when we asked you which plant was Queen Anne's lace?"

Ah.

How to explain it simply? "The lesson was to realize how much you don't know. And that what you don't know may be more dangerous than everything you do know."

Cousin Esme nodded, and said: "Drink your tea, child. You won't get that quality in the dining room on a Saturday."

Then she turned her attention to Marta, and I took a nice mouthful of tea (since it had cooled a bit) and nibbled on my buttered scone. It was a lovely thing, moist and flavorful, with the smallest amount of lift to the dough. Almost like pastry dotted with tart pieces of fruit. I wondered if the cook would share the recipe, and if I could make it in a wood-burning oven. I'd heard about "stoves" but hadn't seen one yet.

"I'll teach her," Cousin Esme said, and I blinked. So, they hadn't known for sure that she'd take me. "You know how much is happening right now, but I lost my herb and potions teacher, and she could definitely teach the first-year students, and perhaps more. Her age doesn't need to be known around the school. I'll do a thorough review later this week. Tell Garda and Eldon that her herbal assistance will cover room and board. We'll set her up with basic ritual work and then talk about whether she'll stay longer or return to your house."

So Momma and Papa are paying for some of this training. I was glad that Cousin Esme thought I had something worth trading. I wondered what my parents had traded—or were still trading— with Marta.

I had not considered that Cousin Esme might be unwilling to teach me. I hoped I could make it worth her time.

My scone disappeared and then I eyed the pile before me. There were a dozen still there, despite the remains of scones on Marta and Esme's plates. After thought, I took another. Two wouldn't seem like too much.

Cousin Esme then said: "Did you design that dress, Alfreda, or did your mother make it?" Her look was a tad sharper than it had been, and took in my feet, slightly tucked back under my own skirt.

"Momma wove the material, after we spun and dyed the wool," I started out. "Marta and I changed it slightly after we visited... Cloudcatcher...to match the high-waisted dress the Squire's daughter was wearing."

"She did it herself," Marta added. "I just double-checked everything new to her, and showed her how to use an awl to make thread holes for her slippers. Her leather interpretation of the silk shoes was masterful."

But they're not as pretty as Jesse Gunnarsson's French slippers. I held my tongue while discussion of American woven goods as compared to British and French materials slipped back and forth around me. I finally sent a good thought to my shoes—I didn't want them to feel unwanted—and told them that I was glad I'd made them, they were so warm and didn't slip a bit on the rug. The tanned leather was a beautiful golden brown, pale as early autumn leaves.

I didn't want to be too different when someone looked over Esme's students.

"Her athame will be ready soon," Marta said. "For her wand, of course she tested for oak, but she doesn't have one yet."

"I think all Schell descendants use oak," Cousin Esme replied, smiling at me again. "Well, Alfreda Sorensson, are you ready to enter the study of ritual magic?"

"Probably not," I admitted.

Cousin Esme blinked.

"I probably have too many holes in my knowing, missing pieces that will be dangerous. But if you and Cousin Marta think I'm ready, then I must be."

Her expression solemn, Cousin Esme said: "She'll do, Marta. I suspect the goddess and the consort protect her. We'll see what we can do to help them out."

I clenched my jaw to prevent a nervous giggle. The idea of helping the Lord and Lady of Light just seemed too silly for words.

If gods needed help looking after me, well....

It's said that the slowest soldier is either a hero or a corpse. I hoped I could learn fast.

I'd already seen enough ghosts.

I didn't want to join them.

THREE

MARTA AND COUSIN ESME HAD HAD TEA and scones long before Marta came in search of me. They'd talked about me, too; I was
certain of that. But even after questioning me, they still had information to trade. I used this time to eat two more of the scones and
try cream so thick a spoon stood up in it, something Marta told me
privately was clotted cream.

"Let us go to the dining room, Alfreda, where I will introduce you
to those students who are neither still asleep nor chose to eat breakfast elsewhere. On Saturday, selected students prepare the meals
so that Mrs. Gardener, our cook, may have a day of rest." Cousin
Esme rose as she spoke, heading for the door, and as we also stood
up I carefully wiped my fingertips on a napkin and glanced quickly at Marta.

No crumbs, tea or cream. Very good, Marta's mind voice said
inside my head.

Now—two more things to mention, she continued as we followed Cousin Esme. *Do you remember what I said about deciding
to bed a boy?*

My mind froze in place like a frightened hare. I hoped I wasn't blushing. I certainly did remember her bringing it up out of the blue. *You said there were good reasons not to do that yet, and asked me to talk with you first if I was tempted.*

Excellent. That request still holds, dear. Please trust me on this—you do NOT *want to start a baby now, and very few forms of birth control are foolproof. The second thing is*—and she looked over her shoulder briefly as she spoke to me. *Don't teach anyone wild magic.*

I felt a weight to the words, as if she were settling them upon me. Of course not.

I was no teacher.

Marta stopped walking and gave me a gentle hug, her cheek momentarily brushing mine. *I'm not dressed impressively enough to meet her current students, so I'll say good-by now. Remember that you are up to any challenge Windward Academy hands to you!*

I love you, I thought to myself, but I did not frame it for her to "hear." I hoped she knew this, but some adults did not like sentimentality from children. I decided to say the words another time.

Marta walked briskly back the way we'd originally come from, leaving me with Cousin Esme, who was moving toward the center of the house. I followed her silently, trying to hold my head high and keep my shoulders from hunching up. *Behold Alfreda Sorensson, a too tall, flat-chested, awkward, thirteen-year-old future Valkyrie.*

Truth.

Still, I was a child of a dual line of famous Northern practitioners. I'd find a place for me here, somewhere.

I cannot hide, I reminded myself. *Only magic can hide me and this is not the moment for magic!*

At least not the moment for my magic. This house reeked of power. It made my shoulders itch.

We stepped into the entry hall. I didn't know where to look. To my right two huge sets of windows flanked what must have been the main entrance of glass double doors. Above us a balcony rimmed almost three quarters of the room, but no grand staircase could be seen. Numerous open-backed chairs lined the walls, and a huge, branched candelabrum seemed to float just below the ceiling.

Cousin Esme continued across the polished stone floor squares to the corner doorway. Glancing over her shoulder, she said: "We generally have breakfast and dinner in the room we are entering. Supper can be taken here or the tea room, or even out on the portico in lovely weather. Saturday, as I said, is the day that students make the meals. I've found that making students responsible for meal preparation can quickly solve many discipline problems."

Another glance revealed no staircase. Discipline problems? So cooking was extra work? Some people were not very good cooks.

Somehow, Cousin Esme knew I wasn't just taking it all in. "Are you looking for something in particular?"

"I thought that fine houses had single, grand staircases? Is this the entrance?"

Cousin Esme smiled and said: "Yes, this is the entry hall. But President Jefferson designed this house, and the architectural principles he prefers do not include a large, single staircase. Fortunately, women's skirts currently do not need double doors to enter a room!" With that, she gestured for me to step into the room ahead of her.

President Jefferson designed this house?

A lovely wood floor stretched away before us, the pale strips and few knots making me think of cherry wood. A good-sized table in the center of the room seated ten, and looked like it could be expanded. Beyond broad glass doors stood between the dining room and another seating area.

Around me whirled a blur of young people, from my little brothers' ages up to at least my own. A sea of faces, and they varied in skin color and severity of dress. In the room beyond, the students looked older. Candles burned up high in wall sconces and on the mantel of the fireplace. Beneath the scent of beeswax I smelled burnt pork and also scorched biscuits. I also recognized the sweetness of oatmeal.

The room was noisy, but not overwhelming. Still, what sounded like spirited conversation abruptly grew quieter as the students realized who had entered the room.

"We have a new student joining the school," Cousin Esme said simply. "This is Miss Sorensson. She has had unusual training up until now, so all of you may see her in at least one class. I hope you will make her feel welcome." Cousin Esme was looking around as she spoke. "Is Miss Rutledge here?"

A dark-haired girl who looked to be my age said: "She was feeling unwell this morning, so she had ginger and willow bark tea in her room. When I stopped there before breakfast, I thought she seemed better."

Cousin Esme's eyebrows rose, and her smile was amused, not re-assuring. "I wanted her to give Miss Sorensson a tour of the house and grounds." My cousin pinned a pretty, plump blonde girl with a look. "When you are finished, Miss Wolfsson, please ask Miss Rut-ledge if she feels well enough to join me in my room." Cousin Esme looked at me and gestured toward the buffet. "Eat whatever you need; we know that growing magicians need fuel!"

Clearly Cousin Esme had her reasons for making students cook the Saturday morning meal. I suspected Miss Rutledge was not re-ally ill, merely avoiding the bad food.

How bad did you have to be to get sentenced to the kitchen on a Saturday?

I also wondered if that itchy feeling I had between my shoulder blades meant that someone was using magic to listen to this entire conversation. Surely practitioners could do that?

Still, I couldn't stop my grin. Since I liked to cook, and had brought with me old trousers and my brother's shirt for dirty work, I was ready for anything from baking to shoveling manure. Perhaps I could manage not to trespass while I was in New York. Just once, could I avoid upsetting people before I even knew the rules?

Cousin Esme smiled up at me. "If she has recovered, I will ask Miss Rutledge to show you the manor after you finish breakfast. She will show you how to find your room. Dinner is at two in the after-noon—there is a bell that rings the time. May you learn here all that you hope for and more." With a gracious nod, Cousin Esme walked out before I could thank her.

I smiled at several children who smiled timidly at me, and then I walked to the buffet table. I found a pan of rashers of bacon, the fat burnt to charcoal, and baked eggs cooked so hard they could be cut from a pan like a dried-up cobbler. *Oh, dear.* Then I found the oatmeal.

Someone made an attempt at a display. A small pitcher of cream, a honey jar, and a cone of precious white cane sugar balanced a bowl of dried fruit. Pride of place went to the oatmeal pot. The dip-per stood on its own in the middle of the cereal, bowls stacked to one side.

Well—some hot water to thin the oatmeal would be in order. As I reached for the dipper, movement at the edge of my vision caught my attention. A small, thin boy of anywhere from eight to twelve suddenly stood at my side. He was dressed neatly in dark knee

breeches, a white shirt and collar, and a blue jean jacket carefully buttoned over all. His dark eyes gave life to a pale face, his dark
hair a bit shaggy. He leaned slightly toward me and whispered: "It
tastes fine!"

"Have you tried it?" I replied, keeping my voice softer than usual.

"I made it. I did everything just like Mrs. Gardener does, I asked
her how. I used five cups of cut oats, and twenty cups of water, and
a little bit of salt, just a pinch!" His gaze was beseeching. Clearly,
getting this right mattered to him.

I wiped a serving off the dipper into my bowl. Round spoons lay
by the plate stack. I picked one up to taste a tiny bit of the cereal.
It was fine, the creamy surface hiding thoroughly cooked grain. I
smiled at the boy. "Excellent."

"Truly?" He studied me anxiously, as if I was putting him off
with a fairy tale.

"Truly. All it needs is a bit of thinning; oatmeal soaks up a great
deal of liquid!" Since there was hot water with the tea, I demonstrated, and soon had a bowl of oatmeal and a cup of fresh tea.

Loaded for bear, I turned back to the young man. "Where do
you suggest I sit?"

The boy seemed momentarily at a loss, but quickly recovered.
"The older students like to sit in the back room. Or you are welcome
to sit here." He gestured to the large table in the center, where a
boy was carefully taking dirty dishes to the opposite buffet table.

Older students, eh? And were any older students supervising
in the kitchen? Did students repeat this punishment, or was once
enough...explaining the quality of most of the food? Did anyone
teach them *how* to cook, for the lord's sake?

What had Cousin Esme said? *I've found that making students
responsible for meal preparation can quickly solve many discipline problems.*

So this was a test. Was the intention to show them that they knew
nothing about work other people did?

Experience is a grand teacher, Grandsir would often exclaim.

Cousin Esme must have had a Grandsir in her life, too.

I started for the large table. "I thank you for the invitation. And
your name is?...."

He flushed. "Daniel Williams, Miss Sorensson." He tidied a place
setting a touch more, laying a clean napkin to the left of the forks—
plural, if you will. I remembered Papa telling me that the secret to

a formal dinner was start from the outside and work your way in. He had said that the fun stuff was at the top—the bread plate and knife, a dessert spoon—although none of those special pieces were laid out here.

"That actually looks good," another boy said, his fair hair and pale blue eyes suggesting he was of Dutch ancestry.

"It is lovely," I assured him. "Mr. Williams has done an excellent job." I hoped it was all right to say that. Since this was punishment, maybe the students didn't want any attention drawn to their efforts? I set down the plate and bowl, and my teacup to the right of the place setting. My skirt moved, and I felt something bump the backs of my legs. Daniel Williams was ahead of me, sliding the chair beneath me. I sat and nodded my thanks to him.

It was like a signal; the others still at the table started eating or talking again, while two boys and one girl got up and headed for the oatmeal. A quick glance told me they'd been drinking sweet tea for breakfast. So were they waiting around for their friends to finish cooking? Waiting for someone to make a mistake? Was everyone expected to show up for the meal?

I surveyed the room and realized something important. No leaders—these students were followers, or misfits. The students who controlled things at this school did not show up for Saturday breakfast.

Daniel Williams grinned fit to bust. I felt he had a right to be proud.

At least two other students ate with their left hands. Good—I liked my tea on my tool-using side. I lifted a crumpled napkin to my left, to make room for my cup and teapot, and found an upside-down bowl. *Well, that won't do.* I slid a nail under the rim to right it, just as Daniel cried: "Don't!"

A growl came from under the bowl.

I slammed the stoneware back down on the table, hearing several gasps and a nervous giggle. Several children started toward us.

The small boy tidying the tables came to me, eyes wide. "I—I apologize, Miss Sorensson. We thought we'd taken all of them back to the kitchen."

"Well, what is it, and how fast does it move?" I asked him. A soft, steady growl continued from under the bowl.

A nibbled lip, a glance at Daniel.... "It's a biscuit," the small boy whispered.

I decided to smile. "So tell me about your biscuit that growls." A few finger taps on the bowl earned me a snarl.

"It has big teeth, too!" a flame-haired little girl at my right elbow volunteered.

"Where do biscuits with teeth come from? They're not considered a threat where my family lives." I tried to keep my voice sounding normal.

The children looked embarrassed.

Several pairs of eyes glanced quickly at the young boy who was the spokesman. I turned to him, trying to look interested but not accusing. The child's face was flushed, his hands clenched—I guessed to resist grabbing for the bowl. He was one of the group who looked underfed, as growing practitioners often did. His sharp features might make an attractive man someday, if one of his spells didn't eat him first.

"I wasn't ever on Saturdays with Miss Wild," he said slowly, stealing a quick glance at me. "So I didn't know how to make biscuits, and no one was there to help with the dough. Saturday cooks usually make biscuits for all three meals."

I nodded.

"I was behind, and I tried to do...just a *little*...bit of magic. To make the dough rise?" His gaze dropped to the floor. "I know we're not supposed to use magic in the kitchen, but it was just a *small* magic. And something went wrong."

"Something always goes wrong," the little girl next to me whispered. She had deep blue eyes, flaming red-gold hair and a pixie look. The lilt to her speech implied an Irish family.

"I had to add more sugar, because the dough started to collapse. I kept thinking I heard purring, and then growls. But there weren't any animals in the kitchen! So I cut biscuits with a cup, tossed pieces of dough on a baking sheet, and made sure they didn't burn."

"And?" I asked when he stopped speaking.

"The biscuits were all jumbled on the pans when I pulled them from the oven," he muttered. "I thought they'd just slid around a little, but they were hopping! By the time I got the basket of biscuits out here, they were popping out of the basket and all over the place, into the trays of eggs, and rooting through the bacon. They didn't like that, though—they just got louder and bounced faster around the room."

This time when he paused, I said: "Did you offer them sugar?" Sugar gave humans quick energy; what gave magical biscuits quick energy?

The boy stared at me, surprised. "Ah, no, miss, we didn't. One found a honey spill and it stopped there, so we could catch it easily."

"If they were happy before, and you heard purring, then it makes sense that what changed in your dough was related to the ingredients, the temperature change, or perhaps to some wild yeast that got into the rising dough." I found a girl with hair the color of clover honey at my left shoulder. "Let's experiment. Would you get some sugar—no, that's too valuable. Get some honey or molasses and drip it on a plate? Bring the plate here and we'll see what happens."

The girl—young woman, really—obliged and returned with a honeyed plate in no time at all. I took the plate from her, and lifted the bowl a tiny bit, setting the plate down next to the opening. The growling was audible...and then there was a whining sound. I dropped the bowl again.

"All right," I said, trying to keep my words formal. "Everyone back up two steps. Mr. Williams, bring me the big serving fork in the bacon pan." Daniel ran to fetch the fork. "Walk, please! Now. It knows we have honey, and it stopped growling. We're going to see if feeding it honey will calm it down. The fork, Mr. Williams."

The boy handed it over, handle first, as if offering me a sword. To the others, I added: "If it attacks me, or tries to make a break for it, I'll jump in as the first defense. You, sir—" I pointed at the fair-haired stocky boy who had just inhaled his oatmeal. "—Go get a teacher and say you need a way to capture and confine a small, magical animal. Everyone else, stand ready with your forks!" The utensils were actually silver, or silver plate. They might break a spell—and their lovely, long double prongs might pin the biscuit to the table.

I lifted the bowl.

Something brown dropped a half-moon over the side of the plate, trying to slurp up the honey. "Bring me the honey jar!" I said, not taking my eyes off the thing.

Lord and Lady, my brothers were going to want one of these things. Shaw and Cousin Cory would want to know how to create one. Marta and Papa would only smile and shake their heads.

Momma would be horrified.

Someone whispered, "I have it!"

"Can you put some on the plate?"

Carefully the young woman to my left pulled up the honey pot wand, smearing the amber mess over the plate. I was impressed that her hand trembled only a tiny bit. The biscuit...merciful Goddess, it *was* a biscuit! The biscuit opened its mouth wider, trying frantically to clean the china.

The big teeth, I could see, actually were ragged clumps of cooked bread, torn apart by the biscuit itself. I watched the little creature, but it was no longer growling. The honey had what it wanted—fast energy—and we had made it happy. It was like smoking bees to raid the combs. The biscuit's movements were slowing even as I heard steps rushing into the room. I kept my eyes on the creature; the last thing we needed was for the biscuit to latch onto someone.

"What is this animal you need caged—" The voice broke off. "Well, well, well, Mr. Smith. I believe I recognize your unique touch. This is a...biscuit?" A small cage appeared to one side of me, and was then set down on top of the biscuit and plate. The tiny creature was apparently glutted—it burped and did not protest when a piece of wood was pushed under it. The cage was tipped so the biscuit slid to the back. Leaving the plate behind, the newcomer snapped closed the bottom of the cage.

The biscuit burped again. The smell of baking bread rolled across us. I could see from expressions on several faces that people wanted to laugh, but they didn't dare. I hazarded a glance at the man holding the cage.

He was fairly young—twenty, say, his face stern—with dark blonde hair, pale blue irises and a trim, healthy physique. He looked prettier than most women I'd seen! A high-waisted jacket, starched shirt with an elaborate necktie, and tight deerskin breeches graced his form. Riding boots finished off the spectacle.

"Thank you," I said calmly, handing the fork to Daniel to return to the buffet.

"You were planning to skewer it if it proved hostile?" the man asked, his words precise, like an educated teacher spoke.

"If necessary," I admitted.

"Professor Tonneman, this is Miss Sorensson." Daniel was already back at my side. "She is a new student. Miss Sorensson, this is the rituals instructor, Professor Tonneman."

Well, I might be from the wild woods, but I knew better than to sit in front of a new teacher. I started to rise, but the man stopped me by resisting the slide of my chair. "No, don't stand. You obviously haven't finished your breakfast." He gave me a long look, longer than I was used to seeing. "No doubt in the next few days Professor Livingston will bring you to me for an evaluation. Whom have you studied with?"

Marta said not to mention Momma's relationship to Esme, but nothing about my training. So, how much.... "I have studied with my mother, Garda Schell Sorensson, as well as Mrs. Donaltsson." I was not yet Cory's pupil, despite his introducing me to grounding and to throwing my thoughts into another's mind. No point boasting of chickens when all I had yet were eggs.

This man didn't need to know that Death had taught me Wild magic, either, unless Esme wanted him to know. I thought that the fewer who knew that, the better for me.

"Marta Helgisdottir Donaltsson?" he asked.

"Yes, sir."

Nodding slowly, his expression thoughtful, Professor Tonneman said to the gathering: "Thank you all for calling me. We'll see how long this biscuit survives, and what it does when it is not looking for food."

"Mr. Williams," I said. "Where are the other biscuits?"

The youngsters exchanged glances.

"And the answer is?" Professor Tonneman said quietly.

Daniel Williams finally said: "In the slops bucket for the pigs. We set a crock on top to keep them from escaping."

The man's eyebrows rose. "Then let us make sure they have not escaped and tracked rotted vegetables throughout the kitchen. Lead on, Mr. Smith."

The boy flinched. "Yes, sir. This way, sir." He disappeared around a corner.

"Miss Sorensson." Another nod, this one sharp, and the rituals professor followed the boy around the corner, the odor of fresh bread clinging to the small cage he was toting. For the first time I heard a door shut. They'd probably had it propped open.

"You hid them in the slops bucket?" I asked softly.

"We didn't know what else to do." Daniel said, his expression a bit worried.

"Ask an older student for help?" I suggested. "Call a teacher? Aren't there spells to prevent magic in the kitchen?" *This will liven up the morning,* I thought, but did not say.

"The fire is spelled so nothing catches fire except wood, and the pump so it won't freeze," Daniel told me. "But otherwise, no one uses magic in the kitchen, except to heat big pots of water. Why would they? It would take more energy than cooking and washing up by hand."

"Well, I suggest you ask an older student or teacher how to take care of little problems like that. You were the practitioners in charge. It was your problem to solve!"

"They would not tell us what to do—only that we should not have done it to start," the tiny redhead's voice was resigned. "We do not get to do fun things like that."

"And your name is?" I asked her.

The child actually grabbed her skirt in each hand and dipped in a curtsy. "I am Moira O'Donnell, Miss."

"There is probably someone whom you could ask," I said. "Did you ask the person in charge of the kitchen?"

Every child's eyes grew larger. So, asking the cook was not a good idea. "She won't know about magic?" I asked hesitantly.

"Oh, no, Mrs. Gardener is a practitioner," Daniel said. "Most people here are—or will be. But she never lets anyone do magic in the kitchen, unless she's asked for it. She says too many things like fire and knives could get caught up in a magic mess."

"And there was that chicken that got up, no head or feathers or anything, and chased the kitchen cat...." Moira murmured to the floor.

"Well, let's finish eating. I'm sure you have other things you want to do today."

"Start dinner," Daniel said gloomily. But his statement seemed to free up the group, and the children resumed their meals or cleaning up.

I remembered the young woman at my shoulder, and turned back around. Our honey bearer waited quietly, a slight smile balancing eyes tinted the soft blue of flax flowers. Small she might be, but her face was that of a woman, not a child, her cheekbones sharp.

Mist clung to her, as if she could call for rain without effort. Magic floated around us in a cloud.

Was it safe to offer her my hand? I rose to my feet.

"Thank you so much for your help with the biscuits with teeth," I started.

"I was happy to assist. I am Miss Smith. I have boundaries duty this morning, but I look forward to furthering our acquaintance, Miss Sorensson."

Was she related to the boy who made biscuits? There was no resemblance. "I look forward to visiting with you," I said, smiling back.

I hoped that was formal enough for this place. The grandeur was a bit intimidating.

"Welcome to Windward." Another smile and a nod, and Miss Smith walked briskly from the dining room, the soft mist immediately obscuring her form.

She was the only one who approached me.

No longer the center of attention, I dug in to get as much cereal in my stomach as I could before anyone else showed up at my elbow. The tea was lovely, with the slightest hint of bergamot in its fragrance. I sipped and listened to the conversation around me. Several children were going back to the kitchen, and I saw a few wands coming out of pant and skirt pockets that had been designed for something long and narrow. Now that the children were back in their own little groups, I was left with fragments of etiquette running through my head. Saturday breakfast was relaxed in more ways than one. I remembered something about whom you spoke to during sit-down dinners....

"Miss Sorensson?" I turned to see the pretty, slightly plump Miss Wolfsson. "Miss Rutledge has gone to Professor Livingston."

"Should I follow?" I asked.

Looking surprised, Miss Wolfsson paused and then said: "I would just wait here—that way a footman could find you."

"Thank you," seemed the best response, which was how I left it. Miss Wolfsson thanked me for my courtesy and moved down the table. After a huddled conference with two other young girls, she headed for the food buffet and soon returned with a bowl of oatmeal.

Apparently thinning the oatmeal had already improved the day for several people, including my possible peers and elders. The students in the back room were now heading for the buffet.

It was interesting that the older students had not appeared while the professor was there. Students being punished cleaned up their own messes, even if it left the place in shambles. Were the older students all off studying or working in some fashion—on boundaries, as Miss Smith put it?

So far, so good. Even on the worst day, the food could be made palatable, and the indoor, sweet-scented water closet was going to be a wonderful gift. If I was lucky, I wouldn't get my skirts dirty as fast as I did going to an outhouse. Cousin Esme—Professor Livingston, I needed to remember that—was willing to teach me ritual magic.

Otherwise? As I saw it, I knew just enough to get myself in trouble. Like, don't talk across the table to people on the other side, only to the people to your left and right. That was a formal thing, but I suspected it was better to be too formal than too casual. Clothing was going to be tricky, what with "carriage gowns" and such, but I figured I had time to assemble things, so I would not borrow trouble worrying about it. Miss Smith's gown was a simple pale green wool garment with long sleeves and a scallop pattern embroidered on the bodice. If necessary I could make something like that.

Now I wondered if I should just sit quietly, or if I should try another tea while I waited for a guide.

The decision was made for me; a slender young woman with blonde curls framing her face entered the room and walked straight to me.

I had no idea what to do. I decided to err on the side of complete courtesy and stood up to greet her.

"Miss Sorensson? I am Margaret Rutledge." The vowels were stretched a bit, the "t" a soft popping sound behind her front teeth. She was English! Her accent was audible but easy to understand, and I suspected it meant she came from a wealthy, educated family.

"I am pleased to meet you," came out of my mouth. "I hope you are feeling better."

"Yes, much better," she replied, her hands clasped loosely before her. She held a blushing brown shawl closed over her pale yellow dress. I took note of how she was hanging onto her shawl.

Miss Rutledge said, "Professor Livingston has asked me to give you a tour of the house and grounds. Have you finished eating?"

"Yes, I have."

"Well, then let us begin with the first floor of the main building. Then the school and dormitory, and finally we will get our coats, and I will show you some of the grounds." Miss Rutledge led me out into the entrance hall.

There followed some of the most bewildering hours of my life. Now, I can laugh at how confused I was, but this house might as well have been a queen's mansion—it was that foreign. No one was currently in the guest bedrooms on the ground floor, so Miss Rutledge led me around to see both of them. One had an octagonal shape, and both had special storage areas above the bed alcove, which I thought quite clever. All the walls were vivid, lovely colors, and the furniture beautifully made, with dark, glossy finishes.

"President Jefferson helped design this house," my guide told me. "He loves building things, and his own home is mostly just how he wants it. So he is happy to make suggestions for his friends, if they want the benefit of his experience."

Cousin Esme knows President Jefferson? I nodded.

Miss Margaret Rutledge did not show me the Livingston private areas. However, an open arch lead to the private library, and from the hallway it was wonderful to see. Sometimes, she told me, students had permission to borrow those books, or to stay in the private library and read.

A greenhouse anchored the south end of the building. Both a large parlor and the entrance hall had unusual things hanging on the walls: gifts to the Livingstons, or things they had acquired in travel.

Occasionally we'd see older students moving around in the main house, but Margaret did not stop to introduce me to any of them. Professor Livingston had said I was to get the tour, and what my cousin wanted she got.

"The school library is in the south wing; we'll go there next," Margaret said. "I will show you the locations of the necessary rooms; we have several in the school wing. They are clearly marked for men or women, and we are expected to honor that convention." She headed for the stairs, because the first floors between wings were only open breezeways. Upstairs, the outbuildings were reached through heavy oak doors that opened easily with a touch of the hand.

"Magic?" I asked her. She looked puzzled, until I said: "Oak is a heavy wood, and these doors are thick. Yet the doors open so smoothly."

"Oh! Yes, it's two kinds of magic—a spell, and also, they are very good doors. They are beautifully balanced."

There was not a lot to see on the second floor. Those halls contained bedrooms for the younger students. "All the younger children are in the south wing, with two older students to keep an eye on them. Once a student reaches thirteen, it's the north wing for them.

"In the north wing, women live on the second floor, men on the third. The doorways are spelled; you cannot go onto the third floor, so do not bother going up there. Men cannot come on the second floor. Few students remain beyond their seventeenth year. The men may go on to college, if their families can give them that luxury."

"And the women?" I asked, after she'd grown silent.

"They return to their families. Most to marry. Alliances are built that way, you know. Daughters of wealthy men seek other wealthy men to marry. Or occasionally a daughter marries into the European nobility."

Yes, I knew about such things. I didn't like them, though.

The hallways seemed wider on the school side, to allow students to reach their next classes quickly, or so I guessed. The library was simply overwhelming. I finally stood and just stared.

I didn't know that so many books existed, much less could be purchased for a small school!

Margaret did not treat me like a rustic. She seemed pleased by my response. "It is wonderful, is it not? It is rare that a small school has such an extensive lending library. The Livingstons value knowledge, and share it with any who will take care of the books. There are even a few people in New York who borrow from this library."

Well, I thought we were in New York, but I decided not to ask that question right now. It did set me wondering, though. Was any of this building someplace else? Not on the same grounds as the house?

Most of the classrooms did not vary. Long tables had slate tops for taking fast notes with chalk, and wooden wings that swung up and across the slate for placing paper and inkwells. Slate stood mounted on stands or the wall for teachers to write upon. Wardrobes held the instructors' materials, and several rooms had no chairs or tables at all. Two classrooms contained their own pumps!

One thing I noticed immediately, as soon as we crossed into the second floor of the south wing. It was much warmer in this hallway, warm enough that I did not need my shawl.

"Is the house being worked on?" I asked as I examined a large window at the end of the second floor. I could not feel any draft from the window or its frame.

"No, why do you ask?" Margaret said quickly.

"This side seems much better insulated than the main house."

Margaret smiled. It was a nice smile, revealing dimples and adding sparkle to her smooth English features. "It's a spell, of course. The Livingstons have created a way to link various power sources into the wings, so the rooms are quite comfortable. They don't heat the parlor, dining areas or the entryway, except from the fireplaces. In case people who are frightened of magic come to the house."

"My room seemed cold this morning," I ventured.

"Professor Livingston had guests this week who were surveying the facilities with a mind to sending their children here for school. The wings are warmer than most other people's homes even without magic. They are very well...chinked, I think the word is. There are few places in the walls for air to sneak in. The Livingstons want the parents to feel comfortable sending their children here."

"Do children without Talent go to school here?" That opened up all kinds of possibilities. I wondered if this privilege was limited to family members of practitioners.

"Yes, they are welcome here. They may even attend classes discussing magic. It is limited to children who have a parent or other family members who do have talent. What if they should have a talented child? Sometimes the power sleeps for a generation or two. Something needs to be in the family lore—a letter in a family Bible. *Something.*"

Margaret seemed a bit upset with this conversation, so I quickly said: "Shall we go get our coats and see the gardens? What I can see out my window is wonderful, even in winter!"

Margaret laughed. "Yes, there are barely words for it! Two labyrinths, one planted for women, and the other for men, and a huge maze! There are even greenhouses for fruits and vegetables. Let's go get our coats."

She led the way out the school door onto a cobbled, covered walkway free of snow. Once inside again, we threaded ourselves up the staircase closest to Professor Livingston's room, and found ourselves on the second floor. This time I saw huge doors to my right, and also looked over the entrance hall below.

"This is?..." I gestured as we passed the doors.

"A moment." Margaret tilted toward the doors, listening. "Unoccupied. They are supposed to put up a warning if it's being used, but sometimes they forget." Margaret opened the door.

"Here is our ballroom, used for big lecture classes, and for dances! You do know how to dance, don't you?"

"I know many country dances," I replied. "I know there are new dances, but there was no one at home to teach me."

"We have a class on dancing and deportment," Margaret said as she pulled the door closed. "Also we learn about all sorts of manners from around the world. It is very useful, since students come from many different countries. Some cultures have rules that dictate manners. For example, you cannot offer wine to a Jew without making sure you have a bottle a rabbi has approved. Neither Jews nor Mohammedans will eat pork. Chinese shopkeepers will never say 'no' to you directly, but you can tell that you're never going to get an answer—much less the answer you want—by how flowery their phrases of regret are."

Continuing to walk down the hall, Margaret gestured above and said, "The area above the ballroom is the dome room. It has been shielded to protect us from any spell casting that goes wrong. We practice ritual and transformation magic up there."

Another large oak door—and where was that door when I left the bedroom this morning?—and we were back in familiar territory. Three doors down on the left, and I was back in my room.

"We do not have enough advanced students right now to double up in rooms, so for now you'll have to sleep alone. I'm sorry." She sounded sincere.

I considered telling her I'd had to sleep alone my entire life, since I had no sisters, but I kept my tongue still. *Don't volunteer information*, I reminded myself. I hung my shawl over a hanger and got my coat and boots.

Margaret had *very* good manners. However astonished she might have been at my heavy sheepskin boots and coat, she only said, "How nice and warm you must be! You will be able to go out on the harder days." Once I was ready, we went down to the sixth room on the left, and Margaret led me into her own room.

The spread on the mattress was textured and white, very elegant, and several pillows on top made an attractive backdrop. She had what I mistook for a handful of rare flowers in a vase on her dresser, but they turned out to be silk.

"How lovely!" I said as she laid her shawl on the foot of the bed and pulled out a heavier cape.

"My mother and grandmother taught me to do that," she said. "They taught me to draw flowers, them to paint them, and finally to form them from silk."

She may have said something else to me, but some metal, oval box frames attached to a pair of slippers caught my eyes. They were open on the heel side at their tops.

"What are those?"

Margaret did look a bit surprised, but said: "Shoe pattens. They lift you out of mud and snow, to keep your boots from becoming soaked or horribly dirty. I'll show you." She pulled out the slippers and took the metal frames with us.

We went outside. While I pulled my gloves on and tucked in my scarf, Margaret balanced against the pillar and slid her boots into the metal scuffs. I thought she'd fall over, but no, she stepped off down the snowy path and headed for the labyrinths and maze.

The landscape was a wonder, even sleeping until spring. Margaret clearly loved the gardens, being full of tidbits of information about them. It turned out that the holly bushes that formed the women's labyrinth were female bushes, except for the ones that framed the entrance, while the men's labyrinth had male bushes, again except for the entrance, where berries could be plainly seen.

"And the difference is?" I asked. There was a section in my Great-Grandmother's book on labyrinths, but I had only glanced at it.

She understood what I meant. "The way it spirals," Margaret said. "The plant in the center is different, too. You'll see them when you walk the paths."

"You can walk either path?" If so, then that meant...what?

"Yes, you can walk both!" Smiling, Margaret went on: "Mostly they are just a beautiful, green walk. They have a use for the oldest students, but my year hasn't studied them yet." She stopped at a wide, green opening in a tall hedge. "This is the maze. Would you like to walk it? With the sun out, it will be a nice outing."

"Do you know the way out, in case I'm not up to solving the puzzle?" I smiled as I said it, because I thought I could solve it. But it would be nice to know that Margaret could get us out in a hurry if we got too cold.

"Yes, I can get us out," she assured me. "There is magic in the maze, but it will not force us to stay in it."

Good. I was a little off-kilter, with the sheer size of this place. I was willing to see still more, but I knew I'd sleep well that night. Why, we'd yet to see the stillroom and kitchen, so, as far as I was concerned, a lot of important things had been left off my tour.

"This maze was formed of yew, a tough plant favored in Europe for mazes and labyrinths," Margaret started as we entered the maze.

Immediately, I felt a strong presence of magic, as if I walked upon a woven path of energy. Eddies swirled about me, like water curling in a stream. I was glad Margaret had warned me, or I would have been alarmed.

It wasn't actually stealing energy from me, but it definitely thought I was interesting. The force of it vibrated in my ears, louder than Margaret's voice and then softer again, pulsing.

We reached a wall, and Margaret headed to the right. I started to follow, and then saw something off to the left. Lord and Lady, was that some sort of magical painting of Marta's house? Smoke rose from the chimney, and there was even Marta off to one side gathering firewood from her pile of split logs. It was like a waist-high pass-through, only I didn't see more of the maze through it, I saw Marta's homestead!

I walked right up to the image, which rose above me to end several feet shy of the hedge's height, and held my hand up to the pulsing, swirling spirals of light. There was nothing threatening about it. Huh. I anchored myself to the bedrock below, and then touched the bubble that expanded toward me.

"Miss Sorensson? Miss Sorensson! Wha...what is the matter?" Margaret was coming closer, I could hear the "snick, snick" of her pattens in the snow.

The clear bubble expanded, as if I blew soapy water through a wooden spool. I felt a tug from it—as if someone had reached out and grabbed my wrist.

Oh-oh.

They are going to carve "fool" on my gravestone, I thought as I tried to hold my ground. My feet slid on the packed snow as the magic pulled me in. *Don't panic!* I grabbed hold of a sturdy yew branch. Perhaps Margaret cou—

I thought I'd be pulled through the opening, but I staggered slightly, as my feet found a path I had not seen.

It was better to walk than be dragged, so I let go of the yew branch. In the end I stood on a snowy path tamped down by human and animal feet. I gazed as if seeing my cousin's home for the first time.

It *was* Marta's house! I turned around, but there was nothing behind me except the trail from Marta's home to the main road.

Of course what I had just walked into was a major spell of some sort. There was no chance of Marta not noticing, even if I could figure out how to get back into the maze. As these thoughts whipped through my mind, Marta looked up from where she was gathering firewood. She was so surprised she dropped the entire armload back on the stack.

I could not think of a single thing to say, except maybe that there was this magic picture and I walked over to see it and....

It seemed I was not required to say anything; not yet.

Marta set her hands on her hips, started shaking her head, and then she burst out laughing. I'm not talking about a gentle titter of amusement. No, this was a big laugh, joyous, full throated, enough laughter to bring tears to your eyes and a stitch to your side.

Maybe the punishment wouldn't be too bad.

I might even find out what I'd just done.

FOUR

There didn't seem to be any reason for me to hold my ground, so I walked toward the woodpile. Marta almost had control of herself; she was brushing a tear from her cheek. I could tell she was still on the edge of laughter; her eyes were bright, her amusement dammed up but bubbling inside.

"I told Esme you'd be through a door before the end of the week," she said. "Esme thought you would be too busy for that to happen." Marta gestured to the woodpile. "Make yourself useful."

I grabbed as much wood as I could balance and followed her inside.

"Do you think the Livingstons would mind if I took my snowshoes back with me?" I said as I stacked the wood in the brick-lined opening to one side of the fireplace. "Miss Rutledge showed me her shoe 'pat-tens', but snowshoes would be better on the grounds."

Marta had her back to me; she made a sound suspiciously like a snort. "Oh, why not? If you need them, they will be there. If not, they can live at the bottom of your wardrobe."

Brushing stray pieces of bark off her gloves, Marta gave me a look and said, "Do you need to go to The Tree?" She had gotten in the habit of calling her outhouse "The Tree," as if there was no other one like it.

"I'm comfortable, Ma'am," was my reply.

"What you need to do next will take an hour or two."

"Well...just in case," I said, and Marta nodded.

"I'll meet you at the trail toward the trap line," she said, and then looked around the room for something. "Ah—here we are." She gestured at the door and then bent over the sideboard table, blocking my view.

Well, I slipped outside and to "The Tree" to handle my business, and then met Marta where a small trail from the house widened to become a deer track. Animals never walk straight, it seems, and this path went two ways. To the right was the last trap line I had worked on, toward water, and to the left went further into the woods. What with the call to Cloudcatcher, and the Hudson clan stealing me away, I had spent very little time at Marta's home. I did not remember ever walking deeper into the forest along this particular path.

Marta turned toward me, and I saw that she had two rolls of canvas in her hands. One she tucked under her arm, and the other she pulled free of its tie and unrolled before me. There were tiny pockets sewn on the inside, with soft flaps of cloth that folded down to prevent the contents from rubbing each other.

Marta nodded to me, and I gently pulled the material aside, revealing rounded wooden sticks. Handles, like the handles of nice stirring spoons.

"Choose one," she told me.

"What is it?" I asked.

"Doesn't matter. Find the one that wants you."

Well...this had just jumped into The Mysteries again. Other people might make such whimsical statements, but not Marta. There was always a second meaning to her humor—and magic behind her whimsy.

The type of wood seemed to vary from very light in color to nearly black. Someone had polished the wood until it was gleaming. Some had satin oil polishes; others, clearly hard wax coats. One looked varnished, of all things.

So...could I handle them? I reached out a couple of fingers to the varnished one, and immediately felt a penetrating cold. From the *wood?* Humph. Then I simply passed my left hand over the pieces. The wood looked like oak, and forgotten knowledge leapt up in my face—Marta had checked me for a wand, back before even

Cloudcatcher had risen into our lives. These were probably different oak wands!

They all *felt* different, even though I wasn't physically touching them. From the cold of the varnished piece to the blazing hot sensation of a darkly stained handle.... "What am I looking for, heat or cold? Or nothing?"

Marta broke into a smile. "Find the one you can't bear to leave behind."

A hint helps.

The third one from the left, sort of a pale golden color, stopped me. It was almost as if the wood had reached out and taken my hand. I continued on, to pass my hand over the entire group, but I returned to the third wand. It just didn't feel right to leave it there all alone.

Now, I know that sounds silly, but there it was—the wand wanted to leave its fellows and go with me. I finally lowered my hand to touch it with thumb and forefinger.

Lovely, liquid warmth stole into my fingers, winding into my hand. This would have made me wary, but I thought Marta would have given me more of a hint, if this was a trap. And if it was, well, she would show me how to get out of it.

I pulled out the handle, and it was, indeed, a wand. It measured about a foot or so, satin polished and rounded, dark at the handle and spiraling up to its white, unstained tip. It was pieced! Another wood had been carefully imbedded into the spiral design, echoing the golden to finally white wood coil all the way to the top.

Just for a moment I wondered which wand Shaw could not leave behind.

Marta chuckled, flipped the protective flap of material over the other handles, and then rolled the canvas carrier up again. "Of course you picked the most expensive one."

Oh, I would hate to leave it! "Should I take another?"

"No, dear, you only take a ritual wand that wants you. You may need more than one wand. This is a very female wand; oak and yew wound together, strength and flexibility. You may need a different wand for defense, and you will make a wand for more personal work. But that's for later." Marta tucked the roll under her right arm, and pulled out the other roll from under her left.

"The athame?" I asked.

"This time you do the choosing," she told me as she untied the roll and let it open across her hand.

I decided I needed something different from the wand, so I wasn't looking for anything in white oak. The wooden handle needed to be strong enough to hold the tang of the blade, and soft enough to be carved to the palm of my hand. I had no interest in a knife that hurt me when I used it.

Again, I saw wood handles, flatter than the wands, but still showing different types of wood, different growth patterns. There were no designs on the hilts. I spied a handle of chestnut, and my hand paused. The chestnut is a tree of majesty, its wood and fruit both useful and very beautiful. Nothing else really caught my interest.

I pulled out the chestnut handle. Even without shaping, it felt good in my left hand. I saw a wave-like pattern in the dagger itself, and a design had been etched along the blade's center line. It looked like the path of the moon, from sliver through full and then back to dark. I turned over the athame. There was only one design on this side. It was a comet, or a shooting star...or both.

My dream came back to me.

"This one," I said aloud. I had no desire to look at the others. This was my first athame.

"There is a carpenter in Philadelphia, I think it is, who can carve the handle for you. It would be worth the price he would charge for his work. You'll carve your own signs and symbols into it afterward, if you want them."

"How do I pay for this?" I said slowly, still looking at the knife. I switched hands, and found it liked my right hand, too.

Marta reached into her pocket and pulled out a small knife sheath, stained black and possessing a tie flap. She tucked the sheath into my pocket.

"Shaw's father Bear Kristinsson made this blade. There are things you can trade him for the work," Marta said. "But that will be later. Now, you must recharge the door to get back through it." She flipped the soft wool over the knife handles, and rolled the pouch on her palm. "Do not forget that you owe me a penny!"

"That's how we got to New York, wasn't it?" I asked, focusing on the most important—to me—part of her words.

"Yes—we went to Windward through the portal at the end of the labyrinth. It's wider than the one you used to get to the front yard."

I tried not to sigh. Here was the hard part. "We have to re-charge the door?"

Marta's twisted smile popped out. "Yes, I'm afraid you do. Come along." She started walking briskly along the trail heading to the left. I hurried to catch up, for the trail was wide enough for two, with care.

Finding north was never a strength of mine, and I quickly got turned around. It wasn't long before I realized we were walking a curving path. "How far into the woods does this track go?"

"Not far. It's a labyrinth, so it coils back upon itself." Marta walked easily, her stride the comfortable rolling pace of someone sure of her direction. I tried to fall into her rhythm, uncertain of the length of the trip.

It only took a couple of minutes to reach the end of the footpath. A small clearing finished the labyrinth, with an ash tree at the center. It was perhaps three feet in diameter, a mature tree, leafless but crowned with high limbs reaching up and out.

"Each time you walk into the clearing is one passage," Marta said. "Pause for a deep breath—it will help you keep up your strength—and then go over here—" She gestured to a thick group of holly. We walked past it and around the corner—and there was the back of Marta's house! "You should take extra energy back to the maze, since you took an unexpected trip. Say...eighty-one cycles."

"Walk it eighty-one times!"

My voice rose, I confess it.

"It will take twenty-seven just to get you back," Marta went on, her expression amused. "Carry your wand in your left hand and your blade in your right. After eighty-one passages, you should have a good idea why I suggested you do that." She touched my cheek with affection. "When you finish, come inside and we'll have supper. You can tell me how you found the door."

Then she turned and walked away. "I'd finish before dark," she added, her voice drifting on the slight breeze. "Carrying a torch changes how the labyrinth stores energy."

I just stood there, so mad I was searching my secret store of swear words to express myself. But no, none of them fit the scene well enough to startle my hope of Heaven by saying them.

Fine, then. How to not lose track while I grumbled through this?

Marta's leading me through the labyrinth might have counted as the first path, but on the chance that I was wrong, I decided to start again. I wondered if it was safe to use the wand to mark each passage....I looked at the wand, and then drew a line in the snow to one side of the labyrinth entrance. The snow melted under the stroke, forming a small pool.

Maybe not the wand.

How to keep my mind from wandering.... I picked up a piece of bark and drew a line. This time, I had a line in the snow. I left the piece of bark in a prominent place, made sure I had a good grip on the wand and blade, and started walking the spiral of the labyrinth.

This worked well enough that by the time I finished the twenty-seventh coil I still had plenty of light. I was doing better knee bends as I went by, scribbling lines of ten strokes before I started a new row. The sun had drifted down to the tops of the trees, hovering over the forest.

Then the labyrinth changed.

Between one step and the next, as I set my foot down for the twenty-eighth passage, I felt power pull at my boot. It wasn't frightening, or even odd. The delicate pull was more like a steady wind pushing just enough into your face that you'd bend your head a fraction to make sure no gusts surprised you. So it was with the labyrinth. I put enough effort into walking that there was no chance of my boot sticking in some manner, tripping me as I moved.

As I finished the second set of twenty-seven, I felt a change in the wand and athame. I always transferred the wand over to my right hand, with the blade, before marking the tick mark in the snow. Then the wand returned to my left hand as I moved to begin the next circuit. This time, I was aware of resistance. The wand and athame did not want to be held together, not even for a moment's convenience.

I looked closely at the two tools, placing my body between them and the sinking sun. Not a doubt—there was a pale golden light coming from the blade of the athame and the tip of the wand. *Hummmm....*

Perhaps I would count the last twenty-seven times through the labyrinth without a tally.

As I walked, daylight grew blue and gray, shadows breeding under trees and shrubs. The sun had dropped halfway down the side of a huge spruce tree just to the right of the path's entrance. Slowly, like snow melting off a roof near the chimney, the yellow light began to dim. Clouds rippled like combed gray wool and hid the blue sky beyond. I had passed the fifteen laps mark when I found myself using the tools like candles, holding them upright and forward. At first, I could not tell if they grew brighter, or the sky merely grew darker.

By the eighteenth circuit, I was sure the glow of the wand and athame had increased. Each time that I walked the spiral, the gleam grew that much brighter. Finally I started to wonder if it was only the tools, or if I was blazing like a torch, too. I found myself impatient, moving faster, even dancing down the curving trail, watching the tools gleam.

The blade was especially interesting, because although the athame was often associated with fire, the rippled effect in this blade made it sometimes look like water, or air moving above a bonfire. I held them out from my body, and tried a spin or two from a country dance. Did more steps charge the labyrinth faster, or confuse it? If you walked backward, could you drain the labyrinth of the energy it held?

I slowed again for the last twenty-seventh lap, the eighty-first walk of the spiral. Both wand and blade now blazed like the moon— no, like tiny stars in my hand, each like a shooting star falling to earth. As I took the last steps around the holly bushes, stopping by the remains of the tally, I turned to face the labyrinth. Holding the tools to either side, I bowed back toward the ash tree and said: "I thank you for the lesson! And I thank you for the strength you shared with me."

As I straightened, I noticed a flicker on the path before me. Peeking farther down to the right, I saw the same thing at the entrance of the spiral. The path glowed. Not a reflection of a hidden moon, or even my tools. Something in the path made it faintly glow white. A clear light, not the murky glow rotting vegetation could have.

Behind me, I heard the door to the cabin open. "Allie! Have you finished?" Marta called.

"Coming, Marta!" The scent of venison and pumpkin pie traveled on the breeze, and I surely did not want to miss the meal waiting for me inside. I hurried around the long cabin, waving the stars in my hands as I tromped through the snow. I must have been a sight as I stumbled back on the shoveled path, but Marta simply returned my smile and opened the door wider.

"You must see that an unexpected draw on either labyrinth could cause problems," Cousin Esme said gently, her dark eyes very serious. "If major spells were being cast at that moment, those both within and without the circle could be injured."

Or killed, I thought but did not volunteer. "Yes, ma'am." Marta had made it very clear over supper that what I'd done could have injured me severely. She had proceeded to treat me to tales of some of the horrible "back blasts" she'd seen caused by spells gone awry. She personally knew practitioners and other magic-users who had been scarred or lost limbs when a spell exploded.

Now I was back at the Livingston estate, standing in Esme's private room on the north end of the main building. I was ready for her to take a few strips of flesh off me. I just hoped they wouldn't be real strips of flesh.

"You had no idea what you were seeing, nor could Miss Rutledge have foreseen that you could see through the cloaking spell. For that reason, I will not punish you for passing through a portal. Later on—in a week or two, perhaps—I will have Miss Rutledge show you some of the tricks of the maze. You may then study the maze and labyrinths and give your class your impression of them." Looking over at Margaret, who stood pale and wan beside me, Esme added, "She needs to be tested immediately. First thing Monday morning—I don't want to chance waiting any longer."

"Yes, Professor Livingston," Margaret said, relief in her voice.

"Have you eaten?" Esme asked me.

"Yes, ma'am," I replied.

"Then you may occupy yourself with the other students in the great room, or your own room. The two candles in your bedroom should be sufficient for either sewing or reading; you may move them both to one table, if needed, but do not move the tables or chest. They are placed to prevent draperies or bed curtains from catching fire."

"Yes, ma'am. Thank you, ma'am." This time I gave her a little dip of a curtsy, like the one the maid had given me. Esme didn't smile, so I didn't think the gesture was out of place. "May I...see more of the farm? I understand you have succession houses, as well as several thoroughbreds?"

Esme momentarily looked thoughtful, and then said, "You will stay on the grounds of the estate. You will not go into the maze. You will only enter a labyrinth if Miss Rutledge accompanies you. You are not required to have an escort to see the home farm, but if you go deep into the barns, dress in your farm work clothing. I trust my field and barn workers with your safety, but they have been known to give new household staff and visitors magical tests of sorts. Be prepared. Mr. Gardener should be told when you are on the property. Do you agree to this?"

"Yes, ma'am," I said, trying not to smile. I could have been left in my room for a month, except for classes and The Tree. Being allowed to walk the grounds would be wonderful!

"Take her back to her room, Miss Rutledge, so she may store her coat and boots...and snowshoes." This time, there was amusement in her voice. "I trust you to keep track of Miss Sorensson. And I bid you both good night."

"Yes, Professor Livingston," Margaret said, tugging lightly on the back of my coat. "Good evening, ma'am." She turned to leave, and didn't let go of my coat until I had also turned toward the door.

Once we were in the hall, I was dying to speak, but I waited until we climbed the narrow stairs and reached my room. When the door to my bedroom was closed, I turned and said, "Miss Rutledge, I am so sorry I frightened you. I should have asked you who painted the clever pictures in the maze. In the future I will be careful to ask about anything unfamiliar before I touch it."

Margaret took a deep breath, and said: "I accept your apology, Miss Sorensson. The maze and labyrinths have been spelled to keep those who are untrained, or have no magic, from accidentally tumbling through to another place. Because I knew of the spell, and had heard you came here especially to learn ritual magic, well...." She paused, and touched a candlewick into life. When she looked back at me, I saw pink sweep from the corners of her mouth to her ears. "It never occurred to me that you might see through the cloaking spell. I apologize for my carelessness. I will work diligently to keep you safe as you learn the path of higher magics."

"Thank you," I said, not sure which part of her speech I should reply to, but glad she wasn't angry with me. "I hope you ate something this afternoon, since I imagine supper is past." I pulled off my sheepskin coat and hung it on its hanger from a hook on the outside of the wardrobe, the better to let the leather dry. I decided not to say anything about the wand and knife...and then I found the long pockets on either side of the coat, under the arms.

I stood there, considering. I had not made those pockets. I doubted my mother made them.

Did Marta?... The night before I came here?...

Now I wanted to look inside all the dresses to see if Marta had also made a place for my wand. But I'd wait until I was alone. I liked what I knew of Miss Rutledge—but I did not yet trust her.

Looking around, I finally noticed that the last piece of furniture was a long desk with two chairs. My room was a small space, but everything a girl needed—heavens, two girls!—could be stored here.

"I never eat supper on Saturday," Margaret said, shaking her head so her curls bounced. "The student meals leave much to be desired. But kitchen duty thoroughly teaches a lesson in humility." She smiled at this, and then continued: "On Saturday and Sunday, my friends and I like to gather in Professor Livingston's work room when she is done with it for the day. One of us reads while the others catch up on mending or needlework. Your timing is impeccable; we start reading *Robinson Crusoe* tonight. Would you like to join us?"

Even if I'd been tired, I would not have turned down her offer. I had no idea how long I would be there, and I did not want to be an outsider looking in on the life of the house and school. "Thank you, I would like that. I have several dresses to hem. Would that be appropriate work?"

"Of course."

I opened the wardrobe to get either the pale indigo cotton gown or the natural linen dress that needed regular hemming. I didn't want to work on silk rolling until I knew my audience was friendly. My time spent in Hudson-on-the-Bend showed me that there were people out there who not only liked mischief—they liked hurting people, in word or deed. And a woman's tongue is one of her few weapons. Some women become masters at it, for good or for ill. I didn't need anyone being disagreeable tonight.

I hope to tread lightly on this world, and leave no harm behind me. It may not be possible, but I can try.

"What a lovely color of blue!" Margaret said, and her voice had both warmed and gone bright.

"Thank you," I replied. "My cousin is very clever with her hands and dye pot. She left the hem and embroidery to me."

Margaret stared, and then blinked, a smile shadowing the corners of her mouth. "I am very impressed, because it looks as if a skilled modiste in London created it!" Her face grew thoughtful, and she added: "You might not mention that she made it. Some people are so high in the instep, they would think badly of you for wearing homemade clothes. But I have seen things that cost more pounds than we can imagine, and they look horrible when worn."

I checked, and my box of needles and pins was on the shelf above the dresses. I peeked in the box. Yes, Marta had included the thread for the dresses. And my stork scissors! Plus a woven rope basket knotted to make an attractive carrier for the box. Momma and Marta both had one. I wondered if Shaw's mother had made them—she had once lived near the sea, where woven furniture was common.

No time like the present to show my skill. I pulled out the natural linen dress, its bodice panel an inset of embroidery in a rose brown thread. It was a basic Celtic weave I had made as a trial. The pins gleamed at the hem, and I blessed Marta for saving me so much time. *I will need dresses here in a hurry*, I thought. I could not wear my gold gown forever.

"You mean we could pretend that I am rich, or eccentric?" I asked, as I pulled off my big sheepskin boots and put on the boots Marta had given me. "Perhaps too many will think of me as the poor country cousin, if they know the truth?"

"Sometimes it is very valuable to not let people know everything about you," Margaret said seriously.

Truth.

It told me something else as well. Margaret was a lovely, decorative, even gracious young woman, but there was also depth to her. And kindness—she could have kept me at arm's length, but had not done so. That was a wonder in itself. But it suggested that, unlike the Hudson compound, this school and farm might be a friendlier place to live and to learn.

"Let us try eccentricity," I said, my syllables measured out in a row to keep me from cramming them together. "It will save time." I didn't plan to explain my words.

Margaret got a glimpse of the bodice while I was pulling on my new shawl. "Did your cousin do this? It is wonderful! Embroidery is respected," she went on. "Your cousin could make good money at this, if she hadn't already set out her shingle!"

"No, I did the needlework on this dress," I said, hooking the sewing basket on my left arm and gathering up the dress so it would not drag.

The response was all I could have hoped for. "Miss Sorensson, you are a master at embroidery! I hope you can teach this to me." Margaret let excitement slip into her voice, so I knew this was a good starting point.

"I will try, and I hope you will share patterns with me." This was a very hard pattern to do well, but someone had had to teach it to my grandmother, who taught my mother, who taught me. "I'm ready. Lead on!"

"This will be great fun!"

And why not? Not everyone would be like the sorcerous Hudson clan. And even the Hudsons had had people of worth among them.

I nodded to Margaret to lead the way.

✣·🖎·✣

It turned out that many young women were waiting in cousin Esme's sitting room. The fire was cheerful, and the room seemed to hold heat well. "In winter, the smaller rooms usually are kept warm with magic," Margaret whispered as we entered the room. "Guests generally don't wander into them."

"We take turns doing the reading," Margaret continued as we wove through the room. "My dear friend Catherin Williams just finished a table runner for her parents, so she will take a break from sewing and read to us this night."

I wondered if these students were invited to Esme's formal evening gatherings. Most looked Margaret's age, sixteen or seventeen, as opposed to my thirteen and a half years.

A lovely, dark-haired young woman with laughing eyes and a genuine smile approached us. "I hoped you could come tonight! And this is our new fellow student?"

"May I introduce you to Miss Alfreda Sorensson?" Margaret turned toward me, her face bright with pleasure. "This is Miss Williams, my valued friend and also the best reader among us."

I gave Catherin my best, "I don't know you, but I'd like to" smile, and nodded my greeting. "I am pleased to meet you. Are you related to the young man named Daniel?"

"He is my younger brother," was Catherin's reply. "He told me of your kindness at breakfast. He was so embarrassed." Her lively eyes were as dark as Daniel's. "The kitchen group did not have an obvious leader, and the result was not unexpected." She gestured over to an unoccupied area, near her own seat. "I have a large branch of candles over here, if you'd like to share my corner."

And so we joined her. We ended up as ten young women, at least two closer in age to me than to Margaret. As Catherin sat down with the large book balanced on the curious adjustable lid of an end table, I finished threading a needle and chose the seam where I would begin to hem. First I hazarded a quick peek. Yes—two long pockets in the side seams, one on each side, one shorter than the other.

I caught myself wondering if anyone here could be as good a friend to me as Idelia had been throughout my childhood.

I also wondered if any of these young women might be my enemy.

Did other people my age think as I did?

They probably did not...unless they were practitioners.

Catherin cleared her throat, and said: "You have noticed, of course, that we have a new student among our numbers. Miss Sorensson arrived last night, and I hope you will make her feel welcome."

I smiled at the faces of way too many strangers. I recognized the pretty but pudgy flaxen-haired girl, Miss Wolfsson, and noticed that one petite young woman had a ghost standing by her side. I blinked, my focus sharpening, but the ghost merely nodded at me and turned back to the needlework being set up. The young woman raised a hand in greeting to me. Oh, it was Miss Smith, the honey bearer, still misty in the soft light. I glanced back at Margaret, and found her flushing as if discomforted in some fashion.

Had I done something wrong?

I followed her line of sight to Miss Smith...and her ghost.

Interesting. Was it the young woman or her ghost that disturbed Margaret? Somehow I didn't think my asking would make Margaret any more comfortable.

"And now, what we have waited for—*The Life and Adventures of Robinson Crusoe*. 'I was born in the year 1632, in the city of York, of good family, tho' not of that country, my father being a foreigner of Bremen....' "

I let my gaze flick up. Everyone seemed to be focused on their needlework. I realized I felt...contented, I think was the right word. I could find myself a place to stand in the swirling waves of students, and learn much. I hoped I could also give gifts to this place. I glanced back down, keeping my head upright as my mother had taught me, discreetly pinched the dress between my knees to keep the material smooth, and started working.

֎

Sunday morning dawned brightly, the sun climbing into a cloudless blue sky. I heard some bustling in the hallway as several students prepared to attend religious services in New York, but I wasn't required to go. It turned out that although a Bishop of New York had been appointed by the Holy Father, he was trapped in Naples in the mess of Napoleon Bonaparte's ship embargo. The bishop had yet to visit his See.

I know you are thinking *Why not take him through a maze?* Well, it happened that there was this nightmare called The Inquisition connected to the Church of Rome. Our leaders who created the Constitution for America did not allow anyone to persecute people for their religion. Though the Salem Accords guaranteed the rights of practitioners even before we had the Constitution and Bill of Rights, no practitioner would offer the Bishop of New York a walk through a maze. Not from Europe. And priests don't practice magic...not officially.

Yes, it is odd that my mother embraced the Church of Rome and raised us as Catholics. I think she did not have faith in the gods of her ancestors, and was looking for powerful protection for us.

I don't think that the powers that be are there just to guard us. I think that they are there to encourage us to be more than we ever imagined.

I do not wish to give up my god. But I do not think that I will remain a member of my mother's church.

֎

After breakfast I found myself back in my room, contemplating the rest of the day. Margaret had told me she would meet me at dinner in mid-afternoon. After the meal she would introduce me to other students, including some of the young men. *There is no difference in our teaching,* Margaret had said. *We will be practitioners, and we will need identical skills, no matter what branch of magic we finally choose for our specialty. The only difference in our study is that as we age we are taught separately, so that we keep our minds on magic and not on society.*

She blushed when she said the last.

Margaret was going to have few secrets from me.

I had a good six hours to myself, no assignments, and as yet no books in my room. Hemming dresses didn't interest me; it could

wait until *Robinson Crusoe* after supper. And I didn't really want
to try to find the library again. I needed fresh air.

I could spend at least three hours poking around the grounds,
as long as I didn't enter the maze or either labyrinth. If I hurried,
I might be able to follow Mr. Gardener, since he'd come back to
the big house to have breakfast with his wife and other servants of
high standing.

I dug out my brother Josh's old wool trousers and a heavy wool
shirt, adding on top an ancient sweater, so worn the color would
be in debate. Buried in the bottom drawer I found a hat my mother
had made for me out of mink fur. The soft, warm pelt was inside,
and thin leather outside. It was pretty ugly, but great while walking
a trap line on a snowy day. I had but to wind my braid up on top of
my head and pull the hat down snug. The paths behind the great
house were shoveled, so I wore my deep warm sheepskin boots and
left the snowshoes in the wardrobe. Finally I found and pulled on
my heavy wool gloves. Ready for almost anything, I strapped my
practitioner bag to my waist, underneath my sweater. After my run-
in with the Hudson clan, I didn't want that pack out of my reach.
This way, I could have fire in a hurry if I needed it for anything.

Eyeballing the candle, I said: "You can go out now."

The candlewick faded into smoke. My only lighting was from the
window, sunlight reflecting off snow, bouncing off the ceiling and
brightening my room.

I caught myself wondering if it was more than a spell...perhaps
a small, magical salamander controlled each candlestick? It sounded as if it should be simple for a practitioner to do. Yet Marta had
always lit candles from a spill touched to the burning logs in the
fireplace. Marta tried never to waste energy in careless magic. *You
never know when you might suddenly need all your strength*, she
had told me.

I had already seen enough strange things in my life to know the
truth of those words.

As for today, there was an entire farm out there, with glass houses of plants, and thoroughbred horses, the ones used as fine saddle
horses and racers. Pulling the bedroom door shut behind me, I tip-
toed down the family and servant staircase and outside.

Once I pulled closed the north door, I paused to inhale deeply,
letting my nose learn the unique scent of Cousin Esme's homestead.

There were pines and other evergreens here, as well as smoke lingering...apple wood, I thought. I could not smell dung, so in winter, at least, the odors of the barns were kept at bay. I'd have to look for pigs and find out if they used spells or just good husbandry.

Speaking of husbandry—I saw a man who looked like Mr. Gardener heading toward the barns and low, gleaming greenhouses. I stopped myself from hollering at him (that might be seen as some form of pestering him) and moved quickly over the packed snow path. My energy was high and my wind good—I made up a lot of the distance before he took a path off to the right, behind what appeared to be the coach house.

I was tempted to stop right there and visit the carriages I could see, but they were closest to the house, just beyond the east wing, and that meant I could easily see them another time. So I waved to someone working on a lapful of leather harness, who gave me a sharp look and an uncertain wave, as if unsure who I might be. Then I hurried around the building to see if I could catch Mr. Gardener.

There was a covered drive between the coach house and what appeared to be a stable. Here was another possible pleasure. I wondered if students were allowed to ride the horses? Or were they too valuable to trust to students? That covered drive would be nice in bad weather. Maybe they led the horses from the carriages to their stalls that way.

I thought I saw Mr. Gardener heading into that covered drive, so I put on speed to catch him.

I took maybe twelve long strides in darkness before I came out the other side of the covered drive. For a moment I saw Mr. Gardener—and then he simply wasn't there. I slowed, and then ran the last three steps. I'd thought his coat was dark brown, but this coat flashed a dark green in a burst of sunlight. Were there stairs, or a driveway that canted southeast? Or—

The first thing that hit me was the smell.

You think of the country as having all kinds of odors, a lot of them overpowering. But in truth, when you got past smoke, fresh-turned earth, manure in all its forms and the garden compost, everything else came to you on a sweet breeze. A well-tended farm smelled clean and welcoming.

This—this *attack* was a nightmare. I smelled rotting fish, beer and wine gone bad, fresh horse and pig manure—and more unwashed bodies than I cared to stand among. The smell of fresh vomit and sweat sewed the scene together, and as I passed the stable gate on the other side, I found myself among a crowd of people, mostly men, and a couple of women my mother would blanch to know I'd seen. The smell of roasting beef and bread baking was almost lost in the faint breeze of sea air. Yes, sea air—I could smell salt.

I knew that ocean water burned in a wound, because of salt.

I took two steps backward and bumped painfully against a brick wall, holding my ears to muffle the sound. *How can they stand the noise?*

Then I panicked.

I wasn't near the maze! I wasn't in the labyrinths! Leaning back, I tried to keep the streaming crowd from sweeping me along in their wake.

Where in God's green earth was I?

FIVE

I DIDN'T KNOW WHAT TO THINK, I didn't know what to do—I didn't know how far away from the Livingston estate I was, I couldn't remember what the estate was named—*What is its name? What? Westward—no, Windward.* I tried to draw air into my lungs through my mouth. My nose had no interest in breathing. I didn't blame it, but I needed air so I could think.

Why hadn't Margaret told me that there were other portals on the estate? Why hadn't Cousin Esme mentioned them? Were these smaller ones so well-guarded they couldn't imagine I would run into them? Was this someone's idea of a joke to test the newest student?

Mr. Gardener's work clothing was dark brown. I saw a flash of deep green, before that fellow slipped away. *Who was I following?*

I thought of the larks my oldest brother and his friends had gotten into, and it occurred to me that I might have found the way the oldest boys could escape to town.

That thought steadied me a bit, and I stopped shaking. This was probably the port of New York.

Probably.

But if portals could go *anywhere*....

It took several minutes, I guess, for me to stop gasping for breath. The nose finally went to work. Dead fish and salt—I smelled salt. This was near a sea...close enough to smell the sea. Was this place somewhere else on Manhattan Island? Was I all the way to China? I watched the faces of people moving by. Few of them looked lost, or bewildered. Mostly they had the bustle of merchants, or simply looked tired. I pointedly averted my eyes from the women. I'd heard sad and terrible things about women who lost their husbands and had no trade to support their children and themselves. I felt for them, but this was not the time to offer sympathy or charity.

Everyone, whether dressed in rough clothing for dirty work, or dressed for selling their wares to people, looked like they knew where they were going. I looked like a farm boy, so these merchants probably would ignore me. I had to move, though. I didn't know how to look like I belonged, so I needed to hide.

The flow of people moved pretty much in two directions, and I joined the group heading right. There was not much snow to be seen. Icicles hung from wood shingled roofs, and dirty snow formed a large pile at the crossway we approached, but otherwise we plodded through mud and manure. Walkers competed for space with wagons loaded high with barrels marked as salt or sugar, wine or ale. One cart had huge sacks perched precariously in a heap, a few seams bulging with raw wool. That driver was in a hurry and had a temper—he was as likely to snap his whip near the walkers as near the ears of his horses.

The buildings towered over us, making me uncomfortable. I felt trapped among so many people, despite a cart path twice the width of any I'd seen back home. Daylight seemed darker, dirtier, and the place felt very foreign.

I was listening so hard I'm surprised my ears didn't cramp from strain. Most of what I heard was English, either our smoother American words or the sharper-edged speech from England herself. I recognized French and German, but otherwise the languages used around me were a mystery. And the noise! Our monthly market back in Sun-Return was silent in comparison. I looked frantically for any kind of hint as to where I was, but so far, I saw only signs for barrel-making—and for selling to agents. I had no idea who "agents" were.

The signs were in English. That was good.

We walkers passed wood sidewalks rimming water and huge boats—*ships*, I reminded myself. On salt water, the big ones were called ships. The masts on those ships rose far above the crowded buildings. Men with rolling carts filled with fish pushed their burdens before them, crying their wares.

No one was loading or unloading anything from those ships. This fact actually made me feel a bit better. I knew that President Madison had an embargo in place.

The crowd jostled me, but no one did any yelling at me, so I kept my head down and my feet moving. We reached a cross street with posters hammered to an upright board.

I snaked toward it, and eventually reached the signboard, taking hold of it to keep from being pushed on. I gulped a few deep breaths of air and thinned a tiny little peephole through my mental walls to watch for anyone unfriendly looking at me. *Lord and Lady, these people have messy minds*, I thought. The river of thoughts was like a waterfall of sound.

Then I scrutinized the signboard.

One of the handbills kindly told me that the *SOLSTICE of New Haven, whereof James Edwards is master, is bound from New York to New Haven. The ship requires two more crewmen. Healthy, seasoned sailors of good character should arrive at SOLSTICE in Berth 23 before high tide Thursday next.* The sign looked new—the snow had not made any of the text puddle from too much cold water.

I was at the port of New York!

My height was suddenly a good thing; I looked around to get my bearings, and saw brick buildings on several of the corners. Well-dressed men in their Sunday best entered the buildings, even as others left. The ones leaving had one of three expressions on their face—pleased, annoyed or somewhere in-between. Probably something like horse trading going on—

"Yeah goin' to grip that board all day?" said a rough voice behind me.

I dropped my heels and stepped to one side. "My apologies, sir— I am in sore need of information."

"Well, this is a good place for information," the man conceded as he tilted his head to read the posters. His clothes were cut simply but clean, and even mended on one elbow with a leather patch. "Lost yeah berth?"

"I'm supposed to find the house of Dr. Livingston, the place called Windward?" It was daring, but I had to get away from all these minds and noises if I was going to yell for instructions or for help. I had a low voice for a woman, and prayed that these people would see what they expected to see—a young man getting his bearings in a new port.

The man flicked his gaze to me, his dark brown eyes taking me in all of a piece. He was maybe my father's age, in work if not in years, his face tanned and creased from years of sun and wind. "New here?" His voice was resonant, and I guessed he could be heard on the windy deck of a boat.

I felt no darkness, no dangerous thoughts hidden even from himself. "Yes, sir. I am expected at Windward, but we got separated in the mess down by the fish market."

"Aye, it's messy," he agreed, smiling faintly. "Well, no one posts maps down here, boy. They're too valuable; someone would walk off with them first thing. Yeah want to go down to the Broad Way." Turning, the man pointed a chapped, tanned hand in a new direction. "Yeah go past Water, Pearl, William, and Nassau, big streets all of them. Keep an eye peeled for livestock—if they can't control the damn pigs and geese, they should not own any, eh? Pearl—Queen Street—has the crushed oyster shells on the road. Broadway is big, with fine houses, like this here Wall Street. Broadway is graded, too. Turn this way—" The man pointed all the way to his right. "And keep going. Past the fancy houses, past the Park Row gardens and the big green place. Yeah'll reach the green land that comes to a point, right before yeah...and there yeah lose me." He grinned. "I've never been farther up the island than that. I think where the green ends, yeah go left for Broadway, and right on a twist to the dividing street. But I don' know for sure. More than that, yeah need to ask again."

"Thank you very much," I said loudly, trying to make myself heard.

"I have a lad about yeah age and size," was his answer. "I help yeah, and please God someone will help him sometime." He leaned forward slightly. "Yeah don't walk like a sailor, so I'll tell yeah this, too. If a couple of burly men start looking yeah way, and they start yelling about yeah being a British sailor that jumped ship? Flee! People know yeah can't be a sailor, yeah walk too straight, but they may not be strong enough or inclined to fight them off for yeah— they might get grabbed, too."

"New York tolerates this?" I knew I was gaping like a greenhorn, but I didn't remember ever hearing about this.

"The watch can't be everywhere," was his reply. "And there was President Jefferson's first embargo, and then his second embargo—President Madison has his work cut out for him. Useless, all of it. I smell war in the air." He straightened, his gaze flitting over the crowd. "They grab most from merchant ships, the British fleet does...but they've snatched a few here. They get hold of yeah, yeah'll find yeahself on a boat for England."

"The people expecting me would come after me," I told him, "but I thank you for your warning." I cut things off there, afraid that something in my speech or manner might make him suspicious.

He nodded once my way, and then with a last poke at the SOL-STICE manifest, he moved on down the docks.

I have a plan, I told myself. *It will change—plans always change—but it makes me look like I know where I'm going.* I rested one hand in the pocket sewn into my trousers, scratched my neck like my brother Josh always did when he was puzzled, and then marched myself down Wall Street with Shaw's long stride.

It did occur to me to wonder if that man had reasons to send me down this street. But the direction made as much sense as any.

The city was...how do I explain a city? It was as if someone smashed together all the buildings on a big farm, some on top of each other, many built of dark red brick. It looked as if everything that happened on a farm happened in the city—but not all in one place. The street by the docks was a pit of mud, although the store-fronts had stone or brick walkways before them. I wondered what would happen if the temperature dropped suddenly. Did the city grade the street at night? How could they drive with those deep ruts frozen into the path?

I drank it all in as I walked, still nervous, but aware of a strange feeling of freedom in this unexpected jaunt. I didn't have to shorten my stride, or wait patiently behind folk strolling along. I could slip past them with a "Pardon" and no one seemed to think anything of it. I wondered if Marta had ever walked down a city street in broad daylight wearing trousers.

My breath quickened.

It was exhilarating.

Wall Street had some lovely buildings. Some looked like meeting houses, and others taverns or maybe boarding houses, the smell of roasted beef and fresh ale wrestling with the heavy scent of fish and blood. Either a slaughterhouse was close at hand, or something terrible had happened back in those twisted, narrow streets the man had not bothered to name. The openings to those dark holes surely had names, but none were posted. Large paths had their names spelled out on the brick street corners in contrasting colors of brick.

The pale sunlight added no warmth, but at least I could see to avoid horse patties. I already could tell I was going to have to brush these boots a long time to get them clean. Where did they sell all this stock being herded down the streets? Did the taverns need to buy every day, or did they have cold attics or cellars? I hoped to see a few of the Dutch homes I'd heard of, with the stair-stepped roofs that were supposed to look like chains of quilt blocks. I thought I remembered reading that part of the city had burned while the British occupied it during the revolution, so a Dutch building might be hard to find.

I also saw one of the strangest people you ever did hope to see— he wore clothing as brilliant as the songbirds my mother planted sunflowers for, his boots had enormous heels, his coat had long tails hanging down past his knees, and his vest screamed color like a field of wildflowers.

And he had lace on his cuffs and collar! He had spectacles on a gold stick hanging from his vest, too.

I decided that he was my reward for surviving my visit to town. Chances were I could spend an entire letter to Idelia writing about that man.

In truth I should have kept my mind on finding Broadway, and saved looking around like a visitor for another day. I'd left my thin little hole open in the back of my mind, and it was a good thing.

Suddenly I was aware of someone's attention...their complete attention.

That was wrong.

I turned to the right as casually as I could, weaving my way into a narrower street past workmen unloading carts and high wagons. I stooped so I could hide behind the row of men unloading sacks of flour, and watched two sailors step swiftly into the twilight of the back doors of buildings, their heads swiveling as they scanned the crowd. I decided to remain where I was—the workers didn't seem to mind.

I could see that the two burly men pushing their way through the crowd possessed dark, muddy auras.

So they were ill, or bad people, or controlled by something magical. I wanted no part of them, whichever was the true answer.

They weren't stupid—they soon passed the wagon walking the other way, studying faces as they moved. I let them reach Wall Street, and then I slunk past the row of servants' doors.

"You! Sailor! Stop! He's jumped ship!" Someone cried out.

I started weaving through the bustling horde of farmers and tradesmen, ducking sacks of flour on shoulders and dancing around full barrels being rolled. *Look for a hole with a second door.* In this case, I was going to enter from the back and go out the front.

That sailor cursed but I didn't look back. I darted past a drunken man, but someone grabbed at my sleeve. I spun to see dark intent eyes and a big groping hand. He wore a uniform trimmed with bright colors, and I had no doubt he was one of the pair following me.

No knife in his hand.

I grabbed for a piece of sky.

No. I couldn't draw down weather to fight—too many people could be hurt. Then the drunk crashed into us both, knocking the sailor so hard that he staggered. I pushed back, tearing off the red wool cuff on my pursuer's shirt as the drunk rolled over the fellow and squashed him flat.

"I'm terrrribly sooorrry, sor, that I amm, terrrribly soorrry," the drunk said, his breath strong enough to light a fire. The sailor cursed and tried to fight off the man even as the drunk looked my way and winked!

For a moment—just a heartbeat—I saw a flicker of fire in his eyes and the faint image of burning antlers upon his head.

Then I forced my way through the crowd, heading into the nearest open doorway.

Dark, smoky, loud, smelly—*how do people live like this?*

It was a tavern of sorts, although the room was smaller, darker and much smellier than the inn where Marta and I had stayed on our way to Cloudcatcher. Lit candlesticks above the fireplace and in sconces on the wall threw long, black shadows, and the fire was roaring.

There was such a crowd I truly could not have pushed my way to the wall. Men stood or sat on benches, eating from bread trenchers, their mugs of ale gripped protectively in their hands, a few drunk, but everyone seemed to be enjoying themselves, the conversation lively and loud. I chose the only way open to me—I dove under the nearest table.

I got a snoot full of hay, wood chips and old food, grateful none of it had been in someone's stomach. The stench of sour ale, moldy bread and very dead fowl made me sneeze. The hay around me lifted slightly, as if stirred by a breeze—I'd pulled the tiny whirling wind into the tavern!

Too late now. I tightened my grip, narrowing the focus of the swirling breeze. *Don't go anywhere without me,* I told it.

Lord and lady, I was talking to the wind.

Crawling as fast as I could, I slid like a snake among the legs. I got nudged and kicked a few times, but the men weren't mean, just surprised. A couple of fellows started laughing and trying to push themselves enough elbow room to toss some bread at me.

"That fellow jumped ship!" cried a familiar, if breathless, voice, and I knew the sailor was in the tavern. "Stop him!"

I heard scuffling, thuds against the wall, and then someone yelled: "Mind yur hands, limey!"

That was the only warning.

Crash! Then the sound of blows against flesh and wood. Everyone at the table jumped up. Peeking out, I saw one man throw himself onto the solid row of men with their backs to us.

I had to get out of there. Reaching the end, I pushed my way through a leg forest beneath the next table.

Push a man's leg hard in any direction other than forward, and he'll move for you; I guarantee it.

Good thing I was moving fast; abruptly there was more light. Men yelled as they upended the empty table and flung it toward the entrance. *Goddess bless, show me a way out!* More patrons leaped up and threw themselves into battle, their drinks raining upon us. Ducking past heaving, struggling bodies I bolted under the next table.

I brushed against fur.

I recoiled—I didn't want to rile a strange dog!

The curled pile of fur stirred. It was not my breeze. I could make out the flash of golden eyes as the creature stretched, flexing its toes at me.

A cat. It was a huge, dirty cat, large enough to block my path. Unperturbed by humans pushing the table above us every which way, the animal finished unwinding itself and stood. It was much larger than I previously thought, like a small bobcat. The cat started walking away from me, tracing the length of the trestle above us, its long, feathery tail swaying gently above its back. Then it paused, looking back over its shoulder.

I crawled after it as fast as I could.

We reached the end of the row of tables, finding a passageway along the inward wall of the tavern into another area for eating and drinking. It was full and noisy, but the fight hadn't spread. The cat made a beeline for that arch, walking between two sets of legs as if they were no more than the doorframe. I got halfway to my feet and slid between the men, stumbling as I followed the cat through the crowd.

A merchant or two in churchgoing clothes pulled their coats away from me, but no one tried to toss me out of the place. My breeze pushed against my back but I didn't stumble. The cat vanished out the double doors. I straightened and slowed my feet, if not my heartbeat, into the brisk walk of someone with a place to go.

The breeze came right along with me and pulled the tavern doors shut behind it.

I might as well have been invisible. No one commented on my appearance or asked my destination. Once out on the stone sidewalk, I looked either way. From the sounds behind me, I was pretty sure the fight was trying to move into the front room.

Keep moving, Allie. I glanced up at the wall next to me, and was told that this Broad Way establishment had existed since 1790. I was where I wanted to be. I set off quickly to the right.

The cat had not gone far; I caught a brief sighting of the animal's fluffy tail. For whatever reason, the cat was still with me.

The light now had that strange intensity winter sometimes gives us, where you're not positive where the sun is, but it's definitely out there somewhere. Colors of clothing muted, not fading to gray. The sky was an interesting mix of shades—lamb's wool grey, old denim blue and white clouds. It was like pouring milk into tea; the clouds spread along the horizon, making new layers in various concentrations, from dove pale to almost flint.

The brightest color visible anywhere was the tail of the cat—despite the dirt, I could see occasional flickers of gold and autumn russet.

My breeze had popped back up into the sky, like a huge, softly twirling parasol.

Adjusting my sweater and brushing the straw and wood chips from myself, I discovered I still had the ring of red wool I had torn from the sailor's uniform. Somehow I'd looped it on my wrist. Watching the sidewalk dance of two merchants, an elderly woman with a basket and a happy-looking drunk sailor avoiding each other, I pushed the ring down to circle my fingers, and then folded it over to ball it inside my fist.

The woman disappeared, literally *disappeared* between one step and the next.

I stopped so fast the boy behind me bumped me and then cursed as I made my way to the wall of the nearest building. After a moment I relaxed my hand, sliding the frayed cuff back over my wrist so that it touched my skin.

There she was, carefully making her way along, avoiding the cluster of men walking her way, her basket wide and awkward. She could have been the wife of any tradesman of the city, her clothing muted but not ragged. From her posture and walk, I guessed she was older than my mother but not too old to walk safely upon snow and ice. Why they weren't trying to fill the space she occupied, I didn't know, since they didn't seem to notice her, but there it was... the loop of cloth had some sort of spell attached to it.

Was this coincidence? Did those men follow me because they could see my aura, and knew me as a practitioner?

I pulled the cuff off, looking for any writing upon it. There was nothing visible, at least to my eyes. Damaged shirt, damaged cuff... damaged spell? I slid the loop back up to my wrist.

I would wear it until I found the buildings far behind me. I sensed that the damaged spell gave me a small advantage over those sailors...if they *were* sailors.

"Chirrrrp?"

I looked down. The cat sat at my feet. "Was that you?" I asked him.

The next sound could only be described as a trill. The animal stood up and rubbed against my legs. His ears brushed my knees.

"So I belong to you, do I?" I knew cats rubbed their faces on things in their territory. Could this animal speak with birds, or call birds? "Let's go," I told him, stepping toward the road. Now that I knew that someone very alert might be able to find me just because they could see people moving around an open space, I thought walking between road and sidewalk might mean fewer people to avoid.

Could magic users see my whirling wind?

I started walking, looking ahead for landmarks and trying to avoid carts or men carrying large burdens. I needed to find that "green space" the sailor had told me about. It was probably brown or snow-covered right now. And I also needed to find someone who looked like they might know the way to Windward. This brush with magic made me wonder if it was smarter to stay away from power, to avoid even simply mentally yelling for help. If I could find the house by myself, I thought it would be better.

The sharp smell in the air promised more snow coming. I sure hoped I could make it back to Windward before darkness. There were worse things than that portal by the stables disappearing before I could tell Cousin Esme about it.

If the people who created that portal did not know I had passed through it, it might continue to be there, waiting to give someone else passage. Someone the household knew nothing about. Even if students had created the doorway...could an accomplished magic user use it to intrude onto the grounds of Windward?

Someone who was not merely curious...someone who was dangerous?

The talk of war had me uneasy.

But then people tell me I think too much.

❧ 🖎 ❧

In the end, asking the way to Windward was even more remarkable than getting out of town had been. I passed the Park Row gardens, and a huge swath of land without a building upon it. There really was a triangle of open land arrowing back toward New York, and roads going northeast and northwest along the two sides that came to a point. I paused there, looking down first Broad Way and then off to my right, where a path called Division went east for a bit and then seemed to swing up north once more. The cat was still with me, although it had discovered a patch of fresh, unmarked snow. This was cause for a cat celebration; he was bouncing around like a rabbit, occasionally posing for me with tail up and whiskers wide.

So what next? Maybe I needed to return to the last tavern and ask for directions. I heard scuffing snow, and looked over my shoulder.

The person approaching me was dressed in dark, loose trousers and a long-sleeved tunic, bowed under a wide hat woven of straw. I grabbed my right wrist and moved the torn red cuff away from my skin.

Still there.

The cat bouncing across the path caught the strange one's eye. As the face turned up, I saw a fleeting smile at the cat—and then I was spotted. All expression left his face. He—I thought a he—continued toward me, his pace only a hair slower than before. Finally, he stopped.

We were maybe twelve healthy strides apart; I could clearly see that he had ivory colored skin and delicate eyebrows. His eyes and brows were a bit like those of the American natives, but he was much shorter, and he was fair compared to the men I'd seen in my dream.

I'd seen a hat like this.... I felt myself straighten. This person was from China, or some such land!

The cat bounded up to me, trilling. The stranger kept his gaze between the cat and me. Finally, the person bent from the waist toward me, low enough for me to see the top of the hat, but not the brim in the back. I also bowed from the waist.

The Chinese person studied me for a while. His gaze flicked above my head. Then I felt something like the brush of my hair in a light wind swirling around me.

Magic.

So, are you supposed to be here? It was a moment like something out of Marco Polo's tales!

His aura was a reassuring mix of blues, greens, purple and white, void of black or even brown. The cat was a bundle of glittering brown, with bursts of white.

I focused again. He didn't look like someone who would take offense at a question.

"Good afternoon," I said aloud. "Do you know the way to the Livingston estate called Windward?"

"Doktor Livingston?" The voice was a deep tenor, almost definitely male.

An arm snaked out of the flapping material, pointing to the right-hand road. "Windward."

I bowed again, trying for the same height as before. "Thank you." I had to either let the man go on, or turn my back on him and hope it was a good decision. A tendril of myself swirled toward the cat, testing if I could see out of its eyes. The cat promptly raised a paw at me, as if batting at a long piece of grass. Then it went over to the man and rubbed against his legs. A hint of a smile appeared, and he spoke to it, the rise and fall of his speech nothing like any words I had ever heard.

The cat bounded to me, rubbing past my legs. "So, you want me to take him on your say-so?" I murmured to the cat.

The cat trilled at me, and then leapt in the direction the man had pointed.

Trying to hide a sigh, I started off on the right-hand path. I had my whirling wind. A whirling wind was an argument, if I needed an argument.

I knew he was back there, like a shadow in my mind, but he made no attempt to catch up. Since he probably did not know I was female (although his magic might include something that could get past my protection) I figured this fellow made a habit of keeping to himself. When you considered how most colonists treated the different Indian tribes, this foreign fellow's caution was understandable. I didn't think I was in danger, but every time I looked to see what the cat was up to, I gauged whether the distance between the man and me had shrunk.

It had increased.

I figured all was well.

Then I heard the squeak and rattle of a carriage or wagon. Two glossy bay horses pulled a small, elegant carriage, slung in a manner I'd never seen before. I wondered if that made the jostling and bouncing from ruts beneath the snow bearable. Marta told me once that some roads were impassable for a wagon—and more than once, a coach carrying people between places like New York and Philadelphia arrived with broken bones among the passengers.

The carriage slowed as it neared the man. A window slid down, and someone in the carriage called out to him. I could see a genuine smile on the slight man's face as he bowed. After a rapid fluttering of sentences exchanged, the man waved, gesturing for me to come closer.

My momma raised no fools.

"I don't think so, but give them my regards," I said aloud, and wondered if my downdraft of air would fit in a closed carriage. I glanced up—yes, the sky looked still darker than before. I really needed to let that energy return to the winds.

I decided I'd let go after the carriage and the man continued on.

"Boy! Boy!" the man yelled, waving for me to come closer. Pointing at the carriage, he said: "Windward!"

This time I sighed and made no attempt to hide it. Well, I hadn't really expected to get back to the house, bathe and then show up for dinner as if I'd never left the estate. That was too much to hope for. Slowly I started toward the carriage.

After I'd kicked my way through snow back to the carriage, an arm holding a tall, impressive hat folded itself out the window, followed by a head. "Say, there! Li Sung tells me you are heading for Windward?"

This new person was male and middle-aged, with either a well-curled head of white hair or a fine wig.

"Yes, sir, I am going to Windward," I said, giving him a little bow.

"Well, no sense in you both trudging through the snow," was his reply. "Come on in!" The small door popped out, even as the elegantly-dressed driver tied up the horses and sprang down to unfold a set of steps.

"Ah.... Thank you, but I had a bit of trouble in town, and I smell like the floor of a tavern."

The foreign man jumped into the carriage; I heard more conversation, and this time I heard some English. I felt something dive at my leg, and looked down at the cat standing by my feet on the road.

"Well! Since you don't appear drunk, I see you must have some traveler's stories to tell. If you'd rather, sit up top with Edward, but if we want to be on time for dinner, we must make haste." He'd leaned back out the window, a single eyepiece on a chain held to his right eye. "Ah...perhaps you could release that vortex? We don't want a whirling wind above us!"

I blinked. The cat thoroughly rubbed my legs, leaving some of the dirt washed loose by the snow. "I am traveling with a cat."

"I see that!" was his reply. "A fine ship's cat, indeed, though a bit travel worn. Bring him along!"

The tiny whirlwind soared as I nudged it back into the sky.

I looked at the cat. It looked at me. "Are you going to let me pick you up?" I asked it.

My answer was his putting his paws against my leg, stretching so much that his ears reached to my waist. "Chirp!"

That was an order.

I reached down and picked up the cat, rearranging him so his front paws and chest pointed to one side. This was the largest cat I had ever seen, and amazingly heavy. The animal immediately started purring. "You know that some say that if you save the life of someone, you are responsible for them forever," I told him.

Did this make me the responsibility of the cat, or did that only work for humans?

Then I looked up at the driver's high seat. It was quite a ways up.

In the end, the driver got behind me, and with one well-placed shove boosted the cat and me up to the top seat.

The driver's gaze was wary as he climbed back to his seat. I relaxed and studied the snowy trees in the forest beyond. The cat alternated between sitting contentedly and purring, and observing any movement within the trees. A slight wiggle followed these discoveries, as if he was ready for the chase.

"I think he's a little big for you," I murmured to the cat as a fine buck watched us from a distance. A taunt stillness told me the cat was seriously thinking about it, but the buck bounded away into the woods. I would have sworn the cat sighed, but he settled back down on my lap.

We reached the open entrance of stone pillars before the sunlight faded into twilight. Ironwork rose in a high arch above the path; WINDWARD was spelled out in capital letters. I was surprised to see gargoyles sitting on the stone pillars to either side of the archway.

Here I was, back where I'd started from, somewhat the worse for wear, and toting a big, dirty cat. I hadn't lasted two days.

Well. If they were going to pack me off home, I hope they'd feed me—us—first. The big city sure worked up your appetite.

How many times in a day could I apologize to Margaret?

I sighed. And the man next to me chuckled. He had a deep voice and a fine set of white teeth in his tanned face.

"Don't worry, son," he said softly. "Dr. Livingston is much more lenient about these little escapades away from the school than Professor Livingston can be. And you wouldn't want to be at any other school for practitioners. This one is as far as you can go before your majority." He leaned over slightly and added: "And the food is the best ever!"

Clearly he didn't eat there on a Saturday.

"Well, I can stir a soup," I replied. "You can tell me next week if the food was all right."

The driver laughed all the way up the drive to the courtyard.

We turned into the covered drive between barns. As the driver put on a brake, I looked at the wall. The light shimmered like the reflection of sun on water.

The portal I'd come through was still there.

SIX

SOMEONE IN CHARGE NEEDED TO KNOW that I had found an open door in the yard.

The two men from the carriage walked under the sheltered part of the drive, their conversation animated. It was a sight, the lean man wearing a white horsehair wig, in his tall hat and greatcoat of dark green wool, and the short, wiry foreigner bundled in shapeless dark cloth and straw hat. The only sign of wealth the Chinese man revealed was his set of leather boots with lashing nearly to his knees.

Most of their swift conversation seemed to be in what I guessed was Chinese. The wigged gentleman seemed to understand what was being said, and kept his right hand to his single eyeglass piece, watching how the other man gestured.

I waited to be noticed, the cat circling my legs in a way that suggested he wanted food and expected me to find it. *I'm not sure I'll get fed today, much less you*, I thought at the cat. *Hope you're a good mouser.*

The portal did not change while I watched. I could not smell the street, only the odors of fresh manure and the promise of more snow.

Then I noticed another cat, a plush blue tortie with that patched color of fur like a calico faded in the sun. Her eyes one might call amber; if she'd been human I'd have said hazel. She sat in the entranceway of the stable on the right, her full tail curled around her feet, gaze fixed on my strutting companion. When my ship's cat spotted her, I wondered if we were going to have a fight.

My cat-companion promptly sat on my feet, staring back at tortie.

"Not even going to introduce yourself?" I murmured to him.

As day faded into twilight, the lanterns lit in the carriage house and stable. Now the portal was no more than wavering air, the way a freshly plowed field looks in spring.

The tortie's head swiveled, following my gaze to the portal, and she wandered past the conversing men, stopping almost on top of the portal. Then she lifted her right paw, her claws extended, as if feeling heat from a fire.

The gentleman held up his hand, nodding an apology to the foreign gentleman, and looked from the tortie to me. "Oh, your catch, is it? Is that how you ended up in town?"

"Yes, sir. I thought I was following Mr. Gardener to the succession houses, and suddenly I was on the waterfront."

Both men turned toward the portal, lifting their left hands toward it. "Youngster, why don't you go on and clean up, and come to the parlor after you have some supper?" the gentleman said over his right shoulder.

My furry companion was still planted practically on my feet. I bent and scooped him up. "Yes, sir," I said, heading back to the house.

Now could I get inside and to my room without anyone noticing? I needed to duck in through the mudroom by the kitchen. I could not bear to track city dirt in on the rugs. I had not found the tub for baths yet, but I surely needed to know now.

A lantern burned by the kitchen entrance. The heavy wood door swung open, a flood of rich odors flowing out into the cold. Blocking access was an impressive mountain of a woman, her bright gold hair softened by white at her ears and temples. She looked both strong and shrewd, and she managed to have her nose in the air even as she pinned me with her stare. This was not the genial Mrs. Gardener...this was the Empress of the Kitchen.

We looked at each other for a bit, and then I said: "I know he's a sight, but this cat saved me in town, so I think I owe him at least a meal and his chance to fight for a corner of the barn."

"If you think that cat is coming into my kitchen before he has a bath, you are sadly mistaken, young lady," the woman announced. She pointed off in the direction of the huge food sinks, and the pump near them. One candle burned, tossing dark shadows over the entire area—which was spotless, I noted. "Have you ever washed a cat?"

"No, ma'am," I replied.

The woman smiled.

Hell, Hull and Halifax.

I sure hoped Cousin Esme was good at stitching people up.

❧ 🐚 ❧

The cat washing went better than you might expect, if you know anything about cats. My new friend was quite patient, sitting quietly on the wood counter while I went to get hot water and re-filled the cauldron in the fireplace before lugging my own bucket back to the big sink. I pumped up a bucket of cold water, too, and made sure the mixture was comfortable. I didn't reach for the cat until I had found a scrap of old towel and had it ready to dry him off.

Everything was fine until I tried to put the cat into the water. Then he suddenly had as many arms as a heathen goddess, and braced himself on the lip of the sink, suspended like the nest of a Baltimore-bird.

We compromised. He must have decided that this was not going to be too bad—maybe the heat rising against his stomach felt good?—because he let me lower his hind legs into the sink. The cat wasn't as dirty as I'd feared. There was just a lot of old, loose gray hair hanging from his body, and most of it pulled off with only a few cat complaints. Vocal complaints only, luckily—he batted at me a couple of times, but he did not use his claws.

Elizabeth rescued both of us. The young maid who lit the fire my first morning at Windward arrived with a large towel and, wonder of wonders, my slippers! "I made up a bath," she murmured to me, setting down the towel to one side of the sink.

I dried off the cat with the scraps, and then reached for Elizabeth's towel (no mean trick while keeping one hand on a cat). I had to get out of my boots and into those slippers, so I could get cleaned up to see The Doktor, as my Chinese man had called him.

Shaking her head and hiding a smile, Elizabeth made me sit on a wooden chest near the door, and showed me how to use a big metal fork to pull off my boots. "Best pay John to clean them," she whispered, and led me off down a narrow hall that ended up at the back staircase. "I'll clean the sink! This way!"

I headed for my bedroom, towel-wrapped cat in arms. Since all these people couldn't bathe down by the kitchen fire, they must bring the tub to the person. My heart sank down to my toes. What could I do to say thank you to Elizabeth for all her trouble?

"Miss Alfreda! Here!" Elizabeth's hiss stopped me in my tracks. She was gesturing to the room right next to mine, the door open a crack. As I approached, I could feel warm, moist air flowing into the hallway.

I looked around the door. A lit candle sat on a shelf up above our heads, its light glimmering on a wooden chair, a small, polished table, and a long, low surface that glowed like marble.

"You will *love* this," Elizabeth whispered, inviting me with a crook of her finger.

There was a room just for bathing?

"I'll start the fire in your room, and get your robe," Elizabeth said, her smile blossoming. "Better wash your hair, too! Can you do it by yourself?"

"Oh, yes. I had to—no sisters to help me," I told her, setting the bundled cat down on the one chair in the room. "I'm going to owe a lot of favors to whoever got all this water up here!"

Elizabeth took hold of my arm (gingerly, because the sweater was matted with straw and muck) and turned me slightly, pointing to a faucet high above the tub. "There is a tank of water up there that comes from the well."

"But it's hot," I said aloud, staring at the iron pipe.

"We heat bath water when we need it. We don't waste timber keeping it hot!" She reached up to remove a glass chimney from a sconce attached to the wall, and lit the wick of the beeswax candle within with a touch of her finger. Doubled, the light revealed the high ceiling, which looked like painted, embossed metal.

"Is *that* how you heated the water?" I remembered how quickly she had started that fire the previous day.

This time she grinned. "Not quite, but close. I'm a salamander, you know!" With that she bustled off, pulling the door shut behind her.

Salamanders can shape shift into people? Or is this something else?

I have so much to learn.

Now I knew how the King of England lived. Not only the necessary room inside and clean, but a special room for bathing!

I wondered if Elizabeth would teach me how to heat water.

❧ 💮 ❧

By the time I finished pulling on my robe and picking up the cat, Elizabeth was long gone. Grateful I was so close to my own room, I hurried into it and shut the door tightly.

From the jar of spills on the thin mantel above the fireplace I chose one, lit it from the fire, and lit two candles, so I could make sure my face was clean and my hair neat. Then I combed out the long fine mess the Lord and Lady had seen fit to gift me with. Once all the tangles were out, I reached back to plait it into one long braid. I could smell something good—stew, maybe?—and I wanted to get to it.

It was a chicken potpie, one all to myself! I'm embarrassed to say I ate most of the thing, as well as some roasted herbed carrots along the side.

The cat got the rest. He was neat while eating, and then cleaned himself up with his tongue. By firelight plus the two candles, he was a reddish color, his face, bib, and paws white.

A pale hermit cookie hid under the napkin. Was this a special occasion I'd missed, or was there always dessert on Sunday? I took a careful bite. *Oh, my.* Nutmeg and the soft bite of soured cream, and even dried fruit and chopped walnuts. The cat inspected it and then dismissed it as unworthy of his concern.

Who knew what the punishment for my little trip would be? This might be my last sweet for a while.

❧ 💮 ❧

It was fortunate for me that the new style of dress pulled over the head and then tied; I did not need someone to button me into the thing. I chose the new linen dress with the embroidered panel, and hoped that I looked respectable.

I left a tiny pile of dishes on the tray for Elizabeth (the cat had licked the bowl, but only after I placed it on the floor) and was ready to head downstairs when my new cat acquaintance batted at the glass of the window and trilled at me.

"Of course you would want to go outside now," I muttered as I checked to see if I could open the window. If I pulled out pegs that formed some kind of lock, then...yes, I could open it. I got the window up enough that the cat squeezed under the sash. He curled his tail around himself, eyed the nearest tree and then jumped toward it, easily gripping the rough bark of a huge limb.

I was surprised that the tree was close enough to the house for the cat to reach it—out where I lived, most people cleared the trees away from their homes. But he was there, and could go about his cat business at his leisure. "Thank you, cat. Be careful out there. I heard a great horned owl last night."

I knew I might never see him again. But it was interesting, meeting a cat that took a liking to me. I shut the window and replaced the pegs that kept it from sliding. Then I blew out the candles, double-checked the spark guard on the fire screen, and grabbed my new shawl for warmth. It was time to go downstairs and pay the piper. I had no idea how long I would be left kicking my heels, so I thought I'd get started on it.

At the last moment, I grabbed the loop of red fabric I'd torn from that sailor's shirt. Cousin Esme might be curious about it.

ᘒ ⌘ ᘒ

Many chairs sat against the walls of the large entryway, a few narrow tables between groups of them. I took a seat near the parlor door, and was there long enough for my hair to finish drying, and to notice that the room wasn't nearly as cold as I had thought it would be.

The parlor door opened, and a stately young man in very formal clothes stepped out, holding the door mostly closed. "Are you Miss Alfreda Sorensson?" the man asked. He had brilliant white hair neatly combed back from his face, but it didn't look like a wig. And he was nicer-dressed than even the ministers who came to Sun Return to preach.

I stood up to face him. "Yes, sir, I am." I had to lift my chin to meet his gaze.

"Dr. and Professor Livingston will see you now." He reached to open the door for me. His movements were very smooth—no fussiness at all.

"Miss Sorensson," he announced as I moved past him into the warmth of the room. The door shut behind me.

The room was filled with soft light, tinting the shadows in the corners with the warmth of deep browns. A metal candelabrum sat on a tea table by the fireplace, and sconces hung on the walls, their candles glowing with the translucence of beeswax. The fire in the fireplace burned brightly; this "parlor" was easily twice the size of Cousin Esme's sitting room.

Standing by the fire itself was a tall man, his dark hair reflecting glints of red. He lifted a single eyeglass to his right eye, and I recognized The Doktor, his heavy coat and wig replaced with lighter weight, trimmer clothing.

The man wore long trousers and a jacket with a swallow's tail to his knees; the clothing was dark except for a snowy white vest, shirt collar, and cuffs. His hair was amazingly short, shorn close to his head like the hair of the soldiers I'd seen in town.

Cousin Esme sat on a small sofa near the fireplace, the tea tray before her, a few cookies left on a plate. Her dress and hair were more formal than I'd ever seen. The dark material had the gleam of silk, and her hair was dressed with tiny silk flowers twined around what glittered like gold.

The third person, the Chinese gentleman, sat with his back to me. His hair was very dark, with a few glittering threads of silver in it.

All right. I was impressed.

But I could talk my way out of a lot of things.

"Come here, Alfreda," Cousin Esme said, lifting her hand in invitation. "It is time for you to meet my husband, Dr. Livingston."

I made a beeline for the fireplace and quickly curtseyed. "Did you create the cork plugs on the chains in the kitchen and bathing room, sir? That is a wonderful invention." It tumbled out before I could even think.

Dr. Livingston laughed, and nodded. "Now I am sure that you are related to Marta Helgisdottir Donaltsson. She never hesitates to ask for information." Looking at me through his eyepiece, he added: "Your disguise was quite good. I did not realize that you were a Schell until I saw the vortex."

I'd have to remember that. Practitioners remember faces, voices...and magical traits. I curtsied again and said: "How do you do, sir?"

Smiling faintly and shaking her head, Cousin Esme turned to the other small sofa. "Alfreda, I wish also to introduce you to our friend Li Sung."

I turned to curtsey, and was surprised when he stood up and bowed to me, the angle precise, his gaze momentarily lowered. "I am pleased to meet next wizard of Schell line," he said clearly. There was the snap of another language under his speech. I wondered if he spoke English even better than this, but did not want me to know.

He was wearing what looked like a loose jacket, fastened with elegant woven knots. It was made of a dark silk...dark blue?...with birds like herons embroidered over it in a lighter thread. His dark silk pantaloons went all the way to his ankles. He wore slippers that reminded me of mine, except they were made of black silk and had no bows.

A single teardrop of a deep green, milky stone hung from a gold wire looped around the back of his left ear.

I met his courtesy with a protracted curtsey. This gentleman was entirely distinguished. He might think I was funny, as Dr. Livingston did, but I wanted to be sure he didn't think that I found *him* amusing.

"You may sit down, Alfreda," Cousin Esme said, gesturing to her side. "We have many things to talk about."

Oh, dear.

Well, I'd expected as much.

❧ 🌑 ❧

Of course they wanted to know about the portal. When did I realize there was a portal? Did I notice as I walked through it, or only after I passed through the opening? Did it close instantly behind me, or only when I tried to return through it? What did I do next?

I told them pretty much everything, except about my Good Friend showing up as the drunk who saved me. Cousin Esme already knew about my Good Friend—she might have told her husband. Aunt Marta was firm about keeping that a private thing, so I told what physically happened and didn't mention any sparking spirit lights. If Dr. Livingston picked at that slub in my weaving, I'd explain more, but only then. Cousin Esme looked closely at the torn cuff, but she did not say anything.

"Where is the cat?" Dr. Livingston asked, glancing at the door as if he expected it to come wandering in.

"It wanted out, so I opened the window of my room and let it out," I replied. "Then I closed the window back up. I didn't think you'd want it left open."

"You were correct," Cousin Esme said, her expression amused. She gave me a long look, and I steeled myself. There was no use making any excuses. I hadn't meant to walk off the property but that would hold no weight in this court. I'd broken a rule, and after my going back to Marta's homestead through the maze, I didn't think she could let this pass without comment.

"Have you been vaccinated for the smallpox?" she asked.

It wasn't at all what I had expected her to say. "I...do not know what you are talking about, ma'am."

"Was your family's farm ever quarantined because of disease?"

"No. ma'am; not that I remember."

"We require everyone living at Windward to be inoculated with cowpox using Dr. Jenner's method," Dr. Livingston said, lowering his eyeglass and lifting a cup to take a sip of tea. "It is not overly painful. Most importantly, you are unlikely to catch the disease, and will be protected from smallpox by your exposure to cowpox vaccine. We'll do this tomorrow morning. You will not be contagious, and if you have no ill effects, you will be able to go right on for testing in the magical arts."

Cousin Esme was watching me closely. "Your aunt has had this procedure done," she told me. "I will write to your parents to tell them it has been done for your safety and the safety of everyone here. Going into town without protection means you may have been exposed to smallpox. In truth, Livingston, I think you should inoculate her tonight. The sooner it's done, the less chance that she will contract the illness."

"You may feel a bit ill from it," Dr. Livingston said, "but it's unlikely that you'll get full-blown cowpox from it."

"My family has done," Li Sung announced. "Many die from smallpox. Many. Many children, many elders."

He was trying to be reassuring with information, I decided. "And they all are fine? No one has ever caught smallpox?"

"No smallpox." Li Sung's voice was firm.

"None of our children or staff has ever contracted the disease after being vaccinated." Dr. Livingston had his eyeglass back up, his expression solemn.

Did anyone die? I wasn't sure they'd tell me even if someone *had* died.

"You do not have to do this, Alfreda," Cousin Esme said quietly. "But if you do not, you will need to be isolated until we are sure you have not caught smallpox. Then you may return to Marta's home."

That settled it. Aunt Marta thought that Esme's instruction was important enough to interrupt her own teaching of me. I could not return to her without even trying to learn ritual magic. "Sounds like the best thing to do, then."

Cousin Esme smiled, and her husband visibly relaxed. "Good. Now, let us move on to our next point of discussion. This is the second time in as many days that you have left the property."

There was a pause. I kept my attention on Cousin Esme.

"The first was totally unexpected, and I know that it was unintentional on your part. I spoke with you and with Miss Rutledge, and did not expect a repetition of the problem. Then we have today's incident. This leaves us with a dilemma, Alfreda. On the one hand, you have done us a favor. This portal was unsanctioned. Either someone on the property created it, or someone from the outside is spying on our household. This was an intolerable situation, and your accidental triggering of the portal has caused us to reinforce our protections."

"It might also make you more vulnerable," Dr. Livingston said abruptly. "We don't know if the person who went through that portal knew he was followed. So we're going to need to mark you, my dear. You should not even know you have been touched by magic. But it will let us know if you suddenly leave the property. Someone will be looking for you!" He smiled slightly as he finished speaking.

"The other side of this coin is that we cannot have students wandering off the property without a by-your-leave. You handled this misadventure quite well. But how would our other students have dealt with it? Some of them are very sheltered. They would not have known what to do, how to protect themselves—the older boys might have ended up on a ship bound for Barbados. I shudder to think what could have happened to some of the younger girls."

"Maybe there should be a class in basic protections if someone snatches you?" I replied. "My father taught us what to do if we were lost in the wilderness. Could you teach us what to do in a strange city?"

The three adults turned from me to each other.

"It has merit," Li Sung announced.

"We do have safe houses in cities, but of course you did not know of them. I hate to think that it has come to survival lessons, but should things progress as we fear...." Cousin Esme's voice trailed off, her gaze upon the flickering fire. "Perhaps."

"We do need to deal with the situation as it exists, Mrs. Livingston," the doctor said to his wife.

"Indeed." My cousin looked back at me. "And this concerns not only you, my dear, but also your mentor here at the school, Miss Rutledge. I do not want any of the mentors to think their task is a light one. They are responsible for the new student under their care, until that student is familiar with the school and its rules. So it is necessary, for appearances, to punish you both for this misadventure. It was impossible to keep secret your return from town."

"You'll need to learn how to slip back onto the property," Dr. Livingston tossed in, dropping his eyeglass and reaching for a cookie.

"Dr. Livingston! I would like her to be more familiar with our school before she starts tramping off on errands for you!"

The doctor lifted his eyebrows in response to Cousin Esme's sharp comment but nodded agreement. Li Sung remained still.

"Thinking it over, I believe the best balance for a punishment is to place you both on kitchen duty for this coming Saturday. In fact, Miss Rutledge will be in charge of planning the meals, and you will assist her. I do not know if she has any experience in planning for a large group, but she should. That will be punishment enough. Am I correct that the kitchen holds no terrors for you?"

"Ma'am?"

"You do know something about cooking, do you not?"

"Yes, ma'am."

"Good. You will assist with the three meals served this coming Saturday. For now, we will have my husband inoculate you—" She turned to Dr. Livingston and added: "The usual place for young women." Twisting back to me, she said: "in the back fold of the arm. It is annoying as it heals, but will not be obvious when you wear a sleeveless gown."

As if my mother would allow me to appear, living or dead, in a sleeveless gown!

"If you have no problems with the vaccination, you will report to me tomorrow after breakfast. I will test you further for class placement, and then take you to the advanced teachers for whatever private lessons you may need before learning basic ritual. Your presence here will be less secretive, and attract less attention, if we slide you into the regular classrooms." Cousin Esme smiled at me.

She did not seem angry.

And that, as it is said, was that.

SEVEN

The vaccination turned out to be simple, but I did not get to really see what was done. Cousin Esme took me back to my room to exchange my dress for my robe, although I left on my long chemise. Then she took me down to what I guessed was some kind of private sitting room close to her bedroom.

Dr. Livingston appeared carrying a large black leather satchel that was long and flat at the bottom. I could see that this inoculating business involved a long swab, a needle and a small jar with something moldy-looking in it, but everything was going on behind my back, so that's all I learned right then. The actual vaccinating hurt no more than a cat scratch.

"Thank you," I told Dr. Livingston. I didn't want him to think I wasn't grateful.

"You are welcome, my dear. Good night to you, now. I have a few more things to attend to before bed." That said, he closed up his jars and black medical bag, and left us.

"Let us return to your room," Cousin Esme said, gesturing for me to follow her.

"I can find my way back, Professor Livingston," I said, making sure my robe was securely tied. I waited to see if she would correct me. It felt like "Mrs. Livingston" was her title socially, and "Professor Livingston" was for other times. That was my guess.

Cousin Esme did not correct me.

"The ability to retrace your steps would not surprise me," she replied, opening the door. "But I will be more comfortable once you are back in the female side of the dormitory. Come along!"

❧⁂❧

Cousin Esme took me to the huge oak door leading into the older women's wing. She wasn't taking any chance with me wandering off into some portal in only my robe and slippers. We said good night, and then I went through the doorway and into the wide hall of the girl's dormitory.

Once the great door closed behind me, I stood, aware that the hall was cool but not cold, conscious of something wrong. I could hear someone weeping.

Was the sound real or a ghost?

I know.

I just don't look at the world the way most people do.

Moving slowly down the hall, I realized it was coming from one of the rooms. Sometimes it helps to have someone to share troubles with. So I knocked.

The door was open. Only a crack, but I could see firelight and candlelight within, so I knocked again, so quietly that the door did not even sway.

The gasping sobs grew quieter. "Yes? Who is it?"

It sounded like Miss Rutledge. "Alfreda Sorensson," I said. "Miss Rutledge? May I come in?"

A long pause...and then she said: "Yes."

I pushed open the door, and found her sitting in a rocking chair next to a small fireplace.

She wasn't alone.

There were at least three ghosts standing around her, and I thought I saw a wisp of something ghostly peeping out from the end of her bed curtains.

Of course good manners said I should concentrate on Miss Rutledge, so after noting the ghosts standing around, I looked back at her. Miss Rutledge had grown noticeably paler.

Pushing the door shut behind me, I started toward her. "Are you all right?"

"I...I am fine," she got out faintly, inhaling deeply. This seemed to steady her, so I halted two steps into the bedroom.

One of the ghosts, who seemed young and female, reached over as if to pat her cheek with a wispy handkerchief. Another ghost, also female but a bit older, had knelt down by her chair and was embracing her. This ghost would have been too close to the fire screen if she'd been alive, but the heat did not seem to affect her.

The third ghost was much older, female, and stood looking on severely but not unkindly. The spirit peeping out from the bed curtains was bouncing up and down. I decided it was more of a child, but I wasn't certain if it was male or female. The suggestion of clothing the ghosts wore looked familiar, like things my mother would wear. These were not old ghosts.

Twisting my hands together behind my back, I decided to curtsy to Miss Rutledge. "Please don't cry, Miss Rutledge. I will tell everyone that I was to blame. You are entirely without fault in all of this," I said. I had a feeling that I had caused this, and that Miss Rutledge was not used to being in trouble.

"No, that is not true," she replied, lifting her own handkerchief to her eyes again. "I am supposed to protect you while you become accustomed to the school, and I failed in my duty." Her voice thickened as she added: "If they send me home, I do not know what I will do. My parents will be so disappointed!"

Well, I moved right through those ghosts to get up next to Miss Rutledge. They were cold, like a puff of winter wind, but otherwise they didn't bother me at all. I reached out to take one of her hands. "Surely they won't send you home over me! I'll go home first. I bet you've never been in trouble the entire time you've been here at Windward!" Margaret Rutledge struck me as the kind of young woman who was a good girl. She wasn't tearing her dresses climbing trees or disappearing into the forest to watch animals.

"Nnooo, not—here," she gasped out, trying to control her tears. "But—"

Making a tremendous effort, Margaret got hold of herself, taking another deep breath to calm her tears. Then she gave me a long look. "You kept your passage through the maze a secret, did you not?"

"I didn't want anyone giving you trouble about it," I replied. "It was no one's business but ours."

"You know how to keep secrets," she said, still giving me a long, considering look.

"I can keep a secret," I told her.

"What I am about to reveal to you is a secret," Margaret stated. "No one must know any of it."

"All right, no one will hear it from me. Unless a life is at stake," I added quickly.

Once I kept a secret so well someone almost died over it. I didn't want that ever to happen again.

Margaret took a deep breath and then rushed her fence. "This is my third school! If I am sent away from here, I don't know what my parents will do! They are so ashamed of me!"

That shocked me. I knew I didn't know much about Margaret yet, but you know how you get a feeling about a person? Margaret Rutledge was not a person who did things that embarrassed her parents. "How could they be ashamed of you? My mother would think you were the perfect daughter!" At any rate, Margaret certainly acted like a perfect daughter. I think my mother would have preferred her to me, given a choice.

Margaret shook her head. "Not when she knew what happens when I am around." There was a long moment where she said nothing, merely clutching my hand and using her other hand to wipe away tears. "When...when you walked in, you looked so odd. Why was that?"

Normally I wouldn't tell anyone what I'd seen, but we were at a school mostly for magic users. Even if she didn't have power, she knew it existed.

Still...ghosts upset people.

"I have seen ghosts since I arrived here," I finally said. "I didn't expect to find ghosts keeping you company."

"You saw them?" This was low, her voice tight.

Them. She knew that there was more than one.

I could be vague, too. "Yes."

Suddenly her eyes brimmed; a blink sent tears trickling down her cheeks. "I see them *all the time.* They follow me everywhere! They *talk to me!* I took a tour of a stately home in the Lake District, and I could not hear the housekeeper speak for all the ghosts trying to talk to me!"

"They *talk* to you? What do they say? Do they actually listen to you and answer, or do they just run on like a minister giving a sermon?"

Miss Rutledge laid her crumpled handkerchief down on her knee and started smoothing out its damp corners. "You are not frightened of them?"

Frightened of them? I thought back to my first ghosts. One had been a tiny cat, burrowing in its mistress's skirts. The other had been a frightening apparition, dangerous to anyone whose path it crossed. I said, "Well, some ghosts are very frightening. But most of them are merely a moment in time, like a...a drawing of ice crystals on a window. Sometimes they look real, with all their colors, just like a painting. The scary part is when you turn back around, and they've vanished. No human could move that fast. That's when you know you've seen a ghost."

"Most people are frightened half to death of them," she whispered.

"I think that most people don't see them—they only feel them, or smell perfume or tobacco smoke, and know something has been there. And poltergeists are frightening. You don't know what they'll do, and that's a real reason to fear them," I said, waiting to see what she would say next.

"My grandmother sees ghosts," Miss Rutledge confessed. "She talks to them all the time, as if they are just normal people in the room. Neighbors come from many miles away, hoping she will talk to their loved ones."

"My great-grandmother could read the future," I shared in turn. "People came from days away to talk with her. She always asked them first if they were sure they wanted to know what the future chose to share with them."

"People either fear my grandmother or tell others that she is crazy," Miss Rutledge said flatly. "When my mother found me talking to a little girl ghost in our attic playroom, she was horrified. Ghosts tell me things that are important to them."

"Are they little, simple things, like that they miss their puppy? Or big things, like that their husband killed them and their children?" I asked.

Miss Rutledge gave me a startled look.

"Because the first story just needs you to smile and sympathize with them, as you'd do with someone living. The second is a problem...is dangerous to you and to other people." I tried to think of a way to explain about looking for clues. "Do the ghosts look like they died hundreds of years ago, and their stories probably can't matter to anyone else now, or do the burial clothes look recent—and the killer still might be out there, endangering others?"

"For the most part they have been people who died young. All the ghosts I can see right now died within a few miles of here, of illness or childbed." She looked up at me when she said this, which I thought a hopeful sign.

"Have you met violent ghosts?" I asked her.

Miss Rutledge shuddered visibly. "I visited a castle once. There were hundreds of ghosts, walking the grounds, racing along the tops of the walls, fighting in the courtyard."

"Do you see fetches?" I asked, letting go of her hand and pulling over a heavy chair from the table against the wall.

The young woman nodded. "Even walking down a busy street in London, I will see people dragging their winding sheet behind them."

"Surely there must be some way to learn *not* to see them except when you want to," I murmured.

"That is why I am here," she said softly. "My family sent me where no one knew my talent, in hopes that Professor Livingston could teach me how to control it. A wizard in London locked down my ability to see things, so I could cross through the spiral gates without any spirit attaching itself to me. But he warned my parents that the spell would age and crumble. I just started classes in dealing with the dead. Professor Livingston wanted to work with me before others joined the class."

"So you just started seeing ghosts again?"

"Friday night was when I realized that the spell had finally vanished," she replied. Her eyes were very wide. "Please, you can keep this a secret, can't you?"

"Of course," I told her. "Although talking with ghosts is just another gift. You're lucky to have it. It might come in handy, sometime. I only see them. They don't try to speak with me."

"It's *not* just another gift," she said sharply. "Some people whisper that my grandmother is a necromancer!"

I studied her, silenced by her words.

Necromancy wasn't just seeing ghosts. Being a necromancer meant that you could *command* ghosts, control their movements. You could raise them from their graves, and lay them back down even if they wanted to walk.

Necromancers often served kings, and conjured armies of the dead.

Sometimes it wasn't safe to have strong gifts.

I wasn't ready yet to tell her about the unicorns.

"That's a pretty powerful gift," I agreed. "I can see why you don't want people to know. But Miss Rutledge, no one would think about necromancy first. They'd just think you're one of those people who can see ghosts." I had an awful thought. "Unless your grandmother...do a lot of people know that she talks to ghosts? Is she famous for it?"

"Only once has she ever commanded the dead," Margaret said softly, studying her hands. "At least as far as I know. It was something to do with the war against Emperor Bonaparte. His people tried something with the dead once, at a castle crypt. I do not think he expected it to work. But it did, with terrifying results. My grandmother heard the call for help from one of his magicians."

"What did she do?" This was better than my family's book, *Denizens of the Night!* It never told me any good stories, just facts and definitions.

"She woke my grandfather and my father, who gathered help. It was no small thing, for English practitioners to go to the aid of French magicians. But when things go extremely wrong, nationalities are put aside. They walked through three different mazes to offer help. There, my grandmother, who speaks excellent French, reassured the ghosts, and returned them to their sleep." Margaret shivered, and in response I reached for a log to toss on the fire. She stopped me with a gesture.

"It grows late. Do not waste the fire. Miss Williams will be up from the gathering soon, and we will retire for the night." This was said with dignity.

"Miss Rutledge," I said. "You have nothing to be ashamed of. I will tell no one about your grandmother. But if I were you, I'd learn how to use that gift. I think gifts are given to be mastered. What if you need that gift someday? You need to know how it works!"

"I would be happy if it left me tomorrow," she whispered. "I have nothing to say to the dead."

"But maybe they have things to say to you," I replied. "Someone must speak for them. I see them, but I've never spoken with them. When I laid a ghost, I needed help to figure out what it wanted. It would have been easier for me if you had been there. Maybe no one would have died if you had recognized the kind of ghost it was, and told us what to do."

"Perhaps." She gestured, as if flinging away the conversation. "But we have more pressing problems. We are in charge of meals this coming Saturday. I have never supervised cooking for a gathering larger than ten people." She was wringing her handkerchief again. "This will be embarrassing."

"No, it won't. It may not be fancy, but if last Saturday was a sample of student cooking, I know that we can do better. I've helped out, cooking for barn raisings and weddings and shucking frolics. We just need to ask Mrs. Gardener what she has in the pantry that we can use." I gave her my best smile. "And we have to keep the children from using magic in the kitchen. I don't want to waste time chasing biscuits with teeth!"

A breath of laughter escaped from Margaret. "I confess that I did go to the laboratory to see the biscuits with teeth! They did not seem dangerous, but an entire pan of them hopping about would have been startling!"

"I probably would have hurt myself laughing," I admitted.

"I wish Miss Wild was still here with us," Margaret said softly. "She is an excellent cook, and she always found a way to keep the children entertained and focused on her. She could advise us."

I had heard that name before...at breakfast. The girl who taught them how to make biscuits.

Well, I could make biscuits, and I had entertained my share of children.

"We need a plan," I said, thinking quickly. "I should be with you, because I know about amounts of food for bigger gatherings. We need to speak with Mrs. Gardener. Will she talk to you? I brought that cat in to her kitchen, so right now I am probably not one of her favorites."

"Did she give you points?" Margaret asked. "And what cat is this?"

"She didn't mention anything about points, and the cat was the one who rescued me in the tavern."

"Tavern! Miss Sorensson, you did not go into a *tavern?*"

"Not willingly," I admitted, "but I had a press gang chasing me. I was afraid they would figure out that I was a girl, and that might have caused all sorts of problems."

"Alfreda!" It was the first time she'd used my given name. "You could have been in terrible danger! You are very pretty. There are men who force girls into—into terrible things!"

"I was scared, but not frozen," I told her. "As long as I didn't hit my head and get knocked out, I knew I could protect myself." *Oh-oh…I can't tell her how I know that.* "I have enough magic training for emergencies. But I didn't want anyone to need to rescue me. So I ducked into a tavern and hid under a table. The impressers started a fight…or someone picked a fight with them, I couldn't see what happened. The cat was under the table, and when he got up and wandered off, I just followed him!"

Well, one thing led to another, and finally I just told her the entire tale, beginning to end. It wasn't my best story, but I did have her laughing when I described the cat arguing about his bath. We both were giggling over the cat ordering me to open the window when there was a sound at the door, and in walked Catherin Williams.

"You were missed at evening circle, ladies. I read the next section of *Robinson Crusoe*," she said, shutting the door and setting the book on their large study table. "And here I find you telling humorous tales to each other!"

"Oh, my friend, we so needed to laugh!" Margaret began. "I did not make one of the school rules clear to Miss Sorensson, and Professor Livingston was quite put out! I'm afraid that we are both sentenced to kitchen duty on Saturday."

"Kitchen duty? Good heavens, what happened?" Miss Williams immediately took a folded chair leaning against the wall and opened it, revealing a small rocker. Sitting down, she scooted the rocker over next to us, her expression alight with interest.

"Professor Livingston does not want us to talk about it," I said quickly, and let my face fall into worried lines.

"The time will come when all shall be revealed, my dear friend," Margaret added. "But not now, I think."

"There is no way to keep that a secret, although perhaps you can hold it close for a few days, at least," Catherin said, her expression thoughtful. "It's been a while since any of the older students have had kitchen duty, so Saturday meals have been disastrous for months. The senior boys usually keep order, but they generally can't do anything except roast a few fowls. The last senior girl was Abigail Wild." Catherin's color heightened, and she did not meet either of our gazes.

"Miss Wild was.... She came from a very rural place, somewhere in Massachusetts...perhaps Nantucket? Miss Wild was a talented practitioner, but from very poor origins. It made her a little wild, coming to the school," Margaret said carefully. "Miss Wild knew no other practitioners." Margaret carefully did not meet Catherin Williams' gaze.

You liked her, I thought.

"Was she always pulling pranks, or was it flicking her skirts at the older boys?" I asked, thinking about the occasional older wild ones I'd heard about.

"Both," Catherin said faintly, her cheeks definitely flushed. She was embarrassed just talking about the girl.

"But she is no longer at school?" I said, bringing the conversation back to safer waters.

"No. She finished her training, and returned to her village...we think."

The pause made me wonder if Miss Wild was asked to leave.

Rushing on, Margaret said: "Miss Wild brought us the biscuit recipe, which meant that we had some sort of bread on Saturdays, depending on who was being punished."

"I can bake bread," I announced, "if the weather is fair. If it's damp and sticky, it might be biscuits again, but no teeth this time. We can dice some apples and make apple bread for breakfast. For supper, we could even make bread bowls, if Mrs. Gardener will allow us the flour. We could have corn bread with stew for dinner, and a thick vegetable soup for supper. Or can we use meat for more than one meal? We could have ham with oatmeal for breakfast, and the apple bread. I could make beans to have in the vegetable soup. My mother has a recipe from one of the cousins, a soup from Italy."

Catherin tilted her head slightly, her eyebrows drawing together, while Margaret leaned back in her chair in astonishment.

You'd have thought I had addressed them in Russian.

"Are they expecting something really fancy, like vegetable dishes and sauces?" I asked, my voice fading a bit.

"No! No, not at all. It's just that.... Miss Sorensson, you actually know recipes? You can direct a cook in preparing a dish?" Catherin asked.

Oh.

I had found one of those traps you can't avoid because you don't know it's there. I remembered how funny people were about my mother dyeing her own material, when I was a prisoner at Hudson-on-the-Bend.

"Out west, people usually are trying to tame a corner of forest into a farm. They may spend their money to get more land, or for outfitting the barns with dairy equipment and a plow," I started slowly. "You might hire someone to help when slaughtering time comes, or to spin or card when preparing for weaving. But most people only hire a woman to help where she's needed. They don't hire just a cook." Something occurred to me, and I added: "My aunt has a cook. But my mother is very good with food—with herbs and spices. And I have learned a lot from her."

There was a long pause. "My mother cooks fish," Catherin said slowly, and tension flowed out of her shoulders. "It is what she remembers from the fishing village she grew up in, in Wales, before she met my father and came to the new world." Catherin's gaze moved to the fireplace. "You might not want the Mayflower Compact to know you have that skill, but my family is no stranger to hard work." Lifting her head, she added, "Susannah Bradford and Sara Alden. They can be...difficult."

That didn't sound good.

"Your little brother is a very hard worker," I replied, focusing on what I knew. "His oatmeal was the best part of the meal last Saturday, except for the tea!"

Catherin laughed gently at that. "Oh, Daniel! I don't know how he manages to get kitchen duty almost every week! He was such a quiet boy at home. But if he is there, I am sure you can count on him to pitch in. He never ducks his punishment, if he thinks he deserves it!"

I was surprised that she hadn't asked Daniel why he kept getting in trouble, but maybe she didn't keep as close an eye on her brothers as I did on mine. Or maybe she knew but chose not to tell.

Well...if I paid attention, maybe I could discover what was going on. But right now, I was very tired.

"I think I'd better go to bed," I said. "Professor Livingston will be testing me tomorrow. I didn't want Miss Rutledge to be alone."

"Thank you for staying with me," Margaret said, reaching to grip my hand tightly. "Wear your oldest gown tomorrow, Miss Sorensson. Magical testing is hard on students."

There was no mention of our conversation before Catherin Williams arrived, and I wondered if Catherin knew about the ghosts. Margaret's gaze was intense, as if warning me, or asking something of me.

The world is woven of secrets. I would help carry this one for a while.

That was all right. My shoulders were broad.

※ 🍀 ※

The next morning came much too early. A soft scratching at the door awakened me, and then Elizabeth entered, heading straight for my little fireplace, it sounded like. It felt like a storm was sitting on my head, but it wasn't any worse than some winter days, so I pulled myself upright and wrapped my robe around me.

I heard the "woomph!" of flames, and looked through the curtains to see a small, bright fire burning. Elizabeth was definitely fast! Then I heard water splashing into china.

By the time I was off the bed, Elizabeth was picking up a bucket and a coal scuttle. "I've brought you hot water, Miss Sorensson," she said, nodding at me. "Breakfast is half a notch from now, and if they run out of eggs, you'll just have to make do with toast and pork rashers!" Her hand brushed the candle, lighting it. She pointed, and I could see the tiny slashes running down the side of the candle. *Notches.*

"Do I need to bathe again?" I asked.

"Every other day for girls, unless you have done work that requires bathing every day," she replied, heading for the door. "Don't forget, blow out the candle and flip up the guard on the fire screen before you leave!"

Remembering Margaret's warning from the night before, I pulled out my oldest dress. Elizabeth's handiwork could be seen in its condition. *I* certainly hadn't had time to press it. People didn't seem to wear skirts here, so this old pale green dress would have to do. Maybe skirts were just too old-fashioned for the East. I wondered what I could do to thank Elizabeth....

Breakfast was simple, warm and filling, with plenty of back bacon and fresh cracked-grain bread. The eggs were brought around quickly in tiny cups that held them up like little wooden soldiers. Margaret showed me how to behead my eggshell to get at the partially cooked yolk and hard white. The entire business was messy, but if it meant having eggs in the winter, I would learn the knack.

"Professor Livingston thinks that students learn better if they eat early, as the servants do," Margaret explained as we ate. Her face lost expression as she went on. "My family eats at 10:00 am or later for breakfast. It's the fashionable hour for the first meal." Whacking off the head of a second eggshell, she added, "The food is quite good for a school."

I'd bet my desserts for a month that no one knew she had attended other schools before this one. I kept that information tucked deeply away.

Margaret and Catherin had pulled me over to their table, but I scarcely had time to meet anyone. The older boys apparently were not finished with their lessons and had to go work on papers. Miss Smith was eating when we arrived, and had tea with us while we started our breakfast.

"Only two more weeks of morning boundaries," she said with relief in her voice. "I look forward to morning classes once again!"

"What do you do on boundaries?" I asked quickly. Rebecca Smith's ghostly companion still hovered near her, but the girl did not seem aware of the woman. Both Margaret and I pretended we didn't see the ghost.

Margaret was working hard at a conversation with Catherin. It meant she did not have to look at Rebecca.

I did not want to upset Margaret, but Miss Smith seemed friendly, and I wanted to be friendly back.

"We practice farseeing by watching over the grounds of Windward," Miss Smith replied. "I have learned so much these past two weeks! My ability to hold an image at a distance is much stronger now." Leaning toward me, she said in a lower voice, "Next I get to help with the early night group!"

I could tell that this would be a long conversation.

"I have testing today," I shared in turn.

"Oh, then good luck to you!" she said as she rose to leave.

I suppressed a sigh. It was going to take time to get to know people here, the way they kept running off.

We took our empty dishes to something called a pass-through and gave them to the kitchen staff. Then Catherin took my hand and pulled me through the dining room and out into the entryway. Margaret came running up after us.

"Professor Livingston does the school testing in her sewing room. Have you read for your academic classes yet?" Catherin asked.

"She asked me questions about the mysteries when I arrived, but there has not been any time—" I started.

"Then you will start here. We must go get our books! Good luck!" She pressed my hand before she let go, and Margaret touched my elbow before the two of them headed down the hall toward the back stairs.

They had left me at Professor Livingston's doorway. I wondered if she wanted me this early? In Sun-Return we had a bell that rang to call us to school. Here, people seemed to know where they were expected.

Cousin Esme had mentioned bells. I had not noticed bells yesterday, but then I was paying close attention to other things.

Well. Nothing ventured, nothing gained. I shook my skirts out evenly and scratched on the door.

"Enter," came my cousin's clear voice.

And so I did, shutting the door behind me.

The fire had warmed the little room to a very comfortable level. Cousin Esme sat in her accustomed chair, facing between the door and the fireplace. The only thing different in the room was a desk set near her, its chair welded to it with a bar that rolled underneath, and a large chalkboard mounted on wooden legs.

"Sit down here, Alfreda," she said, gesturing to the chair.

The desk was for students. Its armrest could be on either side of the writing area—the inkwell was centered. My mother had told me once that a lot of practitioners were left-handed.

"Here at Windward we do not pay a great deal of attention to whether students are studying with children their own age," she began. "There are times to be with your age mates, and times to study with others at the same level of learning. Because our students come from such varied backgrounds, it is the simplest way to handle classes. I find that more problems are caused by boredom—forcing children to retake lessons they already know—than by their associating with older and younger children. I note that someone suggested you might wear older clothing today." Esme smiled at me.

"Eventually you, too, will mentor others. For now, let's get you placed into classes and started on your studies." She produced several pieces of paper, already copied out with problems and sentences. "Let's begin with mathematics. I have prepared a sampling of problems and questions for you. In some of my tests, you may find that you know all the answers, or that you do not know many of them at all. I do not expect you to know everything here. There is chalk in the pencil box of the desk. For this test, you may use the large blackboard behind you."

So began the most exhausting morning of my short life.

Starting with one of my weaker suits wasn't my favorite, but I knew this game and was able to do my work. I knew most of what was on her sheet. There were a couple of questions about figuring the trajectory of a boulder thrown from a trebuchet, but since I didn't ever expect to be storming a castle, I wasn't worried about not knowing that one. I also had no idea how to make a bridge strong enough to hold a wagon of wool and a four-horse team.

I wasn't planning on building bridges, either. But you never know. Maybe they would teach me that, too.

Next, Cousin Esme handed me a piece of paper with an invitation written out on it, and a smaller, heavier blank piece of paper. "Turn this into an invitation suitable for mailing to a guest," she said.

Oh, dear. I studied it a while, and then took up a piece of chalk to outline a shape that matched the smaller pressed page. Fortunately, I had seen wedding invitations mailed to my parents, so I wasn't working in the dark. This was probably to determine whether my cursive writing was acceptable yet.

I am left-handed, and some schools will not permit you to write with your left hand. But the tradition in the Schell family was that no one should be forced to use a hand not given to them by God—a fancy way of saying that left-handed children would stay left-handed. Some of my ancestors were left-handed; my great-grandmother Emma had borrowed letters from different styles of writing to make an elegant script for a left hand. Once I'd found her alphabet in *Denizens of the Night,* I had done a lot of copying of it in chalk and in the dirt until I had developed a penmanship that pleased me. But I had not practiced on paper.

"May I write on the back of this?" I asked, indicating the page she had written her invitation upon.

"Yes, you may," Cousin Esme replied. She set a jar of ink into the well, and laid down several goose quills and a tiny knife with a blade that was flat on one side and convex on the other. "Have you ever written with a goose quill before?"

"Yes, ma'am. But my father always sharpens the quills for me."

"Well, you will learn here how to sharpen your own quills," she said. "I think that these two should be sufficient for your needs. I must run an errand, so you work on that, and I will be back in a bit."

And with that, I was alone.

A woman was expected to keep her family's books, recording every cent spent and taken in. A readable hand was essential, and copperplate signatures were admired. Really fancy finishing schools for young women taught fine penmanship.

This was important.

The chalkboard allowed me to work out where I would place words on the card. Centering would be required, and even spacing between words. Deciding how the stiff stationer's card would look did not take very long. The hard part was mastering several of the capital letters in the card. I recognized the French at the end of the invitation, and had no idea where to put it. Finally, I decided to put *répondez s'il vous plaît* at the bottom of the block of writing, centered, in a slightly smaller size.

When my letters felt good, I carefully dipped the pen and practiced the words on the back of the sheet my cousin had given me. She had not given me any sand to help dry the ink, so I hoped I could do this carefully. Since I kept my hand below my words, I wasn't worried about smudging the invitation, only about drips and sputters from the quill.

The finished card was neat, and my imitation of my great-grandmother's cursive looked clear and not unattractive. Some of her letters I had trouble with, like the capital "E," but fortunately I did not need one here.

Once I finished, I capped the ink and left the card to dry in the warm room. I spent the rest of my time looking at the interesting things in Cousin Esme's sitting room. She had a beautiful globe, and a small bookcase containing many old books. I wondered if some of these were her own journals, which was why they were there and not in the family library.

Cousin Esme did not give me enough time to "get into trouble" as my mother often said. She was back by the time the ink was dry, and examined the stiff card intently. Nodding, she set that aside and asked how I was feeling. It seemed abrupt, but then I remembered the vaccination, and said that other than a little achy, I was doing fine.

"Excellent. Then let us move on to reading comprehension and essay work and use of the globe." Several books were set on my desk, and she pointed at the globe.

"Use of the globe" turned out to be simple—did I know where a lot of common places were? Could I find odd places, like Saxe-Gotha-Altenburg? (Saxe-Gotha-Altenburg, if you do not know, was not in one place, like you'd think it would be. It was a Duchy controlled by one man, although it was divided up later. But he had to ride through other people's duchies to visit parts of his own. The Germanic people were always swapping duchies like horses.)

I did a pretty good job with the globe, knowing most of what she wanted and able to find the rest with clues like the sound of the words. Then I found myself reading, and talking about the Bible and Shakespeare's work, which were the major things considered permissible for young ladies to read. (Clearly, some people didn't read certain stories in the Bible, or certain plays. Or young ladies would not get to read them.)

My cousin wanted me to write about what I knew Shakespeare got right in his works about the "Good Neighbors," or the Fair Folk as we call them when they're not around. She also wanted me to examine the Bible for references to magic, but I pointed out that it might take me several days. There was a lot of magic in the Bible, if you knew what to look for, and miracles might be magic, too. After all, God didn't say that Powers did not exist; he said not to consult them. He wanted people to seek enlightenment from only his own priests.

Cousin Esme told me that I had good questions, and that there would be classes where those things could be discussed.

So I picked a couple things to write about in "A Midsummer's Night Dream," and wrote about how Shakespeare gave the concerns of the littlest fairies to the great *daoine sídhe*, and how he got right the ability of the small ones to temporarily beguile Sidhe eyes. I also pointed out that Oberon's own gods punished him for his little trick against his wife. The son she bore from her frolic with Bottom was a member of the court for a long time, a handsome, brilliant young man, who was evidence of Titania's infidelity—something Oberon could not punish, as the court knew of the magic he had ordered used against her. The changeling boy Oberon stole from his wife lived the length of a normal human life, and then died. Changelings tend to keep their youth, but they die untimely.

Oberon had been compelled to look at the results of his "punishment" of Titania for a very long time. Rumor has it that Titania's son still lives.

Cousin Esme gave me an hour to work on it. She had one more thing she wanted to talk about before she let me go to dinner.

"Tell me, Alfreda. If I wished to stuff eggs, also called deviling them, what kind of eggs would be best for this? What would create the most pleasing feast for the stomach and the eyes?"

I blinked. *What?*

EIGHT

I HAD THIS HORRIBLE, SINKING FEELING THAT I'd come to a finishing school for young ladies, but I replied: "Older eggs. The fresher they are, the harder they are to peel after you boil them thoroughly. Mother adds vinegar to the water if she has to boil young eggs. You have to plunge them into cold water after they sit for a quarter hour or so in the boiling water. If you do all that, and then let them cool completely, you can get the shells to crack and roll off cleanly. My mother also pokes a hole in the eggs' bottoms with a pin before boiling them."

"Excellent. You may go to dinner now, and return when you have finished eating. We will discuss some of the rules of magic and herbal medicine then, and also dealing with children."

Oh, bother. Was I going to be watching littles again? I'd spent a lot of time raising my two youngest brothers. Then I remembered that I might get to teach, and I was both excited and scared. Did Cousin Esme plan to let me teach some herb lore?

"Dinner, Alfreda," came my cousin's voice, and I jumped up and dropped a curtsy before rushing from the room.

Once I was inside the dining hall, I felt underdressed for the spread of food before me: tureens of soup, bowls of mashed potatoes and other vegetables, several sauces and pickles, roast chicken, salty southern ham, and a large cooked fish, its head staring at me. After we'd all filled our bowls and plates, the meal was cleared away and another took its place! The second round had cheeses, a savory and a sweet bread, custards, jellies both savory and sweet, and fruit tarts.

Well, I thought that this was pretty special, and asked Margaret if today was a holiday of sorts. She just smiled and said no, that the wealthier students came from homes where they were served *a la française*—the first food on the table when the diners arrived, served in three courses—and that this was a fairly simple meal. I remembered then that New York was on an island, so fish was possible in winter. It seemed like a party to me.

Had she said *three* courses?

Sure enough, when I thought that I could not stuff another bite in, well-dressed young men cleared off the serving tables and set out bowls of dried fruit, fresh apples (slightly wrinkled but still firm) and nuts. I was grateful for the pockets I put in my clothes, so I could slip a few nuts and an apple away for later.

"If it was a party, we would have ice cream or frozen ices with dessert," Catherin said, cracking an English walnut. "Mrs. Gardener is a wonderful cook."

"She certainly is," I said, surveying the remains of the meal. I felt a bit gloomy about what was before us, because there was no way we could set a meal like this on Saturday, but I took heart. No one expected this from us. Maybe we could learn eventually.

I hoped a few more students were going to join us on Saturday. Margaret and I would be serving cold meat and soup if we were the only ones cooking!

Margaret and Catherin were full of questions about what Professor Livingston had tested me against. Since she hadn't said I should be silent, I told them briefly about my morning.

"Oh, I hate calligraphy class," Catherin said, cracking another nut. "My handwriting is serviceable, but no more. I will be in that class until my last day at Windward."

"That was clever, knowing the German duchies," Margaret told me. "Many students are laid low by those questions."

""Back home, whenever I asked too many questions, our teacher made me study the globe," I replied. "I am just lucky that my teacher had brought a recent globe with him when he came to our town."

"You are lucky that you learned something instead of daydreaming," Margaret said, smiling. "Globe work was so boring! I always had old globes to use, so we were making new names to glue over countries."

"Well, I like learning things," was all I could think of to say.

Then we were sent back to classes, or in my case, Cousin Esme's sitting room.

I managed to beat her back to the room.

"Are you ready for magic?" my cousin asked as she sat down.

"I'm not sure I am ever ready for magic," I replied. "But I'm ready to try."

"Very well. Your cousin Mrs. Donaltsson and your mother taught you the second rule of magic first. How did you phrase it?"

"You may not realize how much you don't know," I said quickly.

"That is an appropriately terse manner of phrasing it. Did they tell you the first rule of magic?" Esme's smile was amused, but it didn't seem mean.

I thought before saying, "I don't think so. One time we were doing something, and Aunt Marta told me that one of the rules of magic was 'Pray for potatoes, and grab a hoe.' We had prayed for the goddess's help in something, but then we had the work to finish."

When I looked back at my cousin, I could see that she was fighting laughter. "That...that sounds just like Marta Donaltsson. She likes to cut to the heart of a matter. The more formal way to phrase that rule is: 'Ask for divine guidance before beginning works great and small.' But that's not the first rule."

"I suppose some people think you can just pray for something, and then not do the work," I went on, not sure if my cousin would talk about things the way Marta and I did.

"A common failing of some magicians," Esme agreed. "The truths hidden in the Bible apply in many paths. Faith *and* works are needed."

"So you think Martin Luther was right about how Catholics do too much praying and not enough working?" I asked.

"I think he had some valid points. The See of Rome was very corrupt when he nailed his list to the door of the church. Protestants are doing some good things in their pursuit of truth, but I feel that they are also making mistakes. But that is for a religion and ethics class. Now, we discuss magic. The first rule of magic is this: 'The magic is in the practitioner.'"

I stared at her. "Of course it is. Where else would it be?"

Esme's smile bloomed. "Many people waste years...a lifetime... making or seeking artifacts of power. But if you have no power to share with the items, their value is limited. Placing power in an object can be very dangerous, because it separates you from the power, and it also might give an enemy a focus to use against you. This is one reason powerful dark users are so dangerous. They will not share their power with an artifact, but they might try to steal your power for it. You know you must keep your ritual names secret?"

"Yes, ma'am."

"Good. In truth, Alfreda, the number attached to a rule of magic changes during your lifetime. Different rules will speak to you at different times. One of them is always valuable: 'Expect the Unexpected.'"

Yes. That sounded like a good one. In fact, I would name it the most important one, depending on how much you used magic.

"Now, I wish you to follow me to my solar, where you shall do a few things for me to demonstrate your comprehension of the herbal arts."

Cousin Esme rose and led me to the kitchen wing. There was a flurry of curtsying from the staff, but my cousin flicked her fingers and told them to please continue with their work. She did pause to speak to Mrs. Gardener, but then we went through the kitchen and down a narrow hallway. Ahead I could see a rectangle of light, with a few bars of darkness laid across it.

It was a door of glass, framed by thick wooden pieces. This was very much like the wall of windows on either side of the front door, only it had a handle of its own. My cousin leaned on the wide, finished piece of wrought iron and pushed the door open. The smell of green herbs swept over us like a wave of fragrance.

Inside it was spring; there was no other word for it. The small room had two walls of windows facing East and South, nestled up against two stone outer walls. The roof peaked above us, slanting down to the windowed wall. The ceiling sparkled—every step or so protruded small glass cones, descending maybe a hand's length from the wooden framework above. The cones threw wide, soft circles of light.

Numerous shelves lined both walls of windows, with many pots of green upon them. The shelves rose above us and dropped down nearly to the floor. A strong table anchored the room, with several chairs drawn up to it. One small fireplace filled the narrower of the stone walls, a cheery blaze burning within.

"Welcome to my solar," my cousin said. "This is where I do what herb work I prefer to handle myself. There is also a larger solar where the students work." She closed the door and gestured to the chairs. "I want to remind you that when you speak of your aunt in front of the staff or other students, remember to call her Mrs. Donaltsson. A certain formality is expected of us when speaking of our teachers. When we are alone, it is fine to call her Aunt Marta, as she has given you that privilege."

Actually, my aunt (who was really Papa's cousin, and also mine) allowed me to address her by her Christian name, but I simply said: "Yes, ma'am."

No need for Cousin Esme to know that. No need for anyone to know that.

"We'll start with propagation of herbs. Have you ever potted up starts of peppermint?" she asked me.

"Yes, ma'am," I answered.

"Good. I want you to trim back these peppermint plants, and use these small pots for the new plants," she said, sitting down by the fire.

I lifted the falling limbs of the closest plant, noting the flowers on it. "Do you want to save the seed for spearmint later?" I asked. "Do you start seed spearmint this early?"

Esme gave me one of her "sorting me like a cupboard" looks, as if she could see my bones. "So you know that peppermint seed usually produces the milder spearmint."

"Mints cross with each other all the time," I replied, studying the sealed dye pots set on shelves against the stone wall. Strips of color dangled beneath the containers, and small, stiff cards labeled jars. One set of strips caught my eye. "You can use lily-of-the-valley to get a buff color? How?"

"By using chrome as the mordant instead of alum to set the color," Cousin Esme answered. "We'll get to dyes later. Have you made any preparations yet from herbs?"

"I've made vinaigrettes, cough drops, infused oils, cosmetics, teas, tonics, soaps—" I started.

"Good, good. I have the materials for making many common aids. You may use the containers here, and there's a hook for that pot." She gestured to the artesian arm folded up inside the fireplace. "Make some cough drops, and we could use some more gargle."

"Do you prefer traditional horehound drops, or the family recipe?" I asked. "Butter is nice to grease the pan if you have any to spare. Do you want a soothing gargle or an astringent one?"

"There is oil of orange here if you would like to make some of the family cough drops, but do not teach that recipe to your classmates," my cousin told me. "That has been our recipe for a long time. As for gargles, one batch of both would do nicely. There's a keg of spring water in the corner over there behind you. The butter bell is on the right side of the table. I also would like to ask you some questions while you work."

Of course she was going to watch. And here I was, in her workroom using her equipment. I searched around for the thymes. "Have you already infused the thyme, or shall I start some for tomorrow?"

"Go ahead and start from scratch," she said, leaning back in her chair. "Now, Alfreda, who was Eris and what was her most famous action?"

I blinked and tried to keep my face still. My mother always jumped straight to the Trojan War. She didn't like me knowing what people said caused it.

Of course I found out.

"Ah...she was the Greek goddess of discord, and the thing most people remember about her is that she tossed a golden apple into a circle of goddesses after writing 'For the fairest' on a strip of linen tied to the stem."

⁂

What followed was a *very* long afternoon.

I poured cold water over fresh thyme cuttings, clamped on a tight lid and brought it all to a boil in the scrupulously clean pot sitting on fat legs near the fire. Next I moved the container further from the flames to simmer for a few minutes, and then set it on the firebrick to steep overnight.

While I was starting the cough drops, I told Cousin Esme all I could remember about the Trojan War, which began because a young warrior named Paris was asked to judge which goddess was the fairest of those gathered. They, being Greek goddesses, tried to bribe him with offers of becoming the most powerful man in the world, the wisest man—or the man in possession of the most beautiful woman alive.

The stories say he decided he wanted the most beautiful woman, and so gave the apple to Aphrodite, Goddess of Love. Remembering all the other stories I've read about Aphrodite, I wonder if she was simply the most beautiful goddess, at least to mortal eyes. But apparently he didn't turn down the woman, even if she was a daughter of Zeus and the wife of a very powerful king. So Helen of Troy went down in history as the face that launched a thousand ships, and Paris as the man who destroyed his people over his desire for a woman.

Would Troy have done better if Paris had chosen Hera or Athena instead? Or had sensibly said no bribes are necessary, or even told them that a mere mortal could not choose among such beauty?

That wasn't the story Homer chose to tell. And when the winner tells the story, we rarely know what the loser would have said.

Peppermint propagates through root runners, so I separated out the root clumps, making four and in one case six new plants from the original mass. I kept all the seed heads in a saucer, and the long, straggling legs were pinched back to allow the plants to become bushy.

All the while Cousin Esme questioned me about gods and goddesses (Greek, Norse and Roman) as well as curious tidbits of folklore. Most of what she asked about was things from my great-grandmother's book, *Denizens of the Night,* like black dogs, varieties of ghosts, and how to set up a ritual circle. We talked about Beowulf; about Greek tragedies; about *Bean-Sidhes* and boggarts; and whether black cats are lucky or unlucky (the British think they are unlucky, and Americans think they are lucky...but that opinion changes depending on where you live).

And we talked about herbs. Common herbs, rare herbs, dangerous herbs, herbs that can fool even experts. I made horehound gargle and red raspberry leaf gargle, a digestive tea for gas from fennel seeds, and a moderately-priced cleansing and moisturizing cream my mother had taught me. Olive oil and rose water can be substituted for oil of roses and still make a fine cream, although I prefer peppermint oil. But I don't use face cream yet. I don't like too much flower scent in things. It is overwhelming.

The light was fading and my mind whirling before Cousin Esme said we'd done enough for the day. "Tomorrow you will finish the cough drops. Then you will see several of the other instructors of magic."

"Most of what I know is herbs—and delivering babies," I admitted.

"As your instructors have been of Earth, that makes complete sense," she replied, gesturing for me to rise from before the fireplace. "As I have said, Alfreda, I do not expect you to know everything. You have done fine so far. These tests are to place you in your studies. If all goes well tomorrow, you will receive your books and start classes on Wednesday."

Before we left, my cousin paused and said: "Ah! *Parlez-vous Francais?*"

"*Oui, je parle un peu Francais,*" I replied. "There are French families near Sun-Return, and trappers passed through our region, so I got to practice what I knew."

"Good. We will expand on that knowledge while you are here," Cousin Esme said as she pulled the door to her solar firmly shut. "You may go to supper now, Alfreda. I will prepare a schedule for your activities tomorrow."

I knew a dismissal when I heard one, and with a quick curtsy was on my way to the dining hall. It was a noisier place for supper than for dinner, perhaps because the meal was less formal: big bowls of beef and vegetable stew full of carrots, potatoes, and turnips, and a sourdough bread with rosemary in it that was very nice. Dessert was one fat cookie for each of us, something mild and creamy with a lot of cinnamon and other spices in it.

I sat down at a vacant place, glad to be out from under anyone's eye. If you had told me last year that what I'd done today would make me feel so tired, I would have laughed at you. Was it from that vaccine thing, or a different kind of tired? I had talked to men who went to college, and they said that their studies were often exhausting. I felt like the day had been truly one long test.

"Miss Sorensson!" Margaret and Catherin sat down next to me. "How was the afternoon?"

"Tiring," I admitted, smearing butter on my fresh bread.

"You must come tell us all about it," Catherin said as she reached for her cup of tea. "Since you do not have homework yet, and Margaret and I have finished our papers, you can tell us of your adventures, and I will read you the passage from *Robinson Crusoe* that you missed."

"We won't have sewing circle tonight?" I asked as we settled into our meal.

"Only on the weekends," Margaret said quietly. "Otherwise we should be studying, practicing spells, writing letters home, or mending our clothing or books."

Oh, Lord and Lady, did I have letters to write. I'd tell Marta about the portal in the stable, and how my Good Friend came to help, but Momma did not need to hear that tale. I would tell my parents about Margaret's compliment on my sewing, and the sewing circle, and maybe a few things about my examinations. Josh could hear about the school from momma.

The only other people I would send a letter to would be my good friend Idelia, and to Shaw and to Cousin Cory. The idea of writing to Shaw and Cory made me feel a little shy, but Cory was kin and Shaw was going to be Marta's student in Earth and Water mysteries, so we both had the same teacher. I had to get used to discussing magic with other practitioners.

I might as well start the conversation with people who liked me.

Sometimes I thought that Marta and Shaw were the only people I could really talk to about everything that happened to me. 'Course, Shaw was so shy, I was never positive what he really thought.

But he always listened. And that was a blessing.

$\cdot$ ⚜ $\cdot$

For one of the few times in my life, I sat and just listened to Catherin read from *Robinson Crusoe* that night. My hands did not miss doing needlework. Both Margaret and Catherin seemed impressed that Cousin Esme let me start preparations that needed a second day to finish.

"I would not have known that business about peppermint seed when I came here," Catherin admitted. "And your knowledge of dyes is formidable. Professor Livingston seems to be refining your placement in classes. I imagine you will be in an advanced herbal class. Have you started using herbs in spells yet?"

"Only a few of them. My family's book *Denizens of the Night* has some recipes that I have tried." The book had only recently shown me magical recipes; before that, only a few family medical recipes were visible.

I was resigned to the fact that my book was a different book every time I looked at it, but I hadn't admitted it to anyone yet.

"I think Professor Livingston will want you to practice with a quill pen, but you have really finished with the classes for younger students, Miss Sorensson. You have even read stories, like *Oedipus Rex*, that girls are usually not allowed to read! You are ready to enter Oxford!"

"My Latin is not good enough for Oxford," I said, smiling, "and I need to practice more French."

"Oh! *Trés bien!*" Margaret immediately began to chatter in French, so swiftly that I caught only one word in three. I started laughing and held up my hands to silence her.

"I will need your help for that. I can understand some French when I am visiting at meals and know what people are talking about, but I haven't learned very many French names for herbs or magical items."

"You will! And possibly some Italian or Spanish as well. It is much easier to learn more than one language at once, I found. If you have spoken only English, it takes time to tune your ear for other words," Margaret assured me.

"Oh, I can speak with people from other lands," I replied. "I can speak to people from Norway, and Ireland. Those were family languages. I know enough German to follow a conversation, if people aren't mad and in a hurry. And once I hear French for a while, I am better at it. I just need to retune my ear. It's like playing music, in a way."

"That is very true," Catherin said. "I understand a great deal of Welsh, but it is discouraged in England, so my parents spoke it only at home, privately."

"It is your family's secret language," I suggested.

A slow smile unfurled across Catherin's face. "Yes, I suppose it is," she answered.

Not long after that we bade each other goodnight and agreed to meet for breakfast in the morning. Both Catherin and Margaret promised to wait until evening to wash their hair with me, since I might feel need of that after my day of magical testing.

They certainly had my curiosity up about the magic tests. I had gotten bloody from magic, but not that dirty. I had a feeling this was a whole new order of knowledge coming up.

ɜ·𝒟·ɜ

I was up before the sun the next morning. I wore the same clothing as the day before, since I hadn't gotten it dirty, and put on my
leather pouch with my knife and wooden cup and fire tinder, among
other things. I also dug out my wand and ritual knife and sheath,
and slipped them into their long pockets. So I was sitting quietly in a
chair when Elizabeth arrived with the hot water and basket of wood.

Elizabeth left me with just the water, saying she'd light a fire for
me in the evening. I freshened up and hurried down to my cousin's
solar. If the fire was already burning there, I could finish the cough
drops and have that out of the way before other "testing."

Someone had built up the fire in her solar, and the door was not
locked. I closed it carefully behind me, to keep the heat within.

The infused thyme smelled delightful. I found a small, square
pan on a shelf that would do well for the drops, and coated the inside with butter. Then I took a good-sized iron pot with a heavy
bottom and a tight lid, buttered the inside and strained the thyme
water through a piece of loose muslin into it.

I paused to see if there was water cold enough for what I needed,
and found a corner of the room where a large ceramic jar touched
the stone wall and the window glass.

Ice sheeted the water within. I broke the ice plug and scooped
water with a clean dipper, pouring it into a small metal bowl and
setting it next to the stone wall to keep cold. The ice shards went
into my bowl as well.

Returning to my pot of infused water, I hung the pot on one of
the hooks over the fire. It had a tight lid, so in no time at all I could
hear the water boil.

There was no lack of ingredients on my cousin's shelves; I measured out sugar, oil of orange, and cream of tartar while I waited.
Carefully I swung the pot away from the heat and added my ingredients to the infused water. I stirred the mixture to dissolve the sugar,
and then added a drop of honey, since the family recipe always
worked better with a touch of liquid sweetener. Schell practitioners
did not give honey to babies, not even boiled honey, but this recipe
was made for adult tastes.

Setting the lid down, I pushed the pot back over the fire where it
was quickly boiling again. Now I had to wait for the steam to wash
the sugar crystals on the sides of the pan into the mixture. When

the pot strained to push off the lid, I used a thick pad to remove the cover. My mixture boiled merrily within.

I hunted up a clean wooden spoon, and placed the ice water on the firebrick before the fire. When the heaving mass looked right, I moved it away from the heat, dipped the clean spoon into the pot, and dribbled some syrup into the ice water.

The drop of syrup separated into threads. I tried to dip them out with the handle of the spoon, but there was no bend to them; they slid away from the polished wood.

Perfect. Using the quilted pads and the wire handle, I carefully poured the mixture into the pan I had prepared. While the cough drops began to set, I gathered up everything I'd used that needed to be washed, loaded it into the pot, and set it aside to take to the kitchen. Cousin Esme's solar did not look as if she cleaned pots in it.

Several knives hung near the fireplace. I took one that looked heavy enough and sharp enough, and scored the cooling mixture into squares no larger than a half-inch to a side. It would need a half hour or so to harden to the point where I could turn it out onto Cousin Esme's marble tabletop. But there would be no need to butter the table; the drops would set before then.

Turning, I placed the knife into the empty cooking pot to make its way to the kitchen as a voice said: "Well, you have indeed learned much of the trade."

I jumped, but managed not to cut myself or leap back into the fireplace. It was Cousin Esme, dressed in her indigo gown, already immaculate for the morning.

"Oh, ma'am, I'm sorry, but you startled me!" I said quickly, dipping into a curtsy. "I did not hear you!" And how did she get that heavy door open without my hearing her enter?

Smiling, Esme said: "I was very quiet. I did not want to break your concentration."

I felt my right eyebrow rise.

Her smile wider, Esme continued: "When you have your own workroom, Alfreda, you will set a spell to tell you if anyone enters it. You will also learn how to cast a spell of silence."

"Oh, I pulled you from your breakfast! I'm sorry!" It didn't occur to me that she'd set wards inside her own house. But after I found that portal in the stable, if she hadn't set such wards before, she would do so now.

"I was finished with my scones and tea," she said. "But now you must eat a bit before your first examination."

"The drops need a half hour before they're broken out," I started, gesturing to them. "And the pot—"

"You may take the pot to the kitchen and leave it next to the breakfast dishes," my cousin said. "I am confident that any child of Garda knows how to clean anything set before her. Here is your list of classes today. The movement of students signals the next class. I will turn the drops when the time comes."

The cleaning comment, I decided, was a compliment to my mother, and would also have to go into the letter. Taking the small list in one hand, I grabbed the handle of the pot with the other, thanked Cousin Esme, and wrestled the heavy door open.

❧ 𝕯 ❧

Breakfast was plenty of bacon rashers and fresh bread dipped in egg batter and fried. I knew that dish; my mother made it for birthdays. I could tell that Mrs. Gardener added cream and spices to hers, cinnamon and something else I did not recognize. The bread was oat, and it made a wonderful meal.

Catherin and Margaret arrived before the lines at the food station became long. They both wanted to know what I was assigned to today, and pored over the list with interest.

"Professor Livingston has you seeing almost everyone today. One of us should come find you and take you to your next appointment," Catherin said, and they quickly divided up the list of names between them. "Oh! You will go to Professor Sonneault first!" Immediately she started chattering in French, gesturing to different names on the list. I started to protest, but Margaret, in French, reminded me that I needed to hear French.

"You will like her, I think. She speaks of the many lands she has visited, and how interesting it is to meet people from different cultures." Margaret pointed to the second name on her list. "Professor Shipley is the Ancient Languages teacher," she went on, her words precise. "He teaches us Latin, and the boys who wish to go on to college also learn Greek. I suspect he also knows a lot of other old languages, like Sanskrit and Old Saxon," she added, tilting her head, her voice soft as if this was both a confidence and a secret swapped between old friends. "He has many old books and scrolls in his office, and I don't recognize the languages at all."

"He's dry as a bone," Catherin added, spacing out her words in a low, exaggerated manner, and I stifled a laugh. I thought I knew what Catherin meant, but her string of words sounded funny in French. "You will understand when you meet him. He does not have a use for people who won't properly study languages, since language is 'crucial to advanced magic.'" Once again she lowered her voice and spaced her words with precision. I wondered if Professor Shipley sounded like that. "So if he treats you like a servant, it is not personal—he treats everyone that way until they prove themselves."

"Professor De Lancey is so kind! He teaches Rules, and beginning magic, and also advanced potions and herbs," Margaret said, touching the next name.

"And then Professor Tonneman." Catherin's voice was brighter, and she sat back in her chair, her entire body tense with excitement. "So polished! Such a gentleman! He teaches ritual magic, but that is more advanced work. Professor Brown is not on the list, is she?"

"It says 'Ask Miss Rutledge to introduce you to Professor Brown,'" Margaret read off my list. "I will ask Mrs. Gardener for some cookies to take as a gift. Professor Brown adores sweets. It is not fair that she is so slender and elegant."

That sounded funny, since I thought of both Margaret and Catherin as slender, dainty women. But for now I would defer to their judgment. I would let Margaret arrange a suitable gift for the professor—but why for her, and not the others?

Students were starting to leave. It was time to face my new teachers...professors. I touched the lumps under my clothes that were my wand and athame, wishing I had the slightest idea how to use them.

Foolishness. That was why I was here, to learn these things.

Some things are hard to learn out of a book; that's why I was with Marta. And Marta had her reasons for wanting me here with Cousin Esme.

Someday Marta might even tell me those reasons.

NINE

CATHERIN AND MARGARET WERE RIGHT; Professor Sonneault sparkled like my mother's cherry mead. I was shocked when
I walked into the room Catherin had practically dragged me to,
because Professor Sonneault was taller than me, maybe as tall as
Marta.

Entering Professor Sonneault's classroom, I had the feeling
that the instructors were volunteering the time normally allotted
to prepare for their classes to evaluate me. I found the lady writing French words in a beautiful script on a black slate mounted in
a frame, like a large picture frame or mirror. Like Cousin Esme's
board, it stood on a double tripod of oak legs.

Professor Sonneaut appeared to be my parents' age. Her dress
was from an earlier time, more like what my mother preferred
to wear. Elegant, thin, long stripes of red and white ran from her
shoulders to her white boots, with a petticoat apron of muslin embroidered with tiny flowers tossed over the full skirt that gathered
at her waist.

With her white gloves, red silk flowers, and a snowy white feath-
er plume in her dark hair, she was a striking sight. I gave a tiny
curtsy as I introduced myself, and met her gaze.

It was like brushing against some elusive woodland creature of
power. Her dark eyes held secrets…and no reflection. There was

a stone quarry a few days ride from our home, one that had filled with water. No one knew the depth of it; the bottom could not be seen, even at midday.

Professor Sonneault's eyes were like that, a hard rock quarry filled with clear water and mystery. I also had a brief sensation of being...weighed, somehow.

The moment passed.

Her entire outfit was nothing but a façade. There was nothing soft and fluffy about the French teacher, despite her pretty picture. I would make very sure she knew nothing of my history.

Perhaps I would find that I liked Professor Sonneault.

But I did not trust her.

Quickly she sat down on a well-upholstered chair and gestured that I was to sit upon its mate.

"*Bienvenue!* Welcome to the world of modern languages!" the lady began. "*Parlez-vous français?*"

"*Oui, je parle un peu français.*" Yes, I speak a little French. It seemed like a good idea to qualify my response by adding "a little" to it.

And then we were off. The professor was very clever, slowly increasing her speed as she asked about my home and schooling. I was convinced that I was making a fool of myself, stumbling as I described what I knew of New York and the estate, when Professor Sonneault changed topics, suddenly chattering about the gardens, the mazes, and the home farm, where the produce and animals for the household were grown and raised.

I knew the names of most of the foods and the animals, and was able to talk about how people trapped fur where I lived. Since the DuBose family tanned furs before taking them to market, I knew the names for various fur-bearing creatures and also for foods Mrs. DuBose liked to make, like *coq au vin.*

"Excellent, excellent!" she said at one point. "You must come to the milliner's with me this month and tell me what fur each hat is made from."

"I won't know any milliner terms—" I began.

"In English, Alfreda, you are doing quite well but are not ready for light social conversation yet. We will fix that!" the professor rushed on.

Professor Sonneault was apparently pleased by my poor attempts to keep up with her. At one point she abruptly changed directions, asking me if my name was Swedish, and did I know any German?

I answered her in Norwegian, and then in my careful German. *"Magnifique!"* she said loudly in French, and then dropped right into German.

Here I understood much more than I spoke, so I could answer her *"Ja"* and *"Nein"* at appropriate places.

Italian was clearly a loss. Spanish was better, but not very much. I could demonstrate my two dozen words of Russian, but had no idea how they were spelled or put together. My father told me that the Russian alphabet was different from our own.

"Have you learned anything else that you can converse in?" she finally asked in English.

It was a relief to hear something that I completely understood! In Gaelic I said: "I am blessed with the words of the Emerald Isle, but only my mother's family speaks it."

The lady burst out in a hearty laugh, her hands gesturing in Gallic amusement. She answered me in Gaelic! We had a brief conversation about whether my mother had taught me the art of fine Irish brewing, and if I could make good soda bread.

"Très bien!" she finally said, her fingers slashing sideways. "Already I can see a half-dozen students benefiting from your company. Mademoiselle, Professor Livingston will have a French-English dictionary for you. You are to start thus — six new words of magic or herbs each day. When learning six a day has become comfortable, then we will add in words that pertain to current affairs of the world." Her last words were evenly spaced, as if emphasizing the foreign nature of the English we spoke. Something of her words lingered in the room, almost like an echo.

"You will have conversational French three days a week — *lundi, mercredi et vendredi*," she went on.

Monday, Wednesday and Friday, I translated silently.

"Mardi et jeudi, you begin conversational German. You will have a notebook for grammar, eh? Later will be time for Italian."

"Oui, madame," I said.

"And now, you must go see Professor Shipley. He will teach you the ancient languages." Something about this clearly amused the lady, but she did not explain the joke.

I thanked Professor Sonneault and made my way out into the corridor. Doors opened and children streamed into the hallway, their voices raised in shouts and conversation. Farther down the hall I could see older youths and maidens pushing through the doors to the far staircase and merging into clusters.

Margaret emerged from the crowd, walking swiftly toward me. "You have survived your first class with Professor Sonneault," she said as she reached me. "Congratulations!"

"She was very kind," I replied, leaning back toward the wall to let two small boys push by us. "I will need to get a dictionary from Professor Livingston. I already have work to be done!"

"That means that you are in a higher class than the beginners," Margaret told me, touching my arm lightly and gesturing down the corridor. "We will get your books when there is time. I am sure Professor Livingston will have them delivered to your room soon. They must be spelled, of course."

"The books are spelled?" I asked.

"Every book that belongs to the school is spelled," was her answer. "If the book goes a single foot beyond the boundaries of Windward estate, it begins to shriek. Of course some of the boys must test the spell! Books are valuable, and books of magic even more so. I have heard that an early student had gambling debts and gave the books up as security on his loan. He was quite stunned when the pawnbroker expected a tenfold increase before allowing the boy to redeem his grimoire. The value of the books was much more than that young man expected. Then he was caught among the Livingstons, who owned the books, his father, and the pawnbroker. The school started spelling the books after that incident."

"I would imagine that it was not a pleasant experience," I said, shivering.

"Not at all," Margaret agreed. "Rumor has it that his father paid a thousand pounds to recover the books from the pawnbroker. He was a lord, but even for a lord, that was a great deal of money!"

It was an unimaginable amount of money—I was speechless. How was I going to protect my books? Possessions could be taught to announce their owner—it was one of the spells that had appeared in my *Denizens of the Night*. Could I put the spell on as an overspell, as the temporary custodian of the books?

"Here is Professor Shipley's room," she said, stopping before a heavy door. "I forgot to tell you. If any of the professors release you well before class change, just go to your room. We will come for you there."

"How do we know when class ends?" I asked.

"Class begins on the hour, and lasts forty-five minutes," Margaret said. "That allows enough time to go the farthest distance necessary before the next class. The advanced classes are on the second floor of the school wing, and I think that most of your classes will be there. You have finished most of the early classes, haven't you?"

"I need to learn how to mend quills," I admitted.

"I can teach you that...no, you are left-handed. We'll get a senior student to teach you how to trim them." Margaret's tone was reassuring. "For now, go meet Professor Shipley. Latin is the language of ritual magic. He will need to assign you to a class!" Smiling, she waved farewell as she hurried on to the stairwell.

Well. I took a slow, deep breath to settle myself, and turned the knob of the heavy door. Inside was a room with eight long tables, an aisle down the middle, and a desk in the front of the room, set slightly to one side. At the front, not one but two black slate boards faced the tables. A neatly dressed man was writing with chalk upon one of them, tilting the board so that he wrote on a flat surface.

I made enough noise walking to be sure I would not startle him. As I approached the front of the room, I could see that he was dressed simply compared to Dr. Livingston and the other professor I'd met. More like Dr. Livingston than my uncles in their business best, but this man did not seek attention with his clothing. He was, well, gray.... From boots of dark gray leather to a white satin brocade vest, and everything in-between. His dark hair was silver streaked and a bit shaggy, and his face, as he turned to me, was clean-shaven and sharp-featured, his nose strong but suiting his solemn expression.

His eyes stopped me. They were a deep green, the pupils black and large in the dim light. Staring back at him, I momentarily held my breath.

What kind of practitioner was he? He felt so...remote. As if he was coming back from a far place, and trying to focus on something small and interesting.

In truth, he did not feel like any human I had ever looked at... not at all.

The man blinked, and the sensation vanished.

"You are Alfreda Eldonsdottir Sorensson," he said in a deep voice. "I am called Professor Shipley in this time and place. Have you any Latin or Greek at all?"

"I have started learning prefixes, and suffixes, to use with English," I said, giving him a slight curtsey since we had jumped over the usual "How do you do." "And vocabulary. I have started learning verb forms. All Latin," I added quickly, realizing I had left out that important piece of information. "I do not have any formal Greek, but my family had three books written in Greek—the Bible, *The Iliad,* and *The Odyssey.* I learned many words from comparing the Greek to English versions of the tales. Then I borrowed Greek plays to read, like *Antigone.*"

"Interesting." I could hear all four syllables in how he stressed the word. Yes, Catherin was a skilled mimic—I heard the same slow speech pattern in Professor Shipley's voice. "Let us examine your pronunciation and memory." He handed me his stick of chalk. "Define and pronounce these words."

I did not spend a lot of time that morning with Professor Shipley, but I did so much thinking my head hurt. Every single Latin word I knew was pulled from me, with emphasis on pronunciation. He switched to Greek at one point, and asked me to read from a Greek book he pulled off a bookshelf. It was *The Odyssey,* and it was like seeing an old friend among a crowd of strangers.

"Your accent is execrable," he told me, "But you have gained a great deal of vocabulary and understanding of Greek grammar from your attempts. We will put you with the beginning Greek students. Most of them have less vocabulary than you do, but having one class that is not a strain is not a bad thing." A faint smile flickered across his face, relaxing his mouth, and in that moment he felt human to me. "You have learned most of what is taught in beginning Latin. You shall read this book." He laid a Latin tome before me. "We will arrange another meeting next week, where you will report your progress and ask any questions that you may have. Once you are comfortable with this book, you may join a second year class. A new group will start up in a few weeks. It is possible that you will be ready for it."

"Yes, sir," I said, to let him know I understood the challenge.

Professor Shipley gave me a hard look. "Students who learn Latin for Classics study at university have different goals than we, Miss Sorensson. Simply put, Latin is the primary language of ritual magic. The great spells are written in Latin. If you mispronounce a word—if you write the wrong word—you are saying something else. And in magic, if you are not saying what you mean, you may be saying something dangerous...something fatal. Have I been clear?"

"Yes, sir. A careless practitioner is a dead practitioner."

His eyes crinkled, the corners of his mouth indenting ever so slightly. The professor did not actually smile, but I did feel like I was looking at a real human ...a practitioner. "Precisely."

So ended my first lesson.

❧ ⌘ ❧

This time no rush of students followed me into the hallway. It was very quiet.

Who knew that Latin would be so necessary?

My mother had hoped I would stop before this point, I realized. Otherwise, she would have stressed the Latin vocabulary more. The Latin book clutched to my chest, I headed back toward the house and the women's wing.

I found a tiny fire built in my fireplace, taking the excess chill from the air, and several books on the study table: a French dictionary, a Latin dictionary, a Greek dictionary and even a German dictionary. There was also a book called *Endor's History of Magic,* a huge herbal by someone named Nightroad, a French studies book, a book on ethics, another small book on logic, a book called *The Great Religions of the World,* and a blank book.

The blank book was not a composition book, full of lined paper for writing and taking notes. I saw several composition books waiting in a stack. In this case, the book had page numbers, the quality of paper seemed good, and the binding was made of stiff, smooth, oiled black leather. Several pages had print on them, but the letters appeared faded, as if someone had tried to erase them. Someone had rubbed two words on the spine in what might be gold leaf: *Ars Magica.* Something magic...I reached for the Latin dictionary to check the first word.

I found that I had picked up the French dictionary. Making a face, I started to set it down and then paused. While I had it, I might as well look for my first word of the day. Peppermint seemed to be a reoccurring theme in my life...the French was *menthe poivrée*. Mint was feminine, but pepper was masculine. So, which was peppermint?

I held the dictionary in my hands, savoring the word, the feeling of the book under my fingers.

Something was wrong.

Purposefully, I closed the book, set it down, and picked up the Latin dictionary.

"Ars" meant "art." The Art of Magic? So was it blank, or was there a trick to it? I examined it closely, to see if there was a portion of the book you touched to reveal the trick. The bookplate on the marbled end paper showed the gates and entry trees of Windward, and merely said "From the Library of" above the etching. The engraving was a winter theme, and was beautiful in its stark simplicity.

What was the French word for thyme? It turned out to be *thym*, and was masculine—

"This is ridiculous."

I spoke aloud, to get my own attention. Not that I wasn't interested in doing my lesson. But I had a real mystery in my hands, a book with blank pages, and the French vocabulary was distracting me. I wanted to do a good job, but I wasn't that prompt of a student—

Suddenly I realized what must have happened, and I flushed from head to toe.

"She put a spell on me."

Professor Sonneault had put a spell on me!

I closed the dictionary and pushed it to the far end of the table. Did she do that to everyone? Was it a nudge, or a command?

When was I going to get training so I could keep things like that from happening?

A rapping at the door seized my attention. "Enter," I said.

"Here you are! It is time for brunch," said Catherin Williams, leaning in through the doorway. "Oh, your books have arrived! That is always such fun. I love the feel of a book, especially a new one. Are any of them new?"

I held up the black book with the blank pages.

"That one is always new," she said soberly. "We are given that book once, and are expected to take care of it!"

"How do we read what is inside?" I asked.

She did not deny that the book did have something within it. "Professor Tonneman will explain it to you later. Leave them for now. Come, we are having French minced chicken on toast for brunch!"

"So how long does Professor Sonneault's spell last?" I asked as I double-checked the fireguard and pulled the door shut behind me.

Catherin actually started laughing. She had a beautiful laugh, bright and happy, totally feminine. "Miss Rutledge told me that you would notice the spell quickly! It lasts two to four weeks, depending on how long Professor Sonneault thinks you will need to get into the habit of that homework. Some of the younger children have that spell renewed a few times, if they prove that they will not do their homework without it. Once they know enough words to carry on a conversation, the spell fades and they have to keep up with the others, or be left out of a 'secret language,'" Catherin said as we went downstairs. Margaret caught up with us on the landing, and we went into the dining hall together.

The brunch was finely chopped chicken meat, pecans and onion mixed with salt and a tiny hint of rosemary. It was held together with some mix of eggs and oil. We were served fresh biscuits with it, and the boys put their meat within the biscuit like tiny meat pies. Mashed potatoes of a new variety were served, as well as a precious tangerine!

"Did I not say we ate well?" Margaret asked, her head tilted at me in inquiry.

I nodded, my mouth full.

The quick consensus was that I had done well with Professor Shipley. "He is a hard one," Catherin confided. "I don't think he has a lot of use for the younger students, until he knows if they are going to seriously pursue the craft."

"He teaches elements to older students, as Dr. Livingston and Professor De Lancey do," Margaret said. "I know that he instructs in Air and Water."

He's an odd one, I thought.

"Several of Miss Rutledge's flirts are his students," Catherin said, one side of her mouth curving up in a tiny smile.

"You know we are not supposed to talk about who is learning what field of endeavor," Margaret said primly, avoiding our gazes.

I wondered if another student was actually courting Margaret. Or more than one student? She was certainly pretty, but the wealthy did not marry solely because a woman was attractive...although it did not hurt the chances of marriage.

"You have Professor De Lancey next, and then Professor Tonneman," Catherin said. "I think you will like Professor De Lancey. He teaches magical history, among other things. Professor Tonneman, well...."

"His class is never boring," Margaret offered, as if conceding a truth.

"You are forgiving." Catherin's brows lowered and drew closer together, her delicate chin lifting. "He likes to frighten students, Miss Sorensson. Be on your guard!"

"We are not supposed to talk about entrance tests," Margaret said quietly, glancing to see if she were overheard.

"I knew *that* before I went in. Many students do," Catherin said, as if justifying her words.

I kept eating. I had been frightened several times in my pursuit of magic. If he had something more frightening than an *utburd* stored in his room, I might be worried. But I did not think he would be allowed to injure us, at least not as beginners.

"Can we protect ourselves?" I finally asked.

"He expects it," Catherin replied. "Take your wand!"

I didn't tell them that I hadn't yet used my wand for anything other than accidentally melting snow.

❧ 🐚 ❧

Both Catherin and Margaret took me to Professor De Lancey's classroom.

"Professor De Lancey teaches all his book classes here, beginning and advanced," Margaret said as we reached the door. "He teaches private classes as well, but there is a lot of fieldwork for his private students. The ritual chamber is used for those classes, or outside."

"Makes sense if he's teaching elemental magic of some kind," I replied.

Both girls looked a bit surprised, but Catherin nodded. "My brother is taking classes with Professor De Lancey. The professor is very patient with new students."

"Good." I must have sounded relieved, because Margaret looked hard at me.

"He will like you," Catherin said, her voice light. "He likes students who are eager to learn."

"He values a good heart," Margaret said in turn, squeezing my forearm as she was wont to do. "Just talk to him. He can help you learn what you need if he knows what you know and don't know."

"Sometimes you don't know just how much you don't know," I murmured, looking at the dark door.

"That's why the Second Rule is so important," Catherin told me, giving me the tiniest push. "To keep us always looking for new knowledge, the forgotten step, the unsuspected piece of information that makes all suddenly clear."

"We will see you after class!" Margaret finished, setting her hand lightly between my shoulder blades in farewell.

I was alone. But it would not last; soon other students would be climbing the stairs, heading for their next class. I didn't care for them to find me waiting like a frightened hutch bunny. I turned the handle and pushed open the door.

The light from a burning branch of candles matched the pale winter light from the three heavy windows. A small fire burned in a fireplace set in the outer wall. A man, dressed darkly, sat by the candelabrum, reading a large book laid open on a table.

Without lifting his gaze from his book, the man stood; he read a bit longer then turned toward me, his bearded face smiling. Although his hair had receded to a horseshoe around his head, his eyebrows were thick, several hairs extending from them like the antennae of a butterfly. He was of average height, a few inches shorter than myself, and barrel-chested, as proud as a rooster upon the roof of the barn.

Professor De Lancey looked through me—there was no other way to describe the feeling. His gaze was so focused you could not imagine him overlooking anything about you. This man would be able to pick me out of a market day crowd after this one meeting.

I looked back...and saw flames deep in his pupils.

I blinked and hazarded a quick glance to the side.

No...it could not be the reflection from the candles, or the fire... or the pale winter light. I wasn't sure about any of the other professors I'd met so far, but whatever Professor De Lancey was?

He wasn't a human man.

I'd met a fire lord, once, traveling in the wilderness, pausing in Sun-Return for a few days.

No flames in the eyes of the fire lord.

The long eyebrow hairs, almost like antennae, lifted slightly.

"I am Adolphus De Lancey," he said, his voice as melodious as a choir master's. "And you are Miss Sorensson?"

"Yes, sir," I replied, giving him a slight curtsy.

"Please be seated," he said, gesturing to another chair near the fire. "I am eager to hear what has brought you to Windward. When did you first know that you had a gift for magic?"

"A big wolf came to our town, and before he died, he nipped a few people. The next day we found out it wasn't a sick wolf, but a werewolf. I could hear them, calling on the wind, and I dreamt of one of the attacks as it was happening. So they knew I had The Gift, and needed training."

"And you were sent here?"

"No, sir, at least not then. I studied herbs with my mother and wood lore with my father. Then there was some business with a vampire, and after that I was sent to study with my cousin Marta Helgisdottir Donaltsson."

"Ah. I have met Mrs. Donaltsson. She is a formidable practitioner. Tell me about your herb studies with your mother. I understand that she is a granddaughter of Emma Schell?"

So I told him about studying herbs with my mother, and trapping and tracking with my father, and helping Marta smoke out a very dangerous creature terrorizing a village in the small mountains of the Michigan territory. I did not feel that I could face him as I told my story, so I let my gaze roam from the flames of the fire to the reflected light along the silver buckles on his shoes. His breeches were an older style, ending at the knee, his stockings a bright gold with what looked like a dragon twining up the outside. The silky thread of the dragon was black and deep red, the eyes scarlet and gold.

"It sounds as if your studies were progressing satisfactorily," he finally said. "Why have your family brought you to Windward?"

"Well...there was this nasty bit of business with a sorcerer trying to steal me away," I said vaguely. "I know that when we arrived here my cousin talked with Professor Livingston a long time. Perhaps she would have shared her concerns with Professor Livingston?"

There was silence...a long silence. The fire popped, returning us to the world. Finally Professor De Lancey said softly: "I see. Well, then, shall we talk about the basic tenets of practicing magic? Have you had the seven major rules of magic explained to you?"

"I know some of them," I replied. "I just found out that the first is 'The magic is in the practitioner.' Of course it's in the practitioner. If it was something you could pick up at the general store, it wouldn't be such a terrifying thing, would it?"

The professor gave me a solemn look. "No, no, it wouldn't. Which ones did you know before you came to Windward?"

"You may not realize how much you *don't* know," I said promptly. "It was practically the first thing my mother taught me. I was almost fooled by something simple, but dangerous. I try to remember that when I am faced with something new."

"A good teacher generally teaches a rule when it is needed. A student is more likely to remember the rules, if they are taught when a likely lesson appears. Is that the only one you've taken to heart?"

"Well...there is another one Mar—Mrs. Donaltsson uses a lot, but the way I heard it is not how Professor Livingston says it," I started.

"Yes, 'Ask for divine guidance before beginning works great and small,'" Professor de Lancey said, smiling. "As always, Mrs. Donaltsson's version drives directly to the point of the lesson."

"Professor Livingston told me that one rule is 'Expect the Unexpected.' That seems very important to me. Maybe it should be the first rule?"

"At certain points in life, it *is* the first rule," the professor responded. "That rule is my favorite, because it covers so many other things. The others have long-winded definitions that you will find in your Endor book, but perhaps I can simplify them for you now." He paused, his expression thoughtful, his gaze flicking toward the fireplace. "One way a student of magic could recite one of the others would be to say: 'We are not gods and goddesses. If we forget this, the Universe *will* remind us.'"

My eyebrows rose. I'd felt the hand of the Mother Goddess once...or whatever that overwhelming maternal presence might be. It didn't seem likely that you could confuse a mortal with an immortal. But I was new to this game. *Practitioners would not pass on that lesson if it wasn't useful.*

"The next, equally valuable, is 'One does not dabble in magic.' Can you guess why that is so important?"

Professor Shipley's last words had brought this home to me. I shivered at the implications. "Because magic is not something you can study half-heartedly. It's too dangerous for that. If you do, eventually you'll make a mistake, and the magic will eat you."

"'Eat you'...yes, that dives right to the center of the rule. The last, but far from the least, is: 'Everything is connected to everything else.'"

"Oh, yes, that is truth," I replied, thinking of the golden bands of light weaving the world together.

"So you have already seen that rule in action?" Professor de Lancey said. "What made that lesson so vivid for you?"

I took a sharp breath, my mind a tangle of images. I had learned of the great connection from the angel of Death, one snowy day not so very long ago. I was fighting for my freedom, and maybe even my life. Death had needed a favor, was the simplest way to think of it. Between us, we had attacked an ancient evil, and called it to the Other Side.

It had been a lesson in Wild Magic. I was trying hard not to talk about the Wild Magic, but it was the magic I knew best, and it kept cropping up.

"There were these mushrooms..." I started weakly.

Professor de Lancey laughed. "You took a great chance, child," he said, shaking his head. "Some mushrooms are very dangerous. There is no return from a poorly chosen journey. But yes, a few varieties do give insight into the Great Connections." Still slowly shaking his head, the professor went on. "I generally teach a small class in the spring about the history of magic. You are in time to join that group. If you start reading now, you will be ready for the discussions next week when we begin."

"Yes, sir."

"Miss Sorensson?" he said, tilting his head like a curious crow waiting to see what I would do.

"Sir?"

"How old are you?"

I was surprised that it had taken so long for someone to ask. "Thirteen, sir."

"Ah. Your family found you good tutors for your academic classes, I hear."

There wasn't a simple way to answer that. The teachers who had passed through Sun-Return had been sound, as Papa said, and between their encouragement (or neglect) and my family's belief in education, I had learned all I could.

But there were no tutors. I had learned what I did because I was bored. My mother had not been willing to start teaching me higher magics...but she had learned that I could finish a day's busywork in an hour. And my ways of keeping out of trouble had not suited her ideas of a daughter's schooling.

So I had found my own wisdom. I was a better trapper and tracker than most, and could ride a horse long hours, if need be. I had not wasted much time.

"I am fortunate in my family," I decided to say.

"Yes," he said gently. "You are fortunate." Pulling a watch from a pocket in his vest, Professor de Lancey opened the case and looked at it. "I am going to let you go a few minutes early. Professor Livingston will give you a schedule of classes, after you have completed all your testing. She will note when you are to return to me. Read the first two chapters of Endor's book for our next meeting."

"Yes, Professor," I said.

"And Miss Sorensson—"

"Sir?"

"If you have any questions about what you find in your books, know that you are welcome here at any time to ask those questions." He looked up from his pocket watch, his gaze pinning me to the chair. I felt like he was trying to tell me something...something more than his words conveyed..

He did not make his offer lightly, I thought.

"Thank you, sir. I will remember."

"We will speak again very soon." I could see the fire in his eyes again.

He didn't feel threatening, exactly. But still....

Lady of Light, hold me in the circle of your protection.

❧ⅅ❧

It was quiet in the dark hallway when I left the classroom, so I considered what I would do next. Margaret or Catherin would probably look for me, so....

"You are Alfreda Eldonsdottir Sorensson, yes? Daughter of the Schell line?"

I whirled about. The woman's accent was more Russian than anything else, but not quite that, either.

The carpet was not thick; I should have heard something. But no hint of her approach had reached me. The woman was tiny, her neck slender, her wrists so delicate I had no doubt I could circle my thumb and middle finger around them. Pale skin, dark hair, and a face memorable for its strong jaw, sharp cheekbones, and beautiful nose. It was her eyes that caught your attention—they were the hazel of polished amber.

Now where had I seen...?

Her dress was fashionable but simple, and looked to be a long-sleeved sacque, pulled over the head and tied under the breasts. It was an older style of dress, easy to get into without assistance. I could not make out details, but her high sash and her hair were both dressed with touches of winter, tiny pinecones and bright berries, fresh holly leaves and acorns.

This was not a student, unless Windward took adults as students.

"I am Alfreda Eldonsdottir Sorensson," I said, standing very straight.

"You found the portal in the carriage house," the woman went on, indicating with a flick of her first finger that I was to follow her.

How many people were supposed to know about that? "Yes," I finally told her.

"I am Professor Brown," she said crisply. "Come with me. You will meet Professor Tonneman in the dome room. All testing for ritual is done there. You have your athame and wand?"

"Yes, ma'am, but I haven't used them yet."

The woman abruptly stopped. Fortunately, I was not right on her heels, and did not bump into her. "You have not yet used them? Then why are you being tested by Professor Tonneman?"

"I was sent here to learn ritual magic. My teachers started with herbs and warding, but felt that I needed ritual before I could continue my studies," I said, wishing I'd thought of that phrasing earlier.

"Ah, you have warded? That is good. Come then, I will take you to the dome." Once again she set off with her crisp walk.

I wondered what this professor taught, and why I was not scheduled to see her, but I decided not to inquire. Professor Brown seemed like the kind of person who would ask what she wanted to know. Her eyes, though...I felt certain that I had seen her before.

"You need basic ritual before you can begin training with me. Otherwise all sorts of terrible things can happen. Part of learning magic is learning how to limit magic. Magic without limits is a dangerous thing."

Her speech was precise, but I did not feel the weight of any spell behind it. At a guess, English was not her first language. But I thought I understood her well enough.

Curiosity won out. "What do you teach, Professor?"

"Transformation," she replied, punching the four syllables.

Transformation? I had not even begun to think about transformation. Changing things, maybe even changing self—

The cat. The cat in the barn.

You could become as small as a *cat?*

We pushed through oak doors to the staircase. The dome, I knew, was on the third floor.

The woman stopped me with an upheld hand, shaped like a dancer's, her gaze lifting to meet mine. "Remember. Whenever you are in the dome—whatever is happening is real. Do you understand me? Never assume that something is illusion."

"I...do not have a lot of training in defense," I decided to say.

"Use what you have learned. This is a test not only of learning, but of competency and courage." Again the tiny flick of a finger, and with her other hand she lifted her skirt and started up the stairs.

As we started up the flight leading to the third floor, we could hear doors opening above us, and male voices, most of them low. Professor Brown moved tightly to the railing, continuing to climb as a group of young men flowed past us, nodding respectfully to us, several murmuring, "Professor Brown," as they passed. One of them, a tall, blond youth with a moustache, winked at me, and another with skin the color of ground nutmeg smiled.

Professor Brown nodded once, both acknowledging and dismissing them, I thought.

I had the impression that they were afraid of her.

I turned slightly, glancing over my shoulder. Several of the young men were looking warily over *their* shoulders, but they looked away when they saw my interest.

So far, she didn't frighten me. Tonneman and several of the others worried me, though. Just because they had manners didn't mean that they were truly kind.

I'd have to figure out the students here eventually. For now, I had to find my place with the teachers.

By the time we reached the landing, we were alone. The door to the practice area was ajar; Professor Brown pushed it open. "Tonneman!" she cried, speaking like one man addressing another. "I have brought you your heart's desire!"

Professor Tonneman was erasing a huge piece of slate that covered a section of the wall. The last of the chalk writing disappeared under his rag. Then he turned to us. He wore a different jacket and vest today, but he was still wearing natural deerskin trousers and high boots. Having seen several gentlemen wearing what must be newer fashions, I now placed the professor as a fancy sort of fellow. Not as fussy as that one shocking man in town, but more than anyone else in the school.

Now why had Professor Brown said those words?

The transformation instructor reached behind herself, took hold of my wrist and pulled me forward. "I bring you Alfreda Eldonsdottir Sorensson, a daughter of the Schell line," she announced. Professor Brown broke off momentarily, and then in a softer voice said: "Be careful what you ask for, Tonneman." Releasing me, she gave me a quick smile (though what she meant by it I hadn't a clue) and hurried out, closing the door behind her.

Now, finally, I had reached the ritual professor. In this room was the entire reason for my trip to Windward.

Professor Tonneman liked to frighten students.

Lord and Lady, help me now. I hated like poison to be embarrassed, and I could smell humiliation on the horizon.

TEN

ABOVE ME, THE ROUNDED DOME rose into shadow. Somehow I'd expected the inside of the room to reflect the Italian design of the house, but there were shadowy rafters above us. The huge room of pieced granite sloped into a large, shallow bowl containing a floor of fine, packed white sand and a disk of smooth river gravel in the center. The gravel had the ladder of a good-sized fire laid upon it. Professor Tonneman stood at the lip of the shallow bowl, his hands behind his back.

"Miss Sorensson," he said gravely. "I was not aware that you were meeting with Professor Brown today."

"We met in the hallway, sir," I told him. "She brought me here before I could tell her I was waiting for a guide." I did not bother with a curtsy.

"Professor Brown is nothing if not enthusiastic," was his answer. "Has your book arrived yet?"

"I received a book called *Ars Magica,*" I replied. "Someone told me it was the ritual book."

"Do you have questions about the book?"

"I'd like to know the trick for reading it," I admitted.

"Was it blank?" he asked, starting toward me.

"Most of it. Some of it was very light print, but I could not read the words."

"Indeed? Curious. This suggests that you have some experience with ritual."

"A little bit," I decided to say. "Not enough to...rely upon." I couldn't call my efforts useless. My ability to call upon Death had surely saved my life. And I had helped Marta with wards several times. But you usually don't learn any ritual until you have your wand and athame, and mine had just arrived. "That's why I came to Windward: for ritual training."

"And Latin," he added, giving me a firm look.

So they'd already found time to discuss me. "Now that I know I need it, I will study it," I said.

"Your early scholarship has been formidable," Professor Tonneman said, and I could hear the strength of his accent on the word "formidable." He sounded a touch British, where before he'd merely sounded educated. "I am surprised that your Latin has been so sparse."

"My mother did not want me to study the mysteries." I used the word practitioners chose when speaking to those with other gifts... those without magic. "I suspect that is why she let the Latin and Greek instruction slip by. My older brother was not interested in college, so it was easy to stress other things. It's not like anyone speaks Latin to each other," I offered after thought.

"Actually, you can speak Latin with another person, but it is rarely done. Generally you will find another language that you share first. I became acquainted with a scholar while in Greece, and the only language we had in common was Latin," the man replied. "All knowledge has value. It is knowing when to use your knowledge that can be the trick." Professor Tonneman stopped next to the smooth circle of gravel. "What kind of wards have you set up?"

"Mrs. Donaltsson set up wards throughout a town, using small boxes filled with faceted crystal balls," I told him. "We made a traveling ward and a ward for our house and surrounding land. My cousin did the spell, though. I was inside the circle to place the stones in a velvet-lined box."

"Is that your extent of warding?"

I considered his choice of words. "I helped with a small circle to transport a letter. We were outside that circle."

I decided not to mention that the Goddess had protected us from a nasty demon by burning the circle down to bedrock.

"Anything else?"

Not any other wardings. Just.... "I have called Death a few times."

He tilted his head, as if studying a small problem. "Have you, now? Already?"

I fixed him with a firm look. "I was taught that the first of the major arcana was introducing yourself to the Last Great Healer."

"That is correct." He studied me for a moment. "I need to see you work, to have an appreciation of where you are in your studies. Go ahead and summon Death."

"Odd" was not a strong enough word for how I suddenly felt.

Slowly, I said: "I was taught to only call upon Death when I had a question I could not answer any other way."

"I am the one with the question," he replied. "It is whether or not you have successfully summoned Death."

"People sometimes do not succeed?" I said, letting my gaze wander around the room at the high, round windows up near the dome, and the slate wall against one of the wings of the house.

"It can take numerous attempts to summon Death," he told me, starting back up the bowl toward the lip of the high circle.

Touching the leather pouch tied to my waist, I said: "I will need water for this." Then I remembered I wasn't wearing my hunting knife. It was in my wardrobe. Bother. That meant using the athame.

I had to trust it was an acceptable way to break in the knife. Since a practitioner sometimes uses the athame to draw her own blood, it shouldn't matter if it was the first use.

He gestured toward the wall opposite the slate panel. "There is a barrel of well water there."

I saw the barrel pushed into shadow across the sandy basin. Water was a place to begin. I thought about the ceremony while I went up to the keg. You didn't summon Death for someone else— you summoned him for your own questions. So I needed a question.

I pulled out my carved little egg-shaped cup my brother had made for me, and used my elbow to push the lid of the wooden barrel to one side.

"Not that thing, we will be here until tomorrow. Use this goblet." A large glass suddenly appeared before me, floating above the open keg. It was a beautiful, deep blue, standing upon a pedestal, and lovely as a newly opened flower.

I tucked the oak cup back into my pouch and took the goblet in my hand. It was heavy but not uncomfortably so. The dipper hanging by the barrel was a lovingly carved wooden one, and I used it to fill the goblet.

In truth I was grateful for the larger container. I did *not* want to have to cut myself twice for a glass full of bloody water. Last time I'd been melting snow, though, and snow took up a lot more room. I marched back down to the fire circle, pleased that the center of the sand bowl was flat enough to set the goblet safely.

As I'd noticed, firewood already lay in the center. I didn't care for the arrangement: too many large logs. I set them aside to start a small fire with flint, steel, and tinder from my pouch. I squatted comfortably. It only took two strikes for a spark to catch, and using some twigs and the smallest of the sticks from the firewood, I got my fire burning. Oak and cedar formed this fire, and my nose thought it a good mix. Then I made a tripod of wood to give the fire a place to grow. The rest, fat logs and long ones, I left to one side, in case I needed them later.

You can't be ready for everything, but having tools at hand doesn't hurt.

Now came the painful part, mixing the elements and drawing the circle. This wasn't warding, not as I'd come to Windward to learn. Calling Death was the only time you could perform a ritual with the other planes of existence and not protect yourself with a true ward. That's because once you drew and closed the circle and summoned Death, everything bad shunned the circle.

Apparently the only thing of value Evil has is brains. Even evil things fear Death.

Blood is salty, so I didn't need to add salt to my water. And I could heat the blade of the athame first, energizing it and giving me fire. While I heated the athame, I blew gently across the water, rippling it, giving it the air of my body. I decided to aim for a modest circle, large enough for Death and me, but not huge. Ten feet across should do it, what with the fire between us.

"What kind of ward is this, exactly?" Professor Tonneman asked abruptly.

"Death's ward," I answered.

"I have not heard of 'Death's Ward.'"

His words caused me to look up. Once again he stood at the top of the sandy depression, but now he held a small, elegant wand.

"I don't know any other wards," I reminded him. "But if you draw the circle for Death and call, nothing evil will stay in the area." Standing, I took my beautiful new silver knife and nicked the flesh of my right palm. Enough blood dripped out to cause a stain to spread over the surface of the water in the goblet. Since the cut closed quickly, I didn't worry about applying pressure. I picked up the goblet and started stirring with my athame.

"You learned this ritual from Mrs. Donaltsson?" Professor Tonneman's voice came from somewhere behind me.

Was it my imagination, or had the room darkened? I glanced at the curved wall of windows, mullioned and gracious, overlooking the labyrinths and maze. More snow moving in, perhaps.

Three strides away from the fire felt like a good distance. I took the wet athame and started dribbling my circle. Heavy drops of water spattered the sand, forming dimples like those on the face of the moon.

"She took me out in the woods and told me what to do to summon Death," I finally said. I wondered if he was really interested, or if he was just trying to distract me while I was working. That's what Cousin Esme had been doing while I was working with the herbs, I realized. She'd been trying to distract me, to see if I could work through confusion.

Huh. I'd learned to make a meal while keeping a weather eye on my little brothers. Nobody got burned or beat up when I was in charge.

"Of course you must be fast enough getting the circle up that nothing evil joins you in the circle," came the professor's voice.

True enough. I wasn't dawdling, that was certain, but I was trying to be precise, so I didn't leave anything out or look sloppy. Professor Tonneman's words suggested that I was a bit slow for him, so I dribbled faster, to get the first circle down quickly.

Then the room disappeared.

That sounds silly, but trust me—the room was no longer there. I was someplace dark, and outside the sand bowl was...water? Only the growing fire gave me light to see by.

I could hear the slaps and pops of a fish breaking the surface of a pond. A ripple hit the rim of the great sand bowl I stood in, allowing water to slop over the edge and trickle a foot into the white grains.

I walked a little faster. A quick glance showed a dark line completely around the fire, so I started the second, inner circle, looking up occasionally to see if anything else was changing. I remembered Professor Brown warning me that anything that happened in the ritual room was real.

How could there be water in the room? It was like I was on an island.

My next glance showed that I was not the only living thing present. I could see tiny, glittery orbs reflected beyond the circle. There were pale green dots and red ones of varying sizes. It felt as if a pond full of frogs watched me.

Water. I stood on an island, surrounded by water.

I knew that shine. When I walked out after dark with a torch, the eyes of animals reflected that way.

Dribble, dribble...I resisted pouring the goblet out. I had to make this water last, because I did not trust magic water to finish the circle. And I definitely didn't want to make up the difference in blood. *I must learn that spell to turn dew into water as soon as possible.*

Something splashed. I set the goblet down, the athame still in it, grabbed the front and back of my long skirt and tied the two between my legs, my response not very lady-like as I bared my wool stockings from the knees down, but I'd take the reprimand later. I remembered all too well losing half my skirt while riding to that Twelfth Night delivery. I stuffed my braid down the back of my shirt for luck, and then seized the goblet to finish the inner circle.

If I was going to get grabbed, I wasn't going to be easy pickings.

Somehow I was still in the dome room, because echoes made it hard to tell what direction sounds came from. Or was this a cave? Halfway around the inner circle, the fire still building nicely...I fumbled for a fat log and slid it into the burning pile of wood. Who knew how long this was going to take? I needed light!

Circle complete. For a moment I could not remember which way was East, and panic froze me. Then I remembered, and sprang over to the eastern side, to slice Raphael's sigil into the space between the lines. The archangel who is the great healer first, who holds the trumpet of the Apocalypse, Raphael's name was one I knew as well as my own. Then the warrior general Michael for the south—

Something pale and green flashed. I leapt away from it, careful to remain in the circle. Dropping the athame into the goblet, I grabbed one of the longest logs, whirled and slashed at the dripping, glowing thing—arm. The blow connected with a satisfying, terrifying thud and crunch.

Oh, Lady, it's real, it's real, it's real—

The arm recoiled in a swinging arc, clearly broken from my blow. Light sparkled as drops of water fell from the wet thing. I watched to make sure the circle was not disturbed by it as I continued to move, ready to draw or fight—

I spun to the West, ruled by Gabriel, the prophet angel and the first whom God will tell when the end of Time is come. Harder to draw, longer than his name in English, but I know that one, I've used it more than a few times—

It was a cold, slimy thing that touched my ankle, soaking my stocking with icy water. I'd set down the log to keep writing, and I scrabbled for it, but something small and translucent, mere moonlight, its huge eyes swollen like a frog or dragonfly, had hold of the log and played a tug of war with me. I won back the log, and smacked the thing out of the circle like an errant ball at a child's game.

Of course balls didn't have a mess of arms and legs.

The goblet was still upright. A quick check—I was alone in the circle. I grabbed the goblet and darted to the North, where Uriel, the flame of God and guardian of Paradise, holds forth. But I didn't have that sigil memorized yet, so I needed his name. *I can spell this, a U instead of Gab, come on, Allie—*

Multiple small hands grabbed at my stockings and skirt, as if trying to pull me away from the fire. I slashed the first cross between angel names or sigils, gave back two long steps and drew the second cross—

A well-placed kick behind me drew a high-pitched scream from whatever it was, and I had the log again and swung it like a scythe, clearing my path to the place between the sigils still begging for a cross, and only one more—

Looking around wildly, I lunged between Raphael and Michael, carving that final wet cross into the sand, and as I did so, screaming erupted from the creatures swarming at my legs. I wasn't finished, but already these things didn't like what I was doing.

"Time to leave!" I told them, smacking one holding onto my knee and elbowing another out of the circle. It lunged back—splat! It was as if it had run into a pane of glass. I didn't want to touch any of them, but I wasn't sure I could get rid of them fast enough.

Tobacco. I needed tobacco to finish the invitation. I ground the goblet into the sand by the now-roaring fire, hitting one of the creatures so hard that it soared over the firepit, its trailing tentacles flaming before it hit the water with a crack and a sizzle. My pouch flap lifted, and it was as if the tobacco rushed to my need. I whacked the two remaining things hard, their continuous squeal hurting my ears, and as they released me, I dropped the log, pulled a pinch of tobacco from my inner soft pouch, and tossed it into the flames.

I opened my mouth to speak the opening words, and was stopped by the realization that I needed to identify myself in the ritual—and I sure didn't want to use any of my ritual names in front of this man, whatever his motive for this little game.

Well, in this one ritual, I had an advantage.

Death had given me another name, one I was not afraid to use, not when it was from such a giver. And I knew that in an emergency, Death was not expecting a lot of flowery language.

"I, Alfreda Golden-tongue, call upon Azrael, greatest of healers and teachers, for I have a question that needs answering!" I shouted. "Come to me, solitary angel, for my need is great!" *A question, dear Lord and Lady, I needed a question.*

The screeching increased—and then it stopped. My ears rang as if a mess of church bells was chiming, but there were no more yelping critters, or shiny eyes looking at me.

On the other side of the fire, the smoke formed into the tall, slender man I'd last seen in the depths of winter, in the remains of the compound at Hudson-on-the-Bend. This time Death did not look quite so much like an older Shaw Kristinsson. The dark hair was still there, the black outline of a beard along his jaw, the moustache full and smooth. But his skin was darker this time, the color of cinnamon, not the pale ivory of Shaw's. And his eyes were not the gray Shaw bore; they were dark enough to watch stars die within them.

Swelling, expanding, exploding stars.

Stars were also born within them, I saw, meeting his gaze. Maybe tradition is wrong. Maybe Gabriel is not the angel of time.

Azrael's emotionless face relaxed, as if the angel was thinking about smiling, but didn't want to do so. Death looked to his right, and said softly: "Be careful." Glancing back at me, he twisted fully to his right, the merest crook of a smile on his lips. "Be very careful."

Then he turned back to me, gave me a hint of a nod of greeting, and vanished.

Just that suddenly, daylight filled the room again, pale winter at the windows. The water and its slimy denizens were gone as if they had never existed. I was left with a damp circle and a roaring bonfire.

"Interesting," Professor Tonneman said. He was standing at the rim of the bowl, near his huge slate board, his hands upraised, wand in his left hand.

Straightening from my half-crouch, I said the first thing that came into my head. "You're not afraid of him."

Tonneman turned slightly. "Death? His presence? No. Metaphorically, of course, Death gives me pause. I am no more ready to leave than the next man of my years. But Death retrieves souls, Death does not kill things."

Death is a hunter, too, I could say, but didn't. I did not want to explain to this man a lot of things I knew...things that might contradict teachings he shared with others. I suspected that eventually I would have to tell Professor Tonneman about a few of my gifts. It would be difficult to hide that I knew another way to do magic.

But there was no sense in rushing through woods on a winding deer trail. I did not know this new country; there could be a ravine on the other side, or a huge river.

I wasn't leaving tomorrow, I knew now. I had time to take his measure, and see if he could be trusted with deeper secrets than even his black book might hold.

"Your book has a sophisticated spell upon it," Tonneman said without preamble.

Was he reading my mind?

I checked my personal wards.

No, they were good.

"It hides from you spells that are beyond your ability to cast. Do you have a wand yet?" He was walking toward me as he spoke.

I tugged my skirt free from its bound up state so I could reach the pocket with my wand in it. "Yes. I just got it before I settled in here." That was basically the truth.

"Bring it when Professor Livingston assigns you to a class. You will do fine in the beginner class. Work hard on your Latin vocabulary, Miss Sorensson. I suspect you will not enjoy using Latin rituals you do not understand."

In that, he was correct. I've never cared for using words I didn't fully understand. That has never changed. I'd bring the Latin dictionary with me, too, so I could look up words I didn't know.

Surely I wasn't the only one who needed Latin assistance.

"What were they?" I asked abruptly.

He did not pretend to misunderstand me. "Nursery boggies... hags. Grindylow, Jenny Greenteeth, Black Annis—that ilk."

"Then they were not real." If they weren't real, I was impressed at his ability to create out of legend. The resistance, the *weight* of them had felt very real to me.

Tonneman gave me one of his sharp looks. "Not real? Oh, they are very real, Miss Sorensson. People use hags and nursery boggies to frighten children away from deep water—and as an excuse when they've drowned an elder they can't be bothered with. But they do exist, and if you enter their realm without precaution or respect, you run the risk of becoming their prey."

That knowledge made me feel a bit better. It had all happened so fast, there had been little time to be afraid. But I had hated the feel of those slimy, long-fingered hands.

I preferred fearing realities. It wasn't necessary to make up evils...the world had more than enough of the real thing.

"Until our next class," he said, walking back toward his slate wall. A champion pacer, was Professor Tonneman.

"Sir," I said automatically, and flung the rest of my blood-tinged water into the fire. I'd finish the closing before I left, if only silently. *I thank you, Azrael, for coming to face me in this circle. Farewell, until we meet again.*

There was only one other thing that might bear talking out, but I wasn't sure yet if the professor shared discussions with his students, or only lectures.

Death's words...was he talking to me, the professor, or something else?

Or had he spoken to all of us?

❧⟡❧

I would just as soon forget our early supper that night. The food was as good as always, a simple stew with bread and an apple, but there were too many people around for my taste. I'd never thought of myself as someone who preferred solitude, but turned out that the few students in my one room school had been more than enough company for me.

"I'm sorry I wasn't waiting for you in the hallway," I began as I reached Margaret and Catherin's table. They were already spread out at one of the drop leaf foursomes folded out near the wall. Miss Smith—and her ghost—were also present.

"Professor Brown was there when our class let out," Margaret replied, pouring me a cup of tea. "She explained why you were not waiting."

"I would not have argued with Professor Brown," Catherin said quickly. "She is a force of nature. Always get out of her way or you'll be trampled!"

"Did your day go well?" Miss Smith asked, turning and smiling her shy half-smile, the right corner of her mouth quirking in.

I was momentarily distracted by the ghost also turning my way.

"Yes, I think so," I replied, sitting down. "I am glad the day is over, though. I am tired!"

At least the ghost left me a seat.

"Not at all surprising," Margaret said, and immediately turned to ask Catherin about something from their earlier cultures class.

From this I guessed that they would hold their curiosity about my day until we three were alone, so I applied myself to my dinner.

"Did you have rituals placement today?" Miss Smith asked, leaning slightly in my direction.

"I did," admitted.

"Ah. I thought so, since you are wearing a work dress." After a sip of tea, she continued, "I thought perhaps someone should warn you...it might not occur to Miss Rutledge, as she has such exquisite taste and good timing...."

This sounded like a warning. I looked directly at Miss Smith, letting her know that I was interested.

"There are students here who are quite..." She stopped, and I realized that Miss Smith was upset.

I did not interrupt her.

Finally Miss Smith blurted out what she wanted to say. "If you do not wear at least a carriage dress for dinner, the Mayflower Compact students will find fault."

Catherin had mentioned those students, and not in a good way. "Should I care if they find fault?" I asked.

Miss Smith gave me a blank-faced stare, and then concern lowered her eyebrows slightly, the corners of her mouth deepening.

"You do not want them looking to find fault," she replied, looking down at the teacup in her hands.

"Well, I also didn't want pond slime on a good dress," I said, setting down my bread. "How are these people members of the Mayflower Compact? I thought that was signed in 1620 by the Separatists?"

"Oh, they are descendants of the original settlers," Miss Smith answered, pouring herself another cup of tea.

I hadn't a clue if I was also a descendant of the Separatists.

Not that it had ever mattered in my life.

"And that is important how?" I asked, applying myself to my stew. It was thick with root vegetables, and showed Mrs. Gardener's skill with herbs.

Miss Smith looked taken aback. "If you are not a descendant, they won't talk to you."

I know my eyes grew wider, because I felt my eyebrows twitch. "I hope I don't have to do a class project with them, then. It would be very awkward."

Just a hint of a smile lurked on Miss Smith's lips. She looked bemused.

"I have no idea if I am a descendant. I have family from New England, so I suppose it's possible," I went on. "Are you a descendant?"

"I don't know," she replied. "I have no one left."

"But they watch over you," I told her.

"I hope so."

I smiled at her. "They do. So," I went on. "If they don't talk to us, how is this a problem?"

"They are rich and their clothing is the envy of the school," Miss Smith said.

Ah. That game I knew about.

I was not sure what to say in response. My life was framed by people who feared me, who thought I was odd, who wanted to be my friend because I had magic, and the very few who simply liked to talk with me and share things together.

I had never feared other children. I had just avoided them.

"It helps give them influence," Miss Smith murmured, turning back to her bowl. "I thought you should be warned."

"Thank you," I told her, buttering my bread.

Forewarned is forearmed.

"A new fledgling in tow, Miss Rutledge? Surely you have served your time?" came a murmuring voice behind me.

Margaret stiffened, her face smoothing into her porcelain "hello, stranger" expression she'd worn when I first met her. "I have always enjoyed mentoring, Miss Bradford," she replied, her voice drained of inflection.

Margaret did *not* like Miss Bradford.

If I craned my neck to see who was behind me I would embarrass Margaret. I reached for my tea and waited to be introduced.

"Miss Sorensson, this is Miss Bradford and Miss Alden," Catherin said, nodding in turn.

Now I could twist slightly.

The girls did not move forward. I could see a white dress of multi-layered gauze out of the corner of my eye. Of the other girl I could see nothing.

"I heard that your new fledgling has already put you on the Saturday staff." There was a smothered giggle from somewhere beyond the table.

I considered whether to speak, and what to say.

Margaret responded with a faint smile, barely twitching her lips. "New experiences. I'll be comfortable with the next house party and spare my mother the effort."

"Don't let all the sharing go in one direction," Miss Bradford said, her voice as restful as a river sliding over stones. "I trust that you will give her a few hints as to appropriate meal attire. Good evening."

There was a whisper of material, and the rise and fall of conversation around us resumed.

I flicked a glance Margaret's way. "You were right. Magical testing is hard on students."

A gasp, quickly smothered, came from Catherin's direction. Miss Smith looked puzzled, while Margaret tightly pressed her lips together.

It could have gone worse. I looked over my shoulder and saw two young women moving into the back room. Both were dressed in gauzy white with fine wool shawls, one dark-haired, one a flaming redhead.

I wondered if I could take meals in my room.

❧·⫯·❧

My bedroom was warm, and our tea was just right.

"Miss Sorensson, you are intrepid!" Catherin Williams exclaimed. "First Tonneman's games, and *then* there was Miss Mayflower Compact, the queen bee herself!" Catherin raised her chin and tossed her head as she spoke, reaching to touch an imaginary hat.

Thanks to Catherin, I suspected I might recognize Miss Bradford when I finally saw her face. I didn't feel like that last had gone well, though. I just hadn't wanted Margaret to feel badly.

I hoped Miss Mayflower Compact wasn't going to be a problem. All I wanted was to learn ritual magic and get out of Windward as quickly as possible.

It was long past supper and into our last tea of the night.

I had planned to ask Margaret and Catherin about whether I should confront Professor Sonneault, but I didn't want to mention it in front of strangers. Then the two of them had homework, and I returned to French vocabulary and studied the list of classes I was expected to attend each day. It was complicated, for the order changed daily.

"The reward for success is more work," was Margaret's comment after looking at my list.

Huh. Maybe I should not have been in such a hurry back home to finish my lessons. I was going to be submerged in languages. But now was teatime, with a small plate of macaroons to share among the three of us, and I needed to say something to Catherin, even though I was not positive what "intrepid" meant.

"Well, I don't know about that," I started, shifting on my perch, which was the foot of my high bed. Catherin and Margaret had the chairs, and had brought a tiny folding table to set the sturdy teapot and cups upon.

"She means fearless," Margaret interrupted. Margaret was becoming skilled at reading my face.

"Not at all," I assured Catherin. "I was very frightened. It's just that fear wasn't going to solve anything. I save being scared for later!"

Catherin burst out laughing, but it was happy laughter, so I smiled in turn. I saw deep creases at the corners of Margaret's mouth as her serene smile crossed her lips.

"And I thought *my* first ritual was a trial! I had but a solitary brownie to face, who was trying hard to be helpful. Fortunately it was one that has helped out at the school for years, and it just thought I was touched in the head," Catherin confided, pouring out a tiny amount of hot tea for us all.

"You acted quickly, Miss Sorensson," Margaret went on, offering me the cookie plate. "I do not know if I could have evaded the hag, much less the Grindylows. You should be well-satisfied with your efforts."

"I got the circle up, and Death came at my request, so I am satisfied," I admitted, taking a cookie and passing the plate to Catherin. "I would be happier if I knew what Death was talking about, when he spoke to us. But life is full of mysteries."

"So many possibilities for so few words," Catherin said, adding cream to her tea.

I preferred black tea and an extra cookie, and suited actions to thought. "Well, I will keep an eye out when in that class," I murmured. "I don't know if Death ever gives more than one hint."

"I have met that angel but once, and do not expect to see him again, until my last day," Margaret said, her gaze dropping to her hands. Her voice had that measured dignity people reserved for talking about Death.

"You don't ever expect to need to ask him a question for a patient?" I asked.

"Who would trust me with a patient that ill?" was her response.

I opened my mouth, and then closed it again. In my experience, ill people happened everywhere, and the more you knew about caring for them, the better you could manage your own homestead. All during my youth my parents had had no doctor to call upon. It was only that last year before the werewolf came that a doctor was in our region. Before that, my mother had handled everything as best she could.

This wasn't the time to argue that point with Margaret.

We had our tea and cookies, and then I walked them back to their room, Catherin with the folding table and Margaret with her English tea set tucked in its box. After stopping off at the indoor Tree, I returned to my own nest, and put the two chairs from the table back where they belonged. It was time to think about sleep, for the day had been long, and the senior student who made sure we all went to bed by lights out would be along soon. I had yet to meet her, but I'd been told she had little sense of humor.

Just as well if I kept going to sleep before she did her rounds.

I reached to the top of the dresser, re-arranging the skirt on Ruth, the doll that my good friend Idelia had given me. Tonight I had finally pulled her from my trunk and set her up in solitary splendor. To Ruth, if only silently, I could admit that I was nervous.

The business with the nursery boggies had left me restless and wondering if I would have nightmares. That had happened, in the past. I could handle emergencies, but sometimes the hours after-wards left me jumpy as a long-tailed cat in a market street crowd.

Still, I had to try to sleep. Tomorrow I had real classes.

As I took hold of the heavy curtains to draw them over the window, I glanced down at the garden...and stared.

The maze was glowing.

Not the thick walls woven of yew, but the path of the pattern. It was more than snow reflecting moonlight. This was much closer to the pale fire Marta's labyrinth had put forth.

I pressed my nose against the cold, bubble-flecked glass and squinted, my breath fogging the lower panes. There was no move-ment, not a human to be seen, but at the entrance of the maze was a dark lump. It looked like a sack except for a snaky curl that led beyond the pile itself.

As the glow of the pathway increased, I realized that I *knew* that lump.

It was The Cat.

I went tearing to the wardrobe for my coat.

⁕·🗝·⁕

I kept enough self-possession to know that tossing on my outer clothes was a clear invitation to be stopped by an adult. So I fold-ed my coat over like a bundle for the laundry, and then realized I would need to try strapping my snowshoes to my slippers.

I hauled open the door to the wardrobe...and there were my boots, cleaned, as if nothing had happened to them. *Wonder what this will cost me, in time or work?* I touched the boots, but they seemed perfectly normal.

Boots on, coat tucked under my arm, pouch strapped to my waist, knife and wand still in their slits...I grabbed my hunting knife and tightened the strap around my waist. Then I rushed for the back staircase.

You are not leaving the property, I reminded myself. *You are not going into the maze. Even if The Cat goes into the maze, you are staying OUT of the maze.*

Well, I knew I wasn't going to fool anyone who might still be working in the kitchen, cleaning up for the baker in the morning. Once in the service area I shook out my coat, nodded to a rosy-cheeked blonde girl who was carrying a stack of plates toward the butler's pantry, and then said: "I must fetch The Cat." Without pause I marched to the kitchen door.

To call the night air brisk would trigger laughter. It was so cold that my first breath hurt. I fumbled out my gloves and scarf, and the inside-out hat I wore doing chores around our farm.

The moon gleamed in a pale sickle of light through thick, bare tree branches. In the distance I heard a dog barking, his voice deep and self-important, and closer, a snort that sounded like a horse. Tracks dappled the firm snow—horses, mice, cats, one dog, and a couple of hares. It took me a few crunching steps to get from the kitchen wing to where the labyrinths and maze were placed.

I practically levitated when a great horned owl shrieked. Good thing I wasn't a mouse, or I'd be running. No nerve tonight. Those boggies had gotten to me.

Neither light nor sound disturbed the serene black and white curves of the labyrinth on this side of the maze. I could not remember whether it was the male or female labyrinth to the right, but I sensed energy about it, coiled up like a rattlesnake.

The maze was not silent. I could hear the steady chiming of hoof beats against cobblestones, as if the maze path was paved. Tracks marred the snow visible from the entrance...large ones. Cougar prints, it looked like, from some sort of big cat.

And wind blew. The branches above me were still, etched against the waning moon. But from the tall formal garden I could hear the rush that promised wind or water.

I stopped, considering the scene. No wind where I was...could I use the stirring air or water within the maze? Here I was, outside in a strange place, with no more protection than a hunting knife that was useful only so long as no one knew I had it. Not a cloud in the sky...how far to reach for wind as a weapon?

It was time to grab The Cat and get inside.

The Cat crouched before the entrance, his long, fluffy tail wrapped around himself. His colorful coat looked like a series of black, white and gray swirls. I approached him. A gust of wind scoured the side of my face, stirring my scarf and a few wisps of hair that had escaped from my braid.

It took effort not to reach for that wind, to capture a piece of it for myself.

As if I had spoken, The Cat turned his head toward me, his furry face peering up toward mine. He chirped a friendly greeting.

"Been getting the lie of the land?" I asked him, and then winced. I was once again talking to the animal.

The Cat trilled at me.

"I know you can't answer me, but I can't help but think..." *that you understand most of what I say* sounded just foolish.

Maybe it sounded foolish, and maybe not. Maybe he wasn't just a cat, either.

The glow from the maze had increased, illuminating branches and leaves a good third of the way up the sides of the yew walls. The rush of wind had also increased, but none of the leaves within the maze stirred.

Are you waiting for something...or someone? I wanted to ask.

Was it me you waited for, and can we go back inside now?

The Cat stood up. I took one step back, but he wasn't paying any attention to me. He was watching the maze. I caught movement and turned to face the entrance.

I had been so busy cautioning myself to avoid entering the maze that I hadn't thought about something coming out of it.

At first it looked large, but the closer it came, the smaller it looked, until it seemed to solidify into something about as tall as I am, and as deep as I'm tall. It was as misty as the floor of the maze. Smoke puffed bluish close to the ground by its front feet, but never rose to obscure the creature.

Its legs were long and slender, the feet cloven, the form as dainty as an Arab horse. Two things were different...the long wisps of hair attached to its—his—chin, and the beginnings of a horn, no longer than my hand, protruding from his forehead.

This foal was a unicorn.

My unicorn?

He was the reason I had come to Windward when I did, but I had not had time to think about him much. He couldn't be any older than...I stared. He was months old, at the least. How could it be my unicorn, unless they grow differently than horses?

Of course it made sense that they grew differently from horses.

The tiny unicorn stepped out of the maze, walked right up to me, and shoved his nose against my shoulder. He looked ghostly, but he felt as solid as I am.

Remembering how easily I had been entranced, I wasn't sure what to do. Could a young one do something like that? Where was his mother, or his aunt?

Somewhere out there was also a father, and that might be a really big animal.

Allie! The mind voice was high, like a reed pipe.

I touched his nose.

Oh, I had felt soft things before, but none rivaled the coat of a unicorn. Even through my gloves I could feel my fingers sinking into his thick, soft plush. His mother had been sleek, but not like this... or was that the deception of a spell? *Are you capable of a spell yet, little one, or is this your true form?* His huge eyes were the dark, dark water of his mother, a deep blue, like the elderberries we harvested every year.

The foal paced sideways to look back into the maze. *Gift!*

Hummmm. So was he offering me a gift, or was I supposed to be a gift for someone else? My legs tightened, ready to spring.

Something was walking through the maze. It looked human...or human-shaped. I stepped backward several paces, folding my palm over the hilt of my hunting knife.

He stopped at the mouth of the maze, the wind behind him lifting stray locks of dark hair and ruffling the fringe of his leather jacket. In the pale moonlight, I could not be positive of what I saw, but if it wasn't Shaw Kristinsson, then it was a blessed good imitation. The same long walk, the same alert, slight tilt to the head. Pale and dark, much the way Death had shown himself to me in the remnants of Hudson-on-the-Bend.

But Shaw had gray irises, not black like Azrael's eyes. They could be very dark, but I knew the truth. Sometimes his gaze was as soft as mist, and sometimes it threatened like a thunderhead. Now? His eyes were dark, but not frightening. And the whiskers were gone.

So Shaw had decided to shave off his new whiskers. I wondered if he'd done it because a girl he'd kissed had complained, and I found myself ridiculously annoyed at the thought of that unknown girl. I even forgot to be nervous.

How could I be sure? Was this a doppelganger?

My Good Friend, if he was close by, was silent.

"Which pattern has your mother used to create several quilts?" I said aloud.

He stared at me, the ghost of his smile hesitating. "Irish Chain?" he said finally, his words a question.

That was a true answer. So unless something had been watching me a long time, and was a shapeshifter, this was probably Shaw.

I stepped closer. "Hello! What are you doing out on such a cold night?"

Shaw's face relaxed, his smile growing until I could actually see a flash of teeth. "I'm your postmaster." Touching the horn buttons on his deerskin coat, Shaw opened the top and pulled out a packet of something wrapped in oilcloth. "Cory gathered up everything for you, and then let me practice bringing things through a maze."

It was a good-sized bundle. I extended my hand, but he held on to it tightly. "It's bulky. Let me take it to the door for you."

Well, I wasn't sure. I wasn't supposed to go off the grounds. After that business with the door in the stables, would the Livingstons want to know about everyone who set foot on the property?

"Cory said that he would tell the Livingstons that I was coming," Shaw added, apparently sensing that I was concerned.

Well, someone could have told me, I thought, and then wondered how. How far could thoughts travel? Not from Marta's home to Hudson-on-the-Bend, and I was much farther away from them than that. I suppose you could say that The Cat had told me.

I looked down at The Cat. He ignored us both, scalloping against the leg of the unicorn in the arched back, twisty way that cats do, even as he was touching noses with—

"What is that?" I said, my words strangled.

It took everything I had not to jump back. The pale moonlight had bleached nearly everything in sight, but not the small creature exchanging greetings with The Cat. The animal glowed with its own swirling colors, flickering chicory blue and hints of purple coneflower. It was raccoon-shaped, a bit like a small cat or fox, with a white mask and a dark-and-white-striped tail. The body was very dark, and gleamed as if sunlight was making those gorgeous pale colors—like looking through a tiny rainbow.

"The smoke?" I added quickly, clutching Shaw's arm.

"That's what I was following," he said, setting his hand over mine. "I would have been here earlier, but I saw it, and I had to see if I could get closer. It's a *glenngarseea.*"

"A glen-gar-see-a?" I repeated, not using the Spanish lilt he gave to the word.

"If my *Denizens of the Night* is correct," was Shaw's answer. "You don't see them very often. Not a lot is known about them."

"It hides in smoke?" I asked, loosening my death grip on his arm.

"It's seen most often inside mazes and labyrinths. I was hoping to get a good look at it, so I followed it around."

"So you weren't following the unicorn?" I said, trying to sound normal. Even through two layers of cloth, Shaw's hand was very warm.

"Not at first. But I followed the *glenn* around a corner, and there was the unicorn. He seems to like you." Shaw smiled as he spoke.

I considered telling Shaw that I did not want to hear any unicorn jokes, but then he said: "He knows that you have a good heart. Someone who is pure of heart can always attract a unicorn."

I couldn't really complain about that.

"Have you ever seen a hag?" I blurted out.

Well, that was unexpected.

Seems I was more upset than I knew.

"Only a drawing of one. Why do you ask?" Shaw replied, so of course I had to tell him. When I started talking about green, slimy arms and water dripping on my ritual circle, Shaw actually interrupted. "Start at the beginning." He stepped to one side, moving along the path that separated the house from the formal gardens. I looked back. The unicorn, the *glenngarseea,* and the cat followed in a straight line.

We had our own parade.

I hoped no one was looking out at us.

I glanced up...dark outlines filled the windows.

Oh, well.

I began my story with entering the ritual chamber, and did not finish until I had tossed the last of the bloody water on the fire. Shaw's arm was rigid.

"He's not careful enough of you." There was no tone to Shaw's voice—no rise and fall of syllables at all.

"Oh, I don't think he would have let me get killed," I replied, trying to sound cheerful. Truth was, I might have gotten hurt. But Marta thought this was the fastest way for me to learn ritual protection. So here I would stay.

"But you could have been injured before he stopped the hag," was Shaw's answer. "I doubt he expected you to fight back. Might be he was waiting for you to scream, or break the circle."

"Break the circle?" I probably sounded like my Aunt Dagmar, she of the fancy airs and oh-so-proper behavior. Once you start a ritual, if you're going to break the circle, you might as well kill yourself right there.

All right, that is an exaggeration...but not much of an exaggeration. With a circle, your life might depend on being either inside it, or outside it. When you invited Death, you stayed *inside* the circle. Because who knew what else might show up?

"You could have called wind; you know how," he said, his voice suddenly very soft. Then, louder: "Remember that. Even inside. So you break a few windows. When your life is at stake, you do what is needed. You can earn the money to pay for windows."

"I'm going to really work hard on my Latin," I told him. "I want to learn as much as I can as fast as I can. So I can get back to Marta."

"If you need help, let me know. I'll come to you," Shaw said. "I am always near a labyrinth."

"Let's hope I don't need too much help! You need to do your own work, and there's medicine as well as magic to study, right?" I asked, looking up at him. He was actually taller than me now, by more than half a head.

Shaw smiled, faintly. "Yes. But I will always come. Allie, there's something that occurred to me that maybe Marta didn't think to tell you. Practitioners use wands when they do spells and most rituals. There are people with simple, strong elemental gifts, who can do things just with their hands. But most practitioners need their wands. You can get hurt with greater spells, using your hands."

So careful, his speech, as if our audience could hear us....

Wild magic.

I worked wild magic without a wand.

Hell, Hull and Halifax. I called Death without a wand. Marta let me do that!

Probably she did that to see if I *could* call Death without a wand. Everything a practitioner does has more than one meaning.

It doesn't matter if that practitioner is your teacher.

"I've already met a girl calling herself a salamander," I told him. "Some of the people here have very interesting gifts."

"Write Marta and Cory and tell them what this fellow starts teaching you," Shaw said. "I have a spell to show you, if he doesn't get around to it quickly. It's an Air spell, so you probably haven't had it yet."

"Which one?"

"How to wrap a spell within a spell. It's simple, and useful."

Useful for hiding things, I bet he meant. He might as well have said it aloud. Too late. I'd called Death without a wand; I'd already let Tonneman know that I was stronger than many who used magic.

I said very softly: "I just realized tonight that sometimes I can't grab a whirling wind to protect myself. I don't know this Eastern forest; for a moment I was frightened."

Shaw said, "Animals are similar all across the continent, whether a black bear or a brown one. Indians are different tribes, but alike in one thing—it's safest to assume they don't like colonists. You'll learn how to call wind up, although doing it from nothing is exhausting."

The last was emphasized. Shaw had called wind up from nothing. That meant he'd done a ritual for weather, for Cory....

"Maybe I'm finally getting scared about that test. Sometimes I get scared in little pieces," I admitted.

"Fear is a lot like courage. Sometimes you have to break it down into little pieces to swallow it," was his answer.

That sounded so sensible I felt myself grow calmer. The light from a lantern had appeared at my toes, and I looked up. We were almost to the kitchen door. I turned slightly, looking up at him.

"It's a little late to introduce myself tonight," Shaw said, "I'll come back another time and meet the Livingstons...and your cat. Without the unicorn and the *glenngarseea*," he added, glancing over his shoulder. The unicorn and the odd magical creature looked at us both. The cat promptly leaned into Shaw's leg.

"I'd like that," I blurted out. *I am such a ninny.* "I'll try to be braver."

"You're pretty brave right now," Shaw said, his smile wider as he turned toward me. I was on the house side, and had held on to his right arm as we walked. Now that we were facing each other, Shaw shifted to grip the letter packet in his right arm, and as he did so, he reached into his coat again.

I saw the handle of a wand.

I grew very still.

I'd missed something.

This *was* Shaw...but worrying about that, I'd missed something else. No point in reaching for my wand; I didn't know how to use it yet. But that breeze in the maze? That I could work with!

His grip on the wand was sure, ready to whip it out of his coat. I hoped he'd just drop the letters, and took a step back.

"You concern is gratifying, but unnecessary," came a male voice. "My presence here was to protect a student of Windward. I am no threat."

To the left stood a tall figure with white hair and a young face. The butler?

ELEVEN

"I know him as the butler," I said to Shaw while still watching the tall, elegant man in the voluminous, dark gray cloak. "He's in charge of the entire staff of the house. But they've been so busy testing me, no one has told me his name."

The man smiled slightly and bowed, the angle of his motion as spare as the movement of his lips. "There has been no need for you to know it, until it was certain that you would remain with us. I am called Kymric in this time and place."

Someone else had used those last words. Did folks ever use their real name here?

"So are you Welsh?" Shaw asked, his voice soft and his hand still on his wand.

"So many Celts came to America," was Kymric's reply. "They are the ones who go forth in search of new worlds to conquer."

"Did you follow me?" I asked, keeping my gaze upon him. I wanted his attention on my face, and not noticing that I was drawing a fingerful of power from the maze. "I know when a student leaves the building," was his answer. "I came to make sure that you were safe and not leaving the property."

My tone a bit sharp, I began: "I said that I would not use the maze again until the Livingstons gave me permission."

"The Livingstons should know of my coming," Shaw offered. "I am Shaw Kristinsson."

"Yes, we received a message from your mentor," Kymric replied.

"I can go speak with them now or I can introduce myself another time," Shaw went on. "I'd planned to leave Miss Sorensson's package with the staff, but she saw the maze awaken and came down to investigate."

"Yes," Kymric said, the word low and dry. "Perhaps, Miss Sorensson, you should seek reinforcements in the future before running out to greet maze visitors. Not all who walk the spirit tracks are friendly."

I exchanged glances with the unicorn. The Cat remained at Shaw's feet. Both ignored Kymric.

The *glenngarseea* was nowhere to be seen.

"And then there are wonders," Kymric went on, his voice softening. "I have never seen a unicorn. And to see a foal! We have been blessed."

Shaw glanced at the unicorn and said: "Time for us to go."

The foal stepped up to me and shoved his nose into my shoulder once more, nuzzling my ear. Then he turned and started back toward the maze.

Shaw finally handed me the oilcloth of letters. "Write back," he admonished me as he pressed something tiny into my hand.

"I will—to Marta, and Cory, too," I assured him, closing my fingers over what he gave me.

"Good. I'll see you soon, then." I could tell that he was reluctant to leave me with this strange man, but Shaw was not one to make a scene. He'd already said more than I was used to hearing from him.

Good heavens. We'd be speaking to each other like adults before you knew it.

I decided that the best plan was to walk straight to the kitchen door while Shaw was still close by. In the doorway I kicked the snow from my boots, watching the unicorn set foot upon the floor of the maze. The path began once more to glow as a wisp of dark smoke swirled around the foal's front hooves.

How did they find the door into this maze, from a world of choices?

Turns out I didn't need to dawdle. Kymric was also watching the unicorn, and he did not turn away from the maze until Shaw passed the bushes at the mouth of the path. The light still gleamed, and I knew that if I tried, I would hear the sound of the unicorn's hooves against stone.

A weight landed against my leg, followed by a chirp, and a trill.

"Best dry him off. Mrs. Gardener will not be pleased," Kymric pointed out.

"I'll get a towel," I said, pushing on the heavy wood door to open it.

&-*D*-&

No one asks questions when it's the butler who is escorting you.

Kymric left me at the staircase. When I finally reentered my room, the oilcloth package and a wet cat in my arms, only the fire-light greeted me. I had no memory of extinguishing the candle, and froze in horror at my transgression. Dear goddess, what if it had set something on fire instead of simply going out?

The candle in the center of my study table unexpectedly burst into flame. I approached it warily.

A small, smooth piece of blank paper sat next to the candlestick, a corner caught under the base. Words appeared on the paper, written in beautiful rounded script.

Never leave a candle unattended! Do not put extra stress on the wick spells! If you continue to forget, you will be required to purchase a glass chimney to protect the flame. A first offense is five demerits.

Thank you for your attention.

Good evening.

It was signed *Miss Crowley.*

So. The mysterious senior who kept an eye on the younger senior girls had finally surfaced. She was rightly concerned about the candle.

I didn't know if she would return again, and I already had enough trouble on my plate.

Tomorrow was soon enough to read about unicorns and *glenngarseeas,* much less my letters. A long day beckoned...

I could not resist opening the oil cloth. Hand-folded envelopes spilled out—from Marta, from my parents, from Cory, from Shaw, from Felicity Hudson, from Jeanette and Matthew Hudson, from Idelia... I had a *lot* of letters to write.

I'd forgotten to tell Shaw about the biscuits.

At least I had something to write about.

"*Chirp!*" said The Cat.

"I don't know if you're allowed to stay inside or not," I told him. "But if you do your business in here, you'll be a barn cat the rest of your life."

The Cat purred.

"This is important, Cat. I cannot convince the maids that you are harmless if you misbehave. *Someone* has to follow some rules around here."

I reached into my pocket and pulled out what Shaw had given me. It was a tiny silver coin, smaller than my thumbnail. It looked very ordinary...too ordinary. It was just a little bit too shiny for a coin given in passing.

I wondered what would happen if I threw it.

❧·🌀·❧

In the middle of a crazy quilt of dreams, one stood out starkly. It was twilight; soft, high clouds dappled like fish scales still held the rosy tint from the fallen sun. Shadows loomed around me, for I was in high, rocky mountains, though I had never seen such a place in real life. I climbed among boulders, some larger than my parents' home. As I stepped around a sheer slice of stone, along a narrow corner, I stopped, the path blocked before me. Beyond arm's length a dark mass radiated heat, hidden in the gloom, as if a mountain had belched forth molten rock, now cooling into new land.

Two slits of glowing fire appeared and then widened, like cracks in scorched summer soil.

I smelled sulfur, a cross between strong garlic and rotting eggs. *But I don't smell in dreams, the unicorns were not a dream...*

Are you going to keep our secret? said a voice inside my head. The sound was deep and very, very low, as if a bass singer in the church choir suddenly had a line of scripture to recite.

"I don't know your secrets," I replied.

Yes, you do. Perhaps you do not yet see clearly.

The slits moved...rose into the air. Slowly, like some strange, burning bird, its wings streamlined, the lines of fire hovered above me.

My mouth was as dry as fragments of ancient paper.

Warmth blew over me, a sulfurous gust strong enough to stir my hair and move my skirt.

I had a bad feeling about this.

The glowing slits were widening, becoming more oval, as I craned my neck to see them.

Flame erupted beneath the slits, and I knew that I was looking at the eyes of a dragon...at only part of a dragon. They were never totally in this world in this form, I'd heard. This one was black as mourning, its scales sleek and pieced like a mosaic.

It would be better if you keep our secrets, the creature told me. *Better for all.*

And then it winked at me.

※ ☞ ※

With a gasp I sat upright in bed.

I could still smell the sharp, pure scent of sulfur, as if my mother was burning some to fumigate the house.

Would it be safe to tell anyone about this?

Maybe not.

※ ☞ ※

The boot-boy had staked out a corner of the drying room, away from where sheets and clothing hung dripping. He looked very competent for someone younger than me; his strokes on the napped leather boot were swift and sure, the rag in his hand a spotless white. I'd say he looked Dutch. His fair hair was almost white and his eyes, when he lifted his gaze away from his work, were the color of a morning winter sky.

"How do you get napped leather so clean?" I asked, after waiting politely for him to notice me.

Startled, the boy glanced up at me, and then blushed. "It's a secret, miss," he replied softly. "My Da has things he makes." Then he said: "It's called suede, miss, when leather is napped."

"Is it? Thank you for telling me. You're John, aren't you?"

"Yes, miss, I'm Jan." He pronounced the J more like a Y.

"I am...Miss Sorensson," I started, remembering that I was now a teacher, at least some of the time. "I wanted to thank you for cleaning my boots this past weekend."

"That's why I'm here, miss," he replied, giving the boot a last pass and setting it down carefully on a varnished bench to his right. Then he picked up a dirty boot. "I do all the footwear for the household and the staff. Also some of the students."

"I'm both a teacher and a student," I said. "I need to know if I owe you payment for cleaning the boots."

The boy seemed to suppress a sigh. "I don't charge the teachers, miss. Sometimes the professors give me a bit, for my materials."

"Well, I should also give you a bit, but I don't have coin." Not that I felt I could spend for a service I had not contracted for, anyway. "I'm paid in my classes. Can I give you something else for your time? Some mending, some cooking?"

"What do you teach, miss?" he asked, glancing sideways.

"I teach the youngest students about herbs," I told him, as if I'd been doing it for an age. My first class would come at the end of today, and I was trying hard not to be nervous.

"Herbs?" He sat up straighter. "You teach one of the herb classes? Can you make something for upset stomachs?"

"I can. What's upset your stomach?"

He shook his head. "It's not for me. My older sister has been feeling poorly. I'd like something for her. Her husband, he's a good fellow, but he's only a journeyman. He doesn't make much money."

"All right, I can do that," I said, wondering when I could start my own plants here. I was going to need them. Could I grow them next to my own window, or would Cousin Esme let me have a row in a greenhouse somewhere? "So, what's causing your sister to have an upset stomach? Is she sick with something else? Did she get some bad food?"

"Not sure exactly what it is, miss," he said, his hands quickly smoothing the second black suede boot. "Ever since she started increasing, she—"

"Hold," I said. "Has she told the midwife that she's feeling poorly?"

"Don't know if she has a midwife, miss. Aalt might not go see a midwife until it's time for the baby to come. She's still doing her work, my sister...she just seems tired, and doesn't want to eat."

This was hard. I couldn't give something to this boy for his sister without knowing how far along she was in her pregnancy.

"How long has she been increasing, Jan?" I asked, trying to say his name as he did. "When is the baby due?"

Frowning, Jan paused in his brushing, and the color in his face bloomed again. "I don't know how long, miss. They said the baby was due come Michaelmas Day, but it's her first."

September 29th. That could be the due date, or could be past the date, since it was her first. Most first babies were late, as the woman's body learned what it was supposed to do. Either way, Aalt was early on with this pregnancy, and should not have red raspberry leaf in a tea yet.

But a nice peppermint leaf and ginger root tea? That I could do. It would be a good mixture to show the children early on. I'd already decided to start with a version of my mother's first lesson to me, recognizing Queen Anne's lace from among more dangerous plants. Then we'd work our way into things we could do with peppermint, and finally I'd teach how it grew, how to encourage it—basics that could be shared with other herbs.

"I'll mix up a tea for her, Jan," I said. "I'll need to get permission to set up my own herbs, but with luck I'll have something for her before church on Sunday."

"That would be more than fair trade for your boots, miss," he replied, ducking his head. "I'll owe you a few more cleanings for it!"

"Well, knowing me, I'll need them," I said. "You kept that mess from staining, and I appreciate it." I wasn't positive what he'd used, but I was sure I smelled mink oil around my sheepskin boots.

Well, it was a secret, so I wasn't going to find out today, if ever.

"Thank you, Jan." I nodded my head and started for the dining room. I still had time for some breakfast, and brunch was much too far away.

❧·ⅅ·❧

It turned out that the herb class was designed a lot like Cousin Esme's sanctuary. Slate flooring supported open shelves rising above my head, as in a potter's green room. Here individual student desks reigned, like the one I had sat in to take my tests.

I was grateful for those single desks. If the boys had to reach to smack each other on the back of the head, at least I had a fighting chance of spotting them and separating them.

Two fireplaces warmed the huge space, one at the far end, where decocting and infusing was done, and one at the long side, shared with another chamber. It was a deep fire pit, however, and between that and the roar of the flames, we did not hear the other group. Several large tables with chairs completed the mixing area.

This room had several slates mounted on oak legs, like Cousin Esme's board. My plan was to use long, thin bandages across each corner to tie my great-grandmother's drawings upright. It worked better than I had thought it would, holding the pictures without damaging them. I placed the drawings so that the names of the plants were hidden. Then I closed up my herbal journal to protect the other drawings and found a long stick with a sharpened point and rubber wrapped around the grip.

I'd put on my mother's older green dress. Working with herbs, I didn't want one of the nice dresses. I smoothed my face, because you can't smile for the first month of classes, or the students might run roughshod over you. Then I braced myself for the arrival of my class of eight.

It turned out that I had met three of them. There was tiny Moira O'Donnell, all flaming hair and huge blue eyes, and Daniel Williams, Cathrin's brother. The third student I recognized was "Mr. Smith," the boy who had created the biscuits with teeth. The other five, two girls and three boys, were new to me, though I had seen them in the dining room.

"Welcome to Herbalism," I announced. "I am Miss Sorensson. As we don't know each other yet, I would like you to identify yourselves before you first speak. We're going to start right up here with these herbs. I'd like you to come up and tell me what they are."

Well, I got lucky: in a ragged chorus of voices, mixed with hands up in the air, I heard half a dozen different answers, including two correct ones.

Excellent.

"Everyone sit down, now, and we will talk about it," I said, moving to the blank slate board and picking up some chalk. "Now, Mr. Williams, you said 'Queen Anne's lace'. Which plant is Queen Anne's lace?"

"Ah...all of them?" he suggested.

I wrote the answer down on the board. "Anyone else? Hands please. If you shout I can't hear anyone."

And so it went. I soon had a good-sized list on the vertical slate, ranging from Daniel's guess of "all of them" to a boy who recognized cow parsnip, although he insisted the drawings were wrong because cow parsnip flowers always had a lavender tinge. The herb Angelica cropped up, too.

Moira O'Donnell, the smallest and also the youngest, was actually the closest to a correct answer. "The third one is the Queen," she said. "I don't know what the other ones are."

This provoked a brief skirmish about whether the queen had a single drop of red or purple in its flower petals – or no color at all.

"Miss Sorensson, does the Queen have any color, or is it just white? Is the color red or purple?" Jane Adams asked, her strong, sharp nose and cheekbones and black curls making her look like a foreign princess—which I did not think she was, but at Windward, you could never be sure.

I considered her question, and answered: "Yes."

They all looked puzzled.

"The queen can have a red dot, or a purple dot, or no dot at all."

Several groans and one "Oh, no!" were my reward.

"Now, we have some strong opinions here. My next question for you is this—how sure are you about your answer? Sure enough to eat the roots of the plant you have chosen?"

Silence. One young man's hand moved toward his books, and I said: "I do not want Anathema Nightroad's opinion about these plants, Mr. Evanston. I want yours."

Finally Mr. Ian Riley, the oldest in the class and almost as new to Windward as I was, said: "You're not going to feed us those plants, are you?"

"No."

"Then I don't know which one is the queen, although I suspect that one of them is. You don't look like a person who enjoys the game of asking for something that is not there."

"Mr. Riley changes his vote to 'I don't know,'" I said briskly, writing it on the slate. *A suspicious sort, are we, Mr. Riley?*

The verbal wrestling match went on for a while, and as it briefly died down, I said: "I think it's time to tell you the answer." Using the pointer, I touched the third of the drawings. "This is the queen." Moira clapped her hands together in delight, while several other students looked disappointed. "Now you may take your herbals and search through them for the other herbs. You may come up to the drawings to look again, if you wish. No helping each other with this, and please do not touch the drawings!"

Soon they were all at the board, heads bent over their huge herbals or, in Moira's case, on tiptoe to see a detail about a plant. I studied them all, different in height and build, some of them confident, others shy. It was good to see them all at the board. At least for now, I had their attention.

"Fool's parsley is also called dog poison? One of these is *poisonous*?" a boy exclaimed loudly.

"Not just that one," Daniel muttered, and then clamped his hand over his mouth.

When I finally got them to talk about what they had learned today, it was plain that they were very excited about learning what hemlock looked like, and that cow parsnip could be white or lavender.

It took a while to get them thinking on a larger scale.

We were out of time. I asked: "Which of the Rules of Magic sums up what we have talked about today?"

The closest fire crackled and gave a pop, as it rushed through a drop of resin. The two older girls looked at each other.

"'It is not what we do not know that is dangerous; it is what we do not realize that we do not know that is dangerous,'" Daniel Williams said clearly.

"Or, more simply, 'You may not realize how much you *don't* know.' Thank you, Mr. Williams—that was my meaning. Learning potions of any kind is the other side of learning Latin. If you use the wrong word in a spell, you may endanger your own life. If you use the wrong herb, you may injure or kill a patient. This is a powerful art, ladies and gentlemen. I trust you will treat it with respect. Tonight, look closely at these four plants. Compare their differences and similarities. Tomorrow we will draw peppermint from a living plant, and I will show you the difference between a tea made from fresh ingredients and one made from dried ones. Remember to bring your colored pencils!"

The sound of scraping chairs came through the fire pit from the other class. "And you are excused for today."

They rushed from the room like a wave, sweeping out the door. I leaned back against the solid teacher's desk and sighed. And I thought Latin was going to be the biggest challenge! Even doing that ritual wasn't as hard as keeping the attention of eight children for an hour.

And they wanted to be there...at least I thought they wanted to be there. If the worst that would happen was Mr. Riley constantly arguing with me, I would be fortunate.

Being the adult was hard.

༈·ⅅ·༈

People tell stories of the terror of being in a dark vegetable cellar. Our cold storage areas were always shallow things, scarcely as tall as my mother, and not too deep. I had wondered why people had a problem with them; just leave the doors open, and go down during the day.

Then I saw what a cellar *could* look like.

Saturday approached: the day for my punishment, and Margaret's. We would have to cook. Mrs. Gardener showed us what we could use.

The cellar of Windward was larger than the kitchen and service wing above it, spreading back like a spider's legs in every possible direction. There was even a passage that led to the river, Mrs. Gardener informed us, but that was an exit only. Spells prevented anyone from entering the house through that opening.

No windows, even tiny ones, let light into the cellar. Deck prisms hid in the ceiling, like in Cousin Esme's herb solar, beautiful carved pieces of glass with flat tops and fat, turnip-shaped bottoms that were part of the passageways above, reflecting light into the cellar below.

Before a winter's dawn, however, those prisms were useless. We depended on the footman, Roger, who carried a lantern down a staircase twice the height of a man, and waited at the bottom until we had all safely descended. Mrs. Gardener knew the way, and moved with the surety of a boat in its own harbor. Margaret and I, however, had our skirts to manage on a strange ladder, plus Margaret had brought hard charcoal and writing paper.

I hated skirts. They were designed to make women useless.

The cellars were dark, the walls stone, the ceiling barely taller than Roger. Here I saw the only cobwebs allowed to stand at Windward. "Spiders are our friends, you know," Mrs. Gardener confided as she walked. "They catch tiny insects that might threaten our vegetables and grain."

True enough. But I hated brushing through a web. It took forever to remove the clinging strands from my hair and clothing.

The passageway was fairly narrow—our dresses could catch at any point—and the stone lining the walk was cold through my thin leather slippers. Raw wood shelves and bins, some with the bark still peeling from their edges, held everything needed by a busy household. Containers of vegetables and apples, sacks of grain and

of dried beans, cones of sugar, dried herbs, barrels of fresh eggs pre-
served in salt...almost anything we'd want, except the meat, which
hung in a smokehouse outside.

Several bins glowed. I wanted to ask about that, but decided it
was not the time.

"As you can see, Miss Sorensson, we have plenty of apples. You
are welcome to use as many as you need." She gestured into a small
room off to one side. I ducked in, and the footman held the lamp
higher so I had a tiny gleam of light.

I saw at least three kinds of apples, maybe more. I took one of
each variety, placing them in the pocket of the apron I had tied on
after dressing that morning.

"We can taste them and decide which for the breakfast bread,
and if we want a cobbler for dinner," I said to Margaret.

"All of those are good cooking apples. They hold their shape,"
Mrs. Gardener said, reaching past me and into a bin immediately
to the right of the entrance. "This is a good sauce apple. You might
want some in your cobbler." She handed me a firm green apple with
red stripes. "That's a Northern Spy, that is. It is a new apple in these
parts. You may use up the Rhode Island Greenings, that greenish-
red round one you took. They won't keep much longer; they're at
the end of their life. It's a good, tart cooking apple, those Rhode Island Greenlings. That orange-colored one is a Blenheim Orange.
Doctor Livingston brought that sapling from Blenheim itself, when
they first planted the orchard. Nice, nutty flavor to those. We spell
the lot of them, so they keep longer."

I smiled at the orange apple I held in my hand, wanting to bite
into it right away. I had a feeling that Mrs. Gardener was enjoying
this trip a little too much. Margaret and I did need to eat something
before our first classes.

"Mrs. Gardener, we can't take up your entire morning. Is there
anything in the cellar that we should not use? That you have plans
for?" I asked as I placed the Blenheim Orange into the apron pocket.

"Well," she started, walking back into still another cellar room.
"I would not want you to *use up* anything—except the Rhode Island Greenings. You may use them all. You girls are the first to have
the sense to plan a menu. If you would like, I will look at it before
Saturday."

"I am not sure that we can decide on the menu until Friday night," I said quickly. "We won't know how many hands we have to help until then."

"Well, you already have eight, I can tell you," she said, smiling at us both. "Three of them are young ones, but if you handle them well, they will make themselves useful. Just don't let James Smith wave that wand of his around!"

"I will teach him how to make biscuits without magic," I replied, gently touching Margaret's back as I urged her to turn around.

"Good. I've been itching to have cooking classes, but part of the punishment is to remind them that they don't know everything. Still, it's such a waste of food," Mrs. Gardener said mournfully.

"My mother used to say after a cooking lesson 'That is what the pigs are for,'" Margaret offered.

This idea tickled Mrs. Gardener so much that she burst out laughing. Her response gave me time to capture Roger the footman's attention and start shepherding folk back to the stairs.

"The meat?" I went on.

"No pork on Saturday. If you want beef for stews, I will have the meat brought in on Friday for you," she answered, starting up the long staircase. "We are low on venison right now, so don't use any venison. No roast beef or veal, mind. That's for special occasions."

"Yes, ma'am," I said.

"The salt and pepper?" Margaret asked, and then she and Mrs. Gardener went ahead into the kitchen.

"And how was your first day?" came Cousin Esme's voice behind me.

I tried not to leap into the air, but I suspected she knew I was startled. Facing her, I said: "Good. I kept order in my classroom, and no one was rude."

"They are only rude the first day if they sense weakness," my cousin said, smiling faintly. "There are those on the staff who love gossip. Word of your adventure with a hag got out. Right now I imagine that those most likely to cause trouble know that they are only a few demerits away from being sent down. So they would not intentionally provoke you."

"Sent down where?"

Cousin Esme's smile grew broader. "It means sent back home for the rest of the term. It is a severe punishment, but not as severe as expulsion, when a student is asked to leave and cannot return."

"Where does kitchen duty stand on the scale?" I decided to ask.

"About two-thirds of the way to being sent down," she replied. "So anyone already on the kitchen list will be unlikely to push you this week. Serving kitchen duty wipes out that punishment, so next week, they will have a clean slate!" My cousin paused, and then gestured for me to walk with her. We headed toward the kitchen door. "Alfreda, I must explain something to you," she started quietly, and then raised her voice: "Mrs. Gardener, I am taking Miss Sorensson to my office!"

In moments we were safely tucked into Cousin Esme's sitting room. The fire burned cheerfully, and a pot of tea waited on her tea tray, as well as a dome over a platter, promising some breakfast.

Mmmm. Perhaps even scones?

"I did not want to warn you up front, because I wanted to know what your natural instincts for teaching were," she began, indicating with a lift of her hand that I should pour the tea. "I have placed the most difficult of the youngest students into your herbal class."

I paused in mid-pour, looking up at her.

"They are not a gang of rogues, so do not worry," she went on, lifting the silver dome to expose a pile of warm scones. "If anything, most of them prefer their solitude. But they have problems working within a group. Sometimes it is temper, sometimes it is awkwardness, and other times it is problems stemming from their situations at home. They need patience and a non-threatening class where they can begin to excel. I think that class can be your class. The introductory classes are taught with both boys and girls attending. The advanced classes are segregated by sex, to encourage students' attention on learning and not upon each other."

I handed her a cup, having noticed that my cousin also took her tea without cream or sugar.

"How can I know how to discipline them? No one has explained the system of awards and penalties to me," I said slowly, waiting for her to take her first scone.

"The system is simple. One, five and ten are the numbers, and you are giving merits or demerits. The most common award or punishment is one, and many students never receive either. They may not excel in a manner that gains extra praise, but they also are not punished for infractions. Five is for when the professor or senior boy or girl is extremely displeased, and ten is vast pleasure or displeasure. I suggest you only give out ones because it is safer," she added, her tone serious. "No one can accuse you of favoritism or dislike if you award and penalize in ones. Turn in your sheet of awards or demerits to me in the evening."

"I haven't even met Miss Crowley yet, and she's already very displeased with me," I admitted, taking a roll. It smelled like a cream scone!

"I heard," my cousin said, her voice amused. She sipped her tea. "It involved fire, so I am inclined to let the statement stand. But as it is my school, you will not get sent down this week for things you do not know.

"I pointed this out to Miss Crowley, and she agreed that, owing to her own severe cold, and the fact that we have no student instruction book, it was unfair of her to presume disobedience. In fact," Cousin Esme went on, smiling, "I have suggested that she consider making a small book for new students to read, so that all the rules shall be known. That type of project pleases her. She *will* come to explain the floor rules to you, however, and may ask you to review her book, once it exists, to see if the instructions are clear."

"I would be happy to help her with that project. Although at this rate I will not be sleeping enough hours the next few months. I thought a farm was a busy place, but a school swirls like the butter in a churn," I told her.

"Yes, it is a very busy place, is it not? The most important thing is your ritual and Latin training, of course. But the other classes will be useful to you, and your teaching this class will be very useful to me. I appreciate your willingness to take up the challenge." She placed some clotted cream on her scone, and then continued: "I might have one more small project for you, later this month."

I gave Cousin Esme my best "interested but not too forward" look.

She was not looking at me. The smile changed slightly...it held both thoughtfulness and calculation. Her gaze was on her scone. "Let us see how the weekend progresses."

Of course.

Even punishment was a kind of test.

ॐ·ⅅ·ॐ

"In conclusion, the major purpose of ritual in the life of a practitioner is safety. As you rise in the ranks of spell casters, the intricacy of the spells you learn will increase. The number of safeguards will also increase in number, and to omit any of the precautions is to court disaster. You have no doubt heard stories of what happens to practitioners when a step in a spell is overlooked." Professor Tonneman paused a moment, his gaze moving toward the large window in our small classroom. "Believe them. Few of them are an exaggeration."

The room was cozy, and quite similar to Professor Shipley's class layout. Here I sat among my herbal students, all eight of them, as well as one more person, Miss Wolfsson, the plump blonde girl I had met in the dining room my first morning. Miss Wolfsson and Mr. Riley were the ones closest in age to me. All the others were around Daniel William's age, ten years or so.

It was our first class together, and I caught myself wondering what tests the others had endured. Our instruction was going to be closely watched; when we had "laboratory" upstairs in the dome, Professor Tonneman would have the assistance of Mr. St. John, an older student. I recognized St. John when he smiled. His dark hair and blue eyes framed pleasant, forgettable features, but when he smiled, he held your attention. It was like the approval of the world was offered to you.

I knew St. John only as one of the boys who watched Margaret when she was unaware of his presence. I recognized him as someone who was always in the hallway when we were traveling to our classes.

"Always" was too often for coincidence.

Margaret also snuck glances back at him. She didn't look back at any of the other young men.

"When considering the elements, which basic control would you think should be mastered first?" he asked the group at large as he paced before the desks.

Silence. Then several hands crept up into the air, arms straightening. "Mr. Riley?"

"Lighting a flame," he said briefly.

"You suggest that fire is the most useful," the professor continued. "How would you teach that in its simplest form?"

Well, most everyone stared back at him. Weren't we there for exactly that reason, to learn the rituals?

Finally I raised my hand. He stopped pacing and nodded at me.

"Lighting a candle?" I asked.

"You are not certain?" was Tonneman's reply.

"Well, you would need to keep the fire confined, limited to a specific fuel," I replied. "So a candle makes sense. Also, it can be small and quite portable. You could tuck it into a tool kit."

"As thieves are prone to do," Professor Tonneman went on. "Would you choose fire for your first ritual spell, Miss Sorensson?"

"No." I waited to see if he would ask others his next question, but he kept looking at me, so I added: "I would want to learn how to pull water from the air."

"Indeed. Why water before fire?"

"Because there are lots of ways to keep yourself warm in an emergency, but only liquids can slake your thirst. Water can be just as much a weapon, if needed, when used well. And you never want to be caught short of water when creating a ritual circle. Knowing how to pull water from the air might save you a lot of trouble and even pain." Remembering that hag, I suppressed a shudder. I'd had enough water that time. I never wanted to run a risk of being without it.

"Pain?" Mr. Riley leaned forward on his desk, frowning at me. "Embarrassment, perhaps, but pain? That seems an exaggeration."

"You find her example fanciful, Mr. Riley?" the professor asked.

"It seems like a description from a Gothic novel," Riley said abruptly, leaning back in his chair.

What was a Gothic novel? Was it a story that had Gothic cathedrals in it?

"Miss Sorensson," Professor Tonneman said, beginning to pace again. "When you suggest pain as a result of a ritual, are you speaking of adding a drop of blood to your water before drawing your circle?"

"No, sir. I was thinking that if you were under attack while drawing a circle, you might have to cut a vein to get enough blood to finish the ritual."

Mr. Riley snorted, and I nearly glared at him. But Professor Tonneman had stopped pacing again and was looking at me, so I resisted the temptation.

"Have you ever had to cut yourself to finish a ritual?" he asked me.

"Not yet. But I've had to re-open a cut each time I filled a cup with snow to get enough water to finish a circle. It was not pleasant. Learning how to pull water might keep me from ever having to slash myself."

"Indeed," Tonneman said. "You are constantly resourceful, Miss Sorensson. I think we will start with water, and progress from there into fire. Just to prevent you from opening any veins."

He wasn't quite making fun of me, and I got my wish.

Good enough.

And I now knew that Mr. Riley was going to require detailed explanations in herb class.

Forewarned is forearmed.

⁂

"Visualization and limitation, visualization and limitation," I muttered to myself as I made my way down the back hall to the door near the kitchen. The afternoon ritual laboratory class was going to be outside, to help the students get a feel for the procedure. The first step was grounding, and apparently most of the youngsters didn't have grounding down pat. I no longer had trouble grounding, even when upstairs in a building. The tile pipes for the necessaries at Windward made a straight line to the ground, which helped me find rock in a hurry. So I was going to jump straight to drawing water.

Now if I could only make the water spell work. "See what you want to happen, then narrow your vision to only that reality," I muttered, ignoring a footman, one of those well-dressed, good-looking fellows who worked under Kymric. The dark-haired young man kept his gaze straight ahead as he paused to let me walk past him.

With small spells, the ritual is the grounding and focusing through a wand. That provides both the limitation and protection a circle can give you. I remembered my aunt's traveling wards that we made one morning. Could I set up a circle that protected me from basic dangers? And carry it like piece of jewelry, or a parasol?

Sometimes you couldn't be safe. But I seemed to run into all sorts of odd dangers, so I wanted to take every precaution I could. Then I would never have to reproach myself for being careless with my life or safety.

Cold air hit me like a down pillow as I left the house, large flakes of snow settling on my shoulders. My language classes had gone by in a blur. When I went back to change clothes for ritual, I put on my oldest dress and my boots, with my brother's trousers on underneath. This way I was warm and my feet would stay dry no matter what happened while we practiced.

I was going to need to designate another dress as "old enough for herbs and for burning things." Maybe my old grey dress....

My fellow ritual students were only a few feet down the path, already passing their wands over wooden goblets and murmuring aloud. There were several ways to do this spell, apparently, and most of what I heard suggested that the class was approaching the problem by using their wands and the cups as links to themselves.

Several struggled with the grounding part, since nothing was happening. I heard someone muttering "*influo*," flow in, and then I heard Mr. Smith demand: "*Flue!*"

It was so broad a command that I inhaled sharply, wondering if the blood in his veins would begin racing. But no, apparently he had a handle on the visualization part, because water spurted out of his wand like the flow of a downspout. The glittering, icy fluid swooped into the cup and back out again, spraying Mr. Smith and the snow bank around him with a film of water that immediately turned to ice.

He got the water to come to him in a flow, all right.

He looked as beautiful as a forest after an ice storm, the red in his dark hair glinting like the flash of a cardinal deep in the trees.

I stepped slowly on the thin ice past Mr. Smith, watching Mr. St. John hold his own hands above Mr. Smith's wet coat to help it dry.

That appeared to be a useful spell. I wondered when I would learn it?

Hannah Wolfsson gently moved her wand tip around the rim of a wooden goblet. Each time she finished, a ring of ice broke free of the small vessel and fell to her feet. Once, the ice formed over the outside of the goblet, and the ring fell around her wrist like a bracelet.

Mr. St. John was there to help the class. He made us split up, spreading us out like a string of beads from the main building almost to the carriage house. Each had a wooden goblet. I could see why. A goblet was easier to hang onto, and wood was less likely to break.

So far only Miss Wolfsson and Mr. Riley seemed to be having any luck. Mr. Riley's wand dripped water into his cup. Perspiration ran down the side of his face as he worked. At least I thought it was perspiration. If it wasn't, did it mean that the spell was backing up into his body?

That didn't sound good.

Professor Tonneman was talking about grounding, trying to get the others in position to make an attempt. He strode about as usual, wearing a long black greatcoat and his riding boots, a hat of sable fur upon his head.

I took up a goblet, found a spot away from the group, and stomped the fluffy snow down to make a nice circle to stand on. I shut out his voice and the other students' soft comments or complaints or questions and stared at the goblet's lip.

The rock beneath me took care of anchoring. In fact, I was so anchored that I wondered if I could pull water up through the Earth.

Maybe. But that wasn't the lesson.

Visualization and limitation. Only the rim should produce water, and not until my wand touched it. I imagined the rim of the cup weeping like an eye, and tears swiftly trickling down the inside to fill the goblet. Marta had not simply waved her wand to make water appear; she had rimmed the glass as she walked the circle, as if inhaling all the extra moisture in the air above. So I would do. Snow would no longer fall upon me, because I needed water, not snow. The snow would become my water, pulled right from the air.

Taking out my lovely wand of golden oak, I touched the tip to the open edge of the goblet. Then I traced the smooth wooden lip, imagining water flowing from the wand into the cup. I had seen water rush down into a gopher hole during a spring flood. It had swirled in a spiral. That's what I wanted here, a smooth, swift appearance of water. I could wring the water from the air, like drawing from a cloud to make a waterspout.

Aqua, afflue ad me. Water, flow to me.

Not wild magic, grabbing a handful of power and trying to force a cloud to do my bidding. This was coaxing the water from the air, from the snow...from whatever held more than it needed.

I did feel warmer. I didn't need all that heat in me, but trying to suppress it seemed to slow the process. So I let the heat trickle into the cup as a thin sheet of water ran down the insides, raising the water level within the goblet. Soon I had a full container of water, and I was only a tiny bit tired.

"How are you doing, Miss Soren—ah. Very good. That's one way to dissipate the heat," Mr. St. John said, coming up next to my side. "You've done this before?"

"No. But I know how to ground," I murmured, reaching to put my hand above the goblet.

"Wait!"

I halted short of the vapor, my hand just beginning to open.

"Sometimes the water becomes very hot, hot enough for the steam to burn you. You are aware that can happen?"

I looked at him. Did he think I was a baby? Of course I knew steam could burn you—blister you—and so far in life I'd escaped with only a reddening of my skin. "How else do you get rid of the heat, if you don't want hot water?" I asked. "I didn't think the heat should be left in me."

"No, only Fire mages easily contain the heat. The rest of us direct it somewhere else. You can push it into the air around you," he explained, holding up a goblet to demonstrate. "You'll want to push the energy out through your feet if you can. Heat rises, so this will give you warmth rising around you. To rid yourself of it in a hurry, you can let it flow out of your head."

"That's where body heat usually leaves," I said, watching his goblet fill with water as a soft puff of warm air rose from the ground around us. The weird thing was, the snow under his feet was still there, if a little softer.

St. John used the same motion we all were attempting, sliding the tip of his dark wand around the lip of the goblet.

I said, "Can you just point your wand at the cup and have water flow out as if at a pump? Is that what Mr. Riley is trying?"

"Yes, it is possible. But think of it...eight or nine people trying that at once. The air would become so dry so swiftly that one of us might have a nosebleed!" St. John smiled as he said the words.

I considered it. "Is that how the fire spell works, then? You pull energy from the air around you, and the heat coming from the tip of the wand warms up water, or lights something that burns easily, like paper or a wick?" Glancing around at the other students, I said: "You never start with fire, do you? It would be too dangerous in this group."

St. John's smile was less broad, more relaxed. "Miss Rutledge said you missed little. No, beginners start with earth or water. There's plenty of challenge, but less chance of a catastrophe."

I nodded my agreement as I tried to reverse what I had just done, and cause the water to return slowly to the air. Pulling the moisture out of the water, turning it into vapor so it would dissipate into the air…. *Flamma*, I whispered in my mind.

First the steam increased, white clouds rising from the container. Then the rim of the goblet burst into flames.

TWELVE

"Snowbank!" St. John yelled, his wand flicking up like a pointer. *"Cantamen dissolvatur!"*

Abruptly I heard popping noises around me as ice shattered and water puffed into showers of snow.

I upended the goblet, dropping it rim-down into the pristine snow to my right. An explosive hissing sound assured me that the flames were extinguished. The container continued sinking into the surface of the snowbank, the hot water dissolving the snow cover and heading downhill, finally freezing into a long tongue of ice.

St. John laughed and reached to pick up the container. "Well, now we have one with a fire-hardened lip!" he said cheerfully.

I stared at the hole in the blanket of snow.

It was a good thing I didn't know how to disappear, because I might have never come back.

So much for the control Marta had tried to teach me. I felt tired and very foolish.

St. John touched my shoulder, and I looked up at him. His grin had faded to a faint smile. "Don't be upset, Miss Sorensson. It's a common mistake. You'll just back up to water, and we'll work with it until you feel comfortable."

"Speed comes with practice," Professor Tonneman said as he walked up to us. "I know that it appears as if you should be able merely to reverse the process of drawing down water, but water is keenly affected by temperature, and its form is dictated by how cold or warm the air may be. Do you have any room in your schedule for her, Sinjin?"

I wasn't sure what he was saying, but St. John answered: "I can slide her in to tomorrow's schedule." He said to me, "Perhaps after your classes but before First Herbal?"

"Yes—yes, I can come then. Where should we meet?" I asked, hope smothering my embarrassment.

"Let us remain outside for another lesson or two," St. John said, his expression thoughtful. "Then we can look for available time in the dome."

Well, all right. But I wasn't sure I cared at all for that dome place.

"In the meantime, try it again," he said, handing the wooden goblet back to me. "Fill it slowly. If you work too quickly at this stage, you'll tire yourself out and have no energy for study tonight."

That confirmed it. St. John was now more teacher than student.

"You said something when you told me to toss the cup," I started slowly. "Cahn TAH mehn...?"

"*Cantamen dissolvatur*—let the enchantment be dissolved," St. John said. "Spoken with authority and power, those words break every spell within the sound of your voice. So they must be used carefully. Without focus you could disrupt a school or practitioner's homestead!"

Yes. I could see that.

But it was good to know that there were words for an emergency.

I studied the container in my gloved hand. The white oak goblet now had a dark rim, as if it had been purposefully singed for decoration.

I would think of it as a focus point.

Raising my wand, I began again.

࿔·🝱·࿔

"This tea is strong!" Moira said, setting the mug down on her student table with a thump. "The ginger makes it taste spicy!"

Jane Adams reached with delicate fingers for the mug, which Moira gave up without a fuss. I handed another cup of my brew to the boys to sample from as I poured the balance of the decoction into a pottery jug Cousin Esme had given me. The boys' attention shifted to Mr. Riley. Where his opinion led, they would follow.

"Much stronger than the dried version," Mr. Riley remarked, sipping first the tea made from dried herbs and then the fresh one we'd just finished. "I could see having a cup of the dried tea to settle your stomach after eating too much on a holiday. But this fresh one is so strong, I'd think that only a swig or two would be necessary!"

"You can add the decoction to boiling water, and thin it to have more of a tea," I pointed out. "That works well for patients you can trust to follow directions. But sometimes you have someone who always forgets your instructions, or loses them when you write them out. That's when you make the tea as dilute as you can yet still have it help your patient. People have to work hard at drinking too much of a thin medicinal tea. After a long day of work, they'll be tired, and they may get it wrong. Give them a large jug and tell them to warm a mug's worth at a time."

While the boys worked at mixing up the mugs and then tested whether they could tell the fresh decoction from the one made from dried herbs, I stacked my utensils in a bucket to be returned to the kitchen for washing. Young Mr. Williams wiped up a water spill, and I gave him a faint smile and a nod of thanks.

There I was, smiling before I'd lasted a day. Would I be tough enough to be a teacher?

What was Daniel Williams doing that was getting him kitchen duty every week? I wondered. So far he hadn't done a thing for a teacher to complain about.

"Should we include runners with our peppermint drawings, Miss Sorensson?" Nancy Spenser asked, looking up from her work.

I leaned down to examine her drawing. It was lovingly done, showing that she knew this plant and how to describe it. "I would," I told her. "You can label the runners to remind yourself that to get peppermint, you must plant runner cuttings. Otherwise, the seed from the plant will be milder, more like spearmint."

"Also called 'spiremint,' isn't it?" Mr. Williams asked as he sat down in his seat.

"Yes, spirement is the old name for spearmint," I agreed, "for its narrow spike of flowers. The leaves are shorter, lighter and more wrinkled than peppermint leaves. And remember that once mint has flowered, the leaves become quite mild in scent and flavor!"

"We are out of time, Miss Sorensson," Mr. Riley said abruptly, looking at a pocket watch he'd pulled from his coat pocket.

I was impressed. Perhaps he was the first son of the family to have such a treasure? "Thank you, Mr. Riley. Everyone, use your notes from class and your Nightroad book to label your drawing," I said as my students shuffled papers and books. "You may start reading about other mints for tomorrow. We can look at some of the more exotic mint plants and talk about how they are used. Remember that European pennyroyal is a mint, and a dangerous one at that. Class is dismissed!" As the group roiled like a cloudbank to thunder out the door, I shouted: "Please bring the mugs up here to me before you leave!" In a normal tone, I added: "Mr. Smith, if you will remain a moment?"

The other students vanished, almost like magic, except for Daniel Williams, who hovered by the doorway.

"He's not in trouble, Mr. Williams, you need not remain to defend him," I told Catherin's brother, giving him a firm look. The boys exchanged glances, and then Daniel disappeared into the murk of the hallway.

I turned my attention back to James Smith. I had noticed while we were outside attempting the water spells that Mr. Smith was dark-eyed, but his hair was not dark brown or black. It was some strange color of red that only looked red in glimpses, like sunlight peeking under a cloud.

As far as I knew, that color of hair only showed up among powerful fire mages.

Little Moira appeared to be fire, too, and was clearly sharp as a whip and with the talent to become a strong practitioner.

Mr. Smith had the potential to be in another category altogether.

The boy was high-strung, sensitive, and keenly interested in getting things "right." I wondered at Professor Tonneman's icy verbal discipline. I hated to be publicly embarrassed, and it made me less likely to listen to whoever caused that embarrassment.

Could I get James to relax in the herbal class?

I planned to try.

"Mr. Smith, I noticed that you did not want to help in preparing and boiling the mint and ginger," I started, leaning back against the heavy teacher's desk. "Do you not care for the lab classes?"

He stared at me.

I considered the day. His first attempt at the flowing water spell had caused a geyser of water from his wand, spraying himself and others close by him, and drying the snow around him to light powder. "Or were you worried that you are so tense that we'd have mint tea everywhere?"

A pause, and then a small nod.

"Well, the business with the water spell was uncomfortable, but if you can figure out how you did what you did, that version of the spell might come in handy one day," I said.

"But I never know how I do it," he answered, his voice soft. "Things just...happen."

"Perhaps we can figure out a few things about...how you work. For example, I would like to know how the biscuits last week ended up so...fierce."

If possible, the boy looked even more miserable.

"In trade, I will teach you how to make wonderful biscuits. No one will ever laugh at you again about the biscuits, except your friends when they're just jesting. No one will want to be stricken from the list of people invited over for your biscuits!"

"D—Mr. Williams would like to learn how to make biscuits," he said promptly.

"And Saturday morning I will teach you all how to make biscuits for dinner," I replied. "I meant that I am willing to trade my special tea biscuit recipe for your biscuits with teeth."

"Why?" he asked, and then looked stricken.

I suspected that he had remembered that I was also a teacher.

"I want to make my brothers laugh," I answered with as much sincerity as I could. Under no circumstances could he know that I felt sorry for him, and wanted him to feel better. He would be appalled.

I also thought I'd be a better teacher for him if I could figure out how he saw the world, and what formed his spells.

And my brothers *would* like the biscuits with teeth!

"Have we a bargain?" I asked.

"I...I will try to remember," he said.

"Good." I stood up straight and moved over to the shelves by the working fireplace. "I have small amounts of ingredients here to use for making biscuits. Tell me how you did it."

Silence. I looked over my shoulder.

In the fading day, Mr. Smith actually looked pale. "We're not going to try it again, are we?"

I blinked. "Of course we are. It's the only way to know if we're on the right track. Now, how did you begin?"

"We used much larger amounts of things," he said doubtfully, looking at the containers that I set on the worktable.

"Yes, but we don't want to be chasing an entire pan of biscuits around the house, do we?" I gestured to the small cast iron Dutch oven I had borrowed from Mrs. Gardener (She had acted very disapproving, but I think she secretly wanted to know how he had made the biscuits.) "We will make twelve square biscuits. That will keep them from rolling, at any rate. If we don't let them get to another energy source, they won't be able to do something like hop up the chimney."

"Oh." This thought seemed to reassure the boy. Then, he asked shyly: "Should we write down what we're going to do?"

"An excellent suggestion. That way, if it doesn't work, we'll know what not to do next time."

Mr. Smith got his workbook, and I started setting the ingredients on the table, measured into small containers. "Flour, butter, milk, salt, baking soda, cream of tartar, eggs—"

"Eggs?"

I turned toward him. "You didn't use eggs in your recipe?"

His expression was puzzled. "I didn't know eggs went into biscuits. I didn't know any kind of cream went into biscuits."

I remembered the smell of yeast when that biscuit burped...there was no yeast in biscuits. "Tell me what you used," I said, opening my own notebook and picking up my square English pencil. "I'll write it down."

That James could do. Far from not knowing how he had done it, Mr. Smith immediately rattled off the list of what he had tossed into his biscuit recipe. He'd used several teaspoons of cane sugar, and had no eggs or cream of tartar.

Looking at the list, I was not sure where to begin, because without a proper mix of soda and cream of tartar, or even eggs, there was no way to get these biscuits to rise.

"How did you mix these ingredients up?" I started.

"I stirred the big spoon into the butter and sugar, until it was soft. Then I added the milk, and finally the other things." James reached to set each item next to the other as he spoke.

I stared at him as he worked his way through the ingredients, wondering if he'd gotten the idea from watching his mother bake a cake, and then added more flour.

"Did you grease the pan?" I asked when he paused for breath.

"Oh, yes! Greased and floured it. But that wasn't until the next morning."

Oh, really?

I felt like a hound quivering at a scent. "So what did you do with the dough?"

"I dumped it out on the bread board, and covered it with a clean towel."

Or perhaps he'd wandered through the kitchen and spotted someone baking bread....

"When did you continue?"

"The next morning." Now James looked unhappy. "The dough had barely risen at all! That's when I panicked. I poured more sugar into it, because when things are sweet people usually don't care much about the rest. And then I...took my wand and...encouraged the heap of dough."

"Encouraged," I repeated. "Do you remember what you said?"

"I told it to rise."

Ah.

I didn't know a lot of Latin, but I knew enough to feel uneasy.

"Which word for *rise* did you use?"

The boy kept his gaze on the bowl. "I was in a hurry, and afraid it wouldn't work? So I commanded it. I said *resurge!*"

I thought about what to say next. If he had left the mess on the breadboard, there was always a chance of a few crumbs of leftover yeast there...or even wild yeast, which was always in the air. But wild yeast usually took a few days to start to work on the sponge of dough. Even if he'd used baking soda and cream of tartar, by waiting overnight the dough would have been dead and the gas long escaped.

"Mr. Smith," I started. "The Romans had several words for rise. The one my father taught me when we talked about bread rising was *oriri*, like our English word for Orient. In the east, the sun rises, and in the west—the Occidental lands—the sun sets. But when you want a person to stand up quickly, the command is 'Surge!' You added the prefix 'Re' to the word...which means *back* or *again*."

"Again rise. To give it more emphasis," the boy said.

I was positive he was not a Catholic.

I wasn't sure if he was a Christian.

"*Resurge* is what the English word 'resurrection' comes from," I said, waiting to see if he would understand.

James stared at me.

"Had you noticed that there was no yeast in your recipe? Biscuits don't need yeast, that's why they are so handy to make quickly. There are no hours of preparation with biscuits. You mix the proper amounts of baking soda and cream of tartar, a reaction occurs, and the biscuits rise."

"So the biscuits should not have risen?" James asked faintly.

"No, they should not have risen. But you may have accidentally rolled some yeast crumbs into your dough. Or some wild yeast may have landed on your towel, and gotten on the dough that way. Not enough to matter. The yeast would have bloomed, but not enough to expand the dough." *Probably collapsed happy, if yeast can be happy*, I thought. "But you took a magic wand, channeled all your power to the dough, and told it to resurrect. You ordered it to rise.

"And it did," I finished, watching his face. "At least, I suspect that's what happened. It rose with the force of resurrection."

The boy blanched. "I've...blasphemed," he whispered.

"No! Not at all!" My words rolled right on top of each other. "You ordered something—yeast—to do what it does naturally. You told it to rise, and it did! You didn't try to make something dead come to life. Yeast is a...a seed, in a way. Under the right conditions, it starts to grow. You just rolled that seed into very good soil!"

I wasn't sure that I'd convinced him, but he didn't look quite so stricken. "Should we try this again?" he asked, his voice doubtful.

"If we're going to get the same result, we need to mix up your dough recipe, and then leave it a while with a towel over it. I should also get a few grains of yeast to insert in another lump of dough." I considered. "We can cut the dough in half – yeast in one ball, none in the other. I'll get another Dutch oven as well. Then, this evening, we can see if we can get a response from either lump of dough."

"It doesn't have to rest overnight?" he asked.

"Most yeast dough only needs to rest until it doubles in bulk," I explained, separating his dough into two balls so we could cover them separately. "A few things rest overnight, but I don't think that had anything to do with your biscuits, except for making you panic. We're going to start where you did—find dough that hasn't risen, add sugar, and then you can try your command again."

"So, after supper, then?" he said, his tone distracted.

"Yes. Can you come here at that time?" I waited, because he had not expected this, and if it were a problem, I would try his choice of words myself.

"May I bring Mr. Williams?" he asked.

"Yes, if he sits quietly and watches. At least until the biscuits need catching! But only Daniel," I added quickly. "Let's keep this a secret for now."

I could just imagine my cousin's face if I had a herd of children conjuring scraps of dough all over the place.

Nodding his agreement, Mr. Smith helped me tidy up the table and hearth. While we cleaned, I decided to start my other little project.

"Mr. Smith," I said as I swept the hearth. "Why is it that you end up serving kitchen duty so often?"

The boy was carefully scraping dough off the wooden table with a small wood paddle. "Well...D—Mr. Williams usually ends up on kitchen duty," he said vaguely.

"Yes, I'd noticed that. He's not volunteering, is he?" I asked.

James looked surprised. "No, Miss, he doesn't volunteer...really."

"So how do you end up on kitchen duty? You don't get in trouble because he gets in trouble, do you?"

James actually looked alarmed. "I...get in fights."

"I see. Do these fights have different reasons for starting, or are they usually about the same thing?"

Silence.

"You do realize that if you continue to end up on kitchen duty, Professor Livingston will notice." James stiffened; he was clearly alarmed at the idea of Professor Livingston noticing. "How are you disguising the bruises, by the way? Arnica?"

"Oh, one of the students is good with bruises. Fixes us up right away," he said with a fair attempt at sounding off-handed.

We have a touch healer among us? That was rare, and needed to be carefully nurtured. Touch healers could burn themselves out quickly if not careful with their gifts. I'd have to ask my cousin about that.

"If you need to talk to someone about the fights, just know that I will listen," I said, matching his tone. "I was raised with four brothers. I know how these things happen." I flicked the last of the debris into the fireplace, where it would either burn up in the cinders or be shoveled out during fire tending.

"They keep fooling around with their wands," James said slowly, his back to me. "They want me to burn things. They don't understand."

"That you don't want to burn things?" I said.

"No! I *want* to burn things! It's easy to burn things! The problem is stopping!"

Ah. So...better to be a fighter than known as someone who had no control, or feared loss of control. That made a kind of sense.

"I understand that some of the professors give private lessons," I began. "Have you asked—"

"No! He'll keep me from doing any magic at all!"

"Are you sure of that? Why would that be a bad thing, right now?"

The boy's pale face flushed, and smoke rose from the top of his head.

A pitcher of water remained on the table next to the dough. Any weapon at need.

"It sounds like you need some advice," I said slowly. "I could inquire for you, without using your name." Of course I had at least two, and possibly more fire mages in my class. It could not be kept a secret forever. "Is this something that you are afraid of happening, Mr. Smith? Or something that you are afraid of happening...again?"

The boy seemed to get a grip on himself—the smoke began to dissipate. He studied me for a long moment, as if weighing something. "This is a secret," he finally said.

"I'm good at secrets, unless someone could die if they're not told," I replied, gesturing toward the chairs around the big table. "So weigh that in your telling."

"It already happened," James went on, sounding defeated. He pulled out a high-backed spindle chair and sat down.

I sat down across from him and waited for him to continue speaking. "We were helping to set up some hams in my uncle's smokehouse. He was showing us how he built layers of wood to direct the smoke. I wanted to help by lighting the fire. I've done that before, just laid my hand on a faggot of wood, and the thing bursts into flame like a torch." He fiddled with the wood utensils in the bucket on the edge of the table.

"But...the entire stack caught, fast, even the wet wood. It was so great a fire, so fast, we had to rush out of the shed." He looked up at me. "We didn't shut the door."

So there was plenty of fresh air to feed the fire. "Did you lose just the hams, or the entire shed?"

James closed his eyes. "The entire building. All Uncle's hams and briskets, the bacon...a year's work."

After a protracted silence, I chose my words carefully.

"Sounds like you'll owe him some work or pigs, after you learn your craft," I said gently. "That's why you're here, Mr. Smith, isn't it? A powerful gift requires special teachers."

"They're afraid of me," he whispered. "I have a cousin who teaches all the children in my family, but after that, he wouldn't teach me."

Oh.

What a blessing I have in my family. There was never a hint that they wouldn't teach me...just working out who would handle which lessons.

"Mr. Smith," I went on. "This is a good school to learn how to control powerful gifts. That's why I'm here. My family believes that the Livingstons are the best teachers I could have. This school is not a punishment, no matter how you may have felt when they sent you here. It's a gift, if you want it to be a gift."

"But I'm not making any progress," he whispered.

Yes, you are. "Can I ask one of the older students if he has a suggestion about the fighting? Maybe you and Mr. Williams could say you weren't interested in playing with the wands unless precautions were taken...like having someone ready with water buckets, that sort of thing." This was going to be hard. Children *will* experiment.

The books. If the books screamed when taken off the grounds, surely they had some spells that watched for unsupervised activity? Or smothered unsupervised activity?

"You won't tell anyone that it's me, will you?" If his eyes could actually speak, they would be pleading about now.

"I will not mention your name," I replied.

They might know who I was talking about, but I would not confirm it.

"Go get ready for dinner," I told him. "If you skip tea, we will have time to come here and see what happens tonight."

"Yes, Miss," he told me, standing and picking up the handle of the bucket. "May I carry this to the kitchen for you?"

Lord and Lady, he might turn out as useful as Daniel Williams.

"Thank you, Mr. Smith. I would appreciate your help."

❧ 🖉 ❧

There was time to change for supper. I didn't know if I would see any of the Mayflower Compact, but if they saw me, I would blend into the crowd. There were aprons in the classrooms, and I would wear one while we tried the biscuit recipe.

I studied my lessons, from my French words through reading about the history of magic. There was a theme to magic in the world—it would be misused, and then all magic-users would suffer. Surely a few hopeful stories would show up.

My reward was some of my letters. It took lighting every candle in the room to make out Marta's flowing copperplate. My mother always wrote tightly, like someone trying to save paper. They sent enough news that they crossed the letters, turning them sideways and writing again, end to end, the sentences overlapping perfectly like the arms of a cross mounted on a steeple. Both sides were crossed, the equivalent of four sheets from both of them, and I could tell my mother would have said more, but could not bring herself to use another sheet of paper.

Strange, isn't it? Momma did not have to pay for the letter to be carried by post; she was giving it to Marta for a magical circle. But still, she conserved. We might be Irish, but there had to be some Scottish in there somewhere. We knew how to save when it counted.

I had time to do a lot of thinking. Before I could finish opening letters, I realized that I had made a decision.

I couldn't let James Smith try that spell without taking some precautions. I remembered clearly the ice forming around him...the steam rising off his head. All that beautiful woodwork on the walls, the racks waiting for new pots of herbs...how could I risk James having an accident?

All these thoughts raced through my head as I made my way down the corridor of the older girls' floor. The logical person to ask was my mentor Margaret, wasn't it?

So I knocked on Margaret's door.

"You may enter," came Margaret's voice.

I opened her door and peeked around the edge. Margaret was sitting at her table, sprinkling sand over a letter she'd just finished to blot any extra ink. She looked up, and I saw surprise flit across her face.

"Miss Sorensson. I did not expect to see you before supper. Please, come in." She gestured toward the other straight chair across from her, and at the rocker she and Catherin somehow made fit into the room.

I chose the straight-backed chair, mirroring her position. This was a work visit, not a pleasure one. Folding my hands before me on the table, I launched right into my story.

"Miss Rutledge, I may have started something that is dangerous," I began, "So I came to talk with you about it, and see if it can be done without endangering the household or anyone present."

Margaret stared. "I must confess that I am taken aback," she said. "When I think of your ability to face down things that leave me quaking in my dreams, your unease is disconcerting."

Well.

"I wanted to help a student," I began slowly, "so he will not be afraid to participate in class. Do you know if there are any spells in place to dampen fires?"

"Is this James Smith?" Margaret asked.

"It could be," I replied, trying not to grimace. Some conspirator I was—I started with the part of the tale that gave everything away!

"You convinced him to try a spell?" Margaret looked impressed. "The professors have been trying to get him to calm down for weeks. How did you...no, never mind that," she went on quickly. "Yes, there are spells that will smother a fire. But if he...flashed, then the protections would strain. I can put protections on you and your student; that will make it much less likely that anyone will get hurt."

"Should we move from the beginning herb room to the spell room upstairs?" I hated to suggest that—that room gave me the cold grue—but wasn't that what the room was designed for?

"I think not," she said. "It might make...your student...much more nervous if you did that. Part of why he is talking to you may be because you are so calm about magical mishaps. Going to the rituals room might signal unease."

"He wants another student to be there, too, so we need three protected," I went on.

Margaret's eyebrows lifted over widened eyes. "Oh. Is this his friend Daniel Williams? Then I may need to summon assistance. I should be able to save you and two untrained fire mages, but the room could be scorched. Professor Livingston would not approve."

So they thought that Daniel was a fire mage, too? "Do you think that Professor Livingston knows that there's a touch healer among the younger children?"

Margaret took in a deep breath, and then let it out slowly. "I always assume that Professor Livingston knows about anything important," she finally said. "I had not heard that rumor. Do you know which child?"

"No. But it's someone the boys feel comfortable asking to speed up the healing of their bruises. I think there's more fighting going on than the numbers on Saturday punishment reveal."

A slight smile briefly dimpled Margaret's face. "I will bring this up at the guardians' meeting. We will be on the lookout for any child looking more tired than usual. Young touch healers generally give themselves away eventually."

"Who are the guardians?"

"Senior students who help with the protections on the estate," Margaret replied. "It is good training for the future. We always learn more when we practice what we need to know."

I nodded. Margaret was afraid of her gift with ghosts, but it seemed that her fear did not extend to power in general. That was good. I didn't want her to sit on her talent.

Did this explain the feeling of being watched I always had in the public areas of the house?

"Where should I meet you? Do you need to touch us to put protections on us?"

"Not at all. It is easier with an object or something to focus on, but not impossible to do," she assured me, rising to her feet. "Let us go have dinner, and I will do it right afterwards."

"I need to get some yeast," I remembered aloud as I stood up.

Margaret looked puzzled. "Is yeast used in biscuits? I thought part of their charm was speed in making? That there is no rising time for them?"

I managed a smile. "My student may have accidentally gotten yeast mixed into his dough."

"Ah." A slight lift of the eyebrows, but Margaret was good at saving questions until later. "You get some yeast, then, and I will talk with Sinjin about this." She checked the fire screen and then held her door open for me.

"Do you mean Mr. St. John? Why do people call him that?" I asked, walking through the doorway.

Margaret halted, her eyes wide with surprise. "Oh, it's a nickname of sorts given by young men to their friends with the name St. John. Another name like that is Sinclair—it comes from the last name St. Claire."

With a name like Alfreda Eldonsdottir Sorensson, which is the old way of writing it, I could use a shorter name. "Should I call him Mr. Sin Jin?"

Margaret covered her mouth with her fingers, which I knew meant that she was amused. "I really could not tell you whether to use it that way. Why don't I ask him for you?"

"Thank you," I said gravely.

Names are important. I didn't want to get his wrong.

❧·𝔇·❧

Margaret's place to observe us turned out to be a classroom next to the herb room. When I arrived, I found her arranging chairs around one of the larger study tables. A large, shallow metal bowl of water sat upon the table.

My mentor smiled. "Good, we'll have time to take care of this protection. It occurs to me that there is a basic spell you should have. I will show it to you now, and Sinjin will teach it to you in the week to come. The spell suppresses flame, and will keep your dress from burning should you turn about too close to a fire. It will also give you protection should one of the untrained mages erupt suddenly."

Of course I smiled back. All I could think was *why hadn't someone thought of this before?* The fire protections on the building were strong ones; apparently I was the first student teacher who didn't know such basic spells.

She pulled a long, thin wand from that useful slit in her lovely muslin dress. The wand was pale, and looked as if it had words or symbols stained or burned into it, in a spiral design. Then she touched the skirt of my dress, her gaze flicking away as if her thoughts turned inward.

"There. It's a simple cantrip, and the spell lasts until the dress is washed. It can be made permanent, but that takes another part of a spell."

"How about the person wearing the dress?"

"The house protections should take care of you," Margaret said promptly. "Still...when Sinjin and the others get here, three of us will spell you as well, just to be sure. We know Mr. Smith is a fire mage; we are not certain about Mr. Williams yet. There is no sense in taking the smallest chance."

"Others?" I asked.

"A precaution. In case both boys erupt."

"How are you going to use the bowl?" I asked, gesturing at the table.

She smiled. "Watch." Sitting down, Margaret passed her wand over the bowl, which looked to be made of hammered pewter. The water rippled, reflecting the herb room, the decocting fire low behind its fire screen. "We can watch and hear with this spell, and we'll know if we need to reinforce any of the protections on you or the room. And we will be able to put protections on both of your students."

"Can you look anywhere with this spell?"

"It has to be somewhere you have actually been before," she replied. "And there are protections that can be put up to shield for privacy."

Good. The potential of ritual magic began to sink in. Clearly, it could affect the simplest parts of everyday living.

"I should get ready," I told her. "Can you finish the spells at a distance?"

"Yes, we can," she said, her tone reassuring.

"Thank you again." I started out.

"Thank you for asking." She stood and slid her wand back into her skirt.

That last was interesting, I thought as I walked next door. She did not lay her wand down for the few moments she needed to finish arranging chairs. Best to keep track of it...and keep it out of sight?

I wondered what you could learn about a practitioner by studying their wand and athame?

❧⚜❧

A tiny amount of yeast crumbled into grains and scattered into one of the small balls of dough, kneaded in, and the dough covered again— Shaking my head, I wrote down all that I'd done. Since James had dumped a bunch of sugar in right before his spell, did any time for rising matter at all? He had noticed no difference in his dough when he found it that morning.

I turned to prepare the fire. Actually, coals were best for baking biscuits, and a Dutch oven was best of all. I'd tried earlier to leave the fire so it would produce good coals, and it had not failed me. The kitchen had several cast iron ovens, and Mrs. Gardener had kindly let me select what I wanted.

I'd chosen two small, three-legged ovens, their walls nicely even and seasoned, their lids tight, their bail wire handles deep and with heavy rings that rose above the lid on each side. Each fireplace had a set of long, loose, thick leather gloves for working with Dutch ovens, as well as tongs, so I was prepared for cooking.

In truth, this wasn't exactly cooking. I wasn't sure if the biscuits would even finish cooking. Would we be able to tell if we'd made biscuits with teeth? I carefully set the ovens near the fire to warm slightly, making note of which pot was which. Then I reached out for the apron hanging over in the corner...and paused.

Would the apron burn if a coal exploded? I lifted the apron from its wrought iron hook, turned in the direction of the wall between Margaret and myself, and held up the apron.

Wind breathed past my ear. "It is already spelled." I clearly heard Margaret's popping, precise enunciation.

So, I could hear her, which was both good and a little uncomfortable, but I could work under her eye. As I tied on the apron, the door opened, and James Smith and Daniel Williams slipped into the room.

There was little prep work. James had already told me how much sugar he had added to his biscuits. I had reduced the amount for our small dough, and measured out two containers. Fixing Mr. Williams with a hard eye, I said: "Do not help, do not suggest, do not interfere unless asked. We want to recreate what Mr. Smith did last time."

Daniel nodded, as still as a mouse under a hawk's eye.

James sprinkled his sugar as he had done earlier, folding his biscuit dough several times. The dough lumps ended up at opposite ends of the table. Then he pulled out his wand.

"Did you do anything else between adding the sugar, and the spell?" I said quickly.

"No, miss. Daniel put lard on the trays to grease them, but that's all." He paused, looking at Daniel.

"Mr. Williams, you may take a scoop of lard from that pot for each oven. Place the lids back on!" The boy jumped to his job, while James and I turned back to the dough.

"Perhaps you should start with the one I did not add yeast to," I suggested. "So there is no chance of added yeast getting on the other biscuits?"

Nodding, the boy faced the right-hand lump, balancing himself carefully on the balls of his feet. "All I did was this..." He touched the tip of his wand directly on the dough. "*Resurge!*"

The room suddenly felt small. Both boys noticed the change. Daniel's dark eyes grew round, and James became motionless. I did not feel anything threatening about the magic...it was simply a lot of spell for such a small area.

We should have done this in the ritual dome.

"It feels different in such a small room, gentlemen?" I asked.

"Yes. The ceiling is much lower here. That may be some of it." He glanced at Daniel. "Daniel and Moira helped me roll balls of dough for the pan."

I had brought a biscuit cutter, but it did not surprise me that it would not be needed. "Daniel, you may go ahead and do what you did before, while Mr. Smith finishes his spell."

We left Daniel rolling balls of dough and setting them inside one Dutch oven. James reached for the other clump of dough, which was actually showing a slight increase in size. He flicked his wand, wiping the tip with the towel I'd laid aside, and then touched the last mound of dough. "*Resurge!*"

Again, the feeling of magical energy filled the room. It almost made the air tingle, as if lightning was about to strike. They must have been in a panic to finish cooking, not to notice such magic floating around them.

"Load the ovens, gentlemen, and do not touch the second ball of dough until you have finished with the first!"

I stepped closer to the wall and whispered: "Did doing the spell twice strain any protections?"

Margaret answered: "It seems fine. He touched the dough; that should have kept the spell pointed where he wanted it. Good heavens, he was so unfocused in his choice of words!"

"Yes, he was," I agreed as James slammed the lid on the second oven.

I lifted my eyebrows at him.

"The dough is rising," he said, looking worried.

"Did it start rising before you put it in the oven last time?"

Both boys nodded.

"Do you know how to set a Dutch oven in coals for baking?"

Their response was owl-eyed silence, so I showed them how to arrange a circle of coals beneath and on top of a Dutch oven.

"Two more coals go on top, and two less on the bottom," I said. "There's a trick to knowing how much heat to use, but since we won't dare eat these biscuits, I won't tell you about it today. Just remember never to put coals under the center of the oven. That's a good way to burn food. If we wanted a crunchy top to the biscuits, we'd move all the coals to the lid for the last few minutes or so."

I then gestured to implements hanging on the wall. "A whisk is to brush away ash so that, when you open the lid, ash doesn't fall in the food. Here are tongs for moving coals around, and the pot lifter, and clean bricks to the side to set the lid on—"

"Should we clean up now?" Daniel asked.

I controlled my smile. "Yes, let's do that now." I used my tongs to nudge aside some extra kindling and branches to make sure the wood would not light, and then we rose to clean up the table.

"Are there actually rules for cooking with a Dutch oven?" Daniel asked.

"Not many, but there are a few, and they are the difference between tasty food and sad, tasteless food," I answered, tightly closing the sugar and setting it back upon the supply shelves. "Before we get into Dutch oven baking, Mr. Smith, do you have any questions about what we just did?"

"What will we do if nothing happens?"

"We will study our notes, and see if we can figure out why," I replied.

"And try again?"

"I would like to try again. Another day. If this does not work, we can try letting the dough rest overnight. But I think something will happen."

"Oh, yes," James said, his voice fervent.

"Is anything different from the first time you did this, Mr. Smith? Other than the Dutch ovens, and our actually adding a pinch of yeast to one ball of dough?"

"I don't know if we should feed these to the pigs," Daniel said, frowning. "I don't think the others ended up in the slops, either."

"The older students did something with them in class," James said, his expression less harried. "Perhaps we could look inside one? Sinjin said that they had large holes from expanding. I wondered if they actually had insides like an animal, but Sinjin said no."

Did everyone call Mr. St. John that except me?

Before I could respond, a muffled sound startled us, like the echo of an animal growling in a cave.

"How long did your biscuits take to bake, Mr. Smith?" I asked. *Why hadn't I thought to ask him that question?*

James grew thoughtful. "A quarter hour or so?"

That was too fast for normal biscuits, and this was even quicker. "Perhaps we should check and see what is happening—"

And then the lid on the left-hand pot tilted upwards, shedding coals, as a tremendous roar burst from the Dutch oven.

THIRTEEN

CANTAMEN DISSOLVATUR...

No. This wasn't an emergency. Yet.

I grabbed the loose leather gloves from the corner of the table and hauled them on. The pot lid rose into the air, like a plate balanced on someone's head, revealing the elastic stretch of dough that suggested teeth, with deep pits that could be eyes.

The hair on the back of my neck rose, and I wanted to look away. There were no pupils, so why was the biscuit face so awful?

I slammed the lid back onto the Dutch oven and flipped up the handle with one hand. "Quickly! A stick that will thread the rings!" The lid strained beneath my gloved hand, trying to fly off into the room.

The boys crashed into each other as they fumbled with the kindling, but they each pulled out a thick stick and handed it my way. I grabbed the one with smoother sides and shoved it through the rings. Then I lifted the pot off the coals and set it on the hearth as snarling emerged from the Dutch oven, first echoing, and then muffled. The dough was still expanding, the mouth swallowed by more dough? This was the pot holding the biscuits that I had added yeast to before the boys arrived. As yet, the second container remained silent.

I might never feel quite the same way again about yeast.

"Gentlemen," I said, my heart racing like a thoroughbred on the straightaway. "Last time, did any of your rolls ooze back together to form a loaf with teeth?"

Both boys stared, motionless, at the snarling Dutch oven. Finally Daniel shook his head slowly. James's expression was appalled.

"Any ideas on why we have a loaf with teeth instead of biscuits with teeth?" I asked, stepping back to the fireplace and taking Daniel's stick from his hands. I snapped the remnants of twigs off it. Then I lifted the rings on the second Dutch oven and slid the stick through them.

We could always replace the stick if it burned through.

"It...was swelling so quickly," James finally said. "I was afraid of what was going to happen with the dough. So...I just dropped the entire thing into the pot."

Ah.

"Not quite the same experiment, was it?"

He looked crestfallen. "No."

"But we have determined that a pinch of added yeast does give us roaring biscuits," I said. "Why that happens might require several different investigations. Perhaps you could interest some of the senior students in that question."

A squeak came from the second Dutch oven, followed by a growl and a soft snarl. Both boys turned their heads, looking at the squat, three-legged pot nestled in hot coals.

"Is this more like what happened in the kitchen?" I asked them, looking down at them. They nodded in unison.

"This suggests that there is enough wild yeast around to stir up biscuit dough with magic. At least sweet biscuit dough," I added. "Let's clean up so we can be ready for the biscuits."

Never has a cooking area been scoured so quickly. Once the boys grasped that I still intended to pull out a few biscuits, they had the area so clean I had nothing to do but praise their efforts and set several plates and a honey pot out.

By the time they finished, the biscuits had begun to chorus in their pots, the loaf with teeth a deep bass note to their twittering.

"What shall we do next with them?" I asked as I moved the second pot to the brick hearth.

"We should examine them," Daniel said eagerly. "May we look at the loaf?"

"No. We need a teacher or more experienced students here to examine the loaf," I said, facing down their disappointment. "But we may each take out a biscuit and see what we find." I handed James the leather gloves.

James pulled on the gloves, removed the stick, and promptly stuck his hand in the second pot. He gave us a startled glance as he yanked his right hand out of the Dutch oven with a growling, snarling biscuit attached, gumming him thoroughly.

As I'd hoped, the biscuits could not actually bite. Their soft, stretchy teeth were much more frightening than dangerous.

"Set it on the table, Mr. Smith. Be sure to keep an eye on it!"

❧⚶☙

Biscuits with teeth turned out to be great fun, when adults weren't there to spoil things. When Daniel opened the lid, the biscuits rushed for freedom, so he had to push them back into the big kettle. Our biscuits had turned out more square than round, thanks to Daniel's shaping of them, so they could not roll. But they did hop up and down on their toasted bottoms, chipping themselves in their fury and excitement.

Yeast, it appeared, had one goal in life. Food.

It did not take the boys long to determine that the biscuits would actually throw themselves backwards, balancing on edge, if it would get them a dribble of honey. One biscuit clamped onto a spoon, trying to tug it away from Daniel. I had to laugh; it was just too silly.

"Could we have a race?" James asked. "Do you think we could get them to hop toward us, if we had honey on a plate?"

"I think the problem would be that several of them would take the course in one hop," I replied, rapping my biscuit on the head with a dry spoon to make it stop nibbling at my fingers. "If you can keep them alive until tomorrow, maybe we could have a biscuit race right after breakfast! It's very dark now, and we should not be outside."

"Should we feed the others?" Daniel looked worried.

"We'll need to feed all of them," I told the boys. "But it would be very messy in here. You already need to scrub off the table. Let's drop them back in the pot. Mr. Smith, you go get some hot water and rags. Mr. Williams, sweep up every crumb and flake of ash! I will get us reinforcements to help feed and cage the biscuits until tomorrow."

It was easier said than done, since lifting the lid meant that two other biscuits hopped out. The boys caught them while I dropped the sated ones back into the Dutch oven. Then James went for hot water, Daniel swept, and I slipped out to talk with Margaret (after reminding Daniel not to open up the Dutch oven with the loaf in it.)

I pushed open the door into the next classroom and found it well lit by candelabra. I was greeted by a blast of sound—the pounding of walking sticks against the floor, as our representatives did to approve of speeches in the Congress.

Margaret sat next to the bowl, enthroned in firelight. Smile lines crinkled the corners of her eyes, and her grin flashed a dimple in her right cheek. Catherin sat next to Margaret, clapping with enthusiasm, her beautiful laughter floating above the noise.

Mr. St. John gestured for me to enter as he shut the door behind me. Two other men were also present, one of them very well dressed, his dark, handsome features reminding me of a picture I had seen of the apostles. The second student, blond and tan, was well scrubbed but untidy, as if fancy dressing was beyond him. He sported an impressive, dark blond mustache, one to rival Death's.

It took me a moment to place them. They had passed me on the stairs, as I followed Professor Brown up to the ritual dome.

"Miss Sorensson, you are indeed intrepid!" Catherin said. "I hope you are there to help with all my emergencies!"

"That wasn't an emergency," I replied. "Just boys making mischief."

"You will make a formidable professor or parent of young magicians, Miss Sorensson," Mr. St. John said warmly. "Your calm under trial is commendable." He offered me a chair.

"Goodness, Daniel is *not* looking in the loaf pot! I am astonished," Catherin went on, bent over the bowl. "I was sure he'd peek the moment you left the room."

"Not if he wants to join any more of these investigations," I muttered, glancing at the water.

"And he knows it," the well-dressed young man said, his smile broad. "He won't risk being excluded from the fun! There's a time for such risks, and this is not one of those times." The man bowed slightly from the waist toward me. "I am Joseph, Miss Sorensson. It is a pleasure to make your acquaintance."

So you saw it all? I wanted to ask, but of course they must have been there from the start. So instead I asked: "Can you help confine and feed the biscuits? I think the children should have their chance at racing them. I can't think of any reason why not."

Everyone else looked at Mr. St. John. "Professor Tonneman does not like us to manipulate animals without supervision," he stated. "But I think that encouraging yeast might be a good lesson in what can go right or wrong in transformation of creatures. By all means, let them have their race—and then have them write up a paper on their experience. I don't see a particle of harm in their enjoying the spectacle, but they need to be reminded that it's also work."

Good. Because Tonneman took the biscuits last time, I wasn't sure if the children would be allowed to play with them. "Where shall we bring the pots, then? The dome?"

"Faulkner, will you take charge of this?" Mr. St. John asked.

"Yes," the untidy blond fellow said. "I can restrain them in the corner. We'll need to leave them with a good supply of honey, though. Can't have them eating each other."

"That might be a more lasting lesson," I said without thinking. The biscuits were so voracious. Would they...?

Perhaps. I shivered. *It's only bread dough.*

And yet.

"Oh!" Catherin said in dismay, her fingers touching her lips. "What a terrible idea!"

"True, though," was Mr. St. John's comment.

❧ 🌑 ☙

A shriek echoed throughout the back courtyard, bouncing from the brick walls and ice-coated branches. A dozen darkly-toasted biscuits hopped past me, squeaking and roaring like a pack of gasping children.

My actual students bounded in pursuit, their knit scarves flying like flags, some holding their hats onto their heads. One boy carried his cap clutched in his hand as he brought up the rear.

"Don't fall on them!" I yelled after the group. "If you hit them, they'll crumble!"

"Indeed," Professor Tonneman said, looking into the cage he was carrying. Within were the remains of the loaf with teeth. The loaf had dropped from a great height to the paving stones in the courtyard, breaking the bread into a good half-dozen chunks. These pieces apparently did not have the energy to grow teeth, so the yeast could not feed magically. The small mouth section snapped uselessly at the air, while the eyes kept looking for food.

The teeth hadn't started chewing on the loaf's own fragments yet, but give it time.

The professor had called all the children together to see what happened to the loaf. After their initial chorus of disgust, they had been slightly unsettled by the sight.

Good. I wanted them a bit uneasy about the affair.

And yet? Let them have their race! It never hurt to remember that sometimes magic was *fun*.

St. John gathered the students together, their roaring biscuits bouncing at their feet, to organize another race. I shook my head and searched the sunlit yard for a good viewing position. Crisp air gave us a glorious day, but it was not a morning to stand around in shadow.

"Have they started falling apart yet?" Cousin Esme walked slowly up the shoveled flagstone path, wrapped in a cape of fine dark blue wool trimmed in white fur, a lovely fur hat tilted over one eye.

She had an escort.

It was Shaw!

He wore his walnut-stained deerskin jacket, and deerskin trousers. The scarf around his neck was of natural flicked wool, beiges and browns and blacks: Shaw was dressed to be least in sight in the woods. Dark hair was handy that way.

My cousin smiled as Shaw led her up to me. "Mr. Kristinsson is here to teach you a spell, Miss Sorensson. I think it would be useful for you to know it, and your mastery of the basics should allow you to absorb the lesson swiftly."

Suddenly I wasn't cold anymore.

Earlier someone had brushed off the stone benches in the back courtyard. Cousin Esme settled herself comfortably on one in the morning sunlight.

"There's an open area over between the manor and the carriage house," Shaw said to my cousin. "May we do this spell over there, Professor Livingston?"

Cousin Esme nodded graciously. "I will make sure you do not have an audience. The young ones do not need to know this spell yet." She glanced toward the kitchen.

One of cook's assistants hurried up the snow-covered cobblestone path. The girl, bundled in several long gray shawls, stopped next to my cousin and offered her something small, like pebbles.

"Thank you, Emily." Cousin Esme took the items from her palm. Turning her head toward Shaw, my cousin said: "This might make a good object lesson."

Puzzled, Shaw examined what she held. "Dough balls?"

I stepped closer. Shaw carefully picked up a misshapen pinch of dried dough, such as might be left over after kneading bread, and offered it to me. I held out my cupped palm, and he set the dough in the center of my left hand.

"Might be able to bind the spell," Shaw said. I could see that he was uncertain, a slight frown touching his mouth. According to my *Denizens of the Night*, binding something after a spell casting was more advanced work.

"What do you want to teach me?" I asked. I didn't want merely to see what he had in mind—I wanted to *learn* the spell.

Shaw lifted the flap on his breast pocket, and withdrew something to offer to me.

A ray of sunlight caught the tiny object in his gloved fingers. It shimmered like mottled silk in firelight. I offered my knit glove with its deerskin grip, and Shaw set the item on my palm.

It was a shell, half as long as my first finger, its surface smooth, yet covered with fine ridges. It was like a narrow cone, or a tightly rolled piece of paper just coming loose on one edge, tapering to a point. This shell could hide in the litter of a forest floor, striped in browns, beiges and creams. I lifted it to my ear and sure enough I could hear the whisper of the sea within it.

Though the shell was quite empty, it once held a living thing that built this beautiful, coiling object. I wanted to touch it with my fingers, feel the glass-like glide of the inside, and the tiny lines running the length from mouth to tip, but it was too cold to think about removing my glove.

"Mater says it comes all the way from the Shogunate," Shaw said. "I think it belonged to a snail. Seashells are more worn than forest shells—from sand and salt grinding away at them. What do you think of when you look at it?"

I blinked.

That was a very big question.

I tried to think about both tiny things and huge things. "The endless sea, the variety of life, the perfection of some forms...." What did he want? There was so much hidden in a shell!

"Think about the form. There's a way to hide a spell in a tight package. Practitioners often carry magic on pieces of jewelry, or items of food, or even a pinch of pipe tobacco or snuff. You never know when having a spell ready-made might be useful."

Tobacco? That could be a nasty way to hurt someone. It could happen with food, too, couldn't it?

I studied the shell again, wondering if another creature had adopted it when the first outgrew it....

"It's a labyrinth," I said, lifting my gaze to meet his. "It's a tiny labyrinth."

"Yes," he agreed, glancing away, as if suddenly shy. "It's a labyrinth. And like a labyrinth, it has many uses."

"Can you store energy in a shell?"

Shaw's gray eyes reminded me of chips of ice. "I guess you could at that. What's important is that you can store energy in a spiral. The stronger the material, the more energy it can hold."

"So metal and stone will hold the most?"

"And oak, maybe."

Shrieking rose from the makeshift racecourse along the cobblestone walkway. We were missing a fine biscuit race.

I put it out of my mind. This was important enough that Cousin Esme had allowed Shaw to come teach it to me, long before I would learn it in class.

So I would learn it.

I did wonder why she wanted me to learn it so quickly.

But for now? Something new!

ॐ·ॐ·ॐ

"Are you still grounded and centered?" Shaw asked.

"Yes." I was pretty sure I was...at least I'd done everything that Cousin Cory and Aunt Marta had shown me.

Pressure bumped me, like a big horse thumping you in the chest with its forehead. It gave me a sensation of momentarily floating, as if I was on a wave, but my feet did not move, nor my spine flex.

"Good," was all he said, but I knew he had checked.

Just making sure....

I had my wand clutched in my left hand, and several balls of dough in my right. My gloves were still on, but the shell was back in Shaw's pocket. The shell was just for show—*this is what magic can do,* it seemed to whisper in my mind. It can coil like a string, in perfect symmetry, or tighten like the tiny metal spring in Papa's pocket watch.

How small could a coil of magic become? Could I watch it scrunch down, if I used the other sight Death had taught me that day in the woods outside Hudson-on-the-Bend? Sometime I was going to try.

"Come back to me, Allie," came Shaw's voice into my musings.

"I'm here," I said, steadying my gaze on the gently rolling snow-field between the big house and the barns.

His wand flicked into my line of vision, tiny dark lines showing the grain of the wood, and I lifted mine in response. The grain was too regular for oak. I wondered what his wand was made of, sparking a question.

"I've never done anything with this wand except charge it, and try to fill a goblet with water," I told him. "Is there anything we need to do before I try to use it in a spell?"

Shaw took a step toward me, his gaze caught mine, and his cheeks and neck suddenly flushed. "You do everything you do with... your hands?" he said.

That didn't sound quite right, but I wasn't using my feet, so.... "I think so." His reaction made my cheeks feel warm, and I wondered if I was blushing, too.

For a long moment neither of us spoke. I could hear the children cheering, and a flock of crows scolding them. Deep within the farm a stallion was trumpeting his superiority. Then Shaw said: "Why don't you put away your wand, and I will show you how to do this with your spelling hand."

I looked away from his frosty eyes and slid the wand into my skirt.

He stepped closer. "How do you do wild magic? With your hand, or something else?" It showed how much I trusted him, that I would answer that question.

I held up my left hand. "When I need it."

Shaw's right eyebrow rose. Then he looked away from me. He gestured with his right hand, his left hand and wand relaxed, pointing away from us both. "See the snow devils?"

I leaned slightly to one side, looking down the snow-dusted cobblestone walkway and across drifts covering shrubs and berm. I saw a tiny puff of wind lift snow crystals, swirl them, and let them collapse back onto the landscape.

Shaw flicked his wand suddenly. Then the breeze swelled, and a larger ribbon of snow rose like a waterspout, twisting like a dust devil before it exploded into white powder. Smaller devils twirled in the path of the wind, some of them looking like small funnels, others looking briefly like chaotic balls of yarn.

"Like dancing hoar frost," I said, remembering the white ice crystals that formed at home on cold, clear nights when trees and the very ground were colder than the air.

"There's always a pattern," Shaw replied, his attention focused on the capricious snow. "Find the pattern, and collapse it on itself. Whichever direction it's moving? Push it faster, but start with large movements and make them smaller, tighter. If you can make it so tight there's nowhere else to go, then I have another trick to show you." Turning to look at me, he added: "You must be fast, to see the pattern. You can do it with heat swirling above a fire, or water in a stream, or a dust devil. Sometimes you can do it above a freshly-ploughed field. Pattern and power."

"Pattern and power," I repeated, looking out over the snow. If I swung my arm as if I was making a snow angel.... I saw the next snow devil move, a thicker funnel, and swung my arm like a windmill.

Snow devils rose like morning mist, swirling like waterspouts, creating a soft ground fog. The new cloud bank rose, taller than our heads.

"Less power," Shaw advised. "More focus."

"How can I be focused and make big movements?" I said, stopping what I was doing. The snow devils expanded and relaxed into a soft fall of tiny snowflakes.

"Focus your mind and eyes," he suggested. "Your arm is just to wind up, or unwind, what you're looking at."

Unwind? I thought of that bathtub down the hall from my room, the water careening about as it hurried down a hidden pipe. If I pictured moving it backwards....

The next gust of wind scooped up snow in a wave, swirling it like water in a cup. I watched the movement, seized the snow devil, and froze it, just for a moment. Then it whipped back around like water swirling counter-clockwise. Finally the snow devil collapsed into snowflakes.

"That made more sense," I said aloud, suddenly cold.

There was silence—even the children were quiet—and then Shaw said, "Did you realize that you didn't use your arm to do that?"

I touched the wand in my pocket, and looked at him.

"I do that, too," he added. "You see exactly what you want in your mind, and you make it happen. We have to be careful about that. If we don't give it limits...."

"Magic must have limits. Or it's like a whirling wind," I said promptly. "There's no way to know where it will strike."

"You saw it collapsing after it whirled back around, didn't you?" he asked.

I thought my way through it. "Yes."

Cousin Esme's warm voice suddenly intruded. "That is common for practitioners who prefer their left hands for work." She had come up behind us. "It does not surprise me that you can learn how to do this inside your mind, without moving your hand or wand." In a low voice she added: "It can be very useful to have a practitioner in a group who can wind energy with the mind alone."

A sudden gust of wind sprayed us with fine icy pellets.

"Try again," Shaw said, looking back out over the cold, glittering lawn. "Pattern and power. Wind it to the right—faster, tighter."

Cousin Esme walked away from us again.

It took eight tries, but I got it. I had to watch for a snow devil and then seize it before it either collapsed or flitted away into the air. Then I pretended I was winding yarn, and it worked, once I thought about making that first tiny core of wool.

Once I was winding and unwinding with snow devils, Shaw asked: "Can you do it without a snow devil? Just grab some lines of power and wind them up?"

I found myself wishing I had stuffed extra biscuits into my pockets before leaving breakfast. The edible biscuits, not the roaring ones....

As if I had spoken, Shaw dug into another pocket, pulled out a folded handkerchief, and handed it to me. I unwrapped it and found several pieces of venison jerky inside. I took a piece, and flipped the handkerchief back over the remaining pieces. As he took back the packet, I nodded my thanks and bit carefully into the hank of dried meat.

Soft and seasoned just right. His mother had a good touch with jerky.

I studied the snowbank, watching the wind spray snow flurries into the air and then sprinkle ice crystals in a shimmering veil. Somewhere beyond that frozen landscape was a woven mat of golden threads, binding the universe together.

Death had taught me how to look for the weaving of life. I could find those threads, weave those threads in new ways....

Break those threads.

It was easier in dreams, or when you ate a certain kind of mushroom. But it could be done by, well...just softening your gaze.

I let my vision go unfocused this time, allowing my mind to wander.

First there was a golden glow, as if late afternoon summer light was filtered through the tree branches. Then slender threads of power sprang into place, as if someone had flipped a bolt of Highland plaid across everything before us. The gleaming threads of silver and gold were flexible, filling hollows and arcing over hills, swirling in spots.

I wondered what the swirls meant. They meant something; of that I was sure.

I looked for a place where the lines seemed to run through the air and did not touch a tree. Then I reached with my mind and poked at a thread. It vibrated, like the string of Shaw's violin. The buzz was pleasant.

I grabbed a string of light and whipped it around, as if I was trying to coil it up. Strange sounds echoed in my head, a hive of busy bees. It wasn't a bad feeling, just odd. Suddenly I had golden thread wrapped into a loose bundle, like the flax on the distaff of a spinning wheel. I was going backwards for spinning, except...I was spinning a shell!

But where did the snail start? Did it find something to begin its shell?

I remembered the tiny balls of dough in my right palm.

Holding the image of my golden distaff in my mind, trembling with the effort, I dropped one ball of dough from my right hand into the palm of my left. Then I touched a loose thread to the dough ball.

The dough exploded into dust.

Somehow I hung onto my weaving of light, although the end of the thread flickered like a firefly. I knew I had another dough ball, so I cupped my palms to drop dough into my palm once again. This time I tried looping the thread back into a slipknot, and lassoing the ball.

Gently....

I rolled the dough to my fingertips and back to my palm, pretending I was tangling the center of a ball of yarn. Finally it was large enough that I could start winding figure-eights, shifting the dough a twitch each pass, making the tiny energy package bigger and bigger.

"Allie, I think you can stop winding now." Shaw's voice was very calm, but the sudden pop of my name made me think he really wanted me to leave off what I was doing.

I held onto the dough ball, and released the soft distaff of remaining energy back into the sky.

My palm was full of light. It was like a golden river pebble, smooth and solid. I looked over at Shaw.

He reached carefully and held his gloved hand above mine.

Did I imagine it, or did he wince slightly?

"That's good," he said aloud. "Now check to see what you have."

"I have a ball of light," I told him.

He relaxed, an exhalation of tension. "Oh, you can see the energy? Then you know what's there." He looked over at Cousin Esme, who was back on the bench. "The dough was a good idea, better than a pebble."

"Much better," she said softly. "The dough dissolves into a puff of flour once you have used the energy attached to it. A pebble could be reused, but it also might burst the next time you tried to use it. A gem is much harder, and safer as a focus of power. Noble metal also carries energy well. But something solid could carry your unique energy signature, and possibly be used against you."

As if I would ever have noble metal—

That meant a coin could be used for storage!

I would never pick up a penny off the street, never, ever—

Shaw had given me that halfpenny.

I had a ball of energy in my pocket....

"What can I do with this spell?" I asked aloud.

"Store energy. Store an entire spell someday," Shaw replied.

"How long does it last?"

Shaw turned his head sharply, surprised. "I...I don't know. I've tucked spells inside items for several days."

Ah. So you can carry energy with you. That could be handy.

Not that I was planning to need that energy...not that I knew how to tap it....

"Do you carry extra energy because you might be too tired to pull it from the air?" I went on.

"A practitioner might not have a wand, but she could have jewelry, or tobacco, or a compounded pill, or—"

"A dough ball," I finished, smiling. "Without a wand, what would most folks do with their tiny spell?"

"Say a word, make a gesture, recite a verse—lots of things can ignite a spell. And if worse comes to worst—" Shaw held out his hand for the dough ball.

I dropped it onto his palm. He swung his arm, flinging it into the snow between the manor and the carriage house.

The snow burst like corn from a fireplace, tossing white powder into the air. Ice misted at least six feet above the ground.

Well, that's disturbing.

"Yes," Shaw said, and I realized I had spoken aloud.

FOURTEEN

"IT MUST BE SIMPLE," MARGARET SAID, the "t's" in her words cutting. The empty kitchen echoed slightly—not the actual words, but a tone, humming like a struck bell.

It will be. It had to be-- the children sentenced to kitchen duty might be willing, but other than Daniel and James, their ability to be useful was unknown. At least Daniel could make oatmeal, and James could clean.

I shook my head to clear it, and tried to focus. My entire day had been a struggle. The magic spiral still vibrated within me, inviting me to join its dance.

"Do you know how to cook anything?" I asked as we walked into the deserted kitchen, its clean butcher block tables sanded, its floors swept and washed down. The huge roasting fireplace was banked for the night.

Somehow all week I had resisted that question, but now I needed to know. In all our discussions about food, Margaret had never so much as suggested she could boil water without scorching the teakettle.

My attention shifted to the wall where the soups and stews were made, a brick ledge waist high and more than arm deep, running the length of the wall, every half foot or so a rectangular opening with a woven cast-iron trivet inset above a pit of unlit charcoal. Gleaming copper stock pots sat upon the cast iron trivets, like soldiers in a row.

This could work....

"I can make macaroons and pound cake."

I turned my head toward her, and found Margaret had closed her eyes.

She sounded a little desperate, as if she was leaping for a rope while falling into a creek.

"Those skills will be very useful," I assured her.

Margaret sighed and opened her eyes. "I have written down everything Mrs. Gardener told us," she said, looking down at the notebook she was carrying. "We could have as many as one hundred sixty people a meal, but they never allow the Saturday group to plan for more than eighty."

"Less food to feed the pigs when things go wrong," I said, running a finger along the top of a copper pot. What an amazing pot. It would be an heirloom in my family.

"I would imagine so." She took a deep breath. "I simply want to survive this day and put it into the past as quickly as possible."

I caressed the huge cast iron kettle Mrs. Gardener used for hot cereal. "We are going to live out of soup pots, Margaret Rutledge," I announced. "I am going to teach you how to make lentil soup and a winter beef stew." *But there is nothing to do on Saturday except eat hidden treats or go hungry...* "The curious will come," I went on. "Daniel Williams has told the children that I will teach them how to make biscuits."

Margaret actually looked more pale than usual. "Miss Alden has told me she looks forward to seeing what I make for Saturday." Her expression became set, flinty, as my mother liked to say, determined beyond common sense. "She hoped that the chaos could be kept to a minimum."

My own lips tightened. Those were fighting words.

I had yet to face them, and I was already tired of Miss Alden and Miss Bradford.

Maybe I knew nothing of fashion, but I could make a meal.

I set a hand on her arm. "We know what we will make. You could make cookies for dessert, tiny ones. Is there really a lot of dried coconut?"

"There is a fortune in dried coconut," she said in a low voice. "And no limit on spices or herbs. I never made the connection between having a maze and the ability to get supplies cheaply!"

"I would be surprised if there are not mazes dedicated to going places like the Spice Islands," I replied. "If it is really just opening a door, and the same amount of effort opens it...."

"More energy for more distance," Margaret said absently, still examining her notes. "It is not easy to do, thankfully. Or else armies would move through mazes."

"When you think of the cost of outfitting a sailing ship, the danger...trust men to ruin trade with war," I muttered, heading to the farthest table. Several sacks of large green lentils lay on the counter. "Good, Jan brought them up for us. We need to put these to soak. How many servings of lentil soup for supper?" It would be our last meal of the day, and needed the most preparation. I poured a large amount of the tiny seeds into a copper pot, grabbed a bucket and dipped water out of the big kettle set aside for cooking.

"One hundred sixty bowls," she said firmly.

I turned around and stared, the dripping bucket still in my grip.

So. Margaret did not lack for courage.

My stomach fluttered and I suddenly felt too warm.

If we made twice the amount allowed and no one came, we might be in trouble.

"Then we need that entire sack and more than one pot," I said, and dumped the water into the first tall stock pot. I was pleased that my voice did not tremble. As I moved on to the next pot, Margaret bent over the raw lentils.

"Oh, Miss Sorensson, there are twigs in here!"

I pulled a ladling spoon off a rack and leaned to show her how to skim off the top of a soaking pot.

❧ 💮 ❧

"We usually cut up vegetables over there, because it's the shortest table." Daniel pointed.

"Then we'll put our vegetables over there. This way, gentlemen!" I gestured, and the boys dropped their bushels of carrots and onions on the block of wood.

"I know how to set a table!" one boy shouted in the dining room.

"They are already set, we're not supposed to touch them!" came a girl's response.

In the midst of swirling children, the yelling made me feel right at home. I grabbed two chalk tablets hanging on the wall and hurried into the dining room.

"Who can draw?" I shouted over their argument. The short, solid girl's hand shot up into the air. She had a determined chin, and I noticed the boys did not contradict her. "Here. Choose one place setting and draw where each piece of silverware and china is placed, so we can set up for the staff tomorrow." I waved the other tablet around. "Can you two count everything so we know what we'll need to set up each meal?"

"Even napkins?" the absurdly thin boy with dark hair and eyes asked.

The other boy, dressed in Sunday farmer best, reached for the tablet. "*Everything*. Start counting plates, Johnson."

A job. They all needed a job. I was used to trained people sliding into kitchen work...

I rushed back to the kitchen and found the oldest of the young men. Tall, dark-haired and brown-eyed, still smooth-faced, he was old enough to eye me thoughtfully. Apparently someone had told him that I was also teaching, because he waited for me to speak.

"I understand that you know how to cut up a side of beef," I said.

"Yes, Miss. My uncle is a butcher. Runs a fine shop in—"

"I need at least a hundred pounds of stew meat. No pork. I don't want the fancy, tender cuts. Dice the meat small, about this size." I showed him the length of my nail joint on my thumb. He held up his own hand, and his first joint was about as long.

"I can do it."

I eyed his fine trousers and jacket. "Do you want to wear those clothes to do it in?"

He startled, his body jerking. "You want the meat cut up tonight?"

"Yes. I want to soak it in wine."

Nodding briskly, he said: "I have some clothes I wear...out. I'll go change."

"Out" being the tavern you were caught in.

"Miss Sorensson," Margaret murmured, and I jumped at the sound of her voice. "I don't think the children will be able to keep up the pace that the older boys will attempt."

"No," I agreed. "They can go rest between cleanups. Are we going to have enough help?"

Margaret actually smiled. "I have heard that we will get a few extras tomorrow. Little Moira purposely sauced off to a maid so she could come learn how to make biscuits."

I couldn't help it; I started laughing. "She probably thinks they will be roaring ones."

Margaret looked thoughtful. "I wonder if Professor Livingston would give us permission to teach a class in roaring biscuits?"

"Perhaps once you have worked out the exact spell," came my cousin's voice behind us.

We both jumped, which I was certain was her plan. Cousin Esme liked surprising people. Considering how often life surprises you, I imagine she considered it good training for us.

My cousin looked elegant in a dress of flowing cranberry silk with a brocade jacket, her hair tumbled high and dressed with feathers and holly leaves and berries. "I am impressed. For some reason, none of the kitchen groups have ever gotten together to start the night before, even to set out their tools and root cellar vegetables."

"We felt our results would have a better chance at being edible with some advanced preparation," Margaret said carefully.

Cousin Esme's appearance saved me from having to ask something of Kymric, who might rebuff me. "Professor Livingston, Mrs. Gardener mentioned that the wine shop delivered a barrel Kymric was not pleased with. It is dryer than you care for. May we have some of it to soak the beef cubes?"

"Yes, but only if Miss Rutledge flashes the wine afterward before you add it to your stew. Did you intend to do that?" my cousin asked, her eyebrows lifting slightly.

I was confused—we always boiled when we soaked—but Margaret said, "Yes, Ma'am."

"I was going to put some parsley and thyme in the soup, and bay leaves," I added.

"It sounds very flavorful. You may add herbs to your wine and oil, but the leaves will be crisped by the flash, after you remove the meat. Do not use those soaked herbs in the soup. You may tell Kymric I have approved wine for your beef marinade." With a wave of her hand, she said: "Please, continue," and walked off.

"She'll be back," I muttered to Margaret. There I was, muttering again. "Oil? What kind of oil? Beef suet? Butter? Olive oil?"

"It will get cold quickly in the kitchen. We need something that won't become solid right away."

"Want to try a bit of olive oil with the wine? I wish we could ask my cousin M—Mrs. Donaltsson if we need some cider in here." I knew you needed some acid against the fat, when you soaked meat, and sometimes salt, but this didn't need brining, not with long cooking. Wine was acid, wasn't it?

"We could mix it and taste a bit. If it doesn't taste good to us, then we don't make a bunch for the food," Margaret said.

"We'll need fat for the beef soup, too." I heard raised voices, and wondered if we were going to get more children than I'd planned on. "I'm going to mix the dough for the apple bread now. I don't want to trust to our time tomorrow. Watching them is going to take a lot of effort."

"You're staying up?" Margaret asked.

"The bread is best if it sits a bit before eating."

"Then I might as well make the pound cake now. We should stay up together." She gave me a knowing look, and I felt very junior in the partnership. I had thought one of us sleeping and one working was a better use of our time. "I'll find an apron."

That look....

Chaperones for each other.

I completely forgot the need for a chaperone in the cities. Marta had warned me about that. *Have to pay attention to that, blast it....*

It was as if, deep inside me, my power always knew it could bloom to save me.

Daniel and James appeared as if I'd conjured them.

"We thought you could use more help?"

"We can, indeed. Let's see how good you are with cutting apples."

❧⊕❧

As I finished separating balls of dough into piles on the bread board and covered them for rising, I heard a soft whooshing, like the sound of grain pouring into a chute. A cloud of fine pale flour billowed like mist around me from behind. In my solitary candle-light it looked like fog.

The giggling sounded like James and Daniel. I walked through the wave of flour into the mixing nook where a huge stoneware bowl rested on a pedestal; the boys were easing a medium-sized bowl down on a neighboring table. Everything was covered in a thin film of ground wheat. They were trying to muffle their laughter.

"Do you gentlemen need help?" I asked.

They jumped.

I began to understand why Cousin Esme enjoyed doing that.

Both boys straightened. They had just dumped flour on top of what looked like creamed butter—soft butter and sugar completely mixed together—in the huge bowl. "So you are going to mix this for Miss Rutledge?"

"Yes, Miss Sorensson," Daniel said quickly. "She made a batch, and we are making another. She measured the ingredients."

"No shells," I said, and they both shook their heads violently, flour poofing off their hair.

"She already cracked four pounds of eggs for us," James said quickly.

"Very well. Don't forget to sweep." I left.

Margaret sent me a look of mute entreaty as I approached the table where she worked. Neat rows of small bread tins full of batter lined up before her.

We could do this. "It will be all right," I told her.

Her expression stiffened. She gazed beyond me, and I turned.

In the gloom beyond our candlelight, something large and white moved majestically toward us.

I took a step closer to Margaret.

It fluttered, rippling like curtains in a breeze.

Was this some sort of ghost?

Closer...closer....

The mass shrank and resolved into a small figure swathed in a bed sheet, a pillowcase wrapped like a turban around its head.

I pressed my lips together.

I will not laugh.

Moira's chin was lifted, her lips pressed tightly in a line. "This time we will make something good. They won't have anything to laugh at."

There are many kinds of punishment. The scorn of your peers was one of them.

"Yes, we will make something good," I told her.

"Let's get you an apron so you may move freely," Margaret said, gesturing toward the cloak room.

❧🏵❧

Two meals down, one left to serve.

Goddess, I was so tired. I had respected Mrs. Gardener, but standing in her shoes for a night and day was an experience I did not want to repeat. Her endurance was astounding.

"Is this right, Miss Sorensson?" James asked, pausing with the block scraper in the air.

"That looks good," I answered. "The kitchen staff will sand again next week." I leaned against the pillar in the kitchen and savored the meaty scent of lentils in the supper stew.

The crashing of pans no longer made me wince. Mr. Jones, our meat cutter, had taken on the washing of pans, and was directing his crew of three as they finished up the biscuit trays. We were half-successful with the bread—it was so cold I couldn't get the sourdough to rise, so biscuits loomed for dinner, but the class in biscuit making was a success.

My only concern was that the younger students seemed to feel that learning how to make biscuits and macaroons was a reward for Saturday crew.

I did not think Professor Livingston wanted that response to rules breaking.

But who knew? Cousin Esme always had more than one reason for doing anything, *that* I was convinced of....

"Miss Sorensson! I could not stop those boys from taking the last of the biscuits!" came Moira's voice. She appeared in a warm wool dress of dark green, a real apron tied around her waist, not quite as large as her sheet of last night. Carefully she balanced two nested bread baskets with a butter bell set inside them.

"Your cheese biscuits were just too good," I told her, taking the basket and plate from her and setting the butter bell over on the marble countertop used for making pastry.

It was time to send them all off to rest. If I was exhausted, they were stumbling. I had to avoid even a hint that they were not tough enough to keep going. A group of tired, quarreling children would not make supper go smoothly.

Margaret appeared around the corner, elegant in an old-fashioned apron across her chest and dress front. "There is a first time for everything," she told us, the right side of her mouth crooked in satisfaction. "I could not have imagined the pleasure of escorting Miss Bradford from the dining room before she was pleased to leave."

"She will punish us for it later," whispered Moira, her eyes growing wider as she realized I had heard her.

Margaret's eyes burned holes in her face, but she stepped up to the stew stove, glancing beneath the simmering stock pots to gauge whether more wood was needed.

As she had only learned the level of heat needed a few hours ago, I was quite proud of her. I wasn't sure if the children would retain their kitchen lessons, but Margaret surely would.

"Moira, if you would help dry the last of the dishes, we can go rest our weary feet."

Sighing dramatically, Moira nodded and headed toward the sinks.

The noise level increased behind us.

I did not even turn around.

I raised my voice: "No hitting with the towels!"

The noise dropped. Margaret's smile grew wider.

"Brothers," I explained to her.

"I clearly missed a great deal, never having to work in the kitchen," she replied, coming to me. She lowered her voice. "Professor Livingston is in her sitting room. She'd like to speak with you."

I hung my apron on a nail and smoothed back the escaped threads of my hair. I was wearing the nicest of what I considered my working dresses, a pale gray, high-necked garment with sleeves tighter from the elbow to wrist, and therefore less likely to drag into food. With luck, anything that had splashed was on that apron.

In Cousin Esme's room I found a cheery blaze in the fire loft, but no signs of tea. My cousin stood by her fireplace, beautifully dressed as always. Her expression was serious.

"So you and Miss Rutledge can keep order in a kitchen," she said, her voice warm with amusement. "That is a good thing to know."

I was pretty sure there was a basin of water somewhere in the room.

"Please sit down by the fire, Alfreda. I have asked you here to propose an expedition to you."

Once we were seated, my cousin in her high-backed chair and I on the small caned settee, Cousin Esme gave me a serious look.

"In the past week, I have learned that you are curious, resourceful, intelligent, brave, and have a gift both for making friends and inspiring envy. Your skills in running a home are formidable, and you already have an impressive grasp of magic principles." She smiled faintly. "You have the two-edged gifts of saying exactly what is on your mind, and a strong dose of common sense, which will not endear you to your more romantic peers. I do not think privilege will ever particularly impress you."

Clothes were going to be a problem.

I wasn't sure yet if the Mayflower Compact would also be trouble.

"You also have a gift I think of as 'hiding in plain sight'...the ability to be noticed, or not noticed. It is an impressive gift, considering your height. That is a non-magical form of invisibility, and right now that gift is pure gold to my husband and me. You see, we need a small errand run. I think that you may be the person to accomplish what needs to be done."

Well, this might be interesting. One never knew with adults.

"I am about to tell you something that is a secret. Marta tells me that you are good with secrets...and this one is very important. A small thing in the history of our young country, but something that needs to be...tided up, shall we say." My cousin looked into the fireplace, her face solemn. "Can you keep a secret, Alfreda? A secret that must be kept a long time...perhaps past the natural deaths of the people involved?"

Slowly I said, "I am not good at secrets that might get someone hurt or killed."

"My hope is that this secret will keep people from getting killed," Cousin Esme replied. "We are trying to get our hands on definitive proof of someone's treachery, so that they will be frozen out of the palaces of power. Three attempts have been made to get something, anything, proving this person's untrustworthiness. All have failed. In fact," she went on, *sotto voce*, "We begin to wonder if that failure is intentional." After a moment Cousin Esme continued in a normal tone of voice. "The...professionals...at retrieving information have turned to the magical community in hopes that we can succeed where they have failed."

She turned back to me. "We need to retrieve a message from someone who cannot be connected to this household. It cannot arrive through magic or post. We cannot penetrate by using magic to where this courier will be, because the owner of the house where we hope to find him is a magician, and has magicians working for him."

She leaned toward me. "Our strongest practitioners are known to these magicians. So we are sending a former student of ours, a brilliant lawyer but a minor magical talent. He will attempt to pick up the item, which will be left in a sealed cylinder in an inconspicuous spot.

"This attempt will be made at a large dinner party at an estate not far from here."

"What would you need me to do?" I asked.

"I need you to observe. We have failed to get any magic user through the doorway of Darkwoods. But you look older than you are, and have little ritual training. Ritual training is what imprints upon a practitioner and makes them stand out in the magical world. Your wild magic..." My cousin reached, her hand hovering above mine. I felt warmth, as if we were touching each other. "Wild magic has marked you differently. My hope is that by placing a simple cloaking spell upon you, you would not register as a magician to them.

"And then—" Cousin Esme revealed a smile very similar to the crooked one Marta occasionally wore "—a spell upon your cross would allow us to see if the courier truly attempts to hand off the cylinder to my old student. It may allow us to know if the courier is a double agent, working for two masters. I cannot cross the threshold of Darkwoods—but you can."

"You think I can pretend to be a maid?"

"No." My cousin shook her head, the holly berries in her hair turning momentarily blood red in the firelight. "It sometimes happens at this time of year that servants become ill, or they have family members who are ill. Those servants are told not to return to the house until everyone has recovered. The kitchen staff at Darkwoods estate is very short-handed. Therefore several estates will send over servants to help out during the party."

"Will they take someone from a wizard's house?" I asked.

"They will take someone who is the daughter of a friend from rural Connecticut, in town for an extended visit."

Connecticut?

Connecticut was a place on a map!

"I don't know *a thing* about Connecticut," I told her.

"There will be no time for anyone to question you about specifics of Connecticut," she said, a flick of her fingers dismissing the problem. "You know the life of a busy farmstead—you have stories to tell, if needed. I will lay a spell of suppression upon you. If anyone tries to brush into your mind, they will find the tangled tapestry of a young farm girl, worried about her chickens in the cold, because who knows if her brother will see to their safety? And thinking about a boy who might be making up to another girl in her absence, and what to do with the material her parents gave her as a Christmas gift...."

I smiled in turn. "So they cannot tell what I am really thinking."

"No."

"Or that I can work magic?"

"That is the actual intent of the spell."

I thought a long moment. And realized that this might be...tricky. "Will I be able to work magic, if I need it?"

My cousin's face stilled. "You will only be able to cast magic if things go badly. If your fear overwhelms you or your actual safety becomes paramount, you will be able to break free of the suppression spell. I hope that is not necessary, because I suspect that if you broke through the spell, it would be...noisy."

Ah. Noisy if I used wild magic, in other words. I had little control over anything else yet. Except maybe dough balls, and that would take thought.

"Who will I be looking for?" I asked her. "Or will this person be looking for me?"

"Neither," my cousin replied. "The courier should set down a package, probably a cylinder. And my former student, a tall, red-headed man, will pick up that package during the evening. I will know who we are watching. You will merely try to face toward the party guests at every opportunity. If you do not know what the courier looks like, you cannot give yourself away by your attention toward him."

"But what if someone tidying up sees the package first?" I asked.

"That would be unfortunate, but not catastrophic," was her answer. "If someone tried to open the cylinder, the contents would be destroyed. Professor Lee would know that someone had attempted to pass a message in his home, but would not know who, or why. The courier will leave it someplace inconspicuous, such as behind a vase. Professor Lee collects vases."

"Will I know why?" I didn't think I would, at least not now, but I was going to wonder.

"Not yet," she replied. "Let us say that the men and women who helped this country at its birth were very human. They made mistakes; they were governed by their history and their passions. Some will tell you that a famous duel was rooted in politics. I believe that the duel was rooted in dishonor. We live out here, not in town, because the Manhattan Company, formed to bring clean water to Lower Manhattan, is a sham. Many people will die because of that sleight of hand. The company's aim was banking, not safe water."

Cousin Esme stared into the fireplace again. "Better for now that it be a secret even from you, Alfreda. Suffice it to say that we are looking for proof of further dishonor by famous men...men who do not have the best interests of our young country at heart."

"How will you watch?"

"My husband and I will watch in water, as you have seen done. Miss Rutledge will assist us. We will send you in Livingston's carriage, and retrieve you at the end of the evening. With luck, your presence will allow us to confirm that the courier is truly working for our cause, and we will have our message at last."

"When do you need me to go?"

"Tonight."

Hell, Hull, and Halifax. Exhaustion already clawed at my heels.

"When will you do the spell?"

"Right now, if you are ready."

❧ 𝕯 ❧

I ended up seated upon a chair in a ritual circle called forth by my cousin merely by lifting her hands, palms up. It flared upon the polished wood floor. *Magical fire?* I wondered, but did not dare ask. It might be that the ritual had already begun.

"Now."

Eight perfect, dipped, beeswax candles appeared at the cardinal points, and halfway between each pair of cardinal points. She snapped her fingers, and the candles lit.

How powerful does a practitioner have to be to light candles with a snap?

Nor did she need a wand. I had seen Marta work without a wand. Was that something about family lines...our level of power...the type of ritual?

The fragrance of burning beeswax filled the room, as heady as harvesting combs on a hot summer's day. And then it was as if someone was pouring warm honey over my head, the thick amber wave dripping down my face to pool around me, fresh from a hive, a feeling like raindrops falling between my fingers....

FIFTEEN

It was freezing cold in my corner of the kitchen, but the women working near the roaring fire sweated as if summer ruled outside the country manor. I sent a quick prayer to the Lord and Lady of Light that I would never have to earn my keep by working in such a place.

"'Ware the pot!" an older woman shouted, rushing from fire to worktable with two full copper kettles. I swung sideways and crammed myself between my bench and the wall, out of her way.

The kitchen at Darkwoods estate was barely contained chaos. The workers were as noisy and busy as a flock of wild turkeys settling onto a harvested field. I was properly planted in the magician Lee's home, but I had no idea how I was going to get out into the main spaces of the house.

I had been prepared as if I was a bride, from my gray dress and a clean, starched, full apron to my hair braided and coiled on my head like a crown.

You need to look as if you could run an errand to the front of the house, Dr. Livingston explained, nodding his approval of my attire. *Not a scullery maid, but a go-between. You must listen for opportunity, for a chance to go to the front.*

Scullery maids scrubbed pots; I knew that much.

The low-burning tallow candle sputtering on the soot-blackened beam over the fireplace showed that it had been two hours since I'd arrived. To casual eyes I was just a country girl delivered by carriage to protect her from the biting wind. My oldest shawl hung on a peg in the mudroom. I had been given a huge over-apron and immediately set to work peeling hardboiled eggs.

No wand. They could not risk my being found with one. *We will see what you see, Miss Sorensson,* Margaret told me as she tied my apron with a lovely bow. The spell on the cross around my neck guaranteed that.

They could see...but not communicate. My magic was Cousin Esme's spell of invisibility upon my mind, a veil made of the thoughts of a kitchen maid from Connecticut.

I carried with me two magical weapons, because they would not let me carry my knife. The first, Shaw's coin, I had shown to Cousin Esme. She had studied it intently for a time, and then said, "From Mr. Kristinsson?"

"Yes, ma'am," I had replied.

"A last defense," she said calmly. "Do not throw it inside the house. It smells like fire."

I had gingerly placed it in my right apron pocket.

The other weapon, in my left apron pocket, I kept totally to myself.

It was part of a cake of yeast.

"Are you done with those eggs yet?" the cook called as she strode through the room. She was a big woman, enormously strong, and ruled her small kitchen kingdom with a firm hand. I had not learned her name. I was not important enough to be introduced to the head of the kitchen, so like the other newcomers I called her 'ma'am'. Privately I thought of her as Cook, as some of the workers reverently referred to her.

Spooning the whipped yolk into the last egg half, I said "Yes, ma'am, they're ready!"

"Good girl," was her response as she picked up the tray. "Well done. Go help Lucy with the biscuits." She hurried to give the tray to a young man dressed in formal livery.

I searched for someone baking until a female voice yelled "Over here!"

Once I reached the bread table I found a solid young woman with a tense tilt to her blonde head dumping dough out onto the center of a flour-covered butcher block. She tossed me a tin biscuit cutter and began to roll out her dough.

"Don't let them mix," she warned me, "Yours are the sweet ones for dessert."

I glanced around for a rolling pin as I dipped my hand into the apron and crumbled some yeast into my hand.

The rolling pin lay at the top of the table, along with a bowl of flour. I scooped up a handful of the flour, hiding the yeast on my palm. A quick rub to the rolling pin with the flour and yeast meant dough would not stick to it. I scattered flour and yeast over the board in a tight spiral and then I pulled some dough onto my flour-covered board, letting the yeast settle in.

If I focused my Latin word on the pans waiting for the fire....

Could older bread, already baked, still respond?

Lucy ignored me and worked very fast. I finished lining up my biscuits on the pan as she carried hers over to racks by the monstrous brick oven set into the wall, two oven cavities one on top of the other. I guessed that the upper oven either had a bed for hot coals, or worked solely from rising heat. The girl made sure her pans were closest to the fire.

If I spoke no word, they would remain only fluffy biscuits. But if a distraction was needed, I had planted the seed. Maybe it was a silly thing to do, but I felt better for it.

I reached for a flat wooden paddle to scrape extra dough off the board, and then Cook tapped my right hand and yelled "I need someone to help bring back dishes, come along!"

Thank you, Lady of Light.

Cook took me by the wrist into the hallway under a candle sconce, and I shivered at the contrast in temperature.

"Fancy dress, child," she said in a soft voice laced with English overtones—*not London* was all I guessed. "Are you so pretty in your own kitchen?"

"No, ma'am!" I said quickly, giving her a curtsy. "Since the professor was having a party, I was ordered to look nice, so I could help wherever you needed me!" I was breathless, not like myself at all, but then I was now Anna, a farm girl from Connecticut. It was fine if I sounded different.

"Mrs. Gardener is a gracious lady," Cook said, her tone brisk. "Good thinking on her part. I need you to help Emma bring back dishes from the sideboard. Emma, here is Anna to help you! Show her what needs doing!"

A dark-haired young woman Margaret's age moved out of the gloom. She wore a dark grey gown with a full apron and a cap covering her hair. Emma dipped her knee to the cook, and then took hold of my skirt and tugged. Cook fled back into her kitchen.

"This way, hurry, now!" Emma rushed down the corridor. I kept up as best I could, our footsteps loud on the wood—there was no runner. We crossed onto polished stone, pale and slick, the ceiling above us high and dark. I could feel cold air from somewhere, and a steady draft.

I was so tired it took everything I had to keep up with Emma.

We crossed a huge room into a corridor. Here a long row of large windows and two sets of double doors overlooked the winter night, one door ajar. The windows seemed odd. The frigid night air streamed in around several men talking on a veranda. A blanket of winter white covered a rolling lawn, with the dark, shaggy outline of a labyrinth standing in frosted splendor. The labyrinth pulsed with energy—the entrance curved to the left, a male labyrinth.

Once we passed the doorway, Emma whispered, "These wizardly folk don't seem to notice the cold at all. Do you know wizardly folk?"

"I've never met anyone who called themselves wizardly folk," I said honestly. Practitioners didn't call themselves wizards...did magicians? I wasn't even positive how magicians differed from practitioners.

"People who like magic, and magic likes them," she hissed. "The rule is to ignore them, no matter what they do, and keep to your work!"

I nodded.

The dining room blazed with tall candelabra placed along the center table, and a chandelier above. Many men sat at the long mahogany table, gesturing with cigars and pretty glass drinking vessels. I spotted the only redhead and guessed that he was Cousin Esme's old student. Emma and I crept to the sideboard, where a young man in a suit like Kymric's was setting dishes cleared from the meal on trays.

The trick was to take as many dishes as possible without dropping anything. My trick was to load a tray as slowly as possible, so Cousin Esme could see everyone in the room. I was careful to choose fragile things that could not be piled too high. I had never seen such glasses. They were so clear, it was like looking through a window, or into a pool of rainwater.

"Those go to the butler's pantry," Emma said, pointing with her chin to a door at the other end of the room. "Put them on the table in the back, and then come back here."

The butler's pantry was very dim. I was grateful for the door being open. Plenty of candlelight filtered in from the dining room as I loaded the glasses from my tray onto the broad table against the wall.

My light level diminished by half as a knot of men stood in front of the pantry door, having a spirited argument. I knew better than to try to pass them, but I did my best to see their faces. *I am Cousin Esme's eyes.*

There was another open door, so I grabbed my empty tray and ducked into a grand walkway lined with columns. It was filled with vases, from tiny ones no larger than my hands sitting on pedestals or tables, to vases as tall as me set right on the floor.

It had to be Professor Lee's collection. Whatever did he use them for? Were they filled during the summer with flowers?

Was this were they would leave the package?

"Anna! Where are you?" It was Emma's voice.

I rushed toward the voices, and found myself entering the dining room from yet another doorway. "The other door was blocked by guests," I whispered.

"We must finish clearing here!"

Two more trips to the kitchen—soup bowls and small plates—before I could glance back into the huge corridor of vases....

And there were no vases.

That stopped me in my tracks. I stood in the open doorway, astonished, a cold wind lifting strands of my hair. What had happened to the vases?

"Anna!"

Whirling, I hurried back to the sideboard.

I saw the redhead in passing. He was in a spirited discussion with the man to his right, and the man to his left seemed to be waiting his turn to speak.

This time, walking back down the icy cold hallway to the kitchen, I took the time to scrutinize the labyrinth...and discovered that all the windows in that corridor were portals!

Somehow I managed not to drop the tray I carried. It was all I could do not to stop and look at one of the windows, but I knew that was a bad idea. The portal to Marta's cabin had pulled me right through it. I didn't want to get too close to those windows.

Could Cousin Esme tell that the windows were portals?

I let my vision unfocus as I carried the tray to where the youngest girls were washing all the dishes. The kitchen remained a bastion of normalcy in this unsettling sea of magic. Flickering light, the babble of dozens of people talking, strong smells on the heavy air—but no magic that I could perceive.

The next trip through the dark great room revealed something flapping near the ceiling. I did not recognize any scent, any pattern to the wing beat...but something was up there. I could hear it; I could feel a current of cold from it.

I didn't like that at all.

Back to the bright dining room. The footman had loaded a tray with slightly larger plates and thrust it at me. I took the long way around the table, so Cousin Esme, Dr. Livingston, and Margaret could see who was talking with whom. Once more I trudged to the kitchen, down the ice house masquerading as a hallway.

The kitchen was still chaotic—a swirl of people yelling, ferocious heat, and splashing water. Someone grabbed the tray of plates from me. I had time for a deep breath and then I was handed an empty tray, and I headed back to the dining room via the east hallway. I hoped my apron was still clean. I skimmed along the back wall, a ghost among the well-dressed men walking off their dinner.

Were the Livingstons seeing what they needed to see?

In the murmur of conversation I occasionally caught phrases like "land purchase," or "form a town," or even "another war with Britain" but I ignored them. It took all my concentration to keep moving. My legs felt like stone.

I reached the dining room. Emma was nowhere to be seen. The footman was also absent. I set down the empty tray and picked up a loaded tray of glassware. Fortunately it wasn't ridiculously heavy, so I hauled it up and headed for the butler's pantry...and, I hoped, a door back to those vases.

They were the only vases I'd yet seen. Cousin Esme might want to spot the package, so I needed to at least walk through that room.

I set the glasses down one at a time on the butler's table. Again, guests drifted back and forth before the pantry door. I hung onto my empty tray and slipped through that opposite doorway.

The vases were back, tall and small, some made from heavy clay and others as delicate as one of Professor Lee's wine glasses. Several candles were lit among the many small columns and niches supporting the vases. There was a balcony above tracing the rectangular room. The soft glow of beeswax reflected up under that walkway and cast long shadows from the glass and ceramic. In the room's center the ceiling was a vault filled with darkness and a glint of starlight suggesting high windows.

Two men strolled down the long hall, talking quietly.

I held up my tray and pretended to look for glasses, keeping myself pointed toward the walkers. As I approached a tall vase, I carefully reached to touch a heavy rim.

My finger passed through the rim and down through the throat of the object. *What?*

It was not real.

Were any of them real?

Another current of cold air prompted me to still. Was this huge building so poorly chinked, or was it something else? Cold sank, it was a natural law...the cold air had to be coming from above.

Gently I reached for another vase, staying well back from it. This time my finger touched smooth china.

Real.

Maybe.

I circled the room, past an external set of double doors with many glass panes, past a fine set of windows overlooking the veranda. Glory be, I found three glasses. Quickly I set them on my tray.

Real vases, imaginary ones...there did not seem to be a pattern. Some actual glass vases were tiny, and one was as tall as I. As I took the circuit again, I studied their bases, desperate to view them all before someone came looking for me.

Then I saw something out of place in that tall, narrow room. It looked like a stick in the feeble light.

I had a candidate.

If that was the package, it remained untouched.

I returned with the tray of glasses to the dining room, this time taking some off the big table, trying to face each cluster of men before I headed back to the kitchen.

Emma and I carried dishes two more times, and brought back bowls filled with nuts and fruit. Then we were following men up and down the corridors, picking up dropped nuts and still more glasses.

Every once in a while I made sure to walk past the vase with the stick peeking out behind it.

Still there.

What was wrong?

I watched for the redhead when I passed through the dining room, and he was still stuck with those two men.

"Stuck" was the word.

They would not let him go. Other guests tried to break in, or steer him off down the corridor for conversation. But the men who had sat on either side of him were like burrs attached to his woolen coat.

I knew that the dessert biscuits would go into the brick oven soon. How much longer would this party go on? All night?

As I made another pass through the vase room, the cold breeze playing with my hair, I saw the dark protruding stick at the base of a huge vase.

I wondered if I should pick it up. It looked like it would fit into my wand pocket....

A feeling of warmth flushed through me. It was not the heat of embarrassment; it was the wave of a summer bonfire.

I turned away from that vase to pick up another abandoned glass, and suddenly felt much colder, as if I had stepped outside. Once I had the glass firmly on my tray, I looked back at the shadowy stick.

Warmth moved through me.

We can communicate.

I was convinced Cousin Esme wanted me to pick up that package.

I bent my knees, keeping my head level in case someone came in.

My fingers closed around a long, metal cylinder, and I quickly slipped it into the wand slit in my skirt, my fingers trembling. I tried to keep the feel and thought of it out of my head—I concentrated on the memory of those pans of biscuits, waiting by the fire, just in case I needed them....

As I turned to walk back to the butler's pantry, another gust of air brought the stench of rotten eggs.

The chemicals for building some spells were quite odious.... I glanced up. Something huge and winged soared up toward the few lights of the upper story, curving around as if to swoop again—

RUN! Margaret's silent scream nearly lifted me off the floor. *Hurry, hurry, RUN!*

The winged thing flew between me and the dining room. Abandoning my tray I spun on my toes and rushed for the outer door with its many panes of glass. Could I open the door? Had they shoveled all the verandas for the party? *Please say someone has shoveled any drifting snow!* I threw my weight on the levered door handle and the door sprang open.

What kind of great house was this, that they never locked the doors?

This house has demons guarding it! Margaret's mind shrieked into mine.

How had I heard her? I was not supposed to be able to hear them, or they me! Only what they could see through my cross—

I threw myself out the doorway and whirled to slam the French door shut. Maybe the winged thing had limits. Maybe it could not leave the house.

That did not mean it didn't have friends outside.

I saw its outline against the faint light of candles: huge many-vaned wings like a bat, its legs with spread claws like a stooping eagle. I pushed the glass door until the latch clicked and ran down the long stretch of the covered porch.

Thank you, thank you, Lord and Lady, that I did not see its face.

Sometimes people did not survive seeing a demon's face.

I'd reached a side porch, but I was entirely turned around. I had no clue if I was heading north or south. Low tables scattered along the open porch supported lit candles encased in tall glass containers. The household had prepared for people to come outside, but I could see that on this side, no one had braved the cold for a private chat.

I had to get back inside, or I would be discovered.

I might have already been discovered.

I reached the end of the walkway and staggered, catching myself against the smooth stone railing, for there were two stairs leading down to the snow-covered ground. Where to go? By the bright arcing road of the Milky Way I could see I was on the same side of the house as the labyrinth, but that did not help me. I had no hope of knowing how to use it to get anywhere I wanted to go. It was possible to travel on a labyrinth—somehow we'd used a labyrinth to travel from Marta's home to Esme's.

Margaret?

Silence.

They had told me we could not speak to each other—how had Margaret reached beyond that limitation? It seemed I could not question Margaret or anyone else, and Margaret was no longer speaking to me.

I didn't think they had expected a demon.

Please send the carriage soon.

I'd panicked. How could I fix this?

Taking a deep breath, I stepped off into space, feeling for a stone beneath the ice—and found the starlight blocked. A wall of glittering snow unfurled before me, swirling like a great snow devil. Shrinking back, I dipped my hand into my right apron pocket, fumbling for Shaw's coin, St. John's words rising to my lips—

Starlight shone on a horn, blazing like a candle beckoning through trees.

The wall of flickering snow was...a horse? A huge, slender horse, larger and yet more dainty than the Kristinssons' Arab stallion. No—a horn, not a horse, not a demon, *a unicorn.*

We must hurry. The mind voice ran into my head like water, a swirl of sound, a deep cataract. *Mount.*

"Oh, and how are you going to prove you're not a pooka?" I gasped out, shrinking back.

The creature tossed its head, craning its neck to look toward the labyrinth.

Standing by the entrance to the labyrinth was my Good Friend, luminous in his white stag form...or there stood a spirit alike enough to be his brother. The deer's antlers were not flaming yet—instead, they gleamed like snow under the eye of the new moon. My White Wanderer stood motionless, watching me. I could just make out the flicker of flame in his irises.

It's always a test.

Was the test to mount, or not to mount?

I'd always trusted him, and he gave no call of alarm....

Hurry! The voice of the unicorn rang between my ears like a bell.

I grabbed a handful of mane. Kicking off from the veranda's top step, I managed to get on the great beast's back, my skirt rucking up, my stockings bared to the cold. *Trousers—if I live through this, I will have my own doeskin trousers to wear always!*

The unicorn said, *Hang on.*

With a bound we were airborne, as if the creature had wings, and heading straight for the labyrinth. Color eddied at the labyrinth's entrance, purples and bright pale blues, and a *glenngarseea,* cat-like, raccoon-like, stood there as if he owned the path...as if he was waiting for us.

The unicorn was an inferno, as warm as the White Wanderer, but I was more aware of the surging power of him, the purely animal side of his nature. Whatever else he was, this unicorn was *real.*

My hair whipped free, my necklace dangled down the back of my neck, but I was too busy hanging on to pay it any mind. The weight of the metal case lay against my thigh.

We plunged into the labyrinth, curving around to the left, weaving to the right and then the left, back right again, one more left—and the unicorn leapt over a lowered part of the hedge. I turned my head against the spray of snow, and saw over my shoulder that the *glenngarseea* had seized hold of the unicorn's fluffy tail and was with us.

Soft snow fell. I glimpsed the great house, and then we ghosted toward the back courtyard to a kitchen door I had entered earlier that evening.

"Here?" I whispered.

You have been here. Do not go farther into the house, not for a twelfth of a candlemark. Do not meet yourself.

Myself? I was already here? Then....

"We are in the past?"

We are always in the past.

A distraction, I needed a distraction, just for a few minutes....

I thought of the pans of raw biscuits sliding into the oven, the golden brick of the firebox—I pointed at everything I could use, everything left to me under my cousin's spell, and said, "*Resurge,*" my mind and heart rushing like a waterspout to those pans.

I could feel the swelling from the dough as the pans slid into the oven, and I let them slip away from me.

Good. The great unicorn came to a gentle stop before the kitchen door. *Wait until you hear screams—then rush in.*

What?

A tilt of the beautiful head, a glint of humor in the inky blue eye— *You have told me this story, in your future.*

"Is that why you are here?"

I am here because you are my friend, and I owe you my life.

A tug at my sleeve. The *glenngarseea* perched on the haunches of the great unicorn, looking at me as if trying to speak without a human voice.

I'm in no hurry to see that demon again, I thought at them, still looking at the *glenngarseea.*

The creature had thumbs!

You have no skills yet for demons—leave them to others, the unicorn counseled.

Did my cousin call you? I asked him.

I detected amusement in the unicorn's mind. *No, I came because you needed me. We are bound. If I can come, I will always come. I owe you everything.*

Who are you? Could you ask a unicorn its name?

I am Misu.

Where did...do...we meet? I decided to ask.

We met when you pulled me from my mother's womb.

I delivered my first unicorn a week ago.

The stallion snorted, clearly amused. *That was me.*

Well, I didn't really have anything to say to that....

Are you going to explain sometime? I couldn't resist asking.

He shifted, almost as if he was nervous, and I slid off on the left side, as I would do for a horse. I felt for the metal case still in my right pocket of my gown. My hair was probably a mess, so I pulled the last pins and let the braid fall back down my spine. The *glenngarseea* was no longer up on the unicorn's back.

Could you thank unicorns?

"I am glad that you came." What a strange way to meet someone!

Yes, I will explain, but not tonight. Be silent, and be well, Misu told me, stepping sideways and lifting his beautiful head so the horn easily passed over me. He started to move away, and then paused, looking back at me. *Hide in plain sight*, he suggested, and then leapt, moving toward the labyrinth, his feet scarcely touching the ground. Beyond him the White Wanderer stepped into the labyrinth, a sparkling cloud at his feet, tinged with blue and purple, and I knew the *glenngarseea* was with him.

Mystery upon myst—

A woman screamed.

The biscuits!

Please lady, let it be the biscuits....

I ran to the back entrance and prayed that this crazy house had one more open door.

❧ 𝒟 ❧

By the time I'd passed through the mudroom, the scream had become a three-part chorus of voices in the kitchen.

I entered the kitchen in time to see a biscuit whiz past my nose, hitting a table with a thump before bouncing off and rushing down the floor toward the custard that had been prepared for dessert. Two biscuits rooted in a bowl of sugared strawberries, the fruit brought in from who knew where at an unimaginable expense.

Hide in plain sight.

I shrieked and tossed my arms over my head, as if I was trying to ward off a bat. The young scrubbing girls and the baker promptly did the same, flinging their aprons over their heads and running away from the biscuits to the corridor.

One girl threw her arms around me, and a second plastered herself to my apron. Too late I realized that I was the tallest in the room and that my light gray dress made me bright as moonlight.

"Run!" I yelled, and pointed to the mudroom. More girls fled shrieking except for the youngest one, who remained latched onto my waist. I put an arm around her and hauled her backward into the mudroom.

I grabbed my navy shawl off a hook and tossed it over my head. "We need things to catch them!" I yelled, looking around for a bowl.

"There!" shrieked a girl, pointing toward a milk pail.

That will do, I thought. Anna wouldn't know that the biscuits were harmless. So— *She's a farm girl. She'd try to get away, and then plan a way to retake her kitchen!*

Grabbing the bucket, I spun as a biscuit hopped toward us, a larger biscuit in pursuit. Oh-oh—they couldn't find enough to eat in the kitchen! They were starting on each other!

"Get it, get it!" I yelled, dropping the bucket over the first biscuit as it reached the entrance to the mudroom.

Inspired, several girls grabbed milk and slop buckets to slam on top of the escaping biscuits. A pail caused a rain of carrot peelings, but I doubted the biscuits minded.

The next few minutes were frantic as kitchen helpers wailed, hiding under their aprons, while a couple of footmen chased biscuits, wielding long wooden bars that were commonly used for home defense. The spit boy made a gallant attempt to catch biscuits with his hands. I thought the butler yelled, but I couldn't make out his words.

The girls proved tough, keeping their aprons on their heads and dropping buckets down on top of biscuits. Biscuits splattered into the containers like exploding corn kernels.

Then Cook screeched on a note of sheer terror. I hauled the girls to either side away from the entrance.

"Hide!" I screamed at them, in case it was that demon. Two girls dove behind the garments hanging off pegs. One girl climbed into a window seat. Another surrendered to her fear and threw open the door to the courtyard.

That made more footprints in the courtyard; that was good. I followed her with several more of the kitchen staff on my heels.

Without the warmth of the unicorn, I was grateful for my navy shawl. The youngest member of the kitchen staff clutched me again, as she had nothing but her apron to protect her.

Crack! The noise sounded like an ice dam had broken free. Light flashed brilliantly from somewhere in the house, reflecting in the corner window at the edge of the corridor.

I should not have stopped moving. I was so tired I nearly fell asleep standing up. At first I ignored the babble of voices around me, then I found a place in the questions.

"This is a wizard's house," I finally said. "Who is in charge when magic escapes?"

"Mr. Bennett," voices chorused.

"The butler," came a timid voice from beneath my shawl.

Then we wait.

I hope I did the right thing, taking the package.

Maybe the biscuits were a mistake....

In truth, I was torn between wanting to know what was going on, and thinking that Cousin Esme would want me to keep my head low. So I stood my ground, listening to the sobs and whispers of the staff and the faint thumping of biscuits trying to get out of overturned buckets.

A well-dressed man stepped out of the kitchen doorway, his expression amused. "It's safe!" he called. "We have the biscuits under control!"

"Did you destroy them?" the spit boy asked. He held up a dishtowel that was wiggling like a kitten in a sack. "I caught one!"

"Capital! Bring it along! No, there was something else in the house that Evans destroyed—" He brought himself up short.

So you destroyed the demon? I thought. That opened up all sorts of intriguing suggestions. Did the demon belong to Professor Lee, the master of the house, or was it also an intruder?

It was definitely not a tale for the staff. I suspected it was hard enough to get the average worker to serve in a haunted house. How difficult to keep staff in a magician's house?

At least keep a staff without their own magic.

Cautiously we moved back toward the door.

The kitchen was full of men in fine clothes, turning over buckets and using dishcloths to seize biscuits and haul them up for inspection, amid laughter and joking.

Around me teary and worried faces made it clear that the kitchen staff was still tense.

Somewhere behind me, I heard Emma's voice whisper "Wizards!" in a disgusted voice.

It was Emma who had the ear of every kitchen worker, for Cook was still trying to calm down. "Something huge was flying in the great hall," Emma reported. "It followed me to the kitchen, swooping at me like a scolding jay."

"What was it?" one footman asked.

Emma shuddered and shook her head. "I did not stop running to look. Never look at magic. It's too risky."

This time you were right, I thought.

"Anna? Anna, a carriage came for you!" came a boy's bellow.

Praise Lord and Lady, they came for me. I unwound the little dark-haired girl clinging to me. "It's all right," I told her. "You can go back to your friends now." I smiled to reassure her, though I didn't like leaving so many young ones in a house that had had a demon running loose, but there wasn't anything I could do about it.

No one here was going to listen to Anna. And I had to get out of here with the cylinder. The redhead and the courier would just have to wonder what happened to it, until they heard from the Livingstons.

Cook had surfaced. Her hair was tightly pinned, her skirts in proper order and her apron smooth. The queen of the kitchen was once more in control.

"Thank you for your hard work, Anna," the woman said, giving me a firm look.

"Thank you, ma'am," I managed, giving her a quick curtsy.

Out into the courtyard, I was stopped by a blast of icy wind. A storm was building, tiny pellets of snow swirling everywhere. I pulled my shawl over my face and walked to the side of the dark carriage. I didn't even wait for the coachman, I just pulled open the door and used the piled snow to climb in.

They could wake me at Windward.

The vehicle started moving. The carriage windows were cracked open at the top, wind whistling through. I sat in the dark gripping my hands tightly and thinking *Anna, Anna.* I was still Anna until I was back inside Windward's grounds.

A dry voice came out of the darkness. "We have examined three servants so far. We still have not discovered who was responsible for the mischief tonight. You are candidate number four."

⁂ 𝕯 ⁂

I gasped out loud.

This is the way a rabbit feels in the dark forest....

"You are not from the farm we are visiting!" I sounded breathless, which was Anna's voice.

A faint glow started within the carriage, slowly bringing the moving room into focus. One tiny star of pale blue light bobbed and fluttered between us in the wind whistling through the open windows.

We were moving—only the coachman would hear me scream.

"Where are we going?" I demanded as a man's dark greatcoat became visible. The scarf wrapped around his neck was pale, as was his face. He looked like he was older than Professor Tonneman and younger than my father. Other than that, I could see only that he was wearing a heavy wool coat and a well-tended beaver hat.

He didn't feel like he was there. I felt nothing at all, no psychic mark that told me another human was sharing the carriage.

Yet the tiny blue light danced on his gloved hand. The light, at least, was real, and made him look like a corpse.

"We are not going anywhere," was the response.

Then his magic rose with the strength of a winter storm, lashing at me. I felt like an onion, my top sliced off and my layers peeling away. I dropped my soul anchor into the earth, letting the thin thread play out with the slowly moving carriage laboring through the snow.

Images rushed at me, of digging up papery bulbs from my mother's garden, the smell of fresh dirt and garlic and hot wind swirling around me. I saw my hands setting noose traps and skinning animals for their pelts. The first time I used a bow to kill a deer, the metallic taste of blood on my tongue as I bit my lip. I'd cried for the death, but I'd gutted and skinned that deer, even as my parents taught me how to hang the meat to smoke. Collecting eggs in the dark, the shells smooth and warm, setting the sweet milk out in pans to let the cream rise, riding to my aunt's on our mule, the hot, damp animal moving beneath me—

"Damn the gods, not another false trail." His voice was so even as he dug deeper, coming closer to my family, to Marta, to Shaw, to Margaret—

He's not going to stop.

No.

Words floated up within like smoke, words I had played with but never used.

My magic sprang through my cousin's ward with all the force I had inside me.

Cantamen dissolvatur.

Our flickering star of light silently expanded, dissolving into the sparkle of fireflies. The man gasped hoarsely, throwing up his other arm to protect his eyes.

Mentally I grabbed a passing gust of wind, coiling it like a spring. Yanking, I hauled the swirling power down to Earth so fast that I could have started a fire from the friction.

The focus of my storm struck next to the carriage, and we floated free as the crack of thunder rolled over us. There was no up or down, no surface beneath us—and then I landed sprawled across the seat and the floor of the carriage, wedged against the opposite door. The carriage lay on its side. Everything, *everything* was silent.

The man had vanished.

I had to move, fast.

Finally I could hear again, a roaring in my ears resolving into the creaks and groans of a carriage falling apart. I could feel the carriage jerking, actually sliding along on the snow beneath the door I leaned against. The sound of hysterical horses reached me. I had to get out before the driver regained control of his team.

The jarring and bouncing of the crippled carriage came to an abrupt halt, throwing me against my seat. I pulled myself up and carefully felt with my foot for an edge of the seat. When I found it, I stood on it and reached the door above me. Twisting the handle, I pushed, setting my other foot on the opposite seat. One more heave, and I was able to throw open the door.

A small whirlwind spun lazily above the carriage. I smiled up at it. *Bright blessings, Lady, that you have given me an argument.* I flipped the stairs away from me and crawled through doorway and over, perching on the opening while I turned myself around.

Both the horses and coachman were gone, the ends of the cut traces slowly becoming buried by the snowfall.

All right, then. I sat catching my breath and getting a feel for where north lay.

Jumping off the fallen carriage, I landed in heavy snow. It was not very deep, and I staggered to my feet. The remnants of previous cart tracks showed as depressions under fresh snowfall. At least I had help walking a path. My boots could handle it, but my skirt was going to be soaked.

Tears trickled down my face.

I didn't know if I was still scared or relieved.

I didn't know if I had killed the man, and I didn't care.

He had threatened my family.

He might have found Cousin Esme and the school.

They might still find us.

They thought someone spelled the biscuit dough to make mischief.

Windward was not that far away; I had walked farther....

Above me, my friendly whirling wind wove its way through the branches, a parasol of protection over my head. Occasionally I petted the cone of force I held at the base, marveling that it did not drain me or threaten me.

It was like having a stray cat follow you.

Frozen tears hurt my eyes. I scrubbed my face with my shawl until the only dampness on my skin was an occasional snowflake.

Warmth crept through me, all the way to my fingertips and toes, that same heat that inspired me to seize the cylinder. I waited, but nothing else happened.

At least I was not cold anymore.

I didn't know how long I stumbled through the snowfall, sliding through the powder, avoiding chunks of older ice, but finally I could hear a carriage of some kind coming from the south. I moved off the road behind a tree, hoping their coach lamps would not extend far enough to touch me.

The carriage was dark, slowing as it approached my grove of trees. The coachman pulled his horses to a halt just past me. The door flipped open, stairs dropped, and I heard Margaret's soft voice.

"Miss Sorensson? Are you here?"

"She's here." It was Shaw's voice. He hopped out of the carriage, a lit lantern in hand. "Allie?"

Relief trickled through me; for a moment my knees could not hold me upright. I floundered through the snowdrifts. "Here!" I whispered for fear of what might be listening in the darkness beyond.

Shaw offered me a warm hand. He gave me a brief smile, his grip firm. "Are you all right?"

"I am now."

Shaw looked above us. "Do you still need that for protection?"

That? I looked up at the swirling winds curling above us, lifting strands of our hair. *Oh.* Exhaustion nipped at me, like children pinching each other when their mother wasn't looking.

"We might be followed," I managed to get out.

"Do you need a window open, or can you control it without touching it?" he asked, drawing me toward the carriage.

"I'm not sure," I admitted. "I've always touched it."

"Then we'll keep one window open for you so you can talk to it," Shaw replied, offering his arm as support so I could climb in the carriage.

All right.

Did I talk to winds?

I guess I did....

Once I was in the carriage Margaret threw her arms around me and hugged me tightly. "Oh, *Alfreda!*" she said.

That was the second time, wasn't it? That was permission. Only took a week to get on a first name basis. "It's all right, Margaret, I'm all right," I whispered into her ear, hugging her back.

"No one had any idea what he was keeping!" Margaret went on, almost babbling. "Professor Livingston said they would have found another exchange point if they had known!"

"How could I hear you?" I asked as I fumbled with the cross twisted around my neck.

"You heard me?" Margaret sounded surprised.

"You told me to run," I replied. "So I ran!"

"I...don't know how you heard me," she admitted. "I just started screaming as if you could hear me. I was so frightened for you. Perhaps Professor Livingston will know?"

"Sometimes fear takes us to greater heights of power," Shaw suggested from his seat across from us. "Also, you mentor Allie. Maybe that means you know where to find her." In a softer tone, he added: "I always know where she is, too."

Margaret's voice was full of warmth: "*Sometimes* I know where to find her."

My smile blossomed. I was confident that Margaret could find me.

I prayed to the lord and lady that I could find Margaret, if ever need be.

※ 🝣 ※

A small crowd waited for us in the Windward breezeway, including Catherin Williams, who hugged me and Margaret, first separately and then together. John Kymric was there, his white hair a flag in the gloom, and Mrs. Gardener told us to hurry in for dinner and hot chocolate as Kymric said, "Professor Livingston will see you now."

I was sure she would, but I hoped that the complete tale could wait. I was so tired I could barely hold myself up. I wanted to hand over that cylinder and crawl into a warm bed.

The butler swept us along to the front parlor where both the Livingstons waited, along with Li Sung, silent and watching from a seat farther from the fireplace.

I slid my hand into my wand slit and pulled out the cylinder. With a slight bend of the knee, I offered it to my cousin. "I felt such warmth when I looked at it," I told her, "that I thought you wanted me to take it. I hope it wasn't the house tempting me."

"You were correct, I wanted you to take it," Cousin Esme said, taking the cylinder from my palms. She held my hand for a moment. "Good. The link worked to keep you warm." Then she released me and sat back.

"Emerson was too new to the gathering, and was being watched. Even he is not so fascinating that he can't get away for a few moments of privacy. But you were also there, and now we have discovered a way to communicate under heavy defensive spells. Still, I never imagined that Henry Lee was consorting with demons." Dr. Livingston stirred, as if about to speak, but she glanced his way and added: "Lee is too skilled for a demon to simply slip onto his estate."

"Agreed," Dr. Livingston replied, taking a sip from a teacup.

She shook her head even as she gently twisted the cylinder, breaking what I now saw was a seal of wax. I moved to sit next to Margaret on the small couch close to the fire, and Shaw chose to stand near the door, watching us all.

Through my exhaustion I wondered if Cousin Esme had felt the demon, or if Margaret had told her. Could a demon come here? I turned to Margaret, who set her hand gently on my arm and said: "The guardians are watching."

Oh. Relief.

My cousin drew some papers from the cylinder and looked hard at them, tilting them so the candles at her elbow gave her the best light possible. "How did they manage to get hold of these?" she murmured, offering them to her husband. He adjusted his monocle, quickly reading, and then sighed deeply.

"I had hoped that rumor was false," Dr. Livingston said heavily, and turned to Li Sung. "It is definitely Burr's signature."

"So is he traitor, or merely greedy?" Li Sung asked.

"It looks to me as if he is power-hungry," Cousin Esme replied, "but that will be for the administration to decide. The duel made his return to politics unlikely. This will seal that fate."

"So long ago," Dr. Livingston said, shaking his head. "We children looked up to them, the heroes of the revolution."

"Ambition can eat a man up from inside," Li Sung said, his voice quiet.

"Is it what you needed?" I finally asked.

Dr. Livingston was carefully checking each page and then handing them to Li Sung. "Nothing about the general," he finally said.

Cousin Esme gestured in dismissal. "His incompetence will eventually trip him."

"But he has partisans, and at least one follower is a magician," Dr. Livingston responded. "I think of how many soldiers could die under his command."

"We need proof or we can do nothing." Cousin Esme turned back to me. "It is definitely what we needed, Miss Sorensson," she said softly. "We had hoped for even more, but our enemies are very careful with evidence of their deeds. I am amazed that our friend was able to acquire these letters. We have provided our country with a great gift. At least one former patriot with conflicting loyalties will not be working against us from within our government."

"We had no idea that Henry Lee had stooped to summoning demons, for any reason," Dr. Livingston said, gesturing to Margaret to pour from the chocolate pot. "If we had known, we would have sought another means of securing the documents." A tilt of his head, a swift glance under lowered eyelids, and he added: "Li Sung and I will make sure of the defenses, and scatter the magical energies of our fellow conspirators." Nodding to us all, he quickly left the room, my Chinese gentleman (who definitely was some sort of practitioner, too) leading the way.

"You think very quickly on your feet," Cousin Esme said to me, "but I do not want you ever to be so vulnerable again. I think re-arranging your classes will be in order. You will need to move faster with ritual magic."

"Perhaps Sinjin and I could work with her, ma'am?" Margaret said, passing me a cup of chocolate. I was ready to pass it on to Cousin Esme, but she shook her head. So I turned to offer it to Shaw.

He walked into the light, cloaked in that stillness that defined him, and I perceived the continent of America looming behind him, a primeval forest. Shaw was actually wearing clothing such as Professor Tonneman wore, a close-fitting dark woolen coat with thigh-length tails over a red vest and white necktie, and new dark close-fitting buckskins with his boots. If I had not felt the forest I might not have recognized him.

He looked like he belonged in Cousin Esme's parlour.

If I asked him how he did that, would he tell me?

Why was he here?

Carefully he took the cup and saucer from me, his eyes downcast. Our fingers touched.

The sudden heat rushing through me was nothing like Cousin Esme's spell.

"Your tutoring Miss Sorensson is a possibility, Miss Rutledge," Cousin Esme said, calling me back to the room. "I will be discussing it with Professor Tonneman tomorrow. You, Miss Sorensson," she went on, "are to sleep in, as late as your body will allow. You have had a busy two days, and I would not have you injure your health!"

"Sleep and hot water will set me right," I assured her. Margaret smothered a sound and Cousin Esme smiled broadly, so I guessed that I'd said the wrong thing.

"Mrs. Gardener has dinner waiting for us," Margaret said, her voice unsteady with suppressed laughter.

I was so hungry that I had gone beyond hunger.

Her smile softening, my cousin said: "I look forward to your joining me for tea tomorrow afternoon, so I may hear the full tale of your adventures. You have done us a great service, Miss Sorensson. From this point on you do not owe any payment for your instruction. It may be that we will be paying you!"

My mind was a jumble of images. What would I tell her tomorrow? Were there things I should not mention, or did she know all my secrets by now?

Cousin Esme knew about the White Wanderer. Right now I was so tired I couldn't remember if she knew about the unicorn. This was where keeping secrets was hard. You had to remember each story that you told, and who got which story. Eventually you would trip over your own tales.

If I wrote to Marta, would she come see me? Marta kept secrets about me. I really needed to know what she wanted me to share about the wild magic and when to tell it.

Shaw knew about the unicorns, although I did not know if he knew that was why Marta had sent me here. If he was leaving that night, perhaps I could walk him to the maze....

⊱🜍⊰

As it happened, Shaw *was* leaving. By the time Margaret and I finished the cocoa, Shaw had vanished and reappeared, now dressed in his old walnut-stained buckskin jacket and trousers, a package under his arm that I suspected was the fancy clothing he'd been wearing.

"You did not need your coin, Miss Sorensson, did you?" Cousin Esme asked.

"Oh, the coin!" I pulled it from my apron and clutched it between my fingers.

It was just a coin. My words had dissolved the spell within it.

"I used Sin-Sinjin's spell, and the coin lost its power, too," I replied, holding up the coin to Shaw. "The biscuits worked, but I needed power in a hurry, so I used the spell first, and then grabbed the sky."

Shaw's face changed, as if he was about to smile but then didn't, his eyes narrowing ever so slightly. I knew that expression. He was trying not to laugh.

My cousin focused intently on me. "What spell did you learn from Sinjin?"

"*Can*—"

I did not finish the word. Who knew what spells might be working in this room? "The spell to finish all magic?"

Cousin Esme straightened, glancing at Margaret. "I look forward to this story," was all my cousin said aloud. "You are excused from your classes tomorrow, and Miss Rutledge will answer questions for your herb class. I will see you in my parlor for tea tomorrow afternoon."

"Yes, ma'am," I said.

"Go walk Mr. Kristinsson to the maze, and then to the kitchen for dinner, ladies." She flicked her fingers in dismissal. "You are certain you do not need sustenance, Mr. Kristinsson?"

"No, professor, thank you," Shaw said, taking the coin from my fingertips and backing away from the settee.

This time the warmth from his touch was comforting.

We made our way into the front hall, Shaw walking close by my side, where Elizabeth, of all people, waited with my sheepskin coat.

"You shouldn't be up this late," I told her as I reached for my coat.

"You were helping Mrs. Livingston," was her reply. "This is my job!" She took my navy shawl, nodded cheerfully to Margaret, and shyly smiled at Shaw before disappearing to the staircase.

"You don't have to go back out in the cold," Shaw said. "I can find the maze."

"Would you deny us our thanks and pleasure?" Margaret responded.

Shaw straightened; he looked a bit startled.

I needed to pin Margaret down about when I had to pay attention to this chaperone business.

We walked out the kitchen doorway and found that the wind had died down, the snowfall a fine, thick veil obscuring the grounds.

"Must you also walk the labyrinth?" Margaret asked as we strolled down the cobblestone walkway.

"No, I charged the labyrinth before I left," Shaw replied.

"We are grateful that you lent your strength to our need," Margaret told him.

"Why did you come?" I asked.

"You know that I can feel you out there—on the magical plane, Cory thinks," he replied softly. "All night you were getting tense and wary. Finally I couldn't stand it anymore and went through the maze. By then Professor Livingston was sending you energy and told the coachman to take Miss Rutledge and me to find you." He glanced at me out of the corner of his eye. "I figured I could find you. And then when you pulled down wind, well..."

So I'd had not only the Livingstons and Margaret with me, I had Shaw and a unicorn watching out, too. And a tiny creature I had not even read about in my book yet. The powers that be were with me.

If there ever was a next time, I wanted Shaw in on the planning. I knew he could come up with some great distractions.

He probably had a pocket full of exploding halfpennies.

"I didn't have time yesterday to find out, what with cooking and cleanup," I started slowly. "What is the difference between a practitioner and a magician?"

Margaret stopped on the walkway before we reached the first labyrinth. "A practitioner learns all the schools of magic," she said. "A magician does not learn any of the healing arts."

"Hope they have a few friends who are practitioners, then," I murmured.

"Say your good nights," Margaret went on, tucking her scarf closer and looking out over the labyrinth. "I will be here."

So chaperones could give you a little privacy. That was good to know.

Shaw and I walked on to the maze. As soon as we stood before the entrance, I asked Shaw, "I don't think my cousin or Miss Rutledge saw the unicorn. Should I tell them? What do you think?"

Shaw did not speak at first. "I think," he said finally, "that your cousin does not envy you anything except your ability to use wild magic. Telling her about the unicorn won't change that." His silver gaze met mine. "That unicorn interest could be dangerous."

"Yes," I agreed. "That's what Marta fears."

"So far it's been handy."

I felt a smile pull at my lips. It had all happened so fast that I had scarcely had time to enjoy my ride. "A unicorn...it's like harnessing all the speed of your stallion, and all the strength of a draft horse."

He nodded. "I bet there will be another time."

I hoped so. "Thank you for coming. I'm sorry you didn't get to blow anything up."

Shaw burst out laughing. It was a strong laugh, lower in pitch than it used to be, but still laughter that I knew.

"That's all right," he finally said. "I expect I'll get to blow something up another time."

Another time.

I had friends I could count on. That was better than gold.

Impulsively I stood on my toes and kissed his cheek.

"Thank you," I said softly.

I could have sworn I saw him blush.

"I'll be there, unless the sky is falling," he said, his voice low. "It might take me a bit longer, then."

"I'll try to wait for you," I replied.

This time it wasn't hard for him to meet my gaze.

CHIRP!

We both startled, looking down. The Cat was sitting at our feet, looking at us.

"You weren't very much help," I told the cat.

"Did you invite him?" Shaw asked.

It was my turn to laugh. "Since when does a cat need an invitation?"

"Well, it *was* a carriage ride away."

Truth.

I picked up The Cat, who purred and snuggled close to me.

"Write us so we know the whole story," Shaw said. Then he raised his hand in farewell to Margaret and walked into the maze. The packed snow began to glow as he moved deeper into the tall shrubs. Finally he turned a corner, disappearing to my sight, but I watched until the glow from the maze vanished.

I walked back to Margaret, carrying The Cat and wondering if she saw me kiss Shaw.

We walked side by side, back toward the kitchen door.

"I like him," Margaret said, her consonants as always precise.

So do I.

~ Finis ~

AFTERWORD

Sometimes a long story starts with "Once upon a time...."

Sometimes it starts with a grand plan.

In the case of Alfreda's tale, it started with (appropriately) a snip of folklore.

The seeds of *Night Calls* were planted at World Fantasy Con Providence. Jane Yolen was telling a group of us about a series of anthologies she and Martin H. Greenberg were doing for Harper & Row Junior Books. The first one would be about werewolves. We were bouncing questions off her, and I remember that Mike Ford was starting a silly thing about "Billy was a wer-giraffe" that sadly I don't think he ever finished. Although I was enjoying the conversation, I didn't write much short stuff and I hadn't found a toehold in the stream of ideas. Then I asked Jane, "Does the werewolf have to be seen?" She replied that "The werewolf does not have to be seen, but its presence has to be felt."

At that moment, I had two intense visual flashes. One was of a young girl in long skirts, rustic clothing, bundled against cold, bending down and discovering new, withered garlic growing under a windowsill. The other was of that same young girl, now inside, standing on a chair and hanging a braid of garlic over an inside door. At that moment, I knew I had to know more about it. It was so intense I checked with a couple of friends to make sure I hadn't borrowed the images from anywhere else. But Allie sprang from my mind in that instant.

I wrote the story as post apocalyptic science fiction and sold it to Jane. Eventually a reprint of it, now fantasy, appeared in *Amazing Stories Magazine*. Kim Moran insisted that it was fantasy, wasn't it. I decided that he was right.

Finally a novel was born, after I experimented over at *F & SF* with vampires, too!

The *Night Calls* world is an alternative history fantasy. This means that I have made some things easier for my modern audience. Felled trees are called stumps, not butts as many pioneers referred to them. Recipes are not called receipts. On the other hand, there were elderly people who did refer to George Washington as King Washington, even though he refused a crown both in real history and in Allie's world. Those elders came from a time when all rulers were kings. It takes time to change speech patterns.

I hope you have fun figuring out what is history, what is fantasy, and what is folklore.

Though I have written previous stories, and plan to write still more tales, Alfreda Sorensson is my gift back to the universe. Try to leave the world a little better than you found it.

It's what Allie would do.

ABOUT THE AUTHOR

Katharine Eliska Kimbriel, September 16, 2014

Katharine Eliska Kimbriel reinvents herself every decade or so. It's not on purpose, mind you—it seems her path involves overturning the apple cart, collecting new information & varieties of apple seed, and moving on. The one constant she has reached for in life is telling stories.

"I'm interested in how people respond to unusual circumstances. Choice interests me. What is the metaphor for power, for choice? In SF it tends to be technology (good, bad and balanced) while in fantasy the metaphor is magic--who has it, who wants or does not want it, what is done with it, and who/what the person or culture is after the dust has settled. A second metaphor, both grace note and foundation, is the need for and art of healing.

"A trope in fantasy is great power after passing through death. Well, at my crisis point, I didn't die. That means that I'm a wizard now. Who knows what I may yet accomplish?"

Kimbriel was a John W. Campbell Award nominee for best new SF Writer.

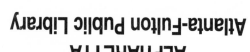

CPSIA infor
Printed in th
LVOW11s11
429949